A WELCOME INVASION

Lil had been kissed before, many times. Awkward kisses, earnest kisses, even a few experienced kisses. But this dark invader of her home, her mind and ultimately, she knew, of her body, created his own lexicon. One her body interpreted even as her mind resisted.

Those lips were as warm and unyielding as the rest of him. But the way they moved—tactile possession in their unhurried exploration. Leisurely he learned her. As if he'd always known her.

Kiss? How banal.

Invasion. Intimacy. Consummation. He'd barely touched her, yet already he'd filled her with his wild strength as surely as if he held her spread-eagled to the bed.

And Lil, stubborn as only one of Scots ancestry can be, tilted her head back to welcome the thrust of his tongue. He dipped, and danced, and tasted the rim of her teeth, lips suckling gently all the while. And she didn't just allow him intimacies she'd allowed no other.

She welcomed them.

THE WOLF OF HASKELL HALL

COLLEEN SHANNON

LOVE SPELL ⬥ NEW YORK CITY

A LOVE SPELL BOOK®

January 2001

Published by

Dorchester Publishing Co., Inc.
276 Fifth Avenue
New York, NY 10001

ISBN 0-505-52412-0

The name "Love Spell" and its logo are trademarks of Dorchester Publishing Co., Inc.

Printed in the United States of America.

Visit us on the web at www.dorchesterpub.com.

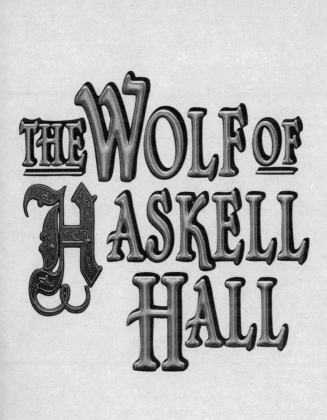

THE WOLF OF HASKELL HALL

Motto: Delilah Haskell, Heiress of Haskell Hall

"I will neither yield to the song of the siren, nor the voice of the hyena, the tears of the crocodile, nor the howling of the wolf."

—George Chapman, *Eastward Ho,* Act V, scene i

Prayer: Ian Griffith, Estate Manager of Haskell Hall

"For one heat, all know, doth drive out another, one passion doth expel another still."

—George Chapman, *Eastward Ho,* Act V, scene i

Chapter One

Cornwall, England, 1878

Pain. Thirst. Hunger. The three demons ran alongside
him in the gloom, dark harbingers leading him to a
future more terribly beguiling with every step he took
deeper into the moor.

Once he had struggled against this fate. He'd traveled to the ends of the earth to avoid it. But neither
the burning sands of the Sahara nor the bone-chilling
cold of an Andean hut had quieted the call of blood
to blood.

Such was the fate of his father.

And his father's father, back into the mists of time
when Druids chanted and danced naked in the . . .

Moonlight.

He lifted his face to the siren call. Now that he

11

accepted his family's curse as a blessing, the wanton moon no longer terrified him. Power surged through him with every alluring ray, making his senses acute to things no mere mortal could understand.

The taste of home upon his tongue with the salt damp of the marsh.

The feel of moss-covered ground beneath his bare feet, springy yet firm.

The touch of mist writhing like a woman's silken skin against his bare torso.

The sight of wild things darting about in the cover of darkness, secure that his flawed human eyes could not see the red glow of their heat. And sounds . . .

The laughter floated toward him, both a taunt and a temptation, drifting on the wind. He lifted his nose and sniffed. Through all the other smells of the fecund Cornish night, he caught the most seductive scent of all: woman. For an instant, he stood where he was, grounded on the soil of home, yet lost in the dilemma of his kind. The remnants of humanity whispered in one ear—

—and demons howled in the other.

Louder, and far more seductive.

Pain . . . a stab so acute that it felt as if his rib cage must expand to hold the muscle and bone his frail human frame could not contain.

Thirst . . . his tongue, unbearably sensitive now, lapped out to taste a pond, but the thin water didn't have the texture and taste he craved.

Hunger . . . it twisted his guts into knots. He bent double, fighting the dark urges, but then the laughter came again. With it, the last of his humanity faded away, a pinprick disappearing into the dark maw of the night.

In one agile bound, he whirled and scaled the tall hedge separating him from his prey. Down, down the slope into the clearing, where the latest Haskell heiress galloped her horse in the moonlight. Her long silvery hair was a banner waving behind her in the stiff breeze, taunting him with the need to catch it and pull her out of the saddle. Unaware of him, she urged the white mare on to faster strides.

Not fast enough.

How easily he kept pace, power surging through him from the tips of his curving fingers to toes growing into claws.

Feet silent on the damp earth, he gained on her with every step.

And then, as he got close enough to leap, all his senses narrowed down to one driving urge.

The need to feed.

He was tensing to spring when he felt the Other bound into step beside him. They bared their fangs at one another, stiff neck hairs bristling as they growled. For an instant, they matched each other step for step, jostling for position as they battled over who would have first taste.

And then, as even her dull human senses came alive to the danger, the woman looked over her shoulder. She screamed, trying to wheel her mount away from them.

But it was too late.

For her.

And for him . . .

13

Three Months Later

Delilah Hortense Haskell Trent drew the light curricle to a halt just inside the wrought-iron gates of Haskell Hall. Delilah and her two servants stared up at the odd mansion.

The Hall glowed like a sanctuary in the gloom illuminated by a half-moon. Lights spilled from every window, as if the servants were determined to do their part to welcome the new mistress. But the bright displays only accentuated the building's sad state of decay.

It was a hodgepodge of architectural styles, from the simple Georgian pilasters and flat front of the central portion, to the fussy Victorian wings on both sides, each capped with octagonal towers. Still, the overall effect might have been charmingly eccentric but for sagging shutters, peeling double front doors, and moldering, ivy-covered stone that needed a good regrouting.

The gravel drive in front, however, was cleanly swept, and the grounds were immaculate.

"Blimey, she's a frowsy bitch, drawers a-droppin' round her knees at the first sign o' interest," came the ribald appraisal from Jeremy, Lil's groom, bodyguard, and favorite general nuisance.

Lil didn't even glance at him, for she'd long since given up trying to make him keep a civil tongue in his head. But he had other qualities she valued more than politesse.

As usual, Safira gave him a censorious look out of slanted, exotic eyes luminous against her burnished

Haitian skin. "Mon, ye have no need to stir up trouble before we even set foot inside the place."

"Trouble don't need stirrin' up here, me dusky beauty," Jeremy retorted. "It follows, bold-like, right through the door with us. I can feel it in me bones."

This time, Safira didn't argue. Her lovely dark eyes got huge as she fingered the talisman at her throat and stared up at the Hall. "Mistress, the little bandy cock could be right, for once. Maybe we should turn around and catch the first boat back to America."

Lil spared them each an amused glance before she clicked her tongue to the horse. "Sometimes I'm not sure which of you is more superstitious. The voodoo priestess or the Cockney sailor who quit the sea because his captain had the temerity to bring his wife aboard."

Neither of them retorted with their usual spunk, so she left off her teasing. It was too late to turn back now. She was in England, the land of her mother's birth, for the first time, and she intended to enjoy every moment.

She had, after all, crossed an ocean to get here, drawn as much by curiosity as by duty. Without her presence, the tiny village of Haskell would fail, or so she was assured by Mr. Randall Cottoway, Esq., of Jasper, Diebold and Cottoway, London solicitors. The estate would be parceled off among various male relatives, the villages and miners likely put out of work, if she did not stake her rightful claim to the inheritance. She, he'd informed her with typical lofty British superiority, was needed back in Cornwall. Surely—he'd made plain with a scornful glance around her mother's overly lavish drawing room—she could afford a few months and a few pounds to save the estate for future Haskell heirs.

"Such a bequest, coming down through the distaff side of the Haskell family, is highly unusual in English law," the solicitor had stated. "Because you are the last known female heir with Haskel blood, if you do not satisfy the terms of the inheritance by living on the property for six months, then everything will finally pass, after three centuries, into the male hands of several distant cousins related only to the patriarchal side of the family." He'd tipped his ridiculous bowler hat, left a packet of papers, and exited, obviously relieved that his duty was done and he could return to civilization.

Like her stoic Scottish father, Lil could be coaxed, she could be cajoled, she could be reasoned with. But she could never be bullied.

Challenged, however, was another matter.

So here she sat in her curricle under the hulking building that seemed to brood down at them. For a craven instant, she felt a quiver of unease shiver down her sword-straight spine. She had much of the sheer practically of her stalwart father, and little of the flighty moodiness of her mother. However, as she stared up at the Hall, a strange foreboding niggled its way through her usual calm, as insidious as the gathering fog.

Had she done the right thing in coming here?

The doors burst open. Light flooded the darkness as smiling servants filed out. She had no time for regrets, or foolish fancies.

16

*   *   *

The next day, Lil sat in the salon partaking of that peculiar English ritual that had been the one legacy her mother seemed to cherish: high tea. Lil had never told her mother, since they always seemed to have plenty to argue about, but like her father, Lil despised the taste of tea. However, since she had no wish to be considered more of a heathen American than she obviously already was to these people, she forced herself to drink it.

As she bit into a cucumber sandwich, Lil had to admit that no one knew better how to make gossip a high art than the English. Even the snooty Denver socialites who'd never accepted the Trents—their scandalous riches actually made, they'd whispered, by Mr. Trent's own hands—could take lessons in hypocrisy from these country ladies.

Mrs. Farquar, of Farquar Hill, gushed, "*So* brave of you to venture here across the sea, all the way to *Cornwall* from America. Of course, I make no doubt that even *our* desolate moors are positively *teeming* with social occasions compared to what you probably knew in . . . now *what* was the name of that town you're from, my dear?"

Biting back the urge to tell the plump little busybody that Denver even had gas lights and paved streets, *really* it did, unlike the parts hereabout, Lil politely wiped the corners of her mouth with her linen napkin and responded, "Denver. Colorado."

"Oh, yes," piped up Mrs. Farquar's horse-faced daughter, "you remember, Maman. That's where all

17

the gold and silver miners moved after they made their fortunes."

Both ladies darted complacent looks at Lil out of the corners of their eyes.

It hadn't taken them long to investigate her background. How had they managed it so quickly in this backwater? Lil's teeth snapped down on a scone this time, but she managed to hold her tongue.

However, Jeremy, who'd been setting a new fire for them in the grate, had no such qualms. Dusting his hands off on his breeches, he said out of the corner of his mouth, "Aye, same place as many a pretty English rose went a scoutin' fer a rich husband if she could get it, and a rich protector if she couldn't." Jeremy raked Miss Farquar with his wintry blue eyes. "Ye could try your luck, gel, but a man'd as lief mount a thoroughbred as a nag, and back ye'd be quick-like, puttin' down yer betters."

Both women goggled at him in shock.

Hiding a smile behind her napkin, Lil gave him a severe look over the linen. When her mouth was straight she lowered the cloth, hoping her voice was sterner than her merry green eyes. "Jeremy, leave the room at once, and never speak to my guests so again!"

As usual, he read her like a book. He gave her his cocky little half salute, and strolled out with his peculiar, rolling gait, not in the least abashed.

"Well, *really!* How do you bear such a . . ." Mrs. Farquar's outrage stopped in mid-spate as she stared at the door. Her daughter did likewise, and the looks on their faces made Lil swivel in her chair in alarm to see what horror stood there.

At first she could make out nothing in the dark hallway, but then the shadow moved into the room and resolved itself into a man.

A very tall, powerful man.

He wore work breeches and calf-high boots that molded his long legs, giving them an obscene clarity and beauty of power and form that would have made a lesser woman than Lil blush. His white lawn shirt was so thin that she could see the shadow of his chest hair, so she knew he must be dark. His face and hair were shaded under a broad-brimmed work hat. And his hands . . . she shivered as she stared at his hands.

The nails were blunt and clean, but his long fingers had a tensile strength and . . . readiness expressed in every flagrantly male sinew of his indomitable frame. And when he walked into the room, he was silent despite his size. He flicked a short quirt against his leg, broadcasting dislike as if he had no more patience for the two gossips than Lil did. His rudeness in not removing his hat spoke loudly of his opinion of them.

Mother and daughter muttered excuses and fled, snapping the drawing room door closed behind them.

Only the sound of the fire crackled, but Lil refused to be intimidated by her own estate manager. For this man could be none other than Ian Griffith. "Why did you not knock, Mr. Griffith?" She glanced at the mantel clock. "You are early for our appointment."

"If you wish, I'll go back out and return in five minutes—mistress." The deep, soft voice put a slight emphasis on the last word, and the intonation gave

19

erotic meaning to the polite usage. Still, he did not remove his hat, and she had the peculiar feeling the omission was as much for his own protection as for hers.

Why would he be afraid of her gaze?

The urge to move her chair away from him almost overcame her, but instead, Lil tilted back her silvery head of fashionably coiffed hair and stared boldly up into the shadow of the hat, her own green gaze steady. She caught the glitter of eyes as he let them wander from her small, slipper-shod feet, up her green taffeta gown, past her full hips and small waist, to her generous bosom, pausing on the vee between her breasts before traveling on to her white throat. The glitter grew brighter as he watched the pulse pound there, but then he whacked the quirt hard against his leg as if to punish his own thoughts, and the glitter snuffed out like a light.

That was why he seemed so threatening, Lil instinctively realized. This man had the measured control of a leashed tiger. It would suffer you to feed it and train it and play with it, only so long as it pleased. But once that power was unleashed, and the wildness broke through . . .

Nonsense. "Remove your hat, if you please." He was just a man, and she was no ninny to be so intimidated.

A sharp intake of breath betrayed his shock at the curt command, but he raised that large, capable hand and pulled off the hat.

It was her turn to gasp. His face was not conventionally handsome. His cheekbones were too high and exotically slanted, his blade of a nose too long, his lips too full and wide. And his eyes . . . she tried to delve into them and take the true measure of this man as she'd had to do so often since her father died, but the amber depths were too opaque and secretive to allow her in. They were fringed with long, dark lashes that would have looked feminine on a less primal face.

Curly midnight hair cascaded over his tanned brow, and long sideburns pointed like accusatory fingers down the sides of his strong, square jaw. As if to emphasize the obvious: I grant favors, if I will it, but I never ask for them. Cross me at your peril.

Every hackle on her body stood on end, and it was all she could do not to leap up and fire him on the spot just to avoid feeling so intimidated. Instead, she managed coolly, "Do you have the books ready for me to examine?"

"Yes, I do." He stalked to a cabinet against the wall and took out two black ledgers.

Lil rose and walked over to the Louis IV desk in pride of place in the middle of the room. The furnishings in the house were as eclectic as the facade, but there were a few priceless pieces, of which this was one. She sat down, expecting him to deposit the ledgers and move away.

Instead, he pulled up a chair. His nostrils flared as he obviously caught the subtle whiff of her perfume, and her own senses went on full alert. He didn't touch her anywhere as he leaned over her shoulder, but she felt his body heat and smelled a faint scent of something indefinable emanating from him, something earthy and primitive that raised her hackles again . . .

. . . and made her long for his touch to soothe them.

The neat columns, written in a bold dark hand, wavered before her gaze. She took a deep breath and tried to concentrate. But she felt the expanse of his shoulders so close that all she had to do was turn and she could investigate their width with her own tingling hands.

She leaped up, knocking over the gilded, spindle-legged chair. "Leave them with me. I will study them later, at my leisure."

An insolent smile tugged at the corners of those full lips as she fled back to her safe seat. She was too off balance to get up and slap it away, as her instincts urged.

"And the rest—mistress?" asked that deep, soft voice. "What of the new pump for the mine? The schoolroom in the village that needs a new roof, and—"

"Not today. I am . . . fatigued." Oh, no. Next she'd make the age-old lady's excuse of the headache. Warily, she watched him rise, pick up the books, and come toward her. She almost leaped up to run, but he only veered around her to put the ledgers back.

To her intense relief, he put his hat back on and shielded her from those steady, unnerving amber eyes. "A true Haskell," he said with mild contempt. "I had hoped that, somehow, you might be different. Good afternoon." Turning on his heel, he stalked out, steps soundless even on the wood floor. The soles of his boots must be as soft as the shank.

Still . . . she had never met such an unsettling man.

She pressed her hand to her hammering heart, vaguely aware that this strange pounding was not just arousal, or fear, or even excitement.

It was a combination of all three. She stood to pour herself a brandy with a shaking hand, thinking the spirits would soothe her agitated nerves. But the smooth burn of the liquor warmed her in unexpected places instead, reminding her of the way Ian Griffith walked, and talked.

And stared at her with secretive, burning eyes.

She tossed her glass into the fire, furious at her own weakness. She strode out of the room, vowing not to think of him again.

She broke her vow before she crossed the floor.

In the ensuing days, to Lil's relief, she didn't have to see Ian Griffith again. For over a week, she had her hands full with the household itself. The former owners had lavished money on the outbuildings, the stables, the greenhouse, even the old chapel on the grounds, but they'd been parsimonious with the interior. Every piece of furniture needed a good stripping and repolishing, every brass fixture needed shining, and the rugs and draperies . . . Lil sneezed just looking at them.

Lil had been unofficial chatelaine of her father's three Colorado homes since she was in her teens, and she knew much of running a household, even one almost as complicated as this. But a mine, the enormous stables that held everything from broodmares to carriage horses to thoroughbreds, the village school, even some of the shops, were also Haskell-owned.

For these, she needed her estate manager. But she refused to fetch him, and he seemed equally content not to come calling.

She wondered where he lived. She wondered if he was married. She wondered why he seemed to dislike the Haskells. And then she wondered, to her own fury, why she bothered wondering.

When the house is ready, she told herself staunchly. It's only that I'm busy. He doesn't intimidate me at all. But she wasn't facing a mirror when she thought it.

Finally, almost two weeks after her arrival, she pulled off her apron and crossed the last item off her list. "Downstairs finished," she said with a weary sigh of satisfaction, blowing a curl off her forehead as she smiled at Mrs. McCavity, the housekeeper. "Now the upstairs. We'll start with the towers—" She broke off at the look on Mrs. McCavity's face. "Yes?"

"Well, milady, that is—"

"I bear no title, Mrs. McCavity. You may call me Delilah."

A horrified look crossed the woman's face. "Sure, and the saints themselves strike me down afore I so disrespect me betters. What was your da a-thinkin' to name ye after a heathen woman?" She blushed as her Irish brogue got the best of her.

Lil laughed. She was always tickled to find the clue to a person's humanity. In her servants. In her friends. Even, on occasion, in her enemies. Everyone had some mannerism, or way of speaking, that betrayed his strengths and weaknesses. The more emotional Jeremy was, the more colorfully he cursed. The more frightened Safira became, the more she retreated into her magic. When Mrs. McCavity was shocked or moved, she reverted to the brogue of her childhood.

And Ian Griffith? How vividly she could visualize that dark, enigmatic face. But she saw no weakness there. And little humanity.

Lil collected her scattered thoughts. The housekeeper looked puzzled, and she'd been so hardworking and kind that Lil felt she had to give the poor woman some explanation as to why her new mistress was so different from the former ladies of the Hall. "If you'd known my pa, you'd understand that he challenged me from the time I was born to be better than a name, a title, an inheritance. 'Delilah,' he would say, 'a name has no more bearing on who we are than money defines what we are. Ye have three scourges to overcome—me trade, your name, and the filthy lucre that will be either the bane o' yer existence or yer deliverance. Take yer weaknesses and make them strengths.' " Lil's smile grew misty as she stared at Mrs. McCavity's attentive face. "I've always done my best to follow his advice. With the result that I fear I am not much welcomed in Denver drawing rooms, and doubtless will not be here, either."

"There you are wrong, mil—ma'am. Money in these parts hides an enormous quantity of sins." Mrs. McCavity ducked her head as if she was sorry she'd spoken so frankly, and she reached for the huge ring of keys at her waist. "Now where do you want to start upstairs?"

"The towers." Lil led the way, but she turned back when she realized the housekeeper had not followed.

"We . . . are not supposed to go into the north tower. The south tower was set up as a governess's suite, but since we currently have no children in the house, it is vacant."

Frowning, Lil scarcely listened to the second half of the explanation. "You are telling me I own this estate and am not allowed to enter parts of my own ancestral home?"

" 'Tis an agreement made many years ago with the Griffith family by the first mistress. So long as a Griffith runs this estate, he may live where he pleases in the house, as he pleases, with no interference from the owners. The Griffiths have lived unmolested in that tower for almost a hundred years."

Lil was appalled. "Such an agreement could not possibly be legally binding. Why, if the house were sold—"

"And morally?"

Lil clamped her mouth shut. No wonder Ian Griffith strode around like he owned the place! In a way, he did.

Without another word, she turned on her heel and led the way upstairs—to the south tower. But as they traversed the connecting hallway, she couldn't help looking in the opposite direction and wondering. Her steps slowed.

Each tower had its own entrance and exit. What guests did Ian Griffith invite inside? How many women had succumbed to his animal magnetism? What did his bed look like? Were his arms and long legs as muscular as they looked? She didn't have to close her eyes to visualize him sprawled on white sheets, all wild dark power and wild dark urges that made a woman—

She caught Mrs. McCavity's gaze. Blushing, she turned sharply in the opposite direction. Would she could turn her thoughts so easily.

That night, even after a soothing soak in the hip-deep copper tub, Lil was still restless. She tossed aside the weighty tome she was trying to read on the biology of Bodmin moor, which lapped at the very foundation of this house. But improving her mind would have to wait for a less stressful day.

She'd worked herself to the point of exhaustion, and had two glasses of sherry that night instead of one, but still she couldn't quiet her overactive imagination. She simply would not be able to sleep until she saw the north tower for herself. Ian Griffith had left word with the butler that he had gone into Bodmin for supplies and would not return until the next day, so she was safe invading his abode.

Wrapping the tie of her sweeping cashmere negligee tightly about her trim waist, shaking back the deep ruffles at her sleeves, she collected the enormous ring of keys the housekeeper had given her. Most were marked, but two, larger and more ornate than the others, were not. One of them had to open the north tower.

She had the right, she told herself, to be sure that illegal activities were not being conducted in her home. If she found an opium pipe, or smuggled goods, or . . . or scandalous pictures or novels . . . well, she'd have every reason to fire the arrogant blackguard.

On the long trek to the opposite wing of the house, her slippers made little sound in the thick carpets, but the lantern she carried threw her shadow upon the wall. Strange the way it danced, in a joyous way quite opposite to the sick, anticipatory queasiness in her stomach.

She looked down. Her hand was shaking.

She stopped. What was wrong with her? She was a woman grown, an experienced woman in every way since she'd made the mistake of letting her former fiancé talk her into his bed. She'd broken off the engagement when she found out that he, despite his greater guile than the others, also only wanted her money. He had not been a kind lover, and she'd had no interest in the act, illicit or sanctified, since.

Which was why her current obsession troubled her so. She took a deep breath, closed her eyes, and visualized her father's bright green eyes smiling at her. "Face yer fears, me darlin', and ye'll be the stronger for it."

"Yes, Pa." Hitching her skirts above her ankles so she could walk faster, she quelled her own foolish fears and hurried into the north wing. Sure enough, the stout oak door that met her, banded with steel like a Norman baron's of old, yielded to one of the ornate keys. She shoved the door inward and listened.

The round stairwell was pitch black, and she heard no sounds above. The entire household was asleep, as she should be at this ungodly hour, so she entered the gloom and shut the door quietly behind her, but left it unlocked.

In the feeble lantern light, the curving stairs and

stone tower seemed to stretch to infinity. Finally she reached another door, this one glossy black and even heavier than the other. She tried the door handle, but it didn't open. She fumbled with the key chain again, and to her relief, the same key that opened the lower door also unlocked this one.

Taking a deep breath, she shoved the heavy portal open. The octagonal space inside was very dark. She quickly lit the gas sconces beside the door, and then the lamp next to the sofa before the fireplace.

She looked around, and some of her suspicions about her manager began to fade. No den of iniquity here. Only a tiny kitchen and dining area in one corner, and a living area across, plus a long table set up before shelves packed with books to make a rudimentary library.

A small but comfortable suite of rooms, a gentleman's retreat, all dark paneling and lush green velvet. Tasteful but spare. None of the heavy empire and rococo style so in vogue in this era when Queen Victoria ruled with a small but indomitable hand. Simple Sheraton writing armoire, marble-topped tables, monkish straight-backed chairs. The only nod to decadence was a plush emerald green silk divan that looked as if it should have a Turkish pasha reclining upon it.

Or a houri.

Wishing she could rid her head of such sensual images, Lil carried the lantern to illuminate the painting above the fireplace mantel. It was a picture of the moors. Because the walls of the tower curved slightly as the angles of the octagon met, it did not rest flat.

Perhaps that accounted for the picture's odd depth and radiance.

The moors she'd seen on the train coming here had never looked like this. Yes, they stretched beyond sight as this one did, and yes, they were filled with intriguing patches of green, where moss or plants relieved the unrelenting brown. And yes, when the sun went down and night ruled, she'd even seen the same luminous, low-lying mist. But that moor had been intimidating, bleak, offering more peril than pleasure.

The same moor depicted in this painting was sensual, glowing with jewel tones of green and sapphire, where lichen-covered rocks dotted the muddy wastes, and pools of blue water reflected back the cloudless sky above. Even the mountains, hazy in the distance, had been added with bold, loving strokes. Here, they were not jagged teeth consuming the sky as they'd seemed to Lil, but hands offering a bounty of life and joy found nowhere else on earth.

Lil stumbled back a step. She wasn't sure why the image was so disquieting and riveting at the same time. Whoever had painted this loved the moors. Loved them as a man loved a woman, or a mother a son.

But there was something else . . . something troubling. She couldn't quite put her finger on it, but the brush strokes were deep, the dollops of paint standing up from the canvas in a style she'd never seen before. As if the painter used violent, passionate strokes to exorcise demons along with his emotions.

Had *he* painted it?

She visualized that primal male face, tried to pic-

ture him wearing a beret, daubing paint upon this canvas. . . . Her mind balked. No, a man who looked as
he did doubtless sported with guns, or horses, or
women. He had the soul of a conqueror, not an artist.

Rubbing at her tingling nape, Lil forced herself to
turn away. She looked at the armoire. She should
search it, set her mind at ease once and for all that
her manager had none of the strange tastes or moti-
vations she suspected. But she couldn't. She already
felt interloper enough.

Blowing out the lamps she'd lit, she walked toward
the door. But something drew her gaze above. A
small circular stair led to another level of the tower,
and she knew that must be the bedroom. She blew
out the last lantern, but even when the lamp she held
was all the light remaining and the spiral stairs were
but an impression upon her unconscious, she still
found herself walking toward them.

She had to see where he slept. Only then could she
get these visions out of her head. She'd set one foot
upon the first rung when the voice came, rough and
low, right over her shoulder.

"If you wanted a tour, all you had to do was ask.
And by all means, I agree with your priorities—bedroom first."

Gasping with fright at the sound of that deep, me-
lodious voice, Lil whirled. Her slipper caught and she
would have fallen if Ian hadn't reached out and
grabbed her. For an instant, every nerve in her body
came alive to the touch of his hard warmth pressed
so scandalously close. Through the thin layers of her
lawn nightgown and fine cashmere robe, she could

31

feel every expansion and contraction of that powerful rib cage.

His breathing had quickened too. Despite the hard, even stare of those impenetrable amber eyes, he was affected by her as well.

Lil stumbled back and fell to her rump upon the third step. The lantern slipped in her nerveless hand, and she would have dropped it if he hadn't taken it and set it on an adjacent table.

The light from below threw his strong face into sharp relief as he drawled, "Would you care to bounce on my bed?"

Cursing her fair skin, hoping he couldn't see her blush in the half-light, Lil retorted, "You mean *my* bed?"

"Oh, you may own the mortar and stone, mistress, but I own the furnishings." His gaze raked over her, lighting upon her bosom like a touch. He might as well have said it: *With time, I will own you too*.

Hoping her throbbing pulse wasn't visible beneath her thin robe, Lil stood and waved him back so she could exit the narrow spiral stair that had her imprisoned. He stood so close that his long legs almost brushed her feet, and . . .

. . . he didn't move. "I am not a dog to obey hand signals. I suggest you put your tongue to good use, or I will give it a better one." And for the first time, a smile stretched that dark face. His white teeth gleamed and he actually leaned closer, running his own tongue against the edge of his teeth in a way that made her mouth tingle.

Strange, how his canines were slightly more prominent than his incisors. . . .

And then she was dumbfounded at his insolence, torn equally between outrage and temptation. She turned away in the only direction open to her—up. If, deep inside, she wasn't quite sure whether she wished to escape him or herself, well, of that no one had to know. Least of all Ian Griffith.

Her former manager. She'd give him his walking papers first thing in the morning.

When she was halfway up the stairs, she stopped and scowled down at him, feeling secure in the distance between them. "I will examine your room for myself. And if I find nothing untoward, I may reconsider my decision to discharge you." She expected him to explode in wrath, or maybe even show a bit of remorse.

His smile only deepened as he nodded that arrogant dark head. "Be my guest. I guarantee you'll be surprised at what you find. But we might as well have truth between us, even from the beginning."

Lil almost ran up the rest of the stairs, holding her skirts high enough so that she didn't trip, but still careful to leave her ankles covered.

The room that came to life in the flare of the gas lamps she lit was unlike any she'd ever seen. Round, simple whitewashed stone. Again, spare, but the velvet bed hangings on the vast fourposter were burgundy, tied back with gold ropes. At the foot of the bed was a bench, and upon the bench was a man's silk dressing gown. It was fiery red, and it had something embroidered on the back, something she

33

couldn't quite make out. Her hands itched with the need to pick it up, but instinctively she knew not to.

Touching his things would lead to touching his person.

So she turned away, and it was then she noticed the easel and canvas set up beneath the enormous curving window. Next to it was a table and a sketch pad. Feeling as if she was finally finding some clue to his secretive personality, she walked toward the table. She was reaching out to pick up the pad when that voice spoke again, right over her shoulder this time.

"Go ahead. Discharge me if you wish."

She started and whirled. How did he walk so silently?

No smile upon that enigmatic face now as he said softly, "But you will still not be rid of me. Any more than I will be rid of you. The Haskell women and the Griffith men have been linked for centuries, Delilah. Your blood is as hot with the bond between us as my own."

Still holding her gaze, he reached around her for the sketchbook. He flipped it open and showed her the top picture, the next, and the next.

Heat started at the top of her head and ran like magma to her toes. The images got progressively more sensual.

And progressively more shocking.

They were all of her. Face only, then bust, then from the waist up. Dressed lightly at first, then only in chemise and stockings. Finally . . . as he flipped

34

through the sketchbook, he ended on a full-length nude.

Of herself. Her arms lifted wantonly toward her lover, her lips ripe with a sensual smile as she lay upon the very bed in this room. Wanting him.

For she knew now, beyond doubt, that he had sketched them. And he had painted the landscape over the mantel. This driven, powerful man was an equally driven, powerful artist, able to appease his own hunger with these wanton images. How had he been able to draw her so accurately? Even the shape of her breasts, the size of her nipples, the triangle between her legs.

All the conflicting feelings troubling her for the past two weeks seemed to coalesce in her mind. Her senses narrowed to a minute speck, and then exploded outward in one glorious emotion.

Fury. Before she put thought to action, her hand lashed out and slapped that arrogant face hard enough to jerk his head to the side.

"You bounder! You have no right to even think of me so, much less—" She broke off with a gasp as he caught the back of her skull in both his powerful hands and tipped her head back. His touch swept through her like a tidal wave.

For a moment she was pristine, like a beach never stepped upon by human foot. And then he shoved her against the wall, pressing into her with his masculine frame that so strangely seemed to fit her own.

And she was marked.

Marked forever after, no matter what came of this night when it seemed only the two of them were awake in all the world. She felt the imprint of him, indelibly stamped through the shivering sands of pride and propriety straight to the bedrock of her soul.

When he kissed her, she tipped her head back to meet him.

And finally, she saw emotion in those strange amber eyes. . . .

Chapter Two

Lil had been kissed before, many times. Awkward kisses, earnest kisses, even a few experienced kisses. But this dark invader of her home, her mind, and ultimately, she knew, of her body, created his own lexicon. One her body interpreted even as her mind resisted.

Those lips were as warm and unyielding as the rest of him. But the way they moved— His exploration was unhurried, as if he'd always known her.

Kiss? How banal.

Invasion. Intimacy. Consummation. He'd barely touched her, yet already he'd filled her with his strength as surely as if he held her spread-eagled to the bed.

And Lil, stubborn as only one of Scots ancestry can be, tilted her head back to welcome the thrust of his tongue. He dipped, and danced, and tasted the rim of her teeth, lips suckling gently all the while. And she didn't just allow him intimacies she'd allowed no other.

She welcomed them.

Curled her tongue shyly around his own, wondering why the moist heat didn't disgust her as it had with the others. When she answered the sexual foreplay so explicitly, the tenor of his embrace changed. During that first kiss, his hands had touched only the back of her skull, cradling it not with tenderness but with surety. As if he knew she knew he had strength enough to crush it—but no need.

He was already in her head.

But when she kissed him back, inexperience made eloquent by passion as great as his own, a shudder ran through that strong frame.

And Lil rejoiced. With a fierceness that almost frightened her. He was not so indomitable after all. He, too, had weaknesses. And he could not exploit hers without exposing his own.

The primitive symmetry was so seductive that Lil pulled her hands free from the heated trap between their bodies. He broke the kiss, looking down at her curiously. He was so much taller that her hands had to trail up from his waist, past his strong chest, over his sturdy collarbone, before she could finally clasp the back of his neck.

His hands went slack upon her head and his eyes went strangely unfocused. As if he needed the touch of her hands upon his flesh the way he needed breath and water. And when she tugged his head down, tilt-

ing it to the side so *she* could kiss *him,* a stronger
shudder wracked him.

The next thing she knew, her robe and nightgown
were open, and his rough palm was learning the generous heft of her breast. Lil gasped into his consuming
lips, but then his tongue thrust again, and the dark
urges went wild within her. She thrust her breast into
his hand. He sensed her need and circled her nipple
gently with his thumb. She was already hard, and the
grazing of that callused thumb made her long for the
feel of his mouth there.

He took her in, suckling her nipple with nothing of
the infant about him. He was all primitive male, tasting her, knowing her, completely.

Almost . . . as if he took his birthright from the tip
of her most vulnerable femininity.

Reject him? Slap him? The thought never crossed
what little mind she had left. She could only slump,
weak, over the strong support of his arm at her back,
and feel her heart fly to meet the gentle suction.

And then something curious happened. He rested
his cheek against her left breast, eyes closed, long
dark lashes like shadows upon his face. As if he didn't
just listen to her heartbeat.

He felt it.

He hungered for it.

He wanted to hold it in his hands and feel its vibrant life.

His mouth opened. His tongue circled the rim of
his teeth. Lil stared down at him, her own eyes dark
with a desperate passion she could not control. For
an instant, it seemed his canines grew to fangs. Still

she could not move. She could only wait, helpless in his grip.

But if she was a victim, so was he.

A moan escaped him, high-pitched, eerie, the sound of a wolf in pain. But when he turned his head to nuzzle between her clothes, the wool and silk dropped to her waist. Both her breasts were bare to him, high, round, firm, and white. Capped by thrusting, blushing nipples pouting for his kiss.

They were so much the essence of woman vulnerable to him, that he drew a deep, shuddering breath. The wildness that had almost overtaken him was buried under the needs of a man for a woman. His expression grew tender. Gently kneading her flesh, he buried his face in her, drawing life, and strength and purity. And Lil was fed too from the bounty of the exchange.

Unbearable hunger one breath, satiated the next. The need only became more acute when she lost the feel of his mouth upon her flesh as he switched from one breast to the other.

The burning ache didn't stop at her breast. It went from her torso, down her legs, to her very toes. And it was so shocking, so atavistically beyond her control, that sanity returned for an instant as that mesmerizing mouth drew away.

For one sobering instant, Delilah, miner's daughter, the doughty Scots heiress, looked down upon that wild black head so intimately placed at her bosom.

With a cry of despair, she caught his thick hair in her hands and pulled his head away, squirming free. Pulling her clothes over her shamed flesh, she ran.

40

Ran as she should have the minute he appeared.

Down the spiral stairs, through the tower, all the long way from one wing to the next. Faster, faster—but far too slow. No matter how fleet her feet, her heart almost burst with the knowledge her mind refused to heed.

Too late.

He had possessed her this night, in every way a man could. The intimate thrust of his manhood into her would be no more invasive or consuming than the feelings rioting through her from the wild tangle of blond hair to the tips of her tingling toes.

The second she reached her room, Lil threw every bolt and lock on the door. A long cheval mirror mocked her, but she turned away, stripped off her clothing, and threw the garments in the fire. Never again could she look at them.

For thirty minutes she scrubbed at her torso, using strong lye soap, not the gentle French perfumed bar, until her skin was red and almost raw. If a hair shirt had been at hand, she would have slept in it.

Finally, the sky pink with dawn's first blush, she pulled on her primmest night rail and climbed into her bed. Even then, she tossed and turned, chaotic images whirling through her confused mind.

Ian, painting upon the moors.

Ian, his lips curled back in a snarl as he listened to her beating heart.

Ian, holding her with a tenderness no man had ever showed her, even her own father.

And it was that last image that brought the tears to her eyes and made the burning ache he'd left in his wake all the more difficult to quell. He gave tenderness so awkwardly, so shyly.

Like a man who'd known little in his own life.

Lil had been attracted to men before; heavens, she'd even slept with one she'd thought herself in love with. But nothing, no sane counsel her father had ever given her, none of the manners that snooty Eastern finishing school had taught her, not even Jeremy's salty oaths or Safira's mysterious philosophies could quiet the torment in her mind and body.

Ian Griffith frightened her.

He thrilled her.

He mystified her.

And as certain as she breathed, the next time he crooked a finger at her, she'd come running.

With a frustrated groan, she pulled the feather pillow over her foolish head.

But still he lurked there, even at the edge of sleep.

And doom . . .

To her great relief, she didn't have to see Ian for several days. As if to make up for her inner weaknesses, she grew firmer with her staff. When Jeremy came to her complaining about the lack of respect he was receiving from the butler, Lil pointed out, "It could be the man feels his dignity is a bit threatened when you persist in addressing him as 'yer ruddy worship.' "

Jeremy growled back, "Could be he deserves it. His brains be scrambled from the thin air up there upon his high horse."

"Then I suggest you learn to relate. Retire to the

stables and study the equine version of dignity. It will come to you faster if you start with the hind end first."

Jeremy's mouth dropped open as she turned on her heel and stalked off. He suspected she'd put him in his place, even if he wasn't quite certain if she'd called him a horse's ass or not.

That very night, in the servants' eating quarters, he glared over his Yorkshire pudding and Cornish pasty at Safira. "What the devil be wrong with Delilah?"

Safira smiled mysteriously. "I fear her Samson has entered her life when she least expects it. But it will be *her* locks that are shorn."

Somewhere in his misspent childhood, Jeremy had spent a few Sundays restless upon his dear departed ma's knee while she read the Bible. "Samson . . . he's that bloke in the lion's den?"

"No, Jeremy. That was Daniel. Samson's the one who had great strength until wicked Delilah discovered the source of his power—his long hair. When it was shorn, he grew weak and the Philistines used him as a slave. But when his hair grew back—"

"I remember now. He used a rock and a slingshot and defeated a giant—"

Safira closed her eyes and muttered some heathen word Jeremy was shrewdly glad he didn't understand. "No. That was David. When his hair grew back, Samson pulled down the temple of the false god and all the Philistines died."

"And Samson?"

"He died too."

Jeremy stared down thoughtfully into his brown ale. "The bloke was barmy in his noodle, too, just like all them Hebrew kings. Death before defeat. What twaddle! Him who lasts, lasts." He was rather proud of his own profundity, but Safira apparently was less impressed.

This time, her muttered oath became an incantation, but she broke off her tirade when Jeremy interrupted, "Anyways, what's all this claptrap got to do with Delilah? Who's a-cuttin' her hair?"

Safira wiped her mouth, rose, and straightened her turban. "Since I do not have the next twenty years for biblical lessons, I will let you decide the matter for yourself." And she stalked off, generous hips swaying.

Jeremy scowled after her, but then he raised his tankard and slurped it dry. He eyed the stable boy and cook's assistant, who'd listened to the exchange. They looked every bit as confused as he was.

His prickly pride a bit mollified, Jeremy filled his tankard again, opining, "Women. Arsk me to time the tides with the phases of the moon, aye. Arsk me to gut a mackerel in one stroke, or tie a half-hitch knot in a typhoon, Johnny on the spot I am! But make sense of a woman's blather? I'd have a better chance of mendin' a spinnaker in a spout with spit."

The cook's assistant had attended the village school, and his eyes lit up. "Alliteration! Ye be an eloquent man for a sailor."

But Jeremy had had quite enough. Shoving his half-touched food to the side, he rose. "Ain't nothin' literal about this godforsaken place, ye arsk me, 'cept that it's a literal friggin' bore!" And he stomped out.

But he made sure he took his tankard with him.

44

*   *   *

Over the next two days, Delilah managed to upset the French cook to the point of quitting, her maid to the point of tears, and Mrs. McCavity to the point of blushing. But when Safira pointed out that she was alienating the staff she needed to run this "great, crumbling pile of moldy stone," Lil sighed and collapsed onto a settee in the salon.

"Oh, Safira, what am I doing here? I . . . miss the mountains." And Papa. And even Mama's silly babble. But they were both lost to her forever. At least, until she departed this earthly vale to join them.

But even as she said it, Lil found her gaze drawn to the enormous arched window that overlooked the moor. In the bright sunlight, Bodmin Moor looked almost as lovely and inviting as that picture Ian had painted. But Lil knew that, just as with Ian, its looks were deceiving.

One unwary step . . . or kiss . . . and disaster would swallow her up.

Or offer, finally, forgetfulness?

Her mellow brown eyes intent upon Lil's expression, Safira shook her head. "Ah, mistress, you do not know the power of what you tinker with. We should leave here with all haste while we can still walk."

Lil's eyes flew to her companion's face. "Whatever do you mean?"

"I have read the bones, and they . . ."

A chill crept up Lil's spine. Safira, who had been educated by a Friends' Society at a School for Immigrants, was never at a loss for words, and she always spoke her mind. Which was why Lil liked her company so much. "They what?"

"He wants you, mistress. As badly as you want him. But some desires have more of the other world than this one in them. If you . . . lie with him, he will consume you, heart, body, and soul."

Even as that chill spread to the marrow of her bones, Lil rose and scowled down at her companion. "This time, you read the bones wrong. Ian Griffith is nothing to me but a valuable employee."

"I said nothing of his name."

Lil pretended not to hear, and swept out of the room.

Alone inside the salon, Safira rocked back and forth and muttered an incantation to the good half of the spirit world. If she loved her mistress less, she'd run screaming from this cursed house on this cursed land in this cursed country.

Late that afternoon, Lil was inspecting the polished silver, finding fault with tiny specks of discoloration, when a footman hurried into the pantry. "A Miss Shelly Holmes is here, madam. She says she was hired by the previous owner to run the stables, and has just now become free of her former obligations. She wishes now to take up her new duties."

Lil glanced at Mrs. McCavity, who spread her hands helplessly. "I know nothing of this."

"Tell her I will be with her directly," Lil replied. "Let her wait in the salon."

Before she went to the salon, Lil took time to wash her hands and be sure her new severe attire befitted the prim and proper heiress of Haskell Hall.

Just over the threshold, she stopped. The woman who stood inside, feet spread, wore breeches of all things, and tapped a short quirt against her leg while she surveyed the room with piercing gray eyes. She was tall, blunt, and unyielding as the mountains behind her in the distance. Lil guessed her age to be between forty and fifty. Her brown hair was braided and wrapped around her head, and her skin was far too brown for the milksop complexion so much the rage at Victoria's court.

When Lil entered, those gray eyes turned from appraising the surroundings to appraising their owner. With the same merciless acuity, she gauged Lil: size, age, value, merit. With one look, Miss Holmes seemed to make up her mind about her potential new employer, for she came forward, large gloved hand outstretched in the new American fashion.

"I regret my tardiness, but it was beyond my control, I assure you." She firmly shook Lil's hand, and then stepped back.

Lil, too, had always been a quick, astute judge of character, and she doubted that much but weather, death, and taxes were beyond this woman's control. Which no doubt accounted for the "Miss."

"Forgive me if I am at somewhat of a loss, but no one informed me of your pending employment."

"I am ever frank to a fault. I confess your predecessor was less than . . . organized."

A small smile curled around Lil's mouth. "A fact I do not quibble with. But perhaps you can acquaint me with the terms of your agreement with her."

Miss Holmes outlined terms that seemed equitable to Lil. The stable was in execrable shape. "Very well. If I may see your references . . ."

They were already waiting on the table before the settee. Lil looked through them quickly. All were glowing, again an incongruity to Lil, for she'd found Englishmen to be even more threatened by strong, independent women than American men.

Except for Ian. He'd probably be delighted if she flew at him, tooth and nail.

Lil stuck the letters back inside the neat leather sleeve. "Very well. I shall see that the quarters above the stable are made ready immediately. I regret that you'll find things in your new domain in rather deplorable condition."

"Quite all right. I relish a challenge. As, it is apparent, do you."

Lil tried, and failed, to hide her surprised look.

Strong white teeth flashed in that angular brown face. "When last I sat in this room, there were spiderwebs on the ceiling, the brass was corroded, and dust hung like a pall over everything. Now, spit and polish everywhere I look. I suspect the stables would have been next on your agenda, so I am glad I arrived when I did, or my services might not have been needed."

"And I suspect I must watch my p's and q's or you will be sitting here in my stead."

A pleasant, deep-timbered laugh shook those broad shoulders. "There you have the wrong of it. I find a drawing room a deadly bore."

"So do I," Lil whispered, leaning forward. "But you won't tell anyone, will you?"

"Oh, I won't need to. You really must learn a bit more duplicity, my dear, so that your life and heart are not such open books."

Before Lil could ask for an explanation, she was given one.

"You are from Colorado, heiress to a fortune in gold, most likely made by your Scottish father. You are very intelligent. You despise hypocrisy and social niceties. Yet you are lonely."

Lil reared back in affront. "How dare you have me investigated!"

"I never heard of you until I arrived at your door. I knew the chit who employed me was dead because I read it in the newspaper, but I assumed, rightly, that the new owner would be in even more need of a competent stable manager."

"Then how . . ."

"You wear a gold nugget necklace. Your father's first strike, I apprehend?"

Clutching the necklace, Lil nodded dumbly. "He told me on his deathbed never to take it off, that it would bring me luck."

"Luck is as much overrated as love, but that's another story. You are obviously American. The largest gold strikes that account for nuggets of that size and purity come from the mountains of Colorado these days. Your accent, though refined, still has a wisp of a Scottish burr about it. And you obviously appreciate my honesty and boldness, which means you despise hypocrisy. As for your intelligence . . . that is as plain as the nose upon my face. Rather prominent, indeed."

Lil was so stunned the woman's reasoning that her voice was squeaky when she finally managed, "And lonely? How do you know that?"

Melancholia darkened those clear gray eyes to charcoal. "Because I see the same expression every day in my own mirror, too."

In that moment, Lil's sense of isolation became a bit less acute. Whether she had found a friend or not, she did not know. But she had certainly found a kindred soul.

Eerily, again Miss Holmes echoed her thoughts. "We are much of a kind, my dear Miss Haskell. Rarities in an age when a woman's worth is gauged by the strength of her womb. We need to think first, and feel later." A smile broke through again. "Quite tiresome to the poor befuddled males of our species who will never understand us."

"But much more amusing as we watch them flail about," Lil pointed out with a wicked smile.

And they shared a laugh that, even in the lengthening shadows of the afternoon, made the house less gloomy.

The next day, when Lil finally saw Ian again, she told herself that she'd quite regained her equilibrium, that it was her turn to watch him "flail about" while she coolly dissected him with her green eyes.

But, as usual, Ian Griffith proved that he would not comply with her expectations.

He walked into her drawing room as she sat before the window embroidering. With Shelly ensconced in the stables, and the household running like a top, all that remained for her to manage now were the outlying buildings, the lands, the mine, and the village. All of which would require Ian's tutelage. So she'd decided to pursue ladylike occupations to shore up her icy reserve.

No matter how much of a silly ninny he made her feel, he was still a common laborer, and she was the mistress of the manor. Even in America, such a divide was seldom crossed. In England, crossing wasn't even contemplated.

As she selected the silks for the woodland design she'd decided upon, she looked down at the drawing of the wolf. Now why had she picked just that amber shade for the eyes?

She sensed him more than heard him.

When she looked up from her embroidery frame, *he* stood there. Looking at her with eyes the exact shade of amber of the silk in her hand. She had to fight a blush and the urge to hide the telltale color, but she only tilted her head back and let her eyes clash with his.

"Next time kindly do me the courtesy of knocking, or announcing your presence in some other fashion."

"Why? So you can take time to put up more false barriers between us?"

"No. So you can avoid being shot. My nerves are strained by all this talk of wild hounds scavenging the countryside." She was glad to see the half smile flickering on his lips fade as he looked at the pistol next to her on the table.

"Nerves? You have plenty to spare, I should think."

"And I shall need every one, just to tolerate your impudence. Now state your business, or get out."

To her shock, he only walked closer, his eyes glowing in the gloom as he stood near an armoire, where the sun could not reach. "Perhaps I came here to tell you that your tenants wish to meet you. That it is high time you ventured from your sanctuary. You need to see the moors, the farms, the village."

"I will so inform you when I am ready." And it won't be with you as guide. She was quite determined upon that. Safira's predictions had always amused her, but this time, she wouldn't take any chances, especially as he'd almost seduced her the other time they'd been alone. She turned a cold shoulder to him, stabbing her needle into the outline of a tree.

His lips curled as he observed her severe profile. Thick silvery hair sleeked back into a knot. Austere black bombazine dress buttoned to her neck, no hint of a bustle. Mouth pursed grimly, as if she feared what she might say—or do.

"It will not work, you know," Ian said softly.

She kept her head down, though she could do little about the color rising to her cheeks under the nearly physical impact of his gaze. "What on earth are you talking about?"

"The more you try to pretend you're a prude, the faster you will come to my bed."

Her green eyes flashed up to meet his. "You overstep the bounds, sirrah. Get out of my drawing room or . . ."

"Or what? Fire me, then. I much prefer our trysts on the moor. You have had life too easy up until now.

I know a place deep in the moor, between bogs and tors, where there's a patch of earth God forgot to take away with Eden. There, I will lay you bare before my eyes alone. You will know the utter joy of softness on your backside, hardness at your front. Then, my naive little heiress, you will truly learn the meaning of life—soft and hard. Good and bad. Joy and pain. All intertwined and inseparable." He leaned forward. "Like us, and the bond we share."

The words ran over her like rough silk, abrading all her covered skin beneath the prudish clothes. But he didn't have to know that her nipples stood erect with temptation. He forgot to mention life's most treacherous lesson—how to figure out the difference between guile and honesty. He was masterful at both, but Lil had always been a quick learner.

Stabbing her needle into the eye of the wolf, she rose and faced him unflinchingly even when that amber gaze trailed over her like flame. "I prefer you learn your own lesson. With your backside upon the moor, you'd have softness behind—and softness in front." Wondering if she'd lost the last little piece of her mind, Lil walked up to him.

So close the tips of her slippers brushed the tips of his boots.

Only a broken dream separated them. Or a whisper of hope . . .

Steadily, Lil held that shocked amber gaze. "Sometimes, life offers only joy. But to get it, you see, you have to give it. You can't twist it, conquer it, or tear it apart. You can only accept it like the gift it is and learn Ian Griffith's hardest lesson." She leaned close until her breath brushed his neck. To her delight, she saw gooseflesh rise on his skin as she drawled, "Humility."

Whisking her skirts gracefully to the side, Lil walked out of her drawing room. And as she closed the door, she heard the bark of his laughter. Surprised, admiring. Almost joyful.

A small smile remained upon her lips for the rest of the day.

A week later, when Lil visited the stables at Shelly's invitation, she wasn't surprised to find all the tack oiled, the very hinges on the stall doors shining, and not a hint of dung anywhere in the barn. The horses gleamed with good health and grooming.

When she was done, Lil looked at her stable mistress severely. "You disappoint me. A week? Would you like to tackle world peace next? Perhaps it might take you a year."

Shelly barked that loud, infectious laugh. "You had me going there for a minute, and it's the rare person who surprises me. But actually, if Victoria Regina would consider stepping aside, I suspect I could contrive quite capably. Though it might take more than a year."

"And they say men are arrogant."

Even Shelly looked shocked at the deep voice that seemed to come from nowhere. They whirled in concert, staring at Ian. They'd heard not a sound, yet he stood on gravel that crunched like bones beneath the stable boys' footsteps.

He appraised Shelly carefully from head to toe. "If

you stay out of my affairs, I shall stay out of yours and leave you to terrorize your little fiefdom. Brutus is mine, by the way. I typically ride every morning at seven. Please see that he's saddled and waiting." And he turned and walked off. Equally soundlessly.

Her gray eyes finally startled, Shelly looked at Lil. "Why do you tolerate him?"

"Until I can find a replacement, I have little choice. According to Mrs. McCavity, the groundskeepers, miners, leaseholders, and villagers all have a fierce loyalty to him."

Frowning, Shelly stared after Ian for a moment. She seemed unsettled, off kilter, but then, with a straightening of her broad shoulders, she replied, " 'Tis your concern, of course. Not mine. But that man is more than an estate manager."

"A smuggler, perhaps? A pirate?" Lil had seen no such evidence in Ian's rooms, but since she couldn't admit she'd been there, she could only say, "As far as I can tell, he does his job, and does it well, so I have no grounds—yet—for his dismissal. But I give you leave to come to me if he makes a nuisance of himself."

Lil turned.

"Do you ride, my dear? I would be happy to show you about the moor myself."

Lil hesitated. She had one fear she'd never been able to control. Not since she was a child. Normally she didn't speak of it, but Shelly would be offended if she didn't understand why the stable owner never availed herself of the stables. "I . . . used to ride. Many years ago. But I lost a dear friend in a riding accident and . . ." She trailed off, looking at Brutus, who'd poked his nose over his stall door. He was a great, fearless black stallion, almost sixteen hands high, and he scared Lil straight into Sunday.

And she'd never seen a mount and master more suited to one another. All darkness, sinew, and power, kept in check only so long as they pleased.

As she watched, Brutus seemed to sense her apprehension, for his nostrils flared. He snorted, and pawed the ground. Lil jumped back.

Shelly went over to him and offered him a sugar lump.

Lil tensed, expecting him to bite, but he only slurped the lump from Shelly's gloved palm. He suffered her touch when she patted the side of his glossy neck. But he didn't seek it, so he reared away as soon as he'd finished chewing.

Very like his master.

Lil turned toward the door.

"You do not strike me as someone subject to irrational fear," Shelly said reasonably, walking Lil to the door.

"Normally, I am not. But this . . . is beyond my control."

"Have you tried to control it?"

"You mean . . . have I ridden? No. But I drive my own curricle on occasion."

"That is not the same. If you like, I can take you up with me on old Betsy over there. If I spur her, she jounces into a trot. She might outrun a rocking horse, but it would be close."

Lil laughed. "If ever I decide to ride again, rest

assured I shall order Betsy." Lil started to walk away, but she noted an odd expression in Shelly's eyes. "Do you wish to say something else?"

Shelly hesitated, which gave Lil some hint of the gravity of the subject. Inexplicably, Lil braced herself.

"I have been around many animals. And I love them all. But any animal, even a domesticated one, can be dangerous if it scents fear. The wise master shows them none, and only then are they tamed to the hand."

Lil stood there staring at that serious brown face. Why did she have the uncanny feeling that they were not talking about horses? And that Shelly had a deeper purpose here than running a stable? "I . . . understand. I think."

"I hope so. Tomorrow then. First thing? We shall ride upon the moors. Once you learn where the bogs are, they're not so frightening. It would be better for you if you learn to navigate there as easily as you do in the house."

Miffed for the first time with her newest employee, Lil turned on her heel. "I have other plans for the morning. I shall notify you, if and when I decide to ride. Good day."

During the short walk back to the house, Lil couldn't shake the strange feeling that Shelly not only had her best interests at heart, but that she feared for her safety.

How could that be?

Perhaps it was time to solve the mystery of what had happened to the former heiress of Haskell Hall.

Chapter Three

During her short tenure, Lil had found the servants to be efficient, hardworking, and honest. At least in matters of the household. But when it came to the history of the Hall, and even more, apparently, the history of the demise of its former owners, the servants were inexplicably affected with various ailments.

Mrs. McCavity grew strangely dumb at Lil's direct question: "How did the previous heiress die?" The housekeeper opened her mouth, but nothing came out. Then she made a garbled excuse and fled.

The butler grew deaf. He continued about his duties, only the tinge of red at his oh-so-proper hairline above his oh-so-proper starched cravat hinting of his discomfiture.

And the French cook seemed blind, for he stared right through her as he yelled at his cook's assistant for not stirring his precious sauce vigorously enough.

By the time lunch came around, Lil was steaming. Whatever the scandal, it must be shocking indeed for the servants to risk her wrath like this. But they didn't know her well enough yet to understand that such resistance only made her more determined. As Pa was fond of saying, the difference between a rich gold miner and a poor one could be summed up in one word: digging. The harder, the longer, the more gold one found.

And since her newest servants seemed to be conspiring to keep her in the dark, she decided it was only fair that she enlist her oldest, most trusted servants—really, Safira and Jeremy were more like friends—to help her cast some light upon the mystery.

Besides, she was tired of eating alone in the great, drafty dining room. As the turtle soup was removed, Lil looked at her friends and said casually, "I keep forgetting to ask the housekeeper, so I was wondering . . . have either of you discussed with the other servants what happened to the former heiress of the estate?"

With unwonted clumsiness, Safira dropped her fork on her plate with a clatter. "Ah, I do not know the other servants here very well, mistress. We do not discuss such topics."

But Lil noted that Safira took a sudden interest in her plate as she spoke. Lil looked at Jeremy.

The minute she saw the redness in his prominent ears, she knew he was lying when he mumbled,

"These blokes be so standoffish, they probably made their own mothers curtsy and sway."

Lil observed that he hadn't answered the question. Her green eyes darkened to the color of polished jade. Cold. Hard. Sharp enough to cut. Lil stood, tossing her napkin beside her untouched main course. There was obviously a conspiracy of silence here. But to involve her own servants . . . Lil spun on her heel. "Jeremy, have my curricle brought around. I'm going to the village."

"But mistress . . ." he whined.

"Instantly!"

Muttering to himself something along the lines that a "man here can't even have a decent meal without having to listen to female blathering," Jeremy stuffed so much bread and meat in his mouth that he looked like a chipmunk. He rose to do her bidding, however.

Lil ducked back around the dining room corner, pulling her driving gloves on as she did so. "I heard that! With the insubordination I've suffered this day, I find myself missing one of the seafaring traditions you always pine for."

"Sailing away on the seven seas?" Jeremy ventured.

Lil smiled sweetly. "No, the cat-o'-nine-tails. Applied to the place you'd feel it least. Your head. Now go!"

Jeremy scurried away. As Lil donned her driving bonnet and her light capelet of green merino wool trimmed with black braid, Safira entered the vestibule. She looked at her mistress with those wise dark eyes that had always seen more deeply and easily into Lil than anyone else.

"Mistress," she said formally, and that was warning enough to Lil that she was treading carefully, "it is not my practice to offer counsel where none was asked, but . . ." She had the grace to blush slightly at Lil's disbelieving look, but went on steadily enough. "But I feel a . . . disturbance in the gloaming between this world and the next."

"Disturbance? You mean you're having bad dreams?" Lil straightened her bonnet with the aid of the hall tree mirror.

"No, I wish it were only that. I feel this . . . foreboding of disaster lurking around every corner of this cursed place. If we do not leave now, within the next few days, I fear it will be too late."

"You know what the solicitor said. Would you have all these people lose their livelihood because I'm craven?" Lil turned to appraise Safira's lovely, worried face.

"If the choice is between that and your own death, then yes, so be it."

Strangely, a shiver climbed up Lil's spine despite the warmth of the capelet. "You have seen this in the bones?"

"No. For the last few days, I have been too afraid to cast them. I smell it in the very walls of this place, and feel it every night when darkness approaches and the moon rides high."

Lil shrugged off her own unease and Safira's warning. "You have been wrong before in these strange premonitions. You thought my father only had a cold, after all. Please see to the straightening of my closet while I am in the village. Things are in a sad mess there, and perhaps once you organize that, you can also sort your feelings to a semblance of normalcy." Lil walked out to wait under the portico, but she took with her the look on Safira's face.

Fear. Sorrow. Almost . . . desperation. As if this time, Safira's premonition was much harder to banish. This time, it took shape and substance, for it walked upon the moors with them.

But the day was lovely, the sky almost as blue overhead as it had been in Ian's picture. Jeremy was, as he played the role of tiger, for once, quiet. Lil savored the scents of moss, and heather, and the salty taste of the damp marsh wind. Despite its bleakness, this place had a curious beauty. One she'd never seen before and would likely never see again, for she knew of no landscape in America like this.

Looking at the seamless blending of greenish-brown-blue moors to the far horizon, where the mountains took on the same strange hues, Lil reflected that she could understand why Ian Griffith was so drawn to this place of his birth. The very air here made one feel . . . wild. Free. As if it would be a joy, in truth, to fling off her clothes and frolic naked in the moss.

The village came in sight, relieving her from her thoughts. It was a shabby little place. Everywhere were signs of neglect, from the tiny, dingy apothecary to the haberdashery with a crooked sign and the smithy, where at least she heard the clang of hammer on anvil.

Hearteningly, she saw other signs of life everywhere she looked. The tiny village school was packed as she drove past, and a mob-capped barmaid bustled between the courtyard and interior of the only public house in the village. She carried tankards of foamy ale and boasted a jouncing bosom that drew more than one ribald eye from the dusty miners and farm workers taking a noontime break.

As Lil slowed, she noted that the barmaid lingered at a particular table half in the shadow of a great tree. She straightened her mobcap with a flirty, natural femininity Lil envied. Lil's mother had possessed that innate understanding of how to best use the only assets females had in a male-oriented world. Lil had none of that artifice, which was one reason, no doubt, her former lover had lost patience with her. Seldom had Lil regretted that lack, but when the barmaid leaned down to whisper in her patron's ear, Lil caught the amber gleam of hungry eyes directed at that overflowing bosom.

Shock and outrage battled for dominance in Lil's mind as she stared at her estate manager.

Bold as brass, Ian sat there, his hat off in the shadow of the great tree, those strange amber eyes glowing like beacons that rivaled the bright new day. And Lil was as surely drawn to them as a ship seeking safe port in a storm.

Safe? Balderdash! If she hadn't been so furious, she might have laughed at the ridiculous notion. And she was a moon-eyed, green girl, despite her advancing years and dabbling in the sensual arts, to romanticize him so.

Lil realized she'd let the lazy carriage horse draw to a stop and graze, but she was too busy analyzing her own strange feelings to care that she was beginning to draw attention by her bizarre behavior.

Furious with the stab of jealousy she could not control, Lil pulled her bonnet strings taut under her chin, almost choking herself, and gripped her reins more firmly. Time to drive on, forget this shocking display of lust right in the middle of town. It was clear how Ian Griffith kept the female denizens of this little village in their places.

With an iron hand indeed!

Still, she was hideously fascinated as Ian pulled the flirtatious barmaid down on his lap and nuzzled her neck.

Suddenly, Lil's pride in her ladylike bonnet and ladylike capelet and ladylike manners felt as constricting as the garments themselves.

"Be we stopping here, mistress?" Jeremy asked hopefully.

"Hmm?" Now the blackguard's huge hand was splayed on the barmaid's generous waist as he whispered in the girl's ear. The girl tossed back her head and laughed. A throaty, sensual laugh that would have sounded natural in bed. It drew every covetous male eye in the place.

And two covetous, ladylike ones.

Perhaps it was the carriage blocking the sunlight.

Perhaps it was the intensity of her own confused emotions.

But something drew Ian's attention. He looked up, only his eyes moving as he continued to nuzzle the side of the girl's neck. Plain as if he spoke it, his taunting gaze said, "Envious? You've only to ask. . . ."

Her mouth dropped open at his temerity, and her green eyes hardened to green agates. To Lil's fury, his dark lashes went down again. He showed no trace of concern or embarrassment. He was impervious to her scorn or anger.

And he kissed the top of one lush breast. Right there, an affront to decency and gentlemanly behavior everywhere.

"Don't mince words, nor action, neither. Now there's a man who should be stridin' a quarterdeck," Jeremy said admiringly.

He seldom offered his ultimate compliment to any landlubber, especially a backward Cornishman, and that only infuriated Lil more.

"Aye, but myself thinks you've the wrong of it a mite." Lil imitated Jeremy's Cockney accent. "He'd look better hangin' from a quarterdeck than stridin' one." And she clucked to the horse, well aware that her progress down the street was followed by those strange amber eyes.

She could feel them.

As they approached a small stone church with a white-cross steeple, Lil observed tartly to Jeremy, "At least I know now where my estate manager disappears to midday. I shall have to dock his wages accordingly, since I shall not pay for such shocking behavior."

"A man's got his appetites, mistress. Even these

65

strange, backward Land's Enders." Jeremy climbed down to offer her a hand off her perch.

"He can satisfy them on his own time," Lil retorted, skirts held with miffed dignity as she walked onto the stone porch of the manse next to the church.

Immediately, Jeremy's expression took on a hunted look as he appraised the tiny church. "Ah, mistress . . . me throat's dry as a desert. Could I . . ." He looked back longingly over his shoulder at the tavern.

"Oh, very well. Meet me back here in an hour." Truth to tell, she didn't want any witnesses to this talk. Surely even if everyone else in this country lied to her, she could count on the vicar for the truth. Perhaps some of Safira's foreboding had worn off on her, for she feared it might be more painful than lies.

But it had to be done. Lil reminded herself of her motto. No pretend crocodile tears, no siren call to lust, not even the false leads the hyenas hereabouts had tried to plant in her way, would distract her from this unpleasant task.

Before she could truly feel herself the heiress of this grim, forbidding place, she *had* to know what had happened to her predecessor. Considering how desperately everyone had tried to keep the information from her, she knew it wasn't pleasant. But how could she arm herself for the future if she had no knowledge of the past?

An hour later, if Lil hadn't been wearing her bonnet, she would have pulled at her hair in frustration. The vicar was away visiting a sick tenant. The vicar's wife was a simpering, silly woman, so intimidated by having the heiress herself in her humble abode that she spilled tea on Lil's dress as she tried to pour it with shaky hands. When Lil gently tried to broach the subject of the former heiress, the little woman turned beet red and snapped her teeth down on a crispy scone still warm from the oven.

"Ladies do not discuss such things," she said after she'd meticulously wiped her mouth and hands on a tiny linen napkin.

Lil almost snapped back that maybe ladies didn't, but she didn't pretend to be one. But luckily, the door to the parsonage opened.

The vicar was as tall and severe as his wife was plump and silly. He nodded when his wife introduced Lil, but his pale blue eyes seemed to penetrate to her spine. "And to what do we owe the pleasure of this unexpected visit?"

His wife opened her mouth, shut it, and looked at Lil. She'd been so busy chattering that she'd never stopped to ask.

Lil cleared her throat. "Might we have a moment of privacy, sir?"

He deposed his long form on the shabby sofa, accepted the cup of tea his wife made just so for him, and then smiled at her. For the first time, his dour countenance softened as he said with genuine fondness, "Letty, would you make more of your delicious meat pasties for the Foster boys?"

Immediately, Letty jumped up, her plump face concerned. "Their mother's confined again? Poor dear." And she was off.

One mystery explained.

Lil had grown up puzzling over the wondrous conundrum that was male-female attraction. Her own parents had been an odd match. This pair seemed equally mismatched, but it was apparent that what Letty lacked in courage, she made up for in kindness. And her husband, it seemed, had enough intelligence for both of them.

"Lady Haskell, do I apprehend that you are here about your predecessor?"

"Why, yes. How did you know? And please, it's Miss Haskell. I am American, after all, merely the daughter of a poor miner."

Shrewdly, he appraised the quality of her garments. "Poor? I think not. But I know most of your servants. Many attend my church quite regularly. They were greatly aggrieved at what happened to the last heiress, and I know that they have formed something similar to the Sicilian code of silence to avoid frightening you off. Your presence is needed more than your enthusiasm, or at least so they believe."

"Surely the village would profit better with both."

Those pale blue eyes warmed slightly. "Here, here. I think perhaps that you are very different from the last heiress, a spoiled girl who insisted on her way. Whether it was safe or not."

Was that a subtle warning? Lil wondered. "And what did she do that was so unsafe?"

He paused to taste a scone, and she sensed the debate behind that calm countenance. "She liked to ride upon the moors. Alone. At night."

Lil laughed. "If that was her grievous sin, you've no fear I shall repeat it. I do not like to ride. And I

68

have never ventured onto the moors after dark." Until today, she hadn't ventured on them at all, but he didn't need to know that.

But he apparently did, for he smiled slightly at her prevarication. "It has been my experience that only when we face what most frightens us do we conquer our fears."

Arrested, Lil stared at him. "Are you related to a Miss Shelly Holmes?" she asked.

"Why, yes. She's my first cousin. I recommended her for her current position."

"I should love to meet the rest of your family." In that, she was quite sincere.

He had Shelly's deep, honking laugh, too. "A trying affair, I'm afraid. All of us invariably attempt to get the best of one another, proposing riddles, solving anagrams, and the like."

With her usual forthrightness, Lil almost spoke her mind, but she bit back the question instead.

"That's quite all right," he replied as if she'd spoken. "It is an odd occupation for one of my bent to choose, but I find that, the more one thinks, the more one needs respite in duty. Caring for the sick. Preparing dull sermons so the children will squirm as is their own duty."

Lil laughed. "Dull? You, sir? This, I doubt. And I shall discover the truth for myself when I attend church this Sunday."

"I shall be quaking in my slippers." His honking laugh joined hers in the tiny room, an easy acknowledgment that, like his cousin, he almost never quaked at anything.

69

They sobered soon enough. He nodded, again as if she'd spoken, and said, "Quite right. Enough roundaboutation. I do not blame you for your fears, Miss Haskell. Or your precautions. Both are well placed." But he hesitated again.

The truth, when it finally came, roiled through her like a tidal wave.

"There is no easy way to say this. So . . . the previous heiress was ripped apart by wolves."

"Wolves? I didn't know there were any left in these parts." She pulled the capelet closer about her shoulders. The room was warm, but still, she was suddenly cold.

"A few are sighted from time to time, closer to the mountains."

"But . . . the mountains are miles away."

Vicar Holmes didn't reply.

"If this was merely an unhappy accident, there's no reason for a conspiracy that has obviously included my own servants. Poor girl. A terrible fate, no doubt—"

"Her heart was eaten."

Her own heart seemed to lodge in her very throat, pounding frantically. "Only . . . h-her heart?"

"So we heard. Miss Haskell, are you all right?"

Lil surged upright again, only then realizing she'd sagged against the sofa back. "Of course. This . . . is why Miss Holmes came here, isn't it?"

"This exact information was not allowed in the papers, but yes. I told her. She's something of an investigator of strange phenomena."

"A hobby?"

70

"A calling. One she excels at."

"And what has she discovered so far?"

"That you will have to ask her. She never talks about her investigations until she's completed them."

Which meant she must be a long way from completing this one, Lil deduced. "Vicar Holmes, I have to know . . . am I in danger, too?"

He hesitated, but then he rose, went to a desk, unlocked a hidden drawer, and retrieved a pile of yellowed newspapers. "These will answer you far better than I."

Her hands shaking, Lil thumbed through them, feeling as if she were, in truth, all thumbs. They were in chronological order. The first account went back to . . . Lil gasped, wondering if she read the faded, brittle paper and strange printing right. "Almost one hundred years ago?"

"Yes. 1779. The first heiress, reputedly the daughter of the last of the male line. Next year will mark the one hundredth anniversary of the first death."

"H-how long did she survive as the heiress?"

"The years vary. Sometimes almost an entire lifetime. Your . . . predecessor died within a few months of taking possession."

"So . . . this has happened repeatedly? The heiresses all die the same way?"

"Yes."

Lil flipped through the rest of the accounts, looking only at dates. By her reckoning, roughly five heiresses had died this way, their throats ripped out, their hearts eaten. All on the moors. All at night. And they were all alone.

Lil tossed the sheaf of papers aside. "But that's preposterous!" Reason began to master fear, and her voice was clear, the hint of Scottish brogue stronger. "Fiction. A legend propagated by people hereabouts to frighten outsiders."

But that didn't make sense, either. These villagers needed her, as the conspiracy proved.

"I wondered about that once, too," he said, interrupting her chaotic thoughts. "But . . . this time, I saw the body myself."

Lil's stiff spine wilted. "But why? No wolf would only eat the heart. It would consume everything if it was hungry enough to approach civilization."

"So one would think." He hesitated, and then he stood and sat beside her. He moved as if he'd catch her shoulders, but he apparently thought better of that and made do with one of her hands instead. "Miss Haskell, a vicar has to become a good judge of character if he is to perform his duties admirably. I sense that you are an unusual young woman, made of sterner stuff than the other unfortunate young woman who inherited this grim place. If so, perhaps you are ready to listen to a story told to me long ago, by a very old woman in this village, on her deathbed. She was a Romany. It is not a pleasant story, but if you are brave enough to thumb your nose at such danger, then you surely have the right to hear it."

Nodding, Lil squeezed his hand. Then she leaned back and braced herself, but her eyes held his steadily.

An admiring gleam in his pale, perspicacious eyes, he said, "It is a very old, sordid tale."

"Lust? Murder? War?"

"All those things, alas. In 1752, the last male heir to the Haskell estates married to produce heirs. But his wife was a sickly creature, and to appease his appetites, he preyed on destitute young women. However, when his eye fell upon a Gypsy girl, at first he tried, by all accounts, to resist her charms."

"How noble of him."

"Quite so. Nobility had little to do with it. Like all good peers of the realm, he wanted no scandal attached to his name. But the passion he felt for this maiden became so virulent that one night during a full moon, when she was bathing in a pool on the moors near the Druid stones and he came upon her . . ." He cleared his throat. "But, as is often the way of such things, passion only bred more passion. On her side as well as his, for ultimately, she grew to love him. But when she was found to be with child . . ."

Lil closed her eyes, sick to her stomach. It was indeed a very old story. "He sent her away."

"He tried. She refused to go. They argued violently one night as her time approached, and her father tracked them to their trysting place at the stones. He'd become suspicious, you see, and when he listened and found his guess of who her lover was confirmed . . . well, his loyalties settled quite naturally on his daughter over his employer. When he threatened to unmask the liaison if Haskell didn't acknowledge the child . . ." He trailed off and looked away.

The scene Lil saw so vividly in her mind's eye brought a tear in sympathy for the girl who'd visited

73

such a terrible wrath upon Lil's own kind. "Was the girl's father killed?"

"Yes. Accidentally, by all accounts, but Haskell panicked and fled, unaware that his lover's labor had started."

"He left her there? By herself? On the moors?"

Her outrage was shared in his face. "Indeed. Her babe was born prematurely. She almost died herself during the birth, and when travelers came upon her and took her to the village, she survived only long enough to give the boy to her grandmother to raise."

Lil frowned. "She had no mother, then?"

"Apparently not." The vicar's tone grew rushed, as if he wanted to get the unpleasant telling over with. "That night, when the moon was full, the old woman used every medicine she knew in an attempt to save her granddaughter, cursing Haskell as she worked. As life faded from the poor girl, she cradled the child her pain and suffering had birthed, and I suppose that it is not so strange that her love for Haskell turned to hatred. With her last breath, it is said, she looked out at the orange harvest moon and cursed the Haskell lineage. She wanted no blood of hers to ever again be mingled with the Haskells'. With her father dead, she begged her grandmother to raise the boy in the Gypsy ways, to keep him far away from the other half of his relatives. The grandmother disappeared into the moors, taking the boy with her."

"And . . . what was the curse?"

"That every Haskell heiress should bear the weight of her torment: lust turned to love, a burning obsession so fierce that it would feel as if her heart were being ripped from her breast. And the moment the words left her lips and her spirit departed this earth, or so it is said, Haskell himself was ripped apart by wolves on his way back to his estate. Since he died without issue, and there were no remaining male relatives, the estate passed to a distant female cousin."

"I might have known this curse upon the females of our line was begun by a man," Lil managed to quip.

Vicar Holmes laughed. "Indeed, as with many things of unpleasant consequence, you can blame the male of our species."

"And the first heiress?"

"Survived to a hale and hearty age. Her daughter was the first to die upon the moors."

"And what became of the boy?"

"No one ever knew. But a few years later, a tradesman set up shop in the village, and his son showed uncommon intellect and an uncommon flair for organization, plus a certain resemblance to Haskell himself. He soon became the heiress's estate manager."

Lil braced herself, her heart thrumming unpleasantly. "Why have you not told me his surname?"

"Because I suspect you already know."

"Griffith," Lil whispered.

He nodded. "No one has ever openly acknowledged that this first estate manager was the Gypsy's son, but so I was told by the old Romany woman, and so it must be, or the first heiress never would have made the agreement that allowed Griffith estate managers to live in the tower. They have Haskell blood, too. Much diluted, many times removed, but surely they have a moral right, if not a legal one, to some small share of the bounty they have toiled so long to harvest."

The memory of Ian's rough words echoed in Lil's ear like her own heartbeat: "The Haskell women and the Griffith men have been linked for centuries, Delilah. Your blood is as hot with the bond between us as my own."

Her hands icy, Lil rubbed her elbows, but she still felt numb from head to foot, even with the warmth of the blazing fire in the small fireplace. Neither her Calvinist upbringing nor her practical nature had ever allowed for such foolishness as curses, blood bonds, or ungodly urges so strong that . . .

"But I don't understand. Why would the Gypsy girl wish such a terrible fate upon those of her own sex? Would it not be more horrid for the Haskell males to die terribly?"

"Remember, she wanted no further mingling of the two lineages, and what better way to keep the heiresses away from Griffith males than to make them fear them? She died because of the terrible power of . . . of . . ."

Sexual obsession. Lil blushed and looked away. She'd had a taste of that power, too, and her sympathy for the girl who'd died so long ago grew.

There was a terrible logic and poetic justice to the girl's curse that, in another time and place, when she didn't feel so terribly trapped in a silken web partly of her own construction, Lil might have appreciated.

Power for the powerless over the powerful.

The Griffiths might be servants to the Haskells, but

in the end, if they truly had a strange dominion over the moors and its wild creatures, could even induce wolves to attack, they had a strength more terrible than any granted by privilege or blue blood. It was the Haskell women who risked everything to trespass upon their territory. But there was one last question she had to ask. "But if the curse is known, why do the heiresses always ride alone upon the moors even when they know what could happen?"

"Not all heiresses have known what I just told you. As to why? That I cannot say. Willfulness. Foolishness. Mayhap even destiny."

"I have never put much credence in curses. Or things that go bump in the night," Lil said, her voice stronger. Really, now that she knew the truth, unpalatable as it was, she felt better. No matter how grim the situation, there was always a remedy. And since she didn't like to ride anyway, and the moors rather frightened her, well, sensible might as well be her middle name.

A flashing memory of her bare bosom lifted to Ian's mouth as he bent her like a bow over his arm made her cheeks redden. Sensible?

She rushed into speech, aware that Vicar Holmes looked at her oddly. "If there are wolves hereabout, we merely need to send huntsmen out to find them. And I assure you I shall not venture out alone into the moors after dark. This 'curse' ends with me." She rose decisively and offered her hand. "But I vastly appreciate your honesty."

He shook her hand gently. "And I your courage. I see why my cousin thinks so highly of you."

"She has said so?"

"In her way." He escorted her to the door. "Please, do visit again, and I promise this time we shall keep the conversation light. I have even been known to play cribbage from time to time."

"I happily reciprocate that enthusiasm. And I hope you and your wife will come to tea at the Hall very soon." At the door, she looked up at him and confessed, "At least now I understand why my current estate manager tends to be so arrogant."

"He is an unusual man, only lately returned from his travels."

Lil frowned. "But . . . he's so much in command, so respected, that I thought he'd lived here all his life."

The vicar walked her outside and helped her into her carriage. "Oh, he did. Until he was twenty. Then he wandered the world for about ten years until he returned home about six months ago. Come see us again soon, my dear, and I shall hope to see you in the front pew this Sunday." Waving, he went back into the parsonage.

As Lil drove toward the tavern to collect Jeremy, she reflected that, whatever her inner conflict at the tale she'd just heard, she could still count on one phlegmatic verity that never wavered under any temptation: subtraction.

If Ian Griffith had returned six months ago, he'd arrived home three months before the last heiress died.

Had there been a strange blood bond between them,

too? Had he sketched her nakedness, tried to seduce her as well?

Who was Ian Griffith, really?

A simple Cornishman of overly lusty appetites?

Or a cosmopolitan wanderer, artist, engineer, lover of beauty with a tormented soul?

And what—or whom—did he remind her of? Those strange eyes, that soundless walk, that magnetism . . . Something tickled at the back of her mind, a childhood memory she hadn't recalled in years. Another myth she'd heard back during a girlhood house party. Her friend's French grandfather had teased the little girls about . . . blast it all, what was it?

But when the tavern came in sight—and she saw, with great relief, that Ian was gone—she let the memory go.

It was, after all, the sensible thing to do. She didn't need to beg for trouble. As Jeremy had said with more prescience than she'd realized at the time, "Trouble follows bold-like, right through the door with us."

Trouble hadn't just followed, it seemed in the ensuing days; it had taken up permanent residence. The mine had a cave-in, so a new pump had to be purchased. Luckily, the miners had not been working that section, so no one was hurt.

The prize stallion, Brutus, jumped out of his pasture and rutted with a tenant farmer's plow mare. He trotted back with a satisfied air about his arched tail and tossing neck. But as Lil watched Shelly halter the great black beast and scold him, she heard one stable boy whisper to another, "No airs about that one, don't matter none how blue his blood be. One quim's good as another, and I ain't sure but what he's not right."

Blushing, Lil moved out of the shade of the barn, and when the boy finally noticed her, he went beet red, tugged his forelock, and ran. Lil decided she'd better have a talk with Jeremy. She knew the source of that philosophy, and she didn't want his ribald sense of humor spoiling these innocent country boys.

Next, the French cook fought with the butler, even threw a knife at the dignified fellow. It took Lil and Mrs. McCavity two days to restore calm.

And it took the carpenter even longer to fix the gash in the wall.

However, as Lil was forced to deal with one domestic crisis after another, she had little time to wonder any further about Ian Griffith, for he was busy, too. And if, every noontide, she'd sneak a glance at her lapel watch and wonder if he'd sought out the tavern and all its delights, no one save her need know.

A week after her visit to the vicar, Lil had visitors herself. She had a kerchief tied about her neck and an apron over her midriff, and was helping Mrs. McCavity sort and cull old staples out of the pantry, when a twittering housemaid found them. "It's the Harbaugh brothers themselves, returned from the Continent! Here to pay their compliments. Mistress." She dropped a belated curtsy on this last.

Even Mrs. McCavity showed a glimmer of excitement. "Have they opened Somerset again?"

"So Mrs. Farquar's maid told Mrs. Thomas's maid who—"

"Yes, yes, more efficient than the post, I know,"

Lil interrupted. "But who are these men?"

"The handsomest young bucks in Cornwall," Mrs. McCavity said, pulling Lil's kerchief off. "Quick, make yourself respectable."

Lil glared at her. "I am not on the marriage mart, thank you very much."

"But they're rich, and handsome, and Thomas is heir to an earldom." There was a sudden tension in the housekeeper's attitude as she muttered, "And Lord knows, those of this household should share in that wealth." She colored under Lil's arrested gaze.

"And why is that?"

"I'm not one to perpetuate gossip," was the prim reply. When Lil still blocked the exit, the housekeeper sighed and admitted, "It's an old story, never verified, of Ian's older sister."

"Sister? I didn't know he had one."

"She died when he was a boy. And that's all I'll say upon the matter. But Thomas Harbaugh wouldn't be who he is today without her."

Lil had tired of the mysterious scandals roiling beneath the serene surface of these moors, and now was not the time to delve further into the latest one. More to the point, she'd seldom met a buck of blue blood she could tolerate, much less be attracted to. "I don't need money, and I have no interest in titles. But if they've come to pay their respects, I should meet them, I suppose."

In the kitchen, Lil paused at a small mirror to straighten her disarranged coif, but it was too badly mangled by the kerchief. And there was a stain of jam upon her sleeve. She'd also worn an old gray gaberdine dress she'd been meaning to give to a home for the widows and orphans, but she'd just have to do.

However, when she set foot inside the drawing room and saw the Harbaugh brothers, she almost backed out again. But they rose immediately, smiling, so she was caught. Preston had the sloe black eyes, perfect features, and curly hair of her favorite poet, Lord Byron. Thomas was as blond as his brother was dark, with dark brows and mahogany-kissed brown eyes that crinkled at the corners from obviously frequent laughter.

And no one needed to tell Lil that they were also both rakes. The efficient way they sized her up in one sweeping glance came only with practice. They bowed gracefully.

Thomas said, "I am pleased to meet you at last, Miss Haskell. I fear we have been remiss in our neighborly duties, but we've only just returned from the Grand Tour."

Preston bowed over her hand. "Charmed, mademoiselle."

Before he could kiss her hand, Lil withdrew it and gave them a polite curtsy, wondering why she was irritated that they didn't address her as "Lady Haskell." Though she detested the affectation herself, she wasn't happy that these smooth gentlemen didn't offer the obvious courtesy to another person of their social rank. Were they subtly trying to snub her?

"You must have been to Paris, too," she said sweetly.

They laughed.

"Yes, and hard it is upon a man's stomach to return to English food," Preston admitted. "Though I've heard you're lucky enough to have a French cook. We're having a ball in a few weeks. You wouldn't want to lend him out, would you?"

"Not unless you wish to have gashes all over your house. He tends to throw knives at whoever upsets him. The dark side of creativity, no doubt." Lil waved them to a settee and took up her station behind the teapot.

"That's why we've come, actually," Thomas said, sipping his tea in a stuffy way Lil secretly detested. He even had one pinkie, decorated by a heavy emerald signet ring, raised in the air. "To invite you to the ball." Thomas nodded at Preston, who took a vellum envelope from his pocket and laid it on a table next to the settee.

"All the gentry roundabout are agog to meet you. Mrs. Farquar has been singing your praises far and wide," Preston said gallantly.

Lil could imagine what "praises" that dreadful woman was spreading, but she only shuddered, finished her half cup of duty tea, and set it quickly aside. Good, strong coffee for her. She'd never get used to these insipid dregs that truly tasted as if made from, well, leaves. "I shall be delighted to attend, assuming, of course, that I have no prior commitments." And she might have to think one up. She'd taken a dislike to society balls in Denver because invariably she was a wallflower at the snooty balls, and a trophy at the ones given by social climbers and brash new millionaires.

83

Here, in a land where tradition was sacred, she'd be a curiosity, no more.

Thomas smiled at her gently. "We promise not to stare. At least, not overtly."

Lil's eyes flew startled, to his face. She smiled ruefully. "Am I that transparent?"

"No. I'm just uncommonly intuitive. For a mere male."

Lil cocked her head and studied his handsome face a bit more closely. "Perhaps you are, at that. Modest, too, I see." There was more to this pampered English blue blood than she'd first supposed, but he was either unaware of, or uncaring about, her own subtle dig.

"People don't stare because they think you're odd, you know," he went on. "It's because they're stunned by your beauty."

Preston nodded, made a picture frame with his thumbs, and said judiciously, "No fairer English rose will ever bloom on our moors—"

"She's American, you idiot," Thomas reminded him under his breath.

"No prettier American wildflower will—"

Laughing, Lil raised her hands in supplication. "Please, sir, the only flour I smell of at the moment is of the wheaten variety." Lil brushed at the flour still clinging to her skirt. "Pantry duty today, which accounts for my appearance."

Thomas's deep male laugh sounded genuine this time. "A wit! I knew our boring country lives had taken a turn for the better the moment I saw you." He looked behind her. His smile faded. His sunny expression grew wintry.

Preston scowled, Byron in a temper tantrum.

Lil turned to look at the doorway.

Ian stood there, his strange eyes glowing in the shadow of his hat as he stared at her guests. Obviously he had no more liking for them than they had for him.

The Harbaugh brothers rose, taking a step to meet him before they checked themselves with automatic, obviously deeply ingrained courtesy.

Wishing she were the true English rose who could wilt and pretend a headache, Lil stood and stepped among the three Cornishmen.

She'd need all her tact to mediate this battle.

Chapter Four

"Get out," Ian said through his teeth. "Keep to your own lands, and mind what's yours."

Even Lil, who didn't put much past him, was shocked at his rudeness. "Mr. Griffith, you will apologize at once!"

He didn't so much as glance at her, dividing his hostile stare equally between the two brothers. "You don't understand. They are not fit company for you. They—"

Preston laughed harshly. "And you are? *You*, who—" He broke off with a wheeze as Thomas elbowed him in the gut.

"At least I don't rape women," Ian snarled.

The hairs rose on Lil's neck as she stared at the brothers.

Thomas went red in the face. For a minute it

seemed he'd strangle with fury, but then he collected
his silver-headed walking cane, tapped it to his temple
in a salute, and said coolly, "We shall be delighted if
you can attend our ball, Miss Haskell. And please feel
free to bring a guest of your own choosing. Good day.
Forgive the untimely interruption." He stalked out,
pushing his sputtering brother before him.

As they left, Lil heard Preston say hotly, "Are you
going to let that bastard talk to us like that? We
should call him out. We should—" Then the door
closed behind them.

Her knees weak, Lil sagged down on the couch,
knocking against the tea tray as she went. The bone
china rattled, and two cups rolled to the rug. She bent
to pick them up, but Ian had already knelt. Their fingers brushed. She shied away, even that small contact
sending a burning tingle up her arm.

He set the cups carefully on the tray and stood. She
had to tilt her head back to see his face, and she didn't
like the way he overshadowed everything, so she
pointed at a chair a safe distance away. When he sat
down, removing his hat to slap it restlessly against
his thigh, she breathed a bit easier. "Why?"

He didn't pretend to misunderstand. He didn't pre-
varicate. He went very still and spoke very softly. "I
don't trust them. They are rakes, unfit for your company. Besides, I don't like the way they look at you."

For a second, Lil was shocked speechless. A rarity
for her. She saw the same thought in his softening
amber eyes, and was so infuriated at the easy way he
read her that she blurted out, "It's less shocking than
the way *you* look at me!"

"Ah, but I have the right."

She blinked. Her hearing was faulty.

Now her sight had failed, too.

She could have sworn he was leaning back at his ease, not in the least abashed at his own temerity. Lil's dazed eyes wandered the room, anywhere so as not to look at that magnetic, indomitably male face that did such queer things to her equilibrium. She had to retaliate, do something to set her tilted world right side up again.

The next thing she knew, her hand acted of its own accord, picked up a delicate bone china teacup—and flung it at his head.

Naturally, he ducked. The cup shattered against the floor.

But it was his laugh that really tipped sensible Delilah, doughty Scots heiress, on her axis. A soft, purring growl, seductive, throaty. He all but dared her to do it again.

And Lil, the extremely unsensible side of Delilah, who was beginning to understand she was heiress to more than a big patch of earth, a village, and a moldy mansion, responded. Using both hands this time, she flung everything within reach at that arrogant head.

The salon door burst open. Panting, as if she'd run, a housemaid stood there. Behind her came the butler. And then Mrs. McCavity. They all stared, mouths agape, at the new heiress. And her target.

Ian didn't even spare them a glance as he easily lifted an arm to deflect the sugar tongs. "Get out," he said.

Mrs. McCavity wavered, "M-miss Haskell?"

"Get out," Delilah agreed through her teeth. This was between Ian and her. Mayhap if he was covered in scones, sugar, tea, and broken china, that overweening male pride would be a bit cockeyed even as it righted her own off-balance world. She picked up the plate, still filled with scones.

Shaking her head, the housekeeper shooed out the accumulated servants and gently closed the door.

Lil hurled the plate. The heavy crockery smashed onto the floor just shy of his feet. Scones went flying, as if they really were filled with air.

To her fury, he caught one with an adroit hand and stuffed it whole into his mouth, eating with enjoyment. Almost cross-eyed with apoplexy, Lil reached blindly for another missile. She was determined to make him wince, make him beg for mercy, or make him run. Somewhere within that indomitable frame were at least a few of the same human frailties he exploited in her.

And she'd find them, by heaven, she'd find them.

The teapot went next, spattering the silk-screened wallpaper with brown splotches. Then the spoons, the sugar bowl, still filled with lumps. But did he wince? No. Did he beg for mercy? Far from it. As for running . . .

He merely lifted a casual arm to ward off the few missiles he couldn't duck, advancing on her step by inexorable step. Laughing all the while. That soft laugh that both made every hair on her body stand on end and that queer weightless sensation in her belly move lower. To the soft center of her she'd spent the last year hardening.

But Ian wouldn't allow her to deny anything—least of all her own nature.

When she picked up the now-empty tray to throw it at him, too, he was close enough to catch her wrist. With easy strength, he removed the tray with his other hand and flung it across the room. It hit a piece of furniture with a clatter, but their eyes never wavered from one another.

"Here I am—mistress. Your favorite target. No need to break all the china in the house. Slap me as hard as you please. But know this. . . ." He leaned so close, those amber eyes became her whole world. "Passion begets passion. I have never hit a woman in my life, and do not plan to start now. But every blow you rain upon me pushes you one step closer to my bed. That's what this is all about, in the end. It is not I you fear and detest. It is yourself."

If Gabriel had flown through the window and blown his trumpet in her ear to warn of the Second Coming, Lil wouldn't have been able to move. She stared into those depthless amber eyes, feeling like a fly that had landed unwisely.

What was his strange allure? On the one hand, shining and golden and promising.

On the other—deadly. But even as glittering gold encased her, pulling her in until she had no breath, no existence beyond Ian, she reveled in the warm doom. Forever would she dwell here, part of him, that moment of flight or fight preserved.

So when he reached out to enfold her in truth as she already was in spirit, she couldn't move. Then she felt the rapid thrum of his heart hammering against hers. She realized he was more affected by their battle of wills than his expression admitted, and the last of her fury dissipated.

With a moan, part agony, part delight, she lifted her face to his kiss.

Doom had never tasted so sweet. . . .

Warm, just as she'd thought. Best of all, when she quit fighting it, deadly amber became honey to sustain her. His lips filled her with golden nectar everywhere they touched. And she could only lie helpless in his embrace, shyly kissing him back, exactly as he'd predicted.

Passion begets passion. . . .

His, as well as hers.

He gave a husky little purr as she pulled his neck down to bury her fingers in his thick black hair and better slant her mouth upon him. And the tender bumblebee kiss became a wasp's sting. His mouth hardened. She felt the sting of his teeth nibbling at the now-tender contours of her lips. He always seemed to have this strange urge to bite her, yet he never broke the skin, and there was something incredibly erotic about the rake of his teeth on her tender skin.

And then, even more arousing and shocking, his tongue swept over the tingling skin, soothing the sting—and inciting a deeper urge. The same urge that made bees pollinate flowers, and flowers cast out their pollen, beginning the cycle anew.

The same cycle she and Ian wanted so badly to celebrate. She felt it in the thrust of his tongue into her mouth, the hardness stabbing into her abdomen, and every particle of femininity she possessed responded. If he had lifted her and crushed her into the couch with his weight, she would not have been able to stop him.

With a harsh, animal-like growl, he lifted his head from the drugging pressure of her mouth. He cupped her face in his hands, breathing hard. His nostrils flared as if he could scent her own arousal. He stared down at her with eyes more flames than amber. "Come to me. Tonight. Before . . ."

Lil took a deep, shuddering breath, and a modicum of sanity returned. "Before?"

He started to reply, but something caught his eye. He stared above her head. A tic appeared in his strong jaw, and then he backed away and said something she'd never expected to hear from him.

"Forgive me. You make me feel things, hope things . . ." He turned and walked out so fast that, in a lesser man, she might have called it running.

Groping for a chair, Lil sat down, and then she followed the direction of his gaze. Whatever had he seen to change his raw male need to raw human despair?

At first she saw nothing, just pictures on the wall, innocuous enough. And a clock. Her eyes wandered, came back. Her legs still shaky, she stood and walked over to the grandfather clock. Above the hands, it had a dial that showed the phases of the moon.

In about five days, the moon would be full.

Lil searched again, but she saw nothing else that could account for his strange moodiness. Why would he be frightened by the moon?

Knowledge she both longed for and feared tapped

like an unwelcome guest at the back of her mind. She pushed back the tendrils of hair that had escaped her prim coiffure. And then she held her hand out in front of her to observe its trembling. As if it belonged to someone else.

Making a fist, she turned and ran, flinging open the door, feeling as if the hounds of hell nipped at her heels. She ran through the foyer, past the startled footman and butler, outside, into the bright sunshine. Drawing deep breaths of the strangely scented air, part marsh, part moss, part blooming things, she finally calmed enough to stroll to the stables.

Miss Holmes seemed to be a walking encyclopedia. Perhaps she would remember the half recollection knocking on a closed corner of Lil's mind. The childhood tale, tied somehow to the phases of the moon. But no matter how hard Lil tried to open that door, it was stuck.

Or she was afraid to face what lay beyond.

For she feared whatever monster lurked there wore Ian's face. . . .

She found her stable manager inspecting tack.

Shelly turned on the wiry little man who'd obviously just polished it. "Can you not see that you left tarnish on the brass? This is not acceptable. Do it again and do it right next time." Shelly turned and strode off, but stopped when she saw Lil. "Hello, my dear. Have you changed your mind about riding?"

Lil shook her head. "I was wondering if you might like to share a cup of tea with me."

Shelly smiled, delighted. "I'm flattered you find my company engaging."

"Not at all," Lil couldn't resist teasing, just to see that confident smile slip.

And it did. But only a bit. It widened again when Lil finished, "Merely engaging, my dear Miss Holmes? Not the half of it. Stimulating, fascinating beyond measure."

That honk of a laugh made a flock of sparrows chirp and fly away from the fence where they'd perched. "Upon my soul, it's the rare man or woman that either impresses me or surprises me. You, my dear Miss Haskell, do both. Come along. I have something I suspect you enjoy far more than tea."

In the cramped but pretty quarters above the stable, Lil soon found herself inhaling God's best aroma: freshly ground and brewed coffee. She sipped again, adding a smidgen more of the thick cream that came from her own cows. "Delicious. Why is it that you are the only one in this place who has figured out how much I miss my coffee?"

"Unlike most of my fellow Britons, I do believe a world outside these isles exists. I have seen it. I have even enjoyed it on occasion. And since I also saw your face when you last shared tea with me, I had the grocer in the village order this for you. You Americans have some peculiar habits, but divided as we are by an ocean, a government, and even our common language, we each enjoy our stimulants."

Lil finished the last drop of coffee and held her cup out for more. "I didn't know the grocer even carried coffee, or I would have ordered it before now." Only when she was braced by her second cup did Lil feel strong enough to broach the true reason for her visit.

She saw curiosity in those intelligent gray eyes, and she knew Shelly had already deduced that this was more than a social call. "Miss Holmes . . ."

"Shelly, please."

"Then do call me Lil. I confess I don't quite like being called Miss Haskell since my father's name was Trent. But no doubt if I remain, I shall become accustomed to it." Lil looked at the bookcase in the corner, which was stuffed with scientific tomes of every type. There was no easy way to say this, so she took a deep breath and blurted out, "Do you know of some significance to the phases of the moon?"

"The tides, of course."

"No, I'm referring to a legend. Something frightening I heard as a child, told to me by a Frenchman."

Shelly froze with her teacup halfway to her lips. "Why are you asking this?"

Lil became interested in the dregs of her coffee. "Curiosity."

"Killed the cat."

Startled, Lil dropped the cup, and a few dots of brown liquid spilled onto the spotless tablecloth. "Whatever do you mean?"

Shelly sighed heavily, and then admitted, "I had hoped it would be a while yet before you heard about this. To give you time to get accustomed to the moors, our ways."

"You wanted me to leap upon a horse and gallop my fears to dust, did you not?" Lil gripped the table edge with both hands. "I am far past the age of being told that if I eat my vegetables, I can have dessert. I can take the palatable and the unpalatable with equal composure. Furthermore, I've spoken to Vicar Holmes in the village, and I know why you came here, and that you are his cousin. If you have knowledge of these peculiar deaths, you have no right to keep that knowledge from me."

"As your employee," Shelly said coolly.

"No. As the only person, other than the two *friends* I brought with me, whom I trust."

Shelly's manner warmed. "For that, I thank you. And I assure you, your trust is not misplaced." She hesitated, rose, and went to a bookshelf, returning with a very old tome entitled *Lycanthropy: Loupe Garoux, Lupe Manaro, and Werewolf: Legends, Myths, And Remedies.*

The minute she saw the title, Lil remembered. "Loupe Garoux! That was it. A creature half man, half wolf . . ." She trailed off. Memory flooded back.

Shelly must have understood, for she took the book out of Lil's limp hands and set it on the table.

Lil scarcely noticed, too intent upon recalling the look on Ian's face when he saw that innocuous dial on the grandfather clock. Rough passion, urgent desire had become . . . fear and frustration. And then he'd bolted out.

"Do you remember how the cycle of the werewolf is governed by the moon? Or so it is said." Shelly had to repeat the sentence before Lil was able to drag herself back to the present.

"The tale frightened me so much when I was a child that I must have blocked it from memory," Lil said. "The closer the lunar cycle to the full moon, the more they change and become . . . inhuman. And then, on the night itself, they have urges they cannot control, do terrible things they often cannot even remember. With the dawn, they become fully human again. Until the next cycle. Do they really . . . eat human flesh?"

"If you believe what you read. I, personally, have never seen evidence they even exist. These stories may well belong with such foolish tales as Coronado's golden city, vampires, and ghosts. All three of which, I might add, I feel that my own previous investigations have disproved."

A glimmer of hope chased the shadows away from Lil's heart. "And what have you learned so far?"

"Very little. I've examined my cousin's evidence from the recent . . . accident. He was fetched, along with the local physician, and they reached the body before the authorities, so he made detailed notes before the burial. According to his measurements, the fang marks looked like those of a wolf, though an unusually large one. The claw marks, too, were consistent with lupine tendencies, though again, abnormally large."

"But if a werewolf is half man, half beast, he'd leave different markings, wouldn't he?" Lil asked hopefully.

"There are so many silly tales intermingled with the scant amount of science I have been able to decipher that these beasts could range from two-legged to four-legged to anything in between. Again, if they really exist."

"But the moon . . . is only five days away from being full."

"Yes."

"Do you plan to do any . . . observation?" Lil's heart pounded in her throat as she tried to imagine traipsing around those dark, desolate wastes at night, with only a full moon to light the way. But she couldn't bear to think of Shelly going alone, either.

"Of course," Shelly said, as if the question were foolish.

"I want to go along."

"Absolutely not! I choose to put myself in danger, but I am quite capable with guns and so on. Do you even know how to fire a rifle?"

"No. But I can learn. I shoot a pistol quite well."

"A pistol would only anger such a beast. You are the last Haskell heiress. Would you have this tidy little village broken up, these people thrown out of their homes once the greedy male cousins get their hands on the estate?"

Lil sighed. "I suppose not. But I cannot just wait for the same curse to befall me."

Shelly patted Lil's white-knuckled hand. "Give me more time to investigate. Once I know what we're dealing with, I am quite sure we can devise a way to stop this creature from striking again. If we have to, we shall kill it. Direct assault on the heart or the brain or an attack with silver implements seem to be the favored ways."

Lil had to close her eyes at the imagery, but that only made the blood and fear she saw in her mind's eye more real. She forced herself to focus on Shelly's homely face again.

"Some lycanthropes apparently fear water," Shelly

added. "From all I can discover, the manner of the transformation is the key to reversing it. If a person becomes a werewolf against his or her will, as long as he or she doesn't taste of human blood, the curse can be revoked."

"How?"

"It depends upon the means of transformation, how long the curse has lasted, and so on. The ideal thing, of course, would be to come upon the creature as it was changing. It would make the entire messy sequence of events so much easier to work out."

The scientific dispassion in Shelly's voice amazed Lil. "Are you not afraid?"

"No, not really. I have my rifle, my mistletoe, my cinders and silver tree leaves to take with me. Surely one of these protections should do the trick. I confess I should truly love to be the first unbiased, scientifically oriented witness to prove werewolves exist."

Lil stood, turning her back upon the ugly black book still squatting like a huge spider on the table. "Science may be your guide, Shelly, but it is not a magical shield against a strength and power we can scarcely comprehend, much less . . ." Again, the horrific images almost overcame Lil, and she had to clutch the chair back for support. "You will take Jeremy and two other men with you, or you will not go upon the moors at all for the next several nights."

Scowling now, Shelly stood, too. "I find that I move much faster and quieter alone—"

"So does the creature you seek." Lil stared back into the taller woman's eyes. "I will not have your death upon my conscience. Is that clear . . . Miss Holmes?"

Standoff. Slate-gray eyes struck sparks off granite-green.

But then Shelly smiled slightly. "You are a re-doubtable young woman indeed. We shall try it your way tomorrow night. If the men are as incompetent as their sort tends to be, the next night I go alone. Is that clear . . . Miss Haskell?"

Since Lil's only other option was to fire this amazing woman, she could only nod begrudgingly.

But if Shelly tried to slip out alone two nights hence, she'd have a very small, very determined shadow trailing behind her. And Lil knew the exact reply she'd make if Shelly turned on her in fury. "You wanted me to face my fears, did you not? And you want no men to accompany you?"

However, as Lil walked back to the mansion, she paused on the gravel drive to look out over the moors. They were flat, and brown, relieved sparingly by un-expected strokes of color. As if an artist's brush had missed the sienna pot and dipped into emerald, forest, turquoise, and . . . there, a lovely pink. A tall flower nodded gaily at her.

"Come, join me," it seemed to say.

As she contemplated those vast wastes, for the first time, Lil began to see some of the beauty Ian had painted so skillfully. That moment of insight terrified her most of all. She turned and ran for the house.

This grim place was proof positive that beauty lurked in unexpected quarters.

But as the fate of the former owners of Haskell Hall

also proved—so did danger. And Lil would forget that dichotomy at her own peril.

As she entered the house, she forced herself to think calmly, as Shelly would think. She knew where to find cinders . . . but mistletoe?

The next night, Lil refused to retire until the investigative team had returned. She tried to read, but ended up pacing the salon. She kept glancing up the stairs, longing to investigate Ian's tower. Just to reassure herself that he had retired long ago, as a hardworking estate manager should. But every time she found her wayward feet approaching the steps, she forced herself to pull back.

She'd snuck into his rooms once and almost ended up in his bed. If he came upon her again in the intimate, quiet darkness when the moon was almost full . . . She whirled and returned to the salon, trying to concentrate on her embroidery.

Finally, well after midnight, she heard a commotion in the foyer and ran to meet the returning party. She stopped short, staring in dismay.

Shelly Holmes, still carrying her rifle, stormed in first. She was muddy from head to toe, and she stopped short of the carpet, dripping brown sludge on the marble entryway. Gray eyes contrasted all the more sharply with her grimy face when she looked over her shoulder at someone behind her. "You, my good man, should return to sailing. I'd suggest the South China Sea . . . no, Easter Island. It's properly isolated, and you should be quite at home with the natives, dancing in grass skirts with half-naked women, communicating in the only way you seem to comprehend—sign language! And civilization will be safe at last!"

Sighing, Lil moved forward a bit so she could see the stoop outside.

Sure enough, Jeremy stood there, even more grimy than Shelly, if that were possible. His pale blue eyes were hopping mad—appropriately enough, for he hopped from foot to foot as if he could not be still. His hobnail boots left muddy footprints as he strode onto the hallway carpet to face his tormentor, hands on his scrawny hips.

"Aye, and so I might, jest so I can escape the airs o' females like ye." He spat on the carpet. "Female! Ye don't even deserve the name. Why, ye could dance bare-bosomed afore me in one o' them grass skirts and the only use I'd have fer ye would be as a broom. Stab me if else."

Since Shelly's eyes narrowed on him as if she were contemplating exactly where to sink the knife, Lil decided she'd better intervene. "I can safely conclude, I suppose, that the hunt was not successful."

Aggrieved, Jeremy turned on his mistress. "Might've been, if this here high and mighty—"

"That's enough, Jeremy!" Lil interrupted sharply. She had a soft spot for the salty sailor, but she knew how trying he could be. "Kindly go to your quarters and compose yourself."

Scowling, he started to stomp across the vestibule to the basement stairs, trailing mud as he went.

"Not that way! Go around the house to the kitchen entrance, and leave your boots at the door."

He stomped outside, grumbling something that might have been, "That one needs a man to ride her, aye, and a dig of the spurs into those scrawny flanks jest to remind her she's the one on bottom." The door slammed shut.

In the abrupt quiet, Lil could hear Shelly's teeth grinding together. Lil took a clean kerchief from her pocket and offered it to her stable manager. Shelly dried off her face.

"I'm almost afraid to ask, but—what happened?"

Shelly wadded the muddy kerchief into a ball. "We were hot on the trail of a set of wolf tracks, even heard howling very close, when that idiot jerked me behind him—off the path, straight into a bog. It took three men to pull me out, and while he was trying to organize things, Jeremy fell in, too. Needless to say, during all the commotion, the wolf disappeared."

With great effort, Lil managed not to smile. "Well, you must admit it was commendable of him to worry so about your safety. He doesn't have much use for the female of our species, but he was still raised to be protective of our, ah, frailties."

"Oh, I know exactly the only use he has for the female of our species. Grass skirts indeed!"

"He's no different there, is he, than any peer in the House of Lords?"

The brown streaks on Shelly's face cracked into a grimace that might have been a smile. Indeed, her white teeth gleamed through the mud. "You leave me speechless."

"Since I have a feeling that affliction shan't last long, I'll take advantage of your condition." Laugh-

103

ing, Lil helped Shelly unlace her boots, linked her arm with her stable manager's, and walked her upstairs. "Come, I know just what you need. A long, hot soak in my copper tub will help you forget Jeremy. I'll have a guest room made up for you. After a long night's sleep, we shall discuss our plan for tomorrow night."

Halfway up the stairs, Shelly stopped abruptly. "What plan?"

"Why, our adventure together. I promised you, as I recall, that if the men in your hunting party proved incompetent, you didn't have to take them again."

"But I said I'd go alone—"

"No, you assumed I'd let you go alone. You wanted me to face my fears, did you not?"

"Now see here, Miss Haskell—"

"I am seeing. Very clearly. Whatever danger lurks outside these walls will not go away if I cower inside and let others put themselves in peril to protect me. Besides . . . I have to know."

Lil looked away from Shelly's gaze, and silently led the way up the rest of the stairs. Shelly hadn't asked her *what* she had to know because she obviously read the truth in Lil's face.

When she met the Wolf of Haskell Hall, would its eyes be amber, its fur lush black, and its scent one her olfactory faculties would recognize before her conscious mind could?

After she'd led Shelly to the guest room and returned to her own room, it was almost two in the morning. Lil sought out her own bed, but she tossed and turned for another hour. Finally, she went to the heavy draperies and moved them aside to stare out at the clear night.

The moon was more than three quarters full. Odd how it never seemed so beguiling over the towering Rockies. Colorado was so scenic: mountains clawing their way to the very sky, aspen trees shimmering in the clean wind, sheer drop-offs displaying lush valleys below. There, the moon was an afterthought. A knickknack God aligned just so to decorate his abode.

Here, the moon ruled supreme. Over the flat moors, it was huge, serene, the focal point of the dark, sere landscape stretching for aeons below. This winsome moon was a siren. It seemed to beckon, to pull the very soul upward. And she finally understood why Cornwall was littered with so many stone altars and monolithic remnants of Druid days.

This moon required homage.

Lil felt it pulling at her mind and will, those very anchors of her being, until she felt a strange floating sensation, as if she had indeed parted the veil between life and death, reality and dream. With the moon shining so brightly, the scene before her seemed to shift subtly. Mayhap she dreamed. Mayhap she only empathized because she, too, was in the ruthless grip of sexual obsession.

But as clearly as if she stood in silent witness, she saw a figure, with the heavy, full clothes of Georgian England. Even the voluminous skirt could not disguise the Gypsy girl's huge stomach. In the distance, the Druid stones, a few more upright than now, glistened with a purity the girl obviously had lost.

Her lovely black eyes glittered under a sheen of tears as she stared up at her handsome, titled lover. Haskell was finely dressed, and perhaps it was the very luxury of his appearance that made the weakness about his mouth so apparent. His eyes shifted away, as if he could not sustain her gaze.

"If I am good enough to lie with, why am I not good enough to wed?" she asked, her voice husky.

Haskell tried to turn away—and came face-to-face with a stocky man with graying hair who ducked out of his listening place behind a tree. He carried a shotgun and a grudge with equal ease. "Bastard!" The outraged father nudged Haskell in the belly with the gun. "You'll get a special license, and get it now, or so help me God—"

"God?" Haskell sneered. "What do you and your get of Satan know of God? She tempted me, she came to my bed willingly."

The Gypsy girl's burnished skin lost all color. The vibrant sparkle in her eyes dulled as her father looked from her back to Haskell.

Staring unseeingly at the desolate moors, but caught in the terrible grip of a vision she needed but did not want, Lil clenched her hands until blood dotted the crescent marks in her palms. If she'd been there, she would have been tempted to use the gun on her own ancestor, possibly putting a period to her own existence, so acute was her fury.

But it was nothing to the father's fury. With a strangled cry, he leveled the shotgun and tightened his finger on the trigger. Haskell reached out to snatch the gun away, but the Gypsy girl was faster. She slammed up the weapon. Both barrels exploded harmlessly toward a tree, and leaves rained down upon them.

The girl's father cast aside the spent weapon and shoved Haskell against the tree, his hands squeezing the taller man's throat.

"Papa, don't!"

The girl pulled at his arms, but she was knocked to the ground when Haskell brought up his knee into his opponent's loins, forcing him back.

They didn't see her roll down a slight slope and come to a dazed stop, her legs and arms obscenely limp and askew, like a rag doll's. Her face twisting with pain, she curled into a ball and cradled her stomach.

The two men had battled their way toward the ruins, neither of them aware of the water breaking between the girl's legs. She struggled to her feet, fluid leaking down her ankles into her shoes, but it didn't show beneath the heavy skirt. She tried to go to the grunting, fighting men, but she could only manage two steps before she stopped, bent, and cradled her enormous stomach.

"Stop it, you fools!" Lil cried. "Help her!" But she could do nothing. For the first time in her privileged, indomitable life, she knew what it meant to be truly helpless.

Then Haskell slammed his forearms up to knock his assailant's hands aside. The girl's father stumbled away. His foot caught a rock, and he fell backward. The sickening thunk as his head hit the Druid altar made Lil wince.

Blood gushed from his wound into the ground, and Lil realized he was dead. His eyes stared sightlessly up at the uncaring moon.

Haskell knelt and felt the man's pulse. His strong face twisted with what might have been guilt, but when the girl's scream rent the night and she flew at him, nails curved into claws, her emotional agony now greater than her physical pain, Haskell reflexively lifted his hands to ward her off.

She fell again, landing on her side. Lil saw her bite her lip as she forced herself to her feet. Under the surreal glow that was so uncaringly lovely, they stared at one another. Her face was so expressive that Lil saw the exact moment when love turned to hatred. The Gypsy looked at her lover's face and then at her father.

Haskell looked at the remains of the man he'd killed. Then the girl staggered over to fall to her knees beside her father. Haskell was left with two choices: comfort her or flee. He did what was most appropriate to his nature.

He ran.

The girl looked over her shoulder in dull resignation at the sound of his retreating footsteps. Her eyes saw him for what he was, and their sick comprehension made Lil clutch her own stomach in sympathy.

The Gypsy girl rocked back and forth on her knees, clutching her belly. She began a singsong chant in Romany that seemed one with the moon, and the bleak landscape, and the Druid stones.

It was an ancient chant, born of an ancient pain.

Lil's eyes watered as she felt the girl's agony made

worse by betrayal. She reached out as if to touch her and comfort her, and the sight of her own hand, shaking against the backdrop of that same ancient moon, brought her back to reality. She blinked. The room came into focus.

She ran for the water pot, nauseous at the full import of what the lass had endured. In that moment, she hated the Haskell blood running in her veins, hated this huge, decaying house that sheltered such shame. As she leaned over the watering pot and vomited, the girl's keening cries seemed to vibrate between the shadow world and Lil's reality.

Despite the terrible legacy that threatened her very life, Lil couldn't hate the girl anymore. No woman was strong enough to survive something so vile with love and faith intact. And what power could counteract such well-justified enmity?

Weak, she leaned over the basin, but then she stood and shakily rinsed her mouth. She combed her hair and braided it. The ritual calmed her enough for her to be able to think. She'd never been subject to visions before, but she'd never had her emotions in such turmoil before, either.

When the terrible power of the vision allowed her to move again, Lil turned toward the door. Perhaps it was true; perhaps she and Ian were linked in a terrible bond begun in blood and pain. Perhaps it was her optimistic nature, or sheer Scots doggedness, but surely she wouldn't see such horrid things for no reason.

It was a warning.

She must not be trapped in the same curse of pride

as her ancestor had been. What matter that Ian Griffith was not of her social rank? He fascinated her more than any man she'd ever met, and while she pursued the liaison at her peril, after tonight, she also had little choice.

She had to embrace the curse to break it.

But first she had to know what she faced. Know beyond any shadow of a doubt, know that yes, it was true. Did he walk so quietly, see so well even in darkness because he was part man, part wolf? Or was he merely a very unusual, enigmatic man no woman could ever civilize, much less tame?

The only way to know for sure was to search his rooms. For if Shelly had tracked a wolf that night, and Ian lay sleeping in his bed, she'd have her answer. If there really were a Wolf of Haskell Hall, it couldn't be Ian.

But if he were gone . . .

Moving slowly, feeling the inexorable urge as surely as if the moon exerted a strange pull on her as well, Lil tied her new silk robe tightly about her slim waist. She picked up her lantern and exited her room for that long trek down the hall to his tower quarters.

And if he were there? Would she be able to escape, virtue intact? Or would the wild urges he incited in her with no more than a look take possession of her?

She smiled grimly. If it were true, as the Bible said, that lusting in the heart was as much a sin as fornication itself, then she was already a sinner many times over.

She might as well enjoy her long, slow slide from virtue into damnation.

Practical? Rational? Wise? Prudent?

Delilah Trent had lived her life by such boundaries.

Lil Haskell scarcely saw the barrier, and if she did, she climbed right over it without breaking stride.

The tower was locked. Lil used her key, wondering if she should knock, but somehow she knew surprise was best.

The rooms were dark. Quiet. The curtains drawn tightly over the moonlight. Lil's lantern threw her shadow on the walls and made it dance, as if her own sensual half had already liberated itself for the pleasure to come.

Lil cocked her head, listening. And then she heard it. A low keening moan, the throaty sound of an animal in pain. Her skin crawled, and she wondered, for a panicked instant, if the wolf had somehow found its way inside the house.

Then she realized the sound came from Ian's bedroom up the spiral stairs.

She ran up the curve so fast the lantern flame flickered wildly, and dashed into the bedroom. She stopped, gasping at what she saw.

Ian Griffith was manacled to his bed by a complicated system of metal chains attached with a hitching mechanism. He was immobilized, wrists anchored to each heavy bedpost. Outraged, Lil looked around to see who could have done such a thing to him, but he was alone. She set the lantern down and inched closer to the bed.

That low, keening moan came again.

It sounded exactly like a wolf groaning in pain. He was bare-chested, the black hair on his chest glistening with sweat, covers wrapped about his waist as he thrashed in the throes of a nightmare.

Lil had to catch the doorjamb to support her weight as she swayed with relief. Obviously, if he was chained to his bed, and from the looks of it, had been for quite some time, he couldn't have howled on the moors tonight. He was not a wolf. Just a very earthy man with a primitive allure that stripped away her own thin veneer of civilization.

The manacles were so tight about his wrists that his hands were growing white. His wrists were raw and red, and she realized, appalled, that his circulation had been cut off. She must get him loose before he hurt himself. She had to feel carefully along the manacle before she found the tiny latch. It was so small that one almost had to know where it was to release it.

She was able to easily unlatch one wrist, and then the other. The awful thought came to her that this was an ingenious restraint system, one obviously devised so a man could latch one arm and then use his teeth to open the latch and attach the other to the chain. When he pulled on the slack, it automatically tightened about a pulley. He must be able to get free in the same manner.

Why had he submitted himself to this? And why would he make it so he could release himself with equal ease? It made no sense.

Unless . . . he'd designed the system to work only with the tactile skill of fingers. Even as the last manacle fell, freeing him, a chill ran up her spine.

Immediately, still sleeping, he drew his wounds to his mouth and licked them.

She backed away a step, for there was something so canine in the way he moved, the way his tongue lapped, that she almost wondered if she could be mistaken. But no, she told herself.

You ninny, even a werewolf can't be in two places at once.

He stopped thrashing, licked his other wrist, and went very still. She assumed he'd fallen into a peaceful sleep. For a stolen instant, she hovered over him, devouring him hungrily with her eyes.

His torso was as broad as she'd suspected, the musculature perfect, lithe, lean, but not bulging. His chest hair was as black as the hair on his head, narrowing to the slim waist that disappeared beneath the covers. And his arms were long, supple, biceps bulging only slightly.

Her hands trembled with the need to touch him, to see if his chest hair was as soft as it looked, but she bit her lip savagely and backed away. Prudent, sensible Delilah told Lil Haskell that it was foolish to even think of having an affair with her estate manager. Why, it would scandalize the entire county.

But Lil's nostrils flared with the wild scent of him. Part man, part sweat, part sandalwood soap. All arousing. Two steps back from the bed, Lil made Delilah stop.

Surely it wouldn't hurt to look a moment longer. Just look. . . .

One of those perfect arms reached out, and long fingers caught her wrist.

Propping himself up on one elbow, Ian drew her gently down on the bed beside him. "Why make do with looking when touching is so much more pleasing? Since you were kind enough to release me from my bonds, Delilah, I can only do the same for you."

And he lay back, pulling her down atop him.

Chapter Five

Lil knew she should scream. She knew she should run. She even knew this was rank folly that would lead to tragedy.

But when she felt the heat of his body, smelled his unique, wild scent, this one defining moment made all else immaterial.

Only feeling mattered.

Again, he showed an eerie ability to empathize with her thoughts. He caught the end of her thick blond braid and used it as a flexible, gleaming golden chain to bind them together. "Ah, Delilah, you release me from the earthly bonds of my enslavement and replace them with ties Samson himself could not break. What hope have I to resist you?"

Ian tugged gently on the long braid, weaving it behind her neck, over his shoulder. Closer, closer, until their torsos brushed. Through the twin layers of silk, she felt the hard muscles, the living vitality of bone and blood.

Blood surged in response. Bones ached with the need to get closer still.

If he had been rough, if he'd pressed her immediately into the bed and mounted her, she perhaps could have resisted him. But his indomitable strength was leashed now, a tiger purring, rubbing against her for her pleasure as well as his own.

Stroke me. Please me. I will not eat you.

The peculiar insight came to her. Remembering the old tale of the lady and the tiger, she realized that, in this case, the two were the same. Disaster lurked in either direction, behind both doorways.

Trembling, fully aware of what she courted, she walked both directions at once, feeling in an atavistic way that only by walking through disaster would she find peace and happiness. For the last heiress, and the last Griffith male, of Haskell Hall.

Most arousing of all, nothing was so seductive as need.

It proved that she, too, had power over this man who was stronger, in mind, body, and soul, than any man she'd ever known.

His heart hammered as hard as hers; the hand gently stroking the curve of her neck trembled; and his eyes, those glowing amber eyes not even darkness could conquer, were dilated with wonder. His own need was raw in his face.

And she was lost.

Worse than lost.

For Delilah reveled in her own fall—seductress seduced.

"Ian," she whispered achingly, burying her lips in the throbbing hollow of his neck. Her tongue flicked shyly into the indentation, and when his heart surged its response, she literally tasted passion. It was an elixir such as none she'd ever known—and it made her ravenous for more.

He kept his trembling hands firmly on her waist as if she were his only anchor in the coming storm. "Delilah, be sure this is what you want. Once our bond of blood is consecrated in this bed, there will be no turning back. My fate will be your fate."

Gibberish. Everything past "be sure this is what you want" was gibberish. How could he even ask?

Want? What a pale word. For this, she had come here, for this, Haskell blood called to Griffith blood. Fate had entered this brooding old mansion with her on that night a few weeks back. She could fight it no longer.

Standing, Lil untied her robe and let the silk fall off her shoulders to pool at her feet. She heard wind howling past the casements. Urgent, a warning, a plea, it moaned through the cracks, rustling the heavy drapes covering the huge window. The outside casements creaked as if they, too, found the forces of nature too much to control.

But when Ian sat up, and the covers fell to his hip, Lil could hear naught but the pounding of her own heart. Dear heaven, he was beautiful.

Broad shoulders, taut, muscular belly, black hair narrowing to a thin, smooth line that disappeared be-

Colleen Shannon

neath the covers. His skin was tanned. He must work often without a shirt. His flesh had a burnished quality, as if he glowed with an inner dormant power he could scarcely contain.

Most arousing of all, even in the dimness of the room, lit only by the flickering lantern, Lil saw the telltale lump in the sheet at the apex of his thighs. He shifted restlessly under her gaze, and the covers fell a bit more, revealing a broadening of the hairline as it met his lower abdomen. Still Lil stared.

For the first time in her life, she knew the meaning of lust.

The thought of all that flagrant maleness, what it wanted, what it could do, incited a deep throbbing in Lil that prepared a way for him. And he'd scarcely touched her yet. . . .

The storm howled, to no avail. Suspended between damnation and delight, Lil and Ian touched only with their eyes. Communicating on that visceral, primitive level, as men and women had done since Eve ate the apple. A very old story, but it was . . .

. . . new to Delilah.

Precious, delicious. And as seductive as the crisp, sweet apple must have been to Eve. But here, bare to her gaze and with all she made him feel, Ian was Adam. Adam as God intended, wild, earthy, elemental, but as human as she was. In this secluded tower grounded on the soil of their ancestors, together, they would fall, or rise. Either way, Ian would be there to catch her and lead her to a bright new day. A day where there were no rumors, no shadows, no fears. No curse.

Only joy given and received in equal measure, compounding with every exchange.

Lil tugged the string at the high neck of her night rail and felt the thin fabric open, wider, wider, baring her shoulders. Another breath, and it would fall to her waist. She reached to tug again, but his voice came, a deep purr of urgency. "No. Come here."

He wanted to do it himself.

Unwrap her like a gift for his pleasure. Independent Delilah should have balked at such rank male arrogance.

But Lil held sway. Traitress Lil, Seductress Lil moved forward and stood docilely before him.

As he reached out to her, his glowing amber eyes were steady upon her, ravenous with a hunger that went beyond reason, or right, or wrong. A hunger that went soul deep and drew her own soul upward to meet it.

But when he touched her, one rough fingertip only, tracing her delicate collarbone, hunger became ache. And when he brought both hands up to knead her upper arms, the gown fell lower still, held in a posture of modesty only by her deep inhalation of shock at his touch.

Her bosom raised with the breath that felt, in truth, as if it were her first.

And her last.

When she exhaled, the gown, too, fell without regret, catching at his hands on her shoulders.

A soft exclamation came from him, and then he rose to his knees on the bed, shifting his grip to her back. With a rustle that sounded like a sigh of satisfaction, the fabric bared her bosom to those slumberous amber eyes. His rough palms stroked her back, neck to tailbone, lightly, soothingly.

Every nerve in her body came to excruciating life. She felt her nipples harden, and she swayed toward him. But he held her gently away, as if he knew once he felt the brush of her skin upon his own, the leashed power surging through him would bound free and consume them both.

Their torsos were so close she could feel the heat of his body. She wanted to look down, to where the covers had bared him, but she was caught in the amber glow of his eyes—moth to flame, fly to sap. He seemed to want to look past flesh, and blood, and bone, to the nerves and impulses of her heart and mind. Far deeper than any man had ever looked. And she wanted to open to him and let him do more than look. . . .

"Are you a virgin, Delilah?" he asked, still stroking her back, still not letting her torso brush his.

She should have been insulted, but she could only shake her head. "Twice. With . . . my former fiancé."

"He was a fool. His loss is my gain. And shortly, it will be yours, too." He moved forward and drew her gently to him at the same time. At last their torsos pressed together.

Tanned skin on pale skin.

Hair against smoothness.

Ian moved his chest from side to side, doubling the sensation of those tactile pleasures. Her nipples hardened further, aching now with delight.

"Do you like this?" he asked softly.

Her eyes drifted shut, and she had to bite her lip to stifle a groan. He laughed.

The primitive male sound seemed to brush every exposed nerve in her body. Acting on instinct, she clasped her arms around his neck and kissed him. Open-mouthed, flaming with all the passion he aroused in her with only a look and a touch.

His body went rigid. He took a harsh breath, seeming to draw his strength from her own lungs, and then he exhaled, giving her the breath of life again.

The symbolism did not escape her even in the heat of the moment. Shortly they would share an even more intimate exchange of life force.

Delilah Trent had never been a convenience, or a vessel for any man. But Lil Haskell yearned to know this one primal man in every way possible to female kind: mind, body, soul. If that made her a vessel, too, so be it.

It was difficult to taste the cup of life without sharing it.

When Ian finally pulled her down on the bed, the nightdress caught at her hips as he drew her to his long, lithe form. She shifted restlessly, needing to feel the power of his legs against her own, but he caught her hands above her head.

"No. Let me unwrap you. You're the best gift I've ever had, Delilah." And he smoothed his rough palms over her shoulders, down her arms, tangled his fingers with hers. Their hands entwined, he helped her push the thin fabric down and off her legs. Inch by slow, luxurious inch. Like a boy who seldom got a present and had to make it last.

Tears stung Lil's eyes. In that moment, the riotous passion quieted, allowing her a moment of clarity. The riptides of lust had pulled her farther and farther from self to a wild shore she could share only with Ian. But this new, quiet vista of possibility was far riskier, its boundaries limited only by her fear of the unknown. For this country of great hope could be entered only by lovers.

Admittance might be granted by her body, but sex was only a symbol for a closeness this unique, powerful man allowed no one.

It was love Ian needed most.

That need was blatant in the slight trembling of his hands, the dilation of his eyes, the hard-won restraint he kept upon himself even though she had been the one to come to him and he knew she was not a virgin.

Her fiancé had offered no such forbearance. As soon as her clothes were off, he was inside her, and five minutes later the deed was done. Leaving her aching, wondering—is that all there is?

Again, eerily, Ian seemed to read her mind. "You will be aching when you leave my bed, Delilah. But not with unfulfilled desire." So saying, he lay back on the soft mattress and pulled her nakedness atop him.

She felt the power of his sex pulsing between them. And even as her body began to tremble again, there was a dangerous fullness in her heart. She would never have believed this arrogant beast capable of such tenderness . . . until now.

He was fully erect with need for her, but still, he contained his baser urges. He stroked her, neck to calves, lingering over the sensitive hollows behind her knees until tingles shot through her like sparks.

How did he know? Where to touch her just so?

The need to please him, too, grew acute. She sat up, knees astride his waist, lifted her arms, and undid her braid, combing through the bountiful silvery waves with her fingers.

Those amber eyes, glowing in the uncertain flicker of the lantern, fixed on her breasts. The nipples thrust at him provocatively, hidden as her hair fell to her waist, only to peep through with impudent cherry tips as she lowered her arms and her hair shifted again.

Ian wrapped his strong hands in the glittering silver bonds and gently tugged. "Look down, Delilah. See what you do to me."

She had deliberately kept her eyes on his face, partly in shyness, partly in fear, for she knew just from the feel of him that . . . but her gaze lowered obediently.

The sight of his virility, proud head red and eager, as if even that part of him preened for her, should have frightened her. He was much larger than her previous lover had been, but she didn't shrink away. Instead, she drew nearer, compelled by the uncontrollable urge to touch.

She clasped her fingers about him, both shocked and delighted at the contrasts he offered. Contrasts in keeping with the complexities of his personality.

Softness upon hardness.

Beating life force, somehow both vulnerable and virile.

Most seductive of all, he was controlled power

leaping in her hand. Biting his own lip so hard he drew blood, he stayed quiescent and let her learn him. Wicked joy took her, a shocking freedom so emboldening that she used both hands.

He arched under her pleasurable torture, pressing his heels into the bed. "Delilah, you are well named," he gritted through his teeth. And then he grabbed handfuls of her hair again, pulling her torso down to his mouth. This time, with no hesitation and little gentleness, he pulled her nipple into his mouth and suckled hungrily. "But it is you, my temptress, who will be shorn." He turned the same loving attention to her other nipple.

She gasped, releasing him as she instinctively tried to move away at the sharp pleasure-pain of the sensation. But he wouldn't allow it. He had both arms about her waist now, holding her down, breasts hanging like ripe fruits before him.

And he tasted . . . forbidden she might be, but she was all the sweeter for it.

Carnality became its own reward.

Gladly Delilah fell.

And Eve's legacy became, in this tousled bed, in the arms of this man part demon, part delight, one to revel in, not fear. She wasn't about to lose Eden; she was about to find it.

With more instinct than skill, she scooted her hips back. Pulling her nipple away from his sweet torture, she positioned him at the pulsing gate to her body.

"Wait . . ." he said, tugging at her waist to keep her still.

She slapped his hands away. "No!" She lifted her

hips slightly and took his thrusting virility inside herself. The tip alone was enough to stretch her but in this topsy-turvy world of two, pain was literally the gateway to pleasure. She eased down slowly, and the fullness invading her was the most intimately arousing thing she'd ever known.

Her fiancé had not even allowed her time to respond, much less the luxury of control.

But Ian . . . this strong, wild, indomitable male lay quiescent for her pleasure. His hands caught fistfuls of sheet and blanket, and she felt his trembling deep inside her own body. But she knew that if she moved to get away, he'd stay still and let her go.

That knowledge was most seductive of all. On some dim, still-defiant level, Delilah warned her to stop, take heed: This awesome control was the most manipulative skill of all. For he'd taken her measure long ago, long before she measured him in this last, best, most intimate way.

Ian Griffith knew the swiftest path to Delilah's heart was through her will.

Only in giving her control, could he gain it.

But such thoughts were, at this moment, shadows in a darkness far beyond the fire and ferocity of this forbidden night. Later, she'd listen. Later.

Her eyes closing, her head falling back on her shoulders, Lil measured those last few inches, feeling herself stretch to accommodate him. And when she held him fully within the core of her body, feeling his pulse in rhythm with her own, she knew that, no matter what came of this coupling, she'd never be the same again.

Bond of blood.

She'd not understood what he meant then. But she knew now. This night would mark them both, ever after. She was so delighted at the thought of leaving her own imprimatur upon this man that she flexed her inner muscles.

He inhaled sharply at the sensation, his hips lifting as he instinctively pressed back. Reaching, as if within the warmth of her essence he found redemption.

"Delilah," he sighed, her name whirling around them like a blessing. "If joy is the talisman against my curse, I will never again fear the darkness when you are near."

Fear the darkness? What did he mean?

But then Delilah was too engrossed in her own reward to wonder, or care, what happened beyond this bed. She slid upward, slowly, and then glided back down upon him, the cadence quickening with each merging.

Assurance grew with every thrust. Perhaps she was inexperienced, but Ian didn't seem to care. She sensed how difficult it was for him to remain still. The deeper he went, the deeper still he seemed to want to go, hips squirming on the bed, knees raising slightly.

As wickedly as her namesake, Delilah made the next thrust faster and harder, concentrating now on one reality: the pressure of his maleness deep inside her body. And like Delilah of the Bible, Lil understood that base this act might be, unconsecrated by church or man, but it was still the most joyous sin any woman could know.

Worth any penance she might have to pay.

The wind howled louder, but she heeded it not.

As if this intimate joining allowed him to read her very thoughts, Ian sighed his own pleasure. His hands came up and cupped her breasts, thumbs tweaking her aroused nipples. Gasping, she angled her hips forward on the downthrust, and the intimate brushing of the base of his aroused maleness against her own aroused femininity was the last impetus she needed.

One more stroke and then . . . glory. Bursting inside her, that strange vista of possibility opening to a nirvana she'd never dreamed of. In this world, the key to which was found only in her strange bonding with this strange man, there was no sin, no sadness, and no pain.

Only elixir, the tasting of which opened the gates of paradise.

Ian entered that world with her, his heels pressing sharply into the bed as he felt her burst upon him. His teasing hands moved to her waist. He lifted and raised her, once, twice, pressing so deeply into her that she knew he quested for that nirvana, too.

The knowledge that he could only find it within her made her own pulsations quicken again. She felt him harden within the silken clasp of her body. Then he burst, too, in potent male fulfillment that bathed them both in joy.

The sensations faded slowly, little darts of pleasure vibrating from him to her and back, as if the strange bond of blood had formed a link beyond their bodies. A forging of minds, even a merging of souls. And the aftermath was almost as pleasurable as the peak.

Colleen Shannon

Unable to bear separation, Lil collapsed upon his chest, resting her cheek upon him. Gently, he stroked her spine from nape to hips, seeming to enjoy the physical closeness as much as the sexual one.

The thudding heartbeat was the same one she could still feel inside her body.

Valiant. Strong. Willful.

As if her own heart drew the best of him to match and meet the tempo of her own. Peace such as none she'd ever known stole over Lil, taking the last of her will with it.

Heiress she might be, employed laborer he might be, but the mysterious link between them was unbreakable now.

And it was good. . . . Sighing, she fell asleep.

Ian's hands stroked for a moment longer, but then his own breath grew even, too. With her still stretched upon him, he slept.

Outside, the eerie storm blew up. Clouds skated across the sky.

For one peaceful, stolen moment, it seemed as if the howling fury of the wind had no power inside the magical circle of light guarding the man and woman in the bed. The defiant flicker of the lantern was valiant enough to keep the darkness out.

Then a strong gust tore the casement open. Wind beat the heavy drapes aside. Clouds disguised, and then revealed, the moon's winsome smile.

Defeated, the lantern blew out. Darkness climbed inside the room, a live thing with a power even the peace of this moment could not repel.

Diana peeked through the flapping draperies. She

128

had the curiosity of a harlot, fingering the curtains aside and caressing the two sleeping figures on the bed.

A short time later, awareness returned to Ian slowly. What was this supple weight upon him? He reached out warily, and memory came flooding back when he touched that silken skin. Delilah.

In his bed. In his arms. Where she belonged. But the thought scarcely left him before tenderness began to change to that other feeling that was becoming increasingly familiar.

Absently, he stroked the soft flesh. This time, the more he touched, the more he wanted to turn this tantalizing form over and rake his teeth against the appetizing neck.

Even as the urge grew, another part of him felt the tenderness passing, and missed it keenly. He knew it was the best feeling life offered. To both man and beast.

Wolves mated for life, after all.

And curse or no, his soul wanted to bond with this woman in every way, too. Intimate ways beyond even sexual congress.

There was a fitful luminescent quality to her skin; she was light and then darkness. The lantern must be about to flicker out, Ian realized, wondering why the nonsensical human thought came so laboriously.

Another part of him hated the heat and light. That strange ability to see even in the darkness was growing again, and the howl outside struck his sensitive eardrums like a blow.

Come, join me. We hunt together, and the one who draws first blood feeds first.

Perhaps because of his satiation, the urge to listen grew more slowly than usual. He was accustomed to awakening alone. His very limbs were lax, so for a very long moment, he was able to ignore the howl even when it came again. More insistently.

Perhaps Delilah was the only talisman he needed.

If I try, I can resist.

He tried. He counted backward in his head. He rubbed the heels of his feet against the soft sheets. He stroked her silken skin, trying to recall how it had made him feel just an hour ago.

But it was too late. He saw the hairs growing on the backs of his hands. The sight jolted him back to full awareness. A muted clattering sound drew his attention.

He turned. Panic assailed him as he realized the wind had blown the window and drapes open.

That was why the moon shone so clearly and temptingly. That was why the howl sounded so loud.

Then the change was upon him.

Panic began to ease with the lengthening of bone and sinew. In its stead came that other feeling, the one both so empowering and so humbling. Strength filled his very marrow until he knew nothing but the urge to bound from the bed and feel the cool marsh beneath his four padded feet. The weight upon him was suddenly distasteful, the scent of human something that drew his gut but not his mind.

His growing snout sniffed, and the smell made his **stomach growl.**

But then Delilah sighed, her arms rising to embrace his thickening neck. A sleepy little smile stretched her lips as she snuggled close. That smile superimposed itself upon a fading memory, a sustaining memory still precious in a corner of his lupine brain.

The woman had smiled at him so. Was it only tonight? And then she gave him pleasure, pleasure even a wolf could recognize and honor.

The memory gave him strength enough to shove her off with his two front legs. With a bound of his powerful hindquarters, still forming as he moved, he leaped across the bedroom to the door. This time, the conflicting urges almost tore him apart.

Part of him wanted to run, to burst outside and smell the scents of home, to hear the sounds of the night. But another part wanted to taste that flesh that was so soft and appetizing.

Half wolf, half man, still forming, he hovered in the doorway, hair still growing along the ridge of his back. The howl came again, and this time, he threw back his head and wailed his answer.

Inside the servants' quarters in the basement, Jeremy was, as usual, winning at the newfangled game of poker that was even taking the royal court by storm. He'd learned it on one of his many trips to America, and his crafty tar's brain had a facility with numbers, perhaps because of all his years of mentally measuring tides, knots, and sails.

The cook's assistant glared at him sourly, and the groom banged his boot against the table leg in frustration.

The shillings, pounds, and pence on the table bounced in a merry harmony that was Jeremy's favorite sound in all the world. Aside from Lil's all too infrequent laughter. Strange how he found that honk of an inelegant laugh from Shelly Holmes even more appealing. . . .

The French cook folded his hands over his ample belly as Jeremy raked in his fourth pot of the night. "Zee luck of zee Irish? Bah. Zee English, zey win at cards in the same way zey conquer the world."

"Aye, matey, ye've the right of it at last. This is a game o'skill, same as billiards," Jeremy responded cheerfully, unaware of the subtle hint that he'd cheated.

"Hmph!" groused the groom. "There's balls aplenty at this table, only they ain't white."

That insult penetrated even Jeremy's thick skull. "No, they're pure iron, as ye'll find to yer displeasure if ye don't leave off insultin' me."

The British tar stared down his Land's End opponents, one by one. Chairs scraped back. Jeremy rolled up his sleeves, as did the groom, but then they both froze at the sound.

Wafting, desolate and eerie, over the moors, so haunting that even the wind paused to listen.

A howl. Rising from a low wail to a long, vibrating cry that raised the hairs on the back of Jeremy's neck. "What's that?"

By way of an answer, the cook went to the one small casement window high above the basement level and made sure it was cranked closed.

The groom blanched and fled, while the cook's assistant bolted out of the common area. Jeremy heard a door down the dark hallway slam and lock.

He knew, then, that no mere wolf had made that cry.

No ordinary wolf, that is. And from the sound of it, it was close. Too close.

Pocketing his winnings, Jeremy hustled to his own small chambers to fetch his gun. A simple British sailor might not understand much of hoity-toity French cooks, or the vagaries of a woman's complex mind. But Jeremy could shoot out the eye of a gull perched on a clipper's mizzenmast.

"About bloody time somethin' interestin' happened around here," he muttered under his breath as he loaded his best shotgun with the heaviest shot he had. "Werewolves indeed! Ain't no such thing. Jest a lone wolf about to meet his maker." But as he ran up the basement stairs toward the entrance, a new sound froze Jeremy in his tracks.

The strangest images ran through his head as he listened to that keening, answering wail. The sound didn't frighten him so, for it was much the same as the other.

It was the source that terrified him.

It came from inside the house. . . .

In the guest room, Shelly Holmes reacted to the same sound by throwing on her clothes. She affixed on her person the various talismans she still had in her possession from the last abortive trip onto the moors. Grabbing up a handful of silver leaf as she went, she hurried to the door.

133

When she reached the landing, she found lights coming on inside the house, one by one. Dawn brushed the sky with silver wings, but as she ran past a tall casement window, she saw the moon, riding high in defiance of the clouds trying so desperately to cover it.

The wind howled like a rabid wolf, too, pounding the casements against the windows, keeping pace with Shelly's running footsteps.

A howl came again outside, closer now.

The one inside answered it, and this time she could pinpoint the source. It sent a chill down her spine and quickened her lope to a flat-out run.

Either a wolf had invaded Ian Griffith's tower . . .

. . . or *he* was the wolf.

The sound brought Delilah awake with a start. Immediately, she felt the emptiness in the big bed. She reached out for him. "Ian?"

A low growl answered.

Drawing the covers to her bare form, she traced the sound to the doorway. Only then did she realize three things.

The lantern had gone out.

The curtains had blown open.

The moon smiled through the windows.

Half jezebel, half virgin, Diana revealed and then hid in darkness the dreamlike shape that stood in the doorway. Shaming the clumsy American temptress for what she'd done.

The growl came again, more savage this time. Twin amber spots glowed at Lil, far too high to be a dog's, but too bright and luminescent in the dark to belong to Ian. "Ian?" she called again, more fearfully this time.

The clouds parted again, and she could see clearly. Fear clutched her about the throat. She drew the covers even higher, as if their frail protection could somehow shield her from that hungry gaze.

A wolf stood in the bedroom doorway.

It had a silvery ruff on its back, and it stood four feet high at the shoulder. The amber eyes were fixed on her, and as she watched, its mouth drew back in a snarl. Enormous fangs were revealed, but the eyes never blinked. They were fixed on her with a covetousness that would have been frightening in a two-legged creature.

In this four-legged, powerful beast, such hunger was terrifying.

The joy of the past night became a melancholy dirge heralding her own doom.

She could deny the truth no longer. Ian Griffith's eyes had that strange glow, and he walked so soundlessly and had such acute senses because he was as cursed as the legend said.

He was the Wolf of Haskell Hall.

But her knowledge came too late. Fate looked her in the eye out of those amber depths. It reverberated up the length of her spine as that low snarl came again.

Tears came to Lil's eyes as she stared at him. Death peered back at her, but still, she could not look away. For hidden in the gaze of that savage hunger, she saw confusion. Hesitation. Every powerful muscle was tensed to spring, but for some reason, he didn't.

If she had been faced with this challenge even a few hours ago, she would have failed to meet it. But the Ian Griffith who'd showed her such tenderness last night lurked still somewhere in that sinew and muscle. The wolf smelled more keenly, so he knew, too, the scent of their lovemaking clinging to the sheets.

Letting the covers drop, Lil rose to her knees in the bed. "Ian, please. I cannot bear it if you leave me like this. Remember? Last night? Think. I know you can still think. I see it in your eyes."

Those unblinking eyes did indeed remain fixed on her, but the snarl that showed his fangs was even more vicious. He padded closer. One step. Two. Then he stopped, every hair on his body bristling. The growl that came this time was savage with hunger. The wolf howled, long, low, and rough.

The prelude to an attack.

It took every fiber of strength she possessed for Lil to remain still, but she knew enough of wolves to realize that the worst thing she could do was run.

Besides, he blocked the door.

There was nowhere to go but outside the window, down a sheer drop of forty feet to the ground. Lil tried again, tears streaming down her face. "Ian, you can break the curse. All you have to do is resist. Please, if not for me, then for yourself. You can break the curse if you try."

A trembling began in those powerful muscles, and the snarl faded. The wolf cocked its head from side to side, as if it tried to listen with ears that heard but did not understand.

A tremulous smile of belief, of total trust, stretched her lips, and though she did not know it, it was very similar to the one she'd worn when she took him inside her body. "See? I wouldn't make much of a meal, anyway."

Hope shimmered in the room, fragile yet ineluctable.

Hope brighter than the moonlight, clearer than the day. It scattered the shadows, leaving no room for curses or things of the night.

Green eyes steadily held amber. For one beating instant of Lil's heart, Ian Griffith appeared in the wolf's eyes.

Then the howl came outside again, so close now that it seemed the other wolf must be in the courtyard.

Lil's bravery fled as she realized two things: There was more than one wolf. And she was the target of both of them.

The amber eyes changed. Humanity faded back to wildness.

Crying out in fear, Lil scrambled for the far corner of the bed.

The tower door burst open, and Jeremy's voice came, sharp with fear, "Mistress? Be ye here?"

"Yes, Jeremy, help!" Lil screamed as the wolf leaped.

In one spring, he was on the bed, fangs bared, snarling savagely as he snapped at her throat.

She had only one recourse, and she took it. She slipped between the edge of the bed and the wall,

137

barely squeezing into the gap. The wolf clawed savagely at the wall, ripping the bedcovers, but the bed was high, and his claws flailed just above her head.

Jeremy ran across the tower. With a last frustrated snarl, the wolf sprang off the bed. Immediately Lil raised herself up so she could see.

The images would be branded forever on her brain.

She saw Jeremy running inside with his shotgun at the ready.

She saw the wolf limned against the moon that smiled bold and brassy through the clearing clouds. Dawn lurked on the horizon, but the pink glow of redemption came too late.

For Lil. And for Ian.

Lil saw the look on Jeremy's face as he leveled the firearm. Forgetful of her nakedness, Lil stood, held out her hands, and cried, "No!"

The retort of the weapon drowned out her plea.

She saw blood appear on the wolf's neck, but much of the shot scattered into the wall behind him. And then he was leaping through the heavy window. For an instant, he was poetry in motion, front feet raised as he bounded over the sill, every sinew in that powerful body strained in flight.

A terrible moment of nothing, and then a heavy weight hit the ground outside and could be heard bounding off. From the sounds of it, Ian was scarcely wounded.

Lil sank down upon the bed, so enervated with relief that Ian had not been badly hurt that it took a moment for the other people crowding into the doorway to impinge upon her awareness. It was the shocked murmurs that drew her first.

Her own lady's maid stared at her with huge eyes.

Lil looked down and saw her own nakedness. She pulled the shredded sheets up, but they were little cover.

And less protection from the condemning eyes.

Chapter Six

It was not in Lil's nature to shrink from anything, but the terrible ending to their glorious lovemaking left her numb. Afraid. And alone. Lil grabbed up a pillow, but it, too, was tattered from the wolf's—Ian's—sharp claws.

Suddenly, under the condemning eyes of the servants she'd begun to consider friends, she felt again the outsider. A coarse American with neither right to nor regard for the estates held at such cost by all the women before her. Women who'd died to safeguard this legacy.

A legacy she'd squandered for a few hours of pleasure . . .

The brisk voice was a salve to Lil's wounded dignity.

"Out! Leave Miss Haskell to compose herself."

Shelly moved her tall form between Lil and the other servants' scandalized gazes.

Jeremy scowled between Lil and Shelly. "And that blasted wolf? If we go look for it now—"

"Too late," Shelly responded coolly. "It will be long gone." Equally coolly, Shelly watched Lil's sigh of relief. Lil knew she should be shamed at her own gladness that Ian had gotten away after he'd tried to kill her, but some feelings went beyond shame. However, she also knew from the look on Shelly's face that she was due a little homily on the subject.

Glancing between Lil and Shelly, Mrs. McCavity tied her robe tightly about her stout waist and shooed the other gawking servants out of the doorway, closing the bedroom door as she went.

The silence weighed heavily upon Lil, for there was someone still present whom she found it even harder to face than Shelly. Never had it been so difficult to meet Jeremy's eyes. The disappointment in that gaze, which had always been so steady and so loving, was almost more than she could bear. But Lil swallowed back her tears and said huskily, "Haven't you ever done something wrong just because you couldn't resist?"

Jeremy opened his mouth to retort, closed it abruptly, and nodded instead. "Aye. But a bottle's embrace and the embrace of a man more demon than human be two different things."

"Have you never known the term 'demon rum'?" Shelly inquired. "Or mayhap 'hypocrite' is more familiar to a man of your sort."

"I'd as lief listen to a magpie as a woman o' yer

141

sort," Jeremy growled, turning on Shelly.

"Then proceed into the moors to look for one. And on the way out, leave the judgment of others to St. Peter and the day of rapture."

"Hmph! That be the kettle calling the pot black. Ye might as well wear a black robe and a white wig, yer bloody honor."

Lil glanced between the pair. If she'd been a bit less emotionally bruised, she might have been amused at their byplay. She was beginning to suspect that, beneath his bluster, Jeremy was attracted to the redoubtable Miss Holmes. He bedded sluts, but had only been in love with one woman that she knew of, and that had been a spinster schoolteacher.

Shelly, however, apparently felt no such ambivalence. "Would that it were so, so I could clap you in irons and toss away the key just so I didn't have to listen to your yammering."

"Yammering, is it?"

Shelly flung the door open and pointed an imperious finger. "Out!"

Jeremy's mouth opened and closed, but he turned on his heel and cradled his shotgun to his side, muttering, "Aye, better a den of howling wolves than a screeching harpy."

He exited. Shelly slammed the door.

Immediately, Lil hopped out of bed and shrugged into her robe. Feeling a bit stronger, she ignored the strange ache in her lower quarters—and the even more painful one in her heart—and faced Shelly. "Get it over with."

Shelly's stern lips softened. "There's obviously no

142

need. Your own conscience is loud enough, I warrant."

Lil's eyes darkened to forest green as she considered that. "No, Shelly. I am so shameless that I do not even feel regret. It was the most intimate experience of my life. Even knowing what he is . . . I do not know if I could resist him the next time."

"That's the curse talking, my dear." When Lil merely stared bleakly into the distance, Shelly grew brisk. "But at the moment, we've other things to worry about. Such as . . . what will we do to quell the gossip?"

Weak-kneed, Lil sank back onto the bed. "I didn't think of that." The tart agreement in Shelly's face almost made Lil laugh. "I assure you, I do still have a brain."

"Perhaps, when Ian Griffith is not in the vicinity."

How could Lil take affront, when Shelly spoke only the truth?

"Now," Shelly continued, "our answer to the inevitable rumors shall be that you were chased by a wolf through the house, into the tower. In fighting him off, your clothes were shredded, and only Jeremy's intervention saved your life."

"No one will believe that poppycock."

"But they won't dare disagree with it, either. At least not to your face. It is not so very far from the truth, after all, which is always the best sort of a lie. More importantly, it will replace one sensational story with a more sensational one. All of Cornwall is agog over the Wolf of Haskell Hall, and the country folk will, if you'll excuse the term, lap it up."

As Shelly obviously intended, this won a laugh from Lil. "Levity? From the redoubtable Miss Holmes? I'm shocked."

"Good. In your condition you shan't have to brace yourself. Has it occurred to you that, now the servants know Ian is also a werewolf, he will not dare show his face around here again?"

Fresh shock coursed through Lil despite the warning. Why had she not thought of that? "But . . . I cannot allow that. He loves the Hall, and it's partly his home, too. No one saw him but Jeremy, and if I ask him to keep it to himself—"

"And how do we explain the wolf tracks outside?"

"We shall erase the tracks." Lil stuck her feet in her slippers and hurried through the suite of rooms, which was beginning to lighten as dawn teased the horizon into a blush. The moon . . . it would soon be gone.

And so would Ian. If she didn't find him fast, he'd flee.

"Miss Haskell," Shelly called, but Lil was already out the door.

As Lil ran down the tower stairs, she knew that when Ian awoke to his manly form again, he'd be ashamed. Maybe he wouldn't remember attacking her, but he'd certainly know that his last memory was falling asleep cradling her in his arms. And the man who'd made love with such tender control must have a visceral attraction to her as deep as her own for him. He'd want to shield her from himself, just as he'd tried to restrain his own baser urges by chaining himself up.

144

Why had she avoided that truth? Who else could have tied him, and why? The answer was both simple and devastating.

She'd refused all whispering remnants of conscience, decency, even sheer self-preservation for one reason: She'd wanted to make love with him. Wanted it like earth needs rain, or hummingbird needs nectar.

That certainty, as troubling as it was, suddenly gave her strength. Mayhap there was a mysterious bond of blood between them, exactly as the curse foretold. But the joy they'd shared last night was a beautiful thing with all the principles of light.

Revealing. Rejuvenating. Bright. And everyone knew that the creatures of the night scurried away from light.

Thirty minutes later, fully dressed and carrying a broom, Lil ignored the butler's disapproving stare and ran outside. Methodically, she swept the wolf's large prints away, through the gravel, past the dirt bordering the fields, onto the pasture. She knew several stable hands watched her curiously, but she ignored them, sweeping back and forth until her arms ached.

The symbolism of the movement was, well, sweepingly apparent. With every stroke, she wiped out the past, leaving a clean slate.

When she reached the edge of the moors, she stopped. The sun beamed down on her happily, as if in sympathy with her earlier thoughts, its brightness chasing the sultry moon back to her den of iniquity. Not a cloud lurked in the brilliant blue sky above.

Still, the sight of those limitless brown flatlands frightened her. Odd that she found the moors both so forbidding and so appealing, all at once.

There, the Gypsy had borne her child alone.

There, the legacy of that forbidden union wandered, a solitary man again.

There, the last heiress of the Hall would have to go to find him.

There, Delilah Haskell Trent would face her own fears—or be overcome by them. Handing the broom to a startled groom, Lil ran back to the house. A bath. She had to have a bath. Maybe then she'd feel strong enough to do this. For the moment, she was only afraid. . . .

Bathed in the healing power of the sunlight, Ian Griffith awoke to himself by slow degrees. For a moment, he reveled, as always, in the feel of the soft moss upon his bare skin. He moved his arms and legs from side to side, realizing next that he was nude. Why was he naked on the moors? True, he often came to the moors with a woman, but he usually dressed and walked her home after their appetites were slaked.

Appetites . . . it was then Ian saw the redness on his hands. He sat up, his head spinning as he realized two things: One, this was his special place, and there was only one woman he'd ever wanted to bring here, the one woman it was disastrous for him to need. Two, he'd apparently broken that rule, for there was someone else here with him.

The girl. Lying unnaturally still in a pool of blood.

She had claw marks from head to toe, her clothes were in tatters, and her torso . . . Ian turned away and gagged. Her hair was so muddy and tangled with leaves that he couldn't tell its color, but from the one glance, he didn't think it was Delilah.

He vomited, but nothing came up but phlegm. It had no red tinge. How long would a raw heart stay in a man's intestines?

Man. Ian tried to laugh bitterly, but only another gag came out. When the dry heaves finally stopped, he forced himself to turn the girl over. Her face was muddy, too, but now he saw black hair, and terror in the open, staring eyes that he'd so recently admired. Only because Delilah watched.

It was the barmaid from the village. He'd dallied with her on several occasions, but he'd never invited her here. Had she come looking for him? Or had he dragged her to his haven while he was . . . not himself?

Shakily, avoiding looking at the girl's gaping rib cage, he got to his feet and carefully inspected the area. This little slice of heaven, where wildflowers grew in profusion, and the pristine waterfall tumbled over a rocky embankment into a spring-fed pool shielded by rocks, would never again be peaceful for him.

His personal paradise was protected on all sides by bogs.

There was only one way in, and one way out.

So far as he knew, he was the only one who could follow that path. Which meant . . . Bile rose in his stomach again, but he forced it back, shakily following his own wolf tracks to that narrow stretch of earth between the quicksand.

He saw no evidence of dragging, but faint signs of small footprints. And his own heavy wolf prints, blurred and repeated, as if he'd paced back and forth. Heaviest there by the stream, almost as if he'd leaped from that rock up above the pool at the base.

The woman must have walked here. Perhaps she'd surprised him drinking at the stream, or . . . he searched his hazy recollection, but those memories were as dim under the murk of despair as they had been all the other times. He didn't remember killing the woman, much less eating her heart, but he didn't remember the first time he'd transitioned, either.

Still, the taste of that last heiress must have been sweet, for his hunger was growing uncontrollable. Bending to the stream, he splashed water on his face and hands, watching blood dye the water red. The color faded to pink as water gurgled and sped on its merry way. Then the blood was gone, part of the earth again, as all living things would one day be.

He stared at his clean but slashed hands. The girl must have fought back with all her strength, clawing him. And he would have clawed back. He wondered why he saw no skin beneath his fingernails. He clenched those powerful hands, stood, and turned away, pulling out the spare clothes he kept shielded under a rock. Her blood was gone, but it would stain his soul forever.

With each full moon, he became less man, more animal. Each occurrence pushed him closer to a precipice. He felt caught in a nightmare of his own design.

With his last strength, he hung in the balance between light and darkness, life and death. The plunge that would rob him of his last claims to manhood was inevitable. Yet, still he fought it with every ounce of his dwindling being, clawing desperately toward the light so close yet so far away.

Was it only last night that he'd awakened to find Delilah hovering over him as she freed him from his bonds? He stared blindly into the bright new day, seeing only the image of his blessing and his curse. Why had he not been strong enough to send her away?

Because she, with her smile, her golden hair, and her inherent optimism, was the very essence of the light he both craved and feared. And her lovemaking . . . a weary smile stretched his lips. That lovely, feminine body, life incarnate, was more than a repository for his male urges. She was a reliquary, too. A keeper of earthly treasures and intangible dreams.

In her body, he found peace. Surcease from the torment of his mind and soul.

And how had he repaid her gift? He knew from the slight ache in his ankles and from a fractured memory that he'd jumped through the tower window.

A drastic step he'd have taken only if threatened, which meant he must have been attacking the very woman who'd given him such pleasure only a few hours before. He could always remember the beginning of the change. He'd shoved Delilah off like an unwelcome blanket, stupidly watching the hairs grow on the backs of his hands, feeling his forelegs form, his spine lengthen.

149

Then a flashing memory of stunned green eyes staring at him in shock and horror. Then . . . nothing. From that moment to this.

But as he dug up the small bag of gold he'd hidden for just this emergency, he reflected wearily that at least there was one good thing to come of this debacle. Now that the truth was out, he certainly couldn't go back.

He'd never again have to face the fear in those lovely, steady green eyes.

Or the knowledge that he'd put it there.

Taking his few belongings and the money pouch with him, he turned to follow the tiny, winding path through the bogs, but then he stopped abruptly and turned back. He couldn't leave the girl's body exposed to the elements and scavengers. He didn't dare take her back to the village, either. But if he just buried her, her family would never know what had happened to her.

He dragged the body down the path to a soft, moss-covered patch of earth, removed her bloody, tattered blouse, and dug a shallow grave in the appropriate manner.

With his hands. Like a dog.

When he was finished, he piled up some stones and fashioned a crude cross from a split tree branch. He tied the girl's bloody, tattered blouse to the cross. He stood, head bowed over her grave, and said a quick prayer. As he stared down at the grave, for a moment he was struck with a feeling so powerful that he staggered.

Envy. At least she knew the peace that passeth all understanding.

Bleakly, he stared at the enormous bog lapping almost at his feet. Almost, he stepped into it, knowing he'd sink without a whimper. But he couldn't do it. Suicide was the act of a coward, and whatever he'd been and done in his lifetime, he'd never been that.

Shouldering his rucksack, he turned away and mechanically got on with the business of living. One foot steadily in front of another, he fled the scene of his crime. At least this time, he walked upright. Where he went, he was not certain.

What he would find, he didn't know.

But one thing was certain. He was lost, as lost on these moors he knew like the back of his hand as he'd once been in the jungles of the Amazon. This labyrinth offered no thread to guide him out. No Ariadne. Not even his temptress Delilah.

In this labyrinth, *he* was the beast. With every monthly gestation of the moon, the creature that was born consumed, piece by piece, all that remained of Ian Griffith.

For two more nights, the moon was full. . . .

Late that afternoon, Delilah pulled the stable boy's breeches over her full hips, ignoring Safira's continual moaning as she rocked back and forth on the edge of the bed. The boy's boots were a bit large, but padded with two pairs of socks, they would do. Pulling on a shirt, a sweater, and an old jacket, Delilah appraised herself critically.

"Well, Safira? I don't look terribly appetizing, do

I?" Lil stuck her hair up under the boy's cap and nodded in satisfaction. How much more practical and comfortable were these clothes than all the laces, frills, and corsets her gender was forced to wear.

Safira only moaned louder before she managed, "M-mistress, do not do this thing, I implore you. How will Jeremy and I get home if something happens to you?"

"You silly goose. Of course I've provided for you in my will. Look on the bright side. If something happens to me, you shan't have to cast the bones for me, argue with me, worry about me—"

Safira's moaning stopped on an indignant hiss. She leaped to her feet so fast that her turban went crooked. "And a fine friend I should be if that's all I cared about!" She nibbled her full lower lip with white teeth, watching her employer warily.

But Lil was touched, not angry. "You know that, all too often, you and Jeremy have been my only friends. Certainly the only two I trust." She straightened Safira's turban. "Now, listen to your own advice. You are always going on about destiny, and how we can flee it only so long before it catches up to us. Well, I merely choose to face it on my own terms. If I am to suffer the same fate as the other heiresses, I prefer to look death in the eye and thumb my nose at it rather than cower in the house and wait for it to claim me." Giving Safira a brisk hug, Lil went to the door.

Trailing along, Safira murmured, "And Jeremy?"

Lil stopped dead. "Of course. Once he gets wind of this, he'll be like a shadow after me. You must distract him, Safira. If he follows us and scares the wolf away again tonight, it won't be the wolf who eats him alive." She and Safira exchanged a wry glance.

Safira's rare, lovely gurgle of laughter filled the air. "Miss Holmes will likely make a meal of him, 'tis true."

Laughing, they walked out together. As if their thoughts had conjured him, Jeremy blocked the hallway, legs spread as they'd often been on the quarterdeck, hands propped on scrawny hips. "What mischief be ye brewin' now, me girls?" His suspicious gaze narrowed on Lil's inappropriate attire.

Lil glued an innocent look to her face and glanced out the window at the darkening gray sky filling with clouds. She stuck the tip of her finger in her mouth, then held the digit up in the air, as if even inside the house she could feel the wind blowing up a gale. "From the feel of the humidity, there is a storm brewing. You'd best stay in tonight. This is a ladies' . . . soiree only."

Jeremy was not amused. "Hmph! And who be a hostin' yer party? The devil himself?" When Lil looked away, Jeremy added severely, "The brewin' storm ain't got naught to do with the weather. Now see here, ye addlepated miss—"

Lil walked straight toward Jeremy. When he stood firm, she faked in one direction and went the other. Then she was running down the stairs, ignoring his stern call to wait. She heard Safira's voice, and knew there wasn't a moment to lose as Jeremy wouldn't be distracted long.

She dashed into the salon and found Shelly awaiting her. "Come, quick! Jeremy's going to try to follow us."

Looking as if she'd been stung by a bee, Shelly bolted up and ran out the door the butler barely managed to open in time. In the courtyard, Lil looked around for her curricle, but saw only two horses, saddled and waiting. One the old mare, the other a spirited gelding. Lil looked from the horses to Shelly.

"You cannot drive a curricle where we're going," Shelly said firmly. "In fact, some of it we may have to manage on foot, but at least we can start on horseback." When Lil opened her mouth to protest, Shelly concluded grimly, "You can ride and keep up with me, or you can stay behind."

Lil's mouth snapped closed. "Who is owner here, might I ask?"

"You might. If there were time for such games." But a smile played about Shelly's lips.

"Oh, very well. But if I fall off, I shall really slow you down." Taking a deep breath, Lil approached the mare, which looked like a mountain to her. The mare turned her head. The soft brown eyes seemed to give Lil an encouraging look, and the creature even snuffled at her hand.

Lil's fears lessened as she patted the velvety muzzle. "Why are some of them so mean?"

"Why are some people so mean?" Shelly countered, cupping her hands to offer Lil a step up. "Horses are all different in personality, too. With the exception of stallions, perhaps. They're rather like rakes. They have one thought in their head."

As Lil moved to step up, she whispered, "Sex? Or food?"

"Both. And usually in that order." Shelly heaved as Lil laughed, and the moment was made far less scary for Lil than it might have been.

Then Lil was straddling the saddle. Shelly adjusted the stirrups as Lil looked around, fascinated. She wasn't accustomed to being so high, and the mare was so gentle and still that Lil's pounding heartbeat slowed enough for her to tease back, "You know they say something similar of us, do you not?"

"No doubt. Let's see . . . they'd say we think of shopping and eating. In that order."

"Sometimes it's a wonder we share the same earth, much less the same bed." Lil blushed as she realized what she'd said, but Shelly only nodded and took her own seat.

As Shelly paused to be sure Lil held the reins correctly, the door burst open and Jeremy exited, Safira panting at his heels as if she'd chased after him. "I'm sorry, mistress, I tried to stop him, but—"

Jeremy blinked up at Lil. "Now I know ye've taken leave o' yer senses. Goin' out in the wilds of this heathen place with only a busybody woman fer protection, on horseback no less."

Shelly didn't dignify him with so much as a scathing glance. Instead, she kneed her gelding toward the gate. The mare lurched after them, and Lil was too busy recalling the rhythms of riding to spare more than a retort. "Jeremy, you nag worse than a woman."

That shut him up. With a last glance over her shoulder, Lil was delighted to see him standing under

155

the portico, mouth gaping at the ultimate insult.

Shelly's honking laugh filled the courtyard. Jeremy gave one last glare at the departing women, turned on his heel in affronted dignity, and stalked inside the house.

But Lil knew him better than that. He'd probably only pause to get his gun. He hated horses, having grown up at sea, but the paths through the moor were so treacherous that, at his tireless, bandy-legged pace, he'd probably keep up with them. After all, he only had to follow their tracks. "If we don't hurry, Jeremy will catch up to us," she said to Shelly.

Sighing, resignation in her strong face, Shelly nodded. "He's a bad penny."

"No, Shelly. He's pure gold behind the tinpot tyrant. You just need to scratch the surface a bit deeper."

Shelly led the way as if she didn't want to discuss the matter further. However, as the two women reached the moors and felt the full force of the wind, Shelly pulled her horse to a stop and turned to Lil. She stuck her hand in her pocket and brought out a handful of cinders, scraping them over Lil's arms, shoulders, and legs, but when she reached for Lil's face, Lil turned her head away.

Under Shelly's disapproving glance, she pulled a looped necklace of silver leaf out of her sweater and showed it to the other woman. "See, I'm prepared, too."

"Your pistol?"

Lil patted her belt. "But no silver bullets. Not that I could . . . bear to use them, anyway."

156

"We may not have a choice, my dear. I will turn and take you back right now if you do not agree that if it comes down to your life or the wolf's, you'll aim for the heart, right through the middle of the rib cage. A shot through the heart is the only way. A wound will simply anger it."

"But . . . you must have a plan beyond just killing it. How could you hope to catch a werewolf alive, otherwise?"

Shelly hesitated, and then she drew a strange contraption out of a holder attached to the side of her saddle. It looked like a collapsing cane. As Shelly pulled, the gleaming metal lengthened in segments, each piece locking onto the next, until it was fully six feet long. Shelly fetched something else out of her saddlebag and tied it to the end. The lowering sun gleamed on the wicked tip of a syringe filled with a cloudy liquid.

"It's a magician's wand," Shelly explained. "Given to me by a master magician after I helped him design several new tricks. Can you guess what I've filled the syringe with?"

"Laudanum?" Lil asked hopefully.

Shelly nodded. "If I can get close enough, there's enough laudanum in this horse syringe to stun three normal wolves, so surely it can stop one werewolf."

"But . . . what if it takes too long to go into effect?"

Shrugging, Shelly carefully collapsed the strange device. "Then I have my rifle, and I shan't hesitate to use it." She capped the syringe and put it back in her bag. "Now we're agreed? You'll use your pistol if you have to?"

Colleen Shannon

Reluctantly, Lil nodded. But as Shelly peered at her through the gloom, she didn't meet those piercing gray eyes. Instead, she reined her docile mare deeper into the moors. It was time to lead, not follow. Shelly seemed to know where she was going, and Lil realized she was retracing her steps of the other night, hoping to come upon the werewolf in a place it frequented.

Lil left the details in Shelly's capable hands, but she wasn't just along for the ride. Somehow, she had to find Ian, and show him she was all right. That even when he was fully a wolf, he'd hesitated to attack her. Somewhere within that frightening, savage form, all sinew, hair, and bone, was the soul of a poet and a dreamer.

She'd reach the best of Ian Griffith even if it meant going through the worst of her own fears.

Some distance back, Jeremy followed the horse tracks, his rolling gait covering the ground swiftly. He had a shotgun strapped to his back, a brace of pistols at his belt, and a sword in one hand. He still felt naked, and none too happy that the sun was tiring of escorting the whirligig earth. But at least that daily dance was something that could be counted on, unlike the whims of a woman.

Much less two women.

Especially two women too smart for their own good.

He'd known the moment he laid eyes on her that Miss Holmes was trouble. It was hardly any wonder the old biddy was a spinster. He tried to picture bedding a woman who spouted theorems instead of nostrums, and wore pants instead of skirts. Even as his mind scoffed at the notion, his lower quarters pricked up in interest, but he only quickened into a lope, as if he could outrun his own thoughts.

He'd never admit it to himself, much less to anyone else, but Jeremy had always had a soft spot for independent, smart women. Mayhap because he was more than a mite that way his own self. That was why he'd followed Delilah back to England, after he'd sworn never to set foot again in the land of his birth. The miss needed him to keep her in hand.

As tonight proved, independence could cross the line into stupidity. How could such smart women set out alone on their merry werewolf hunt?

But they'd be happy enough to see this old salt, he told himself grimly, veering away from a bog just in time, when he pulled their bacon out of the frying pan.

He just hoped he didn't land in the fire in the process. . . .

As abruptly as it had blown up, the wind calmed. Normally Lil would have been glad that the threat of rain had ended. But this was not a normal night. It was her first horseback ride in years, her first venture onto the moors . . . and the first time she hunted a werewolf.

Eerie stillness descended. The clouds dissipated as night crept through the landscape, shading stagnant pools and marshy ground alike. If not for Shelly's lead and the mare's surefootedness as the animal instinctively kept to the firm paths through the quagmires, Lil knew she would have already fallen into a bog.

But as time wore on, the moon peered above the horizon, and the shadows scattered under its glowing smile. Tonight, it had a tinge of orange. Why do you come into my domain? it seemed to ask, peering down on the interlopers.

Clamping down on her thoughts, Lil forced herself to look away from that fascinating, glowing orb. Her nerves were stretched to the limit. They'd already reached and passed the place where Shelly had heard the wolf the night before, and so far, they'd found no trace of tracks. With the moon so bright above, it was easy to see the marks of deer, and birds, even what looked like fox prints.

But nothing large enough, or deep enough, to be wolf tracks. Still, with every rustle of grass and call of night bird, Lil jumped. She was accustomed now to the mare's soothing gait, and without her fear of horses to distract her, other fears clamored more loudly.

Was she mad to come out here after so many others had died on these desolate wastes?

If she met Ian again in his wolf form, would he hesitate this time, or go straight for her throat? And if he did, would she be strong enough to shoot him?

Yet as loudly as common sense protested, her other instincts were more insistent. She could not leave him to his fate. The thought of him awakening, alone, naked, without money or food or a place to go, was enough to keep her facing firmly forward in the saddle. If Shelly's plan worked, they could take him back to the stables, pen him up in one of the steel-barred stalls until the lunar cycle ended.

After that? Well, where there was a curse, there was a cure.

Somehow, she'd find it. With Shelly's help.

Shelly drew to a stop so quickly that Lil jolted forward in the saddle as her mare also stopped abruptly.

"What is it?" Lil whispered.

With a shushing finger to her mouth, Shelly cocked her head, listening.

This time, Lil heard it. A wolf. Howling. They both tried to pinpoint the location. Lil's heart sank. It was over a slight rise, straight past a bog that didn't seem to have any path around it.

But Shelly was undaunted. She dismounted, pulled her rifle over one shoulder, and fixed her strange spear, holding the syringe at the ready. "Stay here," she mouthed, walking toward the bog. It seemed she was going to immerse herself in the foul mud, but then she turned slightly to the side, and Lil made out a narrow sliver of firm ground, shining darker than the bog in the moonlight.

Dismounting, Lil checked her own pistol. It was fully loaded. Sticking the pistol back in her belt, she tied her mare to a tree as Shelly had done, and then followed her stable manager, placing her steps exactly in Shelly's larger boot prints.

Shelly scowled over her shoulder, but Lil merely kept walking. Shelly emerged from the bog and climbed the rocky slope. She topped the rise, pausing to get her bearings, her tall form outlined by the bright backdrop of the moon.

Lil was climbing the slope herself when it happened. One moment, Shelly was upright, getting a firmer grip on her spear. The next, she was gone. No scream, only the bouncing of a few pebbles skidding down the slope to mark her passing.

Her heart in her throat, Lil pulled herself the rest of the way up the slope and peered over. What she saw made her reach for her pistol.

Shelly lay at the base of the slope, her rifle fallen beyond her reach, the spear lying beside her. But she couldn't pick it up because her hands were occupied.

She was desperately trying to hold an enormous wolf away from her throat. Her large hands squeezed the wolf's muscular neck, which was the reason it couldn't growl.

Its silver-tipped ruff standing on end, the wolf bared its huge fangs as it scratched at Shelly's torso, clawing to get free. But thank heavens, Shelly's heavy sheepskin coat repelled even those sharp claws.

Lil recognized that silver-tipped fur, those amber eyes glowing with savagery. It was Ian. And he seemed to have no hesitation in attacking Shelly.

Shelly's arms were weakening. The wolf's teeth snapped together, almost grazing Shelly's throat.

Lil reached for her pistol, but through her tears, she could barely see the pair locked in silent battle. She blinked, trying to steady her shaking hand, trying to make the most difficult choice of her life. . . .

Chapter Seven

But in the end, it was no choice at all. She couldn't let Shelly die. In his human form, Ian would urge her to make the same decision.

Lil dashed her tears away with her sleeve and squeezed the trigger slowly, aiming for that massive rib cage. Before she could fire, Shelly brought her feet up under the wolf's chest and heaved with all her might.

She wasn't strong enough to throw off such a massive weight, but it was enough to make him lurch sideways, slightly off balance. Enough for her to roll free.

Seizing the God-given reprieve, Lil scrambled down the slope and picked up the spear. She tried to sneak up behind him, but his snout lifted and sniffed the air. With a swiftness that amazed her, the wolf spun about—and focused on its new prey. It faced her, growling.

It crept toward her, and she saw the gathered haunches.

The words came of their own accord. "No, Ian. It's Delilah . . . you don't want to do this. Don't succumb to what you are. But think of what we can be. Together."

"Stab him, Lil!" Shelly urged, her voice hoarse. "Or I'll have to shoot him."

But Lil couldn't look away from those glowing amber eyes. The wolf blinked, shaking its head slightly, sniffing the air again, as if it recognized her voice, her scent.

Holding the spear in one hand, Lil reached out with her other. Instinctively.

Not because she wanted to.

Because she had to.

Better she lose a hand than her mind. She had to know, know beyond any shadow of a doubt, that something of the good man who'd made love to her so sweetly and so gently remained inside the lupine madness. Besides, now that she faced this terror of the night, it wasn't so dreadful. Instead, she felt an awful fascination, a wonder at what it would be like to have such primal power and grace. . . .

She heard Shelly's gasp as she crept nearer, her hand held out, palm down, for the wolf to sniff. The animal was so huge, she had to lift her hand instead of lower it, but still, she seemed to startle him, for he backed away a step. She held those wild amber eyes with her own, which though she didn't know it, glowed with a wildness similar to his.

She crooned, "Ian, you know my scent. Just as I know yours. Come back with me to the stables. Let me help you." Her hand was under the black snout now.

So easily he could bite it off. One snap of those massive jaws and . . .

Instead, the wolf's nose quivered as it sniffed again, more deeply. A bit more wildness faded from the amber eyes. For one exhilarating moment, Lil saw recognition, a remnant of humanity, in that steady gaze.

The spear sagged in her hand.

And then the sound came. The long, low howl of the other wolf was so alive with feral menace, it seemed as if the moors themselves had taken form and substance.

A growl came next. Closer.

Ian howled his answer, wildness consuming him again. That terrible hunger grew in Ian's eyes, the amber gaze pinpointing her with menace. Lil snatched her hand back just as the sharp teeth snapped down on the air of her passing.

Tears of despair filling her eyes, Lil backed up.

How could she expect one night of passion to counteract a century of evil? The other wolf must be the dominant male, and he had a far stronger hold on Ian than she ever could. They must hunt together. The quick succession of thoughts came brutally clear and cogent under the transmutation of the alchemist moon.

So easily it changed gold into dross. . . . Blinking the tears away, Lil took a firmer grip on the spear and shook her head as Shelly leveled the rifle. "No. I'll do it."

As Ian gathered on his haunches again, Lil arced forward, shoving the syringe straight into his throat, pressing hard so it would empty.

Ian yelped. Then the makeshift spear snapped in Lil's hands as he growled and yanked free. She had a moment to see that the syringe remained stuck in his throat before he leaped at her. Lil held her hands up to protect her face, tensing for the shot she knew would come.

But it didn't come as expected, from Shelly. It came from the slope above Lil.

With one flashing look, she saw Jeremy silhouetted against the lurid sky. He ran down the slope as she watched, poised to fire again . . .

. . . but there was no need.

The spear dropped from Lil's nerveless hand. The slug had struck Ian squarely in the chest. Blood spurted from the small hole slightly off center in the rib cage. Jeremy scrambled to a stop beside her, still ready to fire.

Whimpering, the wolf fell to the ground in a heap. Quivering, its legs twitching. But Jeremy must have missed the heart, for the bleeding at the chest had already begun to slow. Lil closed her eyes in a quick prayer of gratitude. She could only wonder at the prodigious power and strength that could take such a near mortal wound with so little effect.

The amber eyes blinked, and Lil realized the laudanum was making it dizzy. She spared an angry glance at Jeremy, and then fell to her knees beside Ian, ignoring Jeremy's stern command to get away.

Pulling a clean kerchief from her pocket, Lil pressed on the wound to stop the bleeding. To her amazement, the wound had already begun to close. The great head wavered on the strong neck, and those clear, canny eyes that seemed a part of the night itself grew cloudy. Lil reached out and stroked an ear, surprised at how soft it felt. "Go to sleep, Ian. We'll worry about what to do in the morning. Everything will be all right."

With a peculiar little snort that sounded like relief, Ian dropped his head in her lap. He gave a little whuffle. The tension faded from his body as he inhaled and exhaled deeply, and tears stabbed at the backs of Lil's eyes. She felt Ian's hot breath blowing against the sensitive parts his other persona had brought to such vivid life . . . was it only last night? Ian's logical mind might be victim to the lupine madness, but his olfactory capacities as both man and wolf were connected to passions that didn't require thought.

They only required instinct.

With a similar primitive instinct, Lil realized he recognized her by her scent. Every ounce of the wildness drained from him as, with a soft sigh, Ian went limp, his heavy head still in her lap. Tenderness such as she'd never known made Lil's hand shake as she stroked that thick, soft fur, so warm and dense to her touch. Perhaps there was hope for them yet.

Lil looked up at Shelly—in time to see the second

wolf creeping up on its haunches behind her. "Look out!" Lil screamed.

Shelly turned, but as she leveled her rifle, the second wolf reached out a huge paw and batted it away, its claws digging deeply into her hand.

Lil saw red ooze through the deep slashes in Shelly's glove. Alarm pierced her fear. Automatically, she reached for the silver leaves in her pocket, but Shelly, too, realized the new danger.

Backing away a swift step, she removed crushed silver leaves from her own pocket and slapped them on her wound. She tossed another handful in the wolf's face, but it only snarled, fangs gleaming in the moonlight. Shelly tried her cinders next, but those, too, were ineffectual, not even drawing a sneeze.

Of a much more practical bent, Jeremy raised his rifle. From this angle, he was blocked by Shelly. "Move, gal, get out o' me way!" Jeremy shouted.

But with canny precision, as Shelly moved in one direction, the wolf shadowed her in the opposite direction. He was huge, even larger than Ian. He was also black, but his hair was red-tipped, his snout longer and more menacing. The sounds he made were terrifying enough, but it was the look in those glowing black eyes that froze Lil to her marrow.

Never had she seen hatred so fierce, nor blood lust so pure. The moors could run with rivulets of red, and it still wouldn't be enough to slake this hunger. But was it Shelly he hated? Or any human being?

Setting Ian's head gently on the ground, Lil stood. Jeremy and Shelly had put themselves in danger to protect her, and she couldn't sit helplessly by and watch them die. She touched the pistol in her belt, but suspected the puny slug would only anger the creature. She eyed the tree clinging to this patch of rocky ground, and picked up a fallen limb so heavy she could barely lift it.

The movement drew those inimical black eyes away from Shelly—to Lil. Then the snarl was turned on her. With one bound, the wolf leaped across ten feet. He landed in front of Lil. With all her strength, she lifted the limb and whacked the animal's nose.

Yowling in combined fury and pain, the wolf backed up a step, shaking its head. Shelly had time to pick up her rifle, but she stared down in dismay. It had landed hard against a rock, and the barrel was bent. She tossed the useless weapon away and snatched Jeremy's sword, creeping up on the wolf from the side.

Jeremy hurried to help, too, but in his haste, he tripped over a rock. The rifle flew out of his hands, firing in Shelly's direction as it hit the ground. Shelly went very still as her hat, a neat hole in the crown two inches above her head, sailed through the air from the force of the impact.

Scrambling up as the wolf closed with Lil again, Jeremy raised the shotgun.

"That will only anger him, you idiot," Shelly said through her teeth.

Lil brandished the tree limb again as the wolf snapped at her, but she was exhausted, and the teeth came uncomfortably close to her throat.

Jeremy snatched the sword away from Shelly—and threw it like a spear. The point stuck in the wolf's shoulder. Howling, it spun in a tight circle. Then, with an intelligence that chilled Lil to her marrow, the wolf stopped and carefully bit into the sword hilt, removing the weapon with its teeth. If Lil had debated this animal's origins, she did so no longer. This creature, too, was a werewolf, for surely such craftiness was a human, not a lupine, trait.

It licked its wound—and then bounded across to meet its new opposition. Lil dragged the tree limb with her as she valiantly tried to go to Jeremy's aid.

But Jeremy needed no help running. Spry as a man half his age, he covered the ground in long, loping strides, straight toward the bog.

Disgusted, Shelly watched him run. "I never thought the little banty cock a coward."

"He's not," Lil retorted. "Can't you see he's drawing the wolf away from us?"

Her mouth open now, Shelly watched the wolf gain on Jeremy. "By Jove, I believe you're right. Come on! If we both fire on the beast at the same time, maybe we can scare him off!" Grabbing up Jeremy's still working rifle, Shelly ran after them.

Lil followed, pulling her pistol as she went.

As bright as the moonlight was, Jeremy was still some distance away, and the wolf blended very well with the night. They'd have to get closer to be sure of their aim.

But as hard as they ran, Jeremy was faster.

So was the wolf. It was only three paces behind Jeremy now.

Two . . .

And then, to Lil's immense relief, Jeremy scaled

170

the tree he'd obviously been running for. Using his
hobnail boots for purchase, Jeremy swung his
scrawny weight straight up the bare tree with the remarkable agility of a man who'd climbed more masts
than he could count.

Just as Lil and Shelly drew within firing range, the
wolf surprised them yet again.

It followed Jeremy straight up the tree, its claws
ripping into the bark as it went. The bog lapped beneath the tree on one side. If the limb supporting Jeremy's weight broke . . .

Shelly tried aiming, but she lowered the rifle, defeated. "At this angle, I might hit the little bastard."
She held the rifle in her hand, shifting from one foot
to the other, obviously not liking the feeling of help-
lessness.

Lil noted the bleeding gashes on the back of
Shelly's hand, but the blood loss had slowed. There
was something she needed to remember. Something
to do with the legend of the werewolf. But there was
no time to worry about it now. . . .

Hooting a mocking laugh, Jeremy climbed further
out on the scrawny limb. "Come on, ye ruddy beast.
Ye want a taste? Come and get it. I hope I make ye
choke."

The limb made an ominous creaking sound as the
wolf put one huge paw on it. Below them, the bog
glistened like an earthly maw, wide, gleaming, and
hungry.

Lil covered her eyes. But when she heard Shelly
laugh, she lowered her hands.

"I'll be damned," Shelly murmured on a gurgle of

laughter less honking than usual. "He's got him trapped."

Lil had time for one glance. Jeremy clung to one end of the limb while the wolf slowly climbed out on the other. But with every step, the limb bowed more under its weight. It tried to ease back, but with a savage CRACK! the limb broke. Yelping, the wolf fell straight into the bog.

And Jeremy? He was obviously expecting it, for with an agile leap of his bandy legs, he shoved off and grabbed the next smaller branch above. His feet dangling far above that dark, struggling mass in the bog, Jeremy shouted down, "Can't fly, can ye? Swim, ye bloody bastard. Straight to hell where ye belong!"

Shelly and Lil crept to the edge of the bog and watched the wolf flail at its new, far more formidable enemy.

This one had neither hands nor feet. No blood or bone. It was an amorphous mass that couldn't be bitten or clawed. Instead, the wolf was learning what it felt like to be eaten, for the bog sucked at it more greedily the harder it struggled.

Lil saw its forelegs disappear into the murk, then the powerful neck. . . . Turning away from the terror in those black eyes, Lil instead watched Jeremy as, hand over hand, he worked his way from tree limb to tree limb until he could drop to firm ground.

When they turned away, only the wolf's face was above the bog. A mournful wail followed them. It made Lil shiver, but Jeremy only smiled in satisfaction.

Shelly eyed him as if she'd never seen him before,

and his smile grew teasing. "Didn't think I had brain enough for such a ruse, did ye?" Jeremy leaned close to Shelly and whispered, "I be good at other things, too, ducky."

What might have been a blush reddened Shelly's cheeks, but she only turned away and began to organize what she called a travois. "It's a hauling device used by the Indians of of the American West," she explained, detailing what she wanted them to do.

As Lil followed instructions, she couldn't quell a last glance at the bog beneath the tree. It roiled like oily sludge, as if recently disturbed, but there was no sign of the wolf. She'd never know who he was now, but at least he wouldn't be able to tempt and torment Ian anymore.

Using tree limbs and the heavy piece of rolled canvas Jeremy fetched from Shelly's horse, they constructed the device easily enough. It was getting Ian onto it that was hard. He was limp, and heavy.

But among the three of them, they managed to heave him onto the litter and haul him back up a circuitous path that bypassed the slope, to the horses.

Before they began the trek back, Lil tried to clean Shelly's hand with the water they'd brought along, but Shelly waved her away. "Nonsense. Just a scratch." But Shelly wouldn't meet Lil's eyes as she mounted her gelding.

Nibbling at her lip, Lil stared up at Shelly, but her friend merely glared down at Jeremy. She offered a begrudging hand to him. "Since Lil's mare is pulling the litter, you'll have to ride double with me."

"Hmm . . . sounds like a right attractive offer," Jeremy opined, stroking Shelly's hand before he leaped up behind her. "Make it again, later, ducky."

"Would you stop calling me that? I'm not a duck, a goose, or anything else of an avian persuasion."

"Now don't ruffle them pretty feathers, ducky," Jeremy said, pulling her firmly against his chest. "I'll soon show ye how persuasive I can be."

Lil bit her lip to stifle her laughter at the dazed look on Shelly's face. It was one Lil had seen in her own mirror after her more exasperating encounters with Ian: Shelly had the look of a woman torn between fury and reluctant attraction.

It would be interesting to see who won this battle of wills. Shelly was much smarter, but Jeremy was . . . well, there was no defining what Jeremy was, save his own unique self.

Looking quite content, Jeremy caught the reins and waited for Lil to go first up the path, keeping a suspicious eye on the limp form on the travois. But Ian didn't stir, so Jeremy soon stuck his shotgun back in the holder on his back.

Holding the stable manager against his scrawny chest, Jeremy whistled one of his ditties. Shelly added her own accompaniment: the sound of grinding teeth. But for the moment, she let the little banty cock crow.

It was the strangest end to the strangest night of Lil's life.

Retracing the horse tracks as she led the way home, Lil knew that, as dangerous as the expedition had been, she was glad she'd come. She'd faced her three worst fears this night. The moors. Riding. And the wolves.

As usual, Shelly had been right. Only in facing her fears had Lil overcome them. None terrified her any longer. Often, she looked back at Ian, assuring herself that he was still unconscious, still safe on his way home. He didn't stir. And the more she looked at him, the more beautiful she found his wolf form.

God willing, maybe it would be a new beginning, too. For both the heiress and the Wolf of Haskell Hall.

If she could face her own worst fears, so could Ian.

Somehow, they'd find a way to be together.

There she stood again. A sprite, or a ghost, just on the edge of his consciousness. But every time he reached out to touch her, she turned to smoke in his arms. And with her passing, his arms became legs, his hands forelegs tipped in lethal claws. Fur grew thickly over his body. He threw back his head to call for her, but only a wolf's howl came out.

Long, low, and lonely. The lament of his becoming.

When he lost her, he lost himself. Yet the luxury of choice had long since passed him by.

She was the last heiress, he, the last Griffith male. Their macabre dance of destiny would play out as his ancestress had wished. Either the werewolf would die, or Ian Griffith would die—but only after he'd killed the woman he loved.

Shocked at the revelation that came on that half-awake, half-asleep threshold, Ian opened his eyes. There she was again, her hair as bright as the morning. But this time, she was real, not a dream. With her smooth, fair skin, her silvery hair, even her soft green eyes, she was so much a creature of the verdant day that he could only lie helpless before her and stealthily try to absorb some of that light into his darkness.

She was bending over him, her lovely face concerned, that willful mouth so soft and nurturing that he'd have given the little that remained of his soul to kiss it. Almost afraid, he reached out to touch her, and to his vast relief, his paw was a hand again, and the only lust he felt was carnal.

Memories of the other night seemed all the more vivid in her bright reality. She was life, life incarnate. As precious to him as she'd been when he filled her with his own life essence, trying to imprint himself on her, in her, in the age-old way no woman could forget.

Or any man ... at least, not when the encounter touched more than his body.

He stroked her soft arm, wondering if she felt the near-worship in his touch. Gladness chased the last of his misery away. He didn't know how he came to be here, but to his heartfelt relief, she appeared unhurt. For now, he'd merely bask in the radiance of her presence and forget the night to come.

Green eyes bright with unshed tears locked on his, and this time, it was he who felt naked. What did she seek, looking so deeply into him? Only then did he realize he *was* naked, at least from the waist up. She was doctoring a wound on his chest, and he lay on a cot inside an isolated horse stall, one that had been reinforced for recalcitrant stallions.

He was a man again. For now. . . . He touched the hole in his chest, but she gripped his hand and drew it away, continuing to clean the wound.

"Have you ever heard of the concept of reincarnation?" she asked, smearing a foul-smelling medicinal salve on his wound.

Equally casually, he replied, "Yes, but feel free to refresh my memory."

"I had a Hindu nurse once, and to my Calvinist father's horror, I almost became a Hindu myself. Their religion holds that every creature has a soul."

Ian grew very still, his eyes locked upon her face. Her tone was casual, but her intent was not.

She made a pad out of a clean roll of gauze, her movements efficient. He was not the first man she'd bandaged, and he marveled again at how different this petite American virago was from the insipid heiresses who came before her. "Hinduism holds that every life is one great journey of becoming, and that our deeds in each successive life determine what we become the next time. Only when our deeds are pure does our karma allow us the ultimate oneness in which our souls are liberated."

She pressed the pad to his wound, and helped him sit up. As she wrapped a bandage about his chest to keep the pad in place, she added quietly, "In my next life, I want to be a wolf."

He was half expecting it, but still, the shock of her words jolted through him, part thrill, part foreboding. "And why is that?"

"Twice you could have killed me. Twice you hesitated. I held my very hand before your nose last night, and still you didn't bite. You remembered me, Ian. Even in your savage, four-legged form, you remembered. You chose to listen to your instincts instead of your stomach. I never knew a wolf could think, or reason, or choose right over wrong. And your strength, and beauty, and grace . . . it would not be such a bad end."

He shoved her touch away. "*You* seek it, then! Not knowing from one night to the next whom you've attacked, or what you've eaten, or even if you'll awaken a man or a beast. Good karma? I should hate to see a bad one."

Grabbing his shoulders, she stuck her passionate, flushed face into his. She even shook him slightly. "But it's not your nature to be so savage. You're being drawn into these hunts against your will. Don't you have any memory of the other wolf?" She hesitated, as if she wanted to tell him something, but then she sat back and just stared at him.

Frowning, Ian stared past her hypnotic green eyes to the blue sky beyond the pasture. Some times, just as he felt his consciousness slipping away, he thought he heard a howl, a howl dark with a savage hunger that went beyond any blood lust he'd ever known as either man or wolf.

But then the darkness consumed him, and he knew nothing until he awakened, naked and shivering, a man again. Dreading the next becoming, for each one seemed to last longer and steal more of his human self away. "I . . . don't remember. You think we hunt together?"

"No. I think he strikes first, tempting you to taste. It's almost as if a very human hatred of you has taken shape in the other wolf. He w . . . is a bit larger than you, with red-tipped fur and black eyes. Don't think. Feel. Can you not see him with your instincts?"

But as hard as he tried, Ian saw nothing but the murk of his own shadowy despair. He shook his head, unable to speak past the lump in his throat.

What had he done to earn this steadfast belief in those clear green eyes? Mayhap he had hesitated, briefly, but he must have ultimately attacked, or they would not have shot him. How many more times could he suffer this conversion and still retain an ounce of that goodness she so obviously believed in?

She said staunchly, "We have to find out who he is. If we stop him, I don't believe you'll feel the blood lust so strongly. He . . . calls it up in you."

"And what then?" Ian sank back on the cot, an arm over his eyes to block the sight of that winsome, passionate face. "I've spent years looking for a cure for this curse, even before I couldn't resist the urge to come home. If there is a cure beyond death, I haven't found it." He turned on his side away from temptation. He wanted more than hope, or life, or breath itself, to take her in his arms and bask in her loving warmth and generosity.

But his new feelings demanded that he think of her instead of himself, so he forced the words out. "Leave me, Delilah. Lock me in tonight and don't come near the barn. Do not trust me to be so forbearing again. With every conversion, I become more inhuman. That much, I know."

"You're not alone anymore, Ian." The soft touch of her hand on his shoulder made him shiver, but she was surprisingly strong as she turned him to face her.

Her tremulous smile was the loveliest thing he'd ever seen, and almost, she gave him hope that there was a way out of this for both of them.

She said softly, steadily, "You're not the only one becoming . . . something else. When you made love to me the other night, you did exactly as you warned that first week I came here. You cemented a bond between us that nothing can break. And as you also warned, perhaps I am as shameless as my name. For I'd have it no other way. As long as you return to me by daylight, I will fight the darkness to make you whole. For without you, I am not whole, either."

And Ian, who twice outweighed this indomitable little sprite, felt helpless before her. Trembling with the force of his emotions, he reached out to cup her soft cheek. "Man or wolf, I'm not good enough for you, Delilah. Run. Run back to America and leave me to my fate—"

But she stopped his words in the simple way, the inevitable way—with her mouth. And there, in the warm sunlight that was cold compared to the fire of her generosity and passion, Ian Griffith learned the most important lesson in his becoming.

He learned to hope again . . .

Redemption was sweet on her lips.

For the rake he'd been, and the animal he was in danger of becoming.

And then he couldn't think at all. He pulled her onto his lap and bowed her over his arm, drinking forgetfulness from the bountiful fount of her femininity. And with every precious sip, the wild urges of the wolf receded to the darkness where they belonged.

Only the needs of a man were brave enough to revel in the sunlight with this innocent temptress.

Still, the man had something in common with the wolf: They both wanted to eat her up.

He trailed burning kisses down the smooth column of her neck to the high button of her oh-so-proper gown. Laughter glittered in his deep, dark voice like the sunshine she led him into. "Such prim modesty only makes me long all the more to strip you naked."

Lying against his chest, her arms about his neck, her eyes steady on his face, she replied demurely, "Why do you think I chose this dress?"

His shout of laughter made the horses in the stalls across the way stamp the ground.

A groom quit mucking the stalls to listen to the happy sound, but he quickly returned to his task under Shelly's baleful look.

But Shelly's stern face relaxed into a smile as she, too, listened to the laugh trail off to a chuckle. Sighing with what might have been a twinge of envy in a less formidable personality, she returned to her own job of inspecting a repaired saddle.

Inside the stall, Ian nuzzled Delilah's neck, stabbing his tongue into the vulnerable hollow.

"Show me, then, temptress, what you hide. Fill in the gaps of my memory."

Firmly, she moved his straying hand from her thigh. "You seem quite able to fill in those gaps yourself." She went scarlet as gleaming amber eyes beamed into hers. "That is, I mean, it's full daylight and I'm not so shameless that I—"

"Daylight is safer. For both of us." The laughter was gone.

She mourned her foolish choice of words. But perhaps it was for the best. When he touched her like this, she couldn't think. And never had she needed to think more clearly. She slipped off his lap and moved to a safe distance. Even then, her gaze traveled hungrily over his bare chest.

The bandage didn't spoil his male beauty. It only gave him an even more rakish, indomitable look. In this wounded male form, he was still power curtailed. Twice she'd looked into the wolf's eyes. They were the same color, with the depth of wildness and will, as the eyes that looked at her now with a similar hunger.

And she, heaven help her, found both his personas fascinating and fearful. What did that say of her?

She saw the same thought in his face before he spoke it. "Do not romanticize me in either shape, Delilah. Perhaps this end was inevitable for me. I've been a lone wolf my entire life. Now I must pay the price for that independence. But you don't have to."

"Perhaps not. But I choose to." Turning on her heel away from the stunned look in his eyes, Delilah left the stall and dropped the sturdy bolt on the outside.

He leaped up and grasped the bars, so quick and alert even wounded that she instinctively backed away a pace. "Do not come back tonight. I implore you."

She quickly walked away. He had her at such sixes and sevens that she'd hardly have been human if she hadn't wanted him to wonder, too. Besides, she hadn't made up her own mind about whether to stay with him tonight. Perhaps she was undergoing some strange transformation, too, for fear was fast becoming fascination.

She met Shelly in the yard. Shelly's smile looked strained, and Delilah noted that the stable manager's hand was bandaged now. "How is he?"

"Recovering rapidly," Lil replied. "Too rapidly. I hope the stall holds him tonight."

"Perhaps we should drug him."

"No. Just see that all the hands are sent away. I want no one but myself, you, and Jeremy close enough to hear him."

"Then what? What have you decided to tell the servants?"

"That he's ill, but recuperating, and that within a few days, he'll be able to take over his duties once more."

Skepticism gleamed in the acute gray eyes. "And how do you intend to quiet the gossip?"

"By ignoring it. It shan't be any more lurid than the things they say about me. Since I own this estate, surely it is no one's concern but my own if Ian stays on as estate manager." Lil couldn't avoid staring at that neatly bandaged hand. "Shelly, have you felt any . . . ill effects since the wolf clawed you?"

Uncharacteristically, Shelly turned away without answering. And that alarmed Lil most of all. Lil trailed after her. "Shelly, perhaps we should fetch the doctor. Perhaps your wound is infected."

"Nonsense. It's a scratch, merely. We need to expend our energy on finding the cure for Ian's malady.

I'll speak to my cousin. Perhaps he'll know of some source in the village we haven't thought to check previously." She walked quickly inside the stable. Almost running. Not once had she met Lil's eyes.

And Lil knew then, beyond any shadow of a doubt, that Ian's malady had become Shelly's illness, too. The thought of that magnificent intellect reduced to lupine craftiness was enough to spur Lil on her own mission.

She had the lives of two people she cared about at stake now. Somewhere in this place that had seen the birth of this curse lay the seeds of the remedy. And it was up to the last heiress to find it.

The night passed quietly, to Lil's great relief. If the servants were frightened and suspicious of the growling and the howling issuing from the stables, they took their cue from their mistress and ignored it. Lil had scoured her own library for the rest of that day, but she found nothing relating to wolves, much less werewolves.

By the time night fell and the moon rose, clear and taunting, Lil had once again invaded Ian's quarters. She told herself that it was best she stay there rather than go to the stables again and make Ian's transition even harder. His interests were better served if she found a cure.

But the truth was, she was afraid. Afraid her own terrible fascination with Ian's lupine form would ultimately be their undoing.

If the curse proved too strong, Delilah would be as lost to the wiles of the moon as Ian.

Even as she frantically paged through every book

Ian had on the subject of werewolves, the thoughts crept slyly through the back of her head.

Would it be such a bad fate to be a wolf?

To bound across the earth as if she had wings, fall from a great height and run off, unharmed? To take a near mortal wound and, by the next morning, be virtually healed? To be one with the night, her senses so acute that no dull human could understand the allure of seeing, and smelling, and tasting. To understand, at last, the wonder of rebirth.

And the becoming . . .

A mournful wail raised its homage to the moon, as if chastising her for her weakness. Lil snapped a dusty tome closed. "Delilah Haskell Trent, you've taken leave of your senses!"

She sought her bed, but spent the rest of the night in a chair before the window.

Watching the moon.

Coveting its power and beauty . . .

Chapter Eight

When the full moon passed, the march of days became dull routine again. To Delilah's fury, Ian retook his duties with all the passion he'd once lavished on her. He dealt with his mistress through intermediaries.

A few servants balked at taking orders from him. Two even quit rather than work for a man and a mistress so benighted. But, with Shelly's and Mrs. McCavity's help, within a few days, Lil and Ian had the estate running smoothly again. If people in every village within a fifty-mile radius whispered, for the moment, that was all they could do.

Speculate. Was the curse true? If it was, why did the latest heiress continue to employ Ian Griffith? Was he really a werewolf?

The question uppermost in everyone's mind was

loudest of all, because it was whispered rather than spoken aloud: Who would die next?

But neither of them dignified the lurid curiosity by so much as acknowledging it.

Twice Lil came upon Ian on the grounds, twice he walked away before she could stop him. One evening she went to the tower, but to her fury, he'd changed the locks.

She simmered, she stewed, she vowed to herself she'd fire him and leave him to his fate. But in the end, beneath her fury, she grieved.

It wasn't himself he was protecting, as events soon proved.

One of the groundskeepers and two grooms were sent packing a few days later, all bearing the marks of a brawl. Lil couldn't pin anyone down as to why, so she sought out her one honest-to-a-fault fount of information: Jeremy.

She found him sulking over buttermilk in the kitchen with an expression so sour she wondered if he'd curdled the milk himself. "Jeremy, do you know why Ian fired the grooms and the yard man?"

Jeremy swiped the mustache from his lip. "Aye. I was there."

Lil waited, but he only hunched lower over his glass. "Well? Answer me, if you please."

"Ye got a swelled head enough, if ye arsk me. Like all yer kind." But he sighed at the look on her face and shoved his glass back. "They insulted ye. Ian rammed their nasty talk straight back into their throats with his fist and sent 'em off."

Ignoring the cook's scandalized look at her bourgeois behavior, Lil sat next to Jeremy on the sturdy bench and poured herself a glass of buttermilk. She'd suspected as much. When the cook and his assistants were safely occupied at a distance, she lowered her voice and lamented, "He won't even see me, Jeremy."

"Aye, he be a better man than I give him credit for. Or he loves ye dearly. What does he have to offer ye, him a commoner, and a beastie three nights of the month to boot?"

The simple male perspective Jeremy offered should have made Lil feel better. Maybe Ian did care for her deeply, for she knew beyond doubt that he still wanted her. But her frustration only grew. "How can we find a remedy if he won't let me help him?"

"Mayhap he wants to find the cure himself. Or mayhap he doesn't believe there is one."

Likely the latter, Lil thought, growing more despondent by the minute. And maybe Ian was right. After all, he'd looked for a cure for years, even before he'd returned to the soil that had birthed both man and monster. And who was she, to think she could find what generations of Griffith men had searched for?

The last heiress of Haskell Hall. The last potential victim of the curse. Who had better motivation to end it?

Draining his glass, Jeremy stood. "Mistress, belike we'd all be better off leavin' these backward Land's Enders to their scandals and tragedies and go back to Colorado where we belong. Ye did yer best, but some things were not meant to be."

Surprised, Lil stared up at him. This was most unlike Jeremy. Running away was not in his nature any more than it was in her own. Then she realized that Jeremy stood a bit too tall, his hands propped on his scrawny hips, scowling in offended male pride as he awaited her answer. She had to take another sip of buttermilk to keep from smiling.

She knew he'd tried several times to visit Shelly. Each time, she'd sent him packing. Now the impulses that had taken a Cockney lad of no breeding, no connections, and little money around the world and, on occasion, into the company of potentates and princes, urged him to go back to the safe and familiar. He loved Colorado, too.

"Sad figures we are, the two of us, Jeremy. Stalwarts mooning, if you'll excuse the term, over Samsons who'd as lief jump off a cliff as turn to us for succor." She saw the question trembling on Jeremy's tongue, and added hastily, "Comfort. In a word, old friend, because we have the same temperament, I can tell you confidently that if you run away from Shelly, you'll always regret it."

Jeremy's brows twitched like climbing caterpillars. "Ain't a woman been born yet can make me run nowheres I don't want to be."

"Then go back to Colorado if you must. I stay here to meet my fate, whatever it is. Stubborn I am, maybe even foolish. But all I know is that the curse will die with me and Ian. Either because we're the last of the lines, or because we find a way to break it. I'll pay for your passage if you and Safira wish to go back, but . . . I've never needed the two of you more than now." Lil stood and braced her hands on the sturdy wooden table.

Jeremy's anger had faded to melancholy, but she recognized fierce love and loyalty in those pale blue eyes. God forgive her for exploiting it. If Shelly had been . . . infected, then Shelly needed him, too. If he left and heard that the indomitable woman he'd been so attracted to had turned into the very creature she was trying to study, he'd be devastated. No, it was in Jeremy's best interests to stay, too.

Quietly, Lil said, "You've risked your life for me many times. But now you have to risk something even more precious to one of your bent. Pride is the boon and bane of our existence, Jeremy. It's made us who we are. Two strong people, who can't be bothered with propriety. But strength without compassion is like steel without alloy: We will break, not bend."

His eyes flickered, as if he wanted to look away from her steady green gaze. But then he put his hands on her shoulders and softly kissed her forehead. "If yer pa could see ye now, he'd fair bust his breeches with pride. Ye shame me, me girl. I stay. I promised him on his deathbed I'd die in service to ye, and so I will. Curse or no. No skinny spinster will make me forget me duty." With that pride and determination etched deeply in his face, the banty cock strutted from the kitchen, all but crowing his lust for the one hen in the barnyard who ignored him.

Laughing, in much better spirits and determined to heed her own advice, Lil flew to the tiny mirror on the wall and straightened her coiffure. Besides, she decided with a wicked grin, wolves could be quarry, too. If the huntress was wily enough.

Then, turning aside so she didn't have to see her own blush, Lil undid the top two buttons of her dress. At least, in this regard, both the two-legged and four-legged forms of Ian Griffith had the same weakness.

For the flesh . . .

Her blush deepened as she visualized the two-legged Ian Griffith's seductive, unique method of consummation. Odd how it only left them both hungry for more.

Anticipation was delicious on her tongue. . . .

Search as she might, Lil couldn't find her quarry. She heard raised voices in Shelly's rooms above the stable, and at one point recognized Jeremy's exasperated tones.

The men working the grounds shrugged when she asked about Ian's whereabouts. They were sullen, and she didn't like the way they looked at her, but finally one young lad shyly tugged his cap off and rolled it in his hands.

"Yes?" Lil queried.

"I believe he be in the mine, ma'arm. He were supposed to inspect the new equipment, or so the foreman told me da."

"Thank you, young man." Lil gave him some shillings for his trouble. His eyes got huge, and he grinned, bobbing his head in thanks.

Running back to the house, Lil fetched a shawl and driving gloves. Under the butler's disapproving gaze, she realized her dress was unbuttoned and turned her back to correct that oversight. She said curtly, "I may not arrive back for dinner. Please inform the cook."

Outside, she climbed onto the curricle driver's seat, determined to make the trip alone, despite the impropriety. If she found Ian, she didn't want witnesses. Blushing, she lifted the reins, but Safira came running out.

"Mistress! Mistress, wait."

"Yes, Safira?" Lil turned to her sometime companion, sometime maid.

Safira's dark eyes glittered with tears, but she glanced uneasily at the attentive groom still holding the horse's head. "Do not go into the village today."

"Whyever not?"

Safira folded and unfolded a clean kerchief. "I . . . have seen an omen. The bones point at the moors. Death awaits there."

A chill ran up Lil's spine. All of Safira's omens proved true. Eventually. Lil nodded the groom away. He walked off, glancing curiously over his shoulder. Then she beckoned to Safira until she could be sure none of the other servants milling about heard her quiet, "Whose death?"

"I . . . do not know. But a young woman. She dies . . . like the others." Safira couldn't meet Lil's eyes now.

"When?"

The slim shoulders shrugged. "Please, stay in the house today."

Lil considered the request, but surely she was safe enough now. It was weeks before another full moon.

"I cannot." She had three weeks to find a cure for a curse one hundred years in the making.

Briskly, Lil gripped the reins. "I shall be fine." She patted the pistol in the holster beside her on the seat. She also wore her silverleaf necklace and a pouch of cinders under her clothes, just in case. For all the good that had done a few nights past.

Taking with her the look of dread on Safira's face, Lil was nervous the entire way to the village. At the fork in the road that led to their estate, she saw Thomas and Preston Harbaugh riding toward her. She drew the horse to a stop and smiled as they pulled up beside her.

"Well met, Miss Haskell," Thomas said, tipping his hat. "We were just on our way to see if you'd decided whether to accept our invitation to the ball. Seating arrangements, you know. A bore, but necessary."

Not certain where the impulse came from, but certain somehow she was doing the right thing, Lil smiled back demurely, like a proper heiress of a proper estate to proper gentlemen. Though after Ian's remarks Lil was not certain these men were either proper or gentlemen. "I intended to post my acceptance on the morrow. I do, indeed, plan to attend. But I plan to bring a male guest, if you've no objection. Just so I don't throw your seating arrangements off, you understand. Even a gauche American has some sensibilities about such things."

"Gauche?" Preston expostulated, glancing at his brother as if for confirmation. "If you are gauche, that Farquar chit is positively primitive."

"Not to mention horse-faced and rude," Thomas agreed.

The two brothers burst into laughter.

Lil was not overly fond of either Miss Farquar or her silly mother, but still, she knew any young woman would be hurt to hear herself so described. And it was hardly gentlemanly of these two men of blue blood but purple prose to mock their compatriot to a newcomer.

Since she'd never been good at hiding her emotions, Lil realized Thomas must have seen the glint of disapproval in her eyes, for he stopped laughing and even had the grace to look ashamed. "Sorry to gossip, Miss Haskell. Miss Farquar does tend to . . . run a man to ground, but that's neither here nor there." Embarrassed, he cleared his throat.

Lil's disapproval relaxed into mild amusement. Yes, she could just imagine how determinedly Miss Farquar and her mother pursued the area's two most eligible bachelors. Lil said sweetly, "Then find her a different fox. Perhaps you can find someone new to introduce her to at the ball."

"A capital notion!" Thomas averred. "But it shall come as no surprise to you that I would rather expend my energy on you, instead. There's a great deal to be said for an . . . attachment between us."

Lil had done some investigating herself about his interest in her, and she'd discovered that their lands were joined by a choice finger of property that the Harbaughs had tried on numerous occasions to purchase from the Haskells. It was lovely, tied to the river, and allowed a shortcut to the coast road be-

194

tween the two estates. "Could my parcel at the junction of the roads account for part of my fascination for you?"

Thomas had the good grace to at least look embarrassed, but then he blustered, "Now, see here, you shan't put me off so easily from my true mission—I demand you save at least three dances on your card for me."

"And three for me," Preston added.

Lil picked up her reins again. "I'm quite sure you'll both understand if I, too, have a bit of a problem with commitments. But I shall consider your requests at a more appropriate time."

Thomas pretended to pull a knife out of his heart. "Gauche? Wily. As dangerous as she is lovely." Abruptly, he leaned forward, and all the teasing went out of his face as he said gruffly, "You are a lovely, exciting woman, and it would be a crime against nature itself if you should meet the same end as your predecessors. Be very careful, Miss Haskell. Do not go out on the moors alone. Beautiful women have a tendency to meet . . . unsavory ends there."

"Just like that barmaid who disappeared, what was her name? The comely one with beautiful black hair who worked at the tavern," Preston said.

"Hush, Preston, don't spout such horrors. You'll frighten Miss Haskell needlessly," Thomas rejoined.

"Well, needfully, perhaps. It is unfortunately true that no one has seen the wench for days, and her family has contacted the sheriff about the matter. But so far the man hasn't turned up any trace of her. She didn't so much as pack a new dress, or so it is whispered."

Black hair. Lil remembered the lovely, buxom barmaid Ian had cradled on his lap that first time she went to the village. Her hair had gleamed like a raven's wing. Lil cleared her voice to be sure it was steady. "But, she's not a Haskell. Surely you aren't implying she lies somewhere on the moors, rip—" But she couldn't complete the sentence.

The grim stare exchanged by the brothers punctuated her aborted statement well enough.

"Oh, well, it's too lovely a day to worry about such ugly things," Thomas said. He tipped his hat to her. "But do be careful. You are the most exciting thing that's happened around this backwater in years. We will both look forward to dancing with you at our ball. Good day." They drew aside to give her the road, watching her as she drove off.

The day was one poets would eulogize. Wildflowers preened under the breeze's brazen caress. A hawk keened above, soaring over the trials and tribulations of the tiny earthbound beings below.

But Lil's troubles colored her enjoyment of the day nevertheless. She was still wondering about the waitress when, as she drew close to the tiny, rutted road that led to the mine, she finally saw Ian. He was riding that great brute of a black stallion. Riding as if the hounds of hell chased him.

He pulled up short when he saw her. Brutus reared and snorted, but Ian controlled him with a flick of one strong arm and the flexing of his powerful thighs. The stallion settled down. Ian's muscles bulged beneath his shirt sleeves, and man and stallion were as much a part of this wild place as the toothy mountains chewing the landscape in the distance.

And the smells . . . why was she so susceptible now to scents? It was as if, in sharing his essence with her, Ian had also shared his heightened senses.

Warm earth.

Warmer horse flesh.

Warmest healthy male flesh.

Ian's white shirt clung to his skin with all the loving attention to detail Lil longed to lavish upon him. Lil realized he must have checked the mine equipment himself, for his hands were filthy. As her eyes adjusted to the shade of his wide-brimmed hat, she saw streaks of dirt on his face. But then, like a blow, she saw the expression in his eyes.

She reeled under the impact. All thoughts of the waitress, the brothers, the ball, and her determination to take Ian as her guest, narrowed to something more ephemeral and instinctive than thought, scent, or touch—emotional empathy. An empathy that, incongruously, grew apace with her fears and frustrations. Something had happened to Ian recently, something he hadn't told her about.

If Satan's minions had descended on this remote stretch of road to build a gateway to hell, they could not have cast more blackness upon the land than the stygian night staring out of Ian's eyes.

Endless darkness.

Pain without surcease.

Lil's voice broke under the emotional impact of that look. "Ian, why will you not let me help you? Between the two of us we can—" She broke off with a gasp as, in full daylight, Ian took on his other persona.

Like a wild man, in one smooth movement, he kneed his mount next to the curricle, leaned down, and swept her sidesaddle before him. Then he kicked the stallion into a gallop, sitting on the animal's hindquarters, yet still moving with each powerful stride as if he were, in truth, part of the animal.

Where were they going? For one heart-stopping moment, Lil thought Ian was as subject to the uncontrollable passion between them as she. Did he intend to take her into the wilds, as he'd once threatened, to ravish her?

But then she realized he was riding straight down the road toward the village. And here she was, the foreigner already subject to much gossip and dislike, ankles and calves showing, hat knocked askew, a madman holding her in the clutch of his arms.

About to be paraded through the village she owned.

The thought of yet more scandal, more staring eyes, made her struggle and pull at his iron grip about her waist. But he only held her more tightly in the secure circle of his arms, gripping the reins on each side of her waist.

Lil's teeth jarred together on a garbled protest. He ignored it, hauling her back against his strong chest. The feel of him, the smell of him, made music in her head, but it was a jangled dissonance that matched the jerky rhythm of the horse.

It wasn't passion tensing the strong muscles surrounding her. It was despair. Determination. To prove—what to her?

She felt his hot breath blow on the nape of her neck. Prickles ran through her as he growled, "Be still. Since you persist in playing with matches, you might as well learn the dangers of fire. If you won't listen to me, I'll take you to someone more persuasive."

And question him as she might, that was all he said on the ride into the village. When they wound through the quaint streets, sure enough, every man, woman, and child they passed stopped and stared. Ian seemed to realize, a bit too late, the additional scandal they were causing. He pulled her dress down.

Looking dignified and unruffled under the circumstances was a challenge, especially as she felt her skirts flapping around her calves, but somehow Lil managed. Spine erect, she set her hat back at the proper angle and stared straight ahead as if she arrived in town this way every time she came.

She didn't know whether to be relieved or upset that Ian ignored the whispers and shocked stares as he rode straight to the vicarage.

She'd intended to visit the good man herself, but not using this mode of transport. As Ian pulled the stallion to a stop and slid off the animal's powerful hindquarters, the door to the parsonage opened.

Mrs. Holmes froze on the threshold, her taller husband peering over her shoulder. Both were dressed for an outing. Lil had time for one flashing glimpse of the shocked look on Mrs. Holmes's face and the amused quirk of Vicar Holmes's mouth before Ian pulled her willy-nilly off the horse, not allowing her time to pull her skirts down. In fact, the movement

199

revealed her knees, and the humiliation Lil had stifled exploded into action at the vicar's muffled laugh.

The moment her feet touched the ground, Lil doubled up a small fist and swung at Ian. The easy way he dodged, caught her wrists in a secure but not painful hold, and marched her toward the parsonage steps only angered her more. "You have no right to manhandle me like this. Let me go, you, you—"

Abruptly, he turned her to face him. He bent and stuck his flushed face into hers, saying for her ears alone, "Wolf, I believe, is the appellation you seek. It's time you accept that truth, Delilah. No romantic notions, no generosity on your part can change my nature, or my fate."

Was that actually a sparkle of unshed tears in those fearless eyes? No, that wasn't right, either. Ian had fears aplenty—but in that vulnerable moment, he let her see deeply into the heart and mind he kept so private.

His fears were for her.

The knowledge took the sword out of her hand and turned it into an olive branch. How could she fault his passion when she had only to look at him to go a bit mad herself? Lil braced her small feet, staring straight back into his eyes, wondering what he saw in her own.

The words came easily, after all. "Don't you see it's too late for me to run?" she whispered. "My fate is your fate. You told me so yourself. Would you curse me to everlasting darkness, too?"

With a strangled groan, he tried to turn away, but now it was she who caught his wrist. Lil had forgotten her anger, her humiliation, even their fascinated audience. She knew only the same need that had been driving her since this wild, dangerous man had shown her, in his bed and in his arms, the deepest tenderness any woman could imagine. "Ian, it's you who do not understand. Whether I run back to Colorado, or die on the moors as was foretold, life as I knew it has ended. I'd rather die trying to find a way to end this curse upon both our names that run home a coward and perish one day at a time without you."

There it was again. A strange look to see in a face as indomitable as his, but all the more precious for it.

Tenderness.

Tenderness a woman could dream of, but seldom hope for.

His long-lashed eyes closed, as if he felt her more than saw her, sensed her more than touched her, and Ian reached out one large, strong hand and traced every passionate curve of her face. Forehead, eyelashes, cheekbones, nose, chin, and finally, mouth. He rested his fingertip there, and the trembling contours of her lips seemed to create a similar unsteadiness in him. "Delilah," he whispered.

It was enough. Perhaps through the conduit of their touch, perhaps through the husky purr of his voice, she sensed his yearning to believe her. His need for trust, for contact, for purpose . . .

. . . for hope.

Her own eyes bright with tears, Lil kissed his fingertip and turned to the couple still standing silently on the stoop. She saw from the looks on their faces that they hadn't heard the whispered exchange. But it was also apparent that they didn't need to.

Mrs. Holmes leaned against her husband's shoulder, so moved she needed support, and the vicar's voice was throaty as, gently supporting his wife by her shoulders, he said, "Welcome back to the village, my dear Miss Haskell. I suspected when Ian came to me that I'd see you shortly, too." He looked beyond her to Ian. "Do you want me to show her what we found?"

Ian nodded.

The vicar looked down at his wife. "Lovey, we shall save our visit to the Cromwells for tomorrow, if you've no objection?"

Blowing her nose on a clean kerchief, the vicar's wife stood straight. "Certainly. I shall see you for supper, lovey mine." With a last tremulous smile at Ian and Lil, she went back inside the house.

To distract from her own shyness, Lil instilled a teasing note in her voice. "Lovey? Lovey mine?"

The unflappable vicar actually blushed. "A foolishness granted only by twenty years of happy marriage. I shall . . . hope the same for you one day."

This time, it was Ian and Lil who couldn't look at one another.

"Shall we walk?" the vicar asked, sweeping an arm before him.

Lil preceded them, but with an automatic courtesy surely out of keeping with the common laborer Ian tried to pretend to be, he offered his elbow to her. As they walked, she felt how rigid his arm was, and when she looked up at that strong jaw shadowed by his hat, she saw a muscle tic. Matching his stride to hers, he stared straight ahead, but she felt his dread as they approached the edge of the village and started walking toward a sheltered copse of trees.

Wherever they were going, he was obviously nervous about her reaction at what they would find. Vicar Holmes, walking silently at her other side, seemed grim, too.

Her heart beginning to pound with fear, Lil cleared her throat, but before she was faced with a new mystery, she had another to solve. "Mrs. Holmes wasn't afraid of Ian," she commented to the vicar. "Your wife—she knows about us?"

"Oh, yes. She's as fond of Ian as I am. She has faith that, among the four of us, we can find a cure."

"And the rest of the villagers?"

"A few suspect, but most of the people have known Ian since he was in shortcoats, and they also know how many times he's risked his life for the people hereabouts. Did you know that during a mine cave-in, he insisted on being the one to climb through the tunnel they made through very unstable rubble? To test its safety before he led the men out himself?"

The man under discussion obviously didn't like it, for he pulled his arm away and hurried ahead, but Lil was amused to see his reddened cheeks. Odd how he'd rather be taken for a savage than a saint.

Relieved of his distracting presence, Lil felt the vicar's earlier comment hit her with belated impact.

The four of them. Vicar Holmes didn't know Shelly had been bitten.

Lil hesitated, glancing at Ian, then the vicar, wondering if she should voice her own suspicions and betray Shelly's secret, but the vicar was Shelly's cousin, after all. He and Ian both needed to know. Lil rushed through the unpleasant truth, "Shelly was scratched the other night."

Turning, his face going ashen, Ian stopped cold. "Did I—?"

"No. The other wolf. Do you have any idea who he is, Ian?"

Rapidly, Ian started walking again.

The vicar sighed at his reaction and confided softly to Lil, "I have my suspicions, but haven't been able to confirm them. When and if I can, you shall be the first to know. Shelly . . . dear heaven, I cannot imagine another person in this world who would so hate to lose her self-control and become . . ." He swallowed as if he couldn't say it.

"Perhaps that's why she has the most hope," Lil countered. "You see, sir, I believe, from the two contacts I've had with these creatures, that the personality of the human is somehow transferred into that of the wolf. In other words, if a man—or woman—is basically decent and honorable as a person, he remains so in his otherworldly form. Twice Ian could have killed me with ease, and twice he hesitated."

"That theory would postulate, then, that the other wolf must be as evil and cunning in his human form as he is in his lupine being."

"Yes." Lil stopped as they reached their goal. At first she was confused, for she saw nothing but a wild tangle of growth beneath the trees. But then her eyes adjusted to the shade from the bright sunshine. She made out crude crosses, a few homemade headstones of brickwork, even one of carved granite. But it was so covered with ivy that she couldn't make out the name.

She was standing in a cemetery. A very neglected cemetery. Set apart from the town.

These poor people were as isolated in death as they'd been in life. It must be a Gypsy cemetery.

Knowing she was right from the look on Ian's face, Lil knelt at a grave slightly apart from the others. It bore a simple headstone half covered beneath moss. Part of the moss had been recently ripped away, and she could just make out an inscription. But the words were strange; she didn't understand them. But the date . . . the year the gypsy girl died. Lil traced the crude block letters with her fingertip. They weren't Latin.

"Romany," Ian said.

Lil looked up at him, standing so tall and invincible over his ancestor's grave. He'd removed his hat, and as he stared down, with her increasing sensitivity to his thoughts, she read the mix of emotions behind his expressionless face. He wanted to hate the woman who'd visited this curse upon his name.

But he couldn't.

He felt a great sadness, regret that she was no more respected or honored in death than she'd been in her pain and suffering. Feeling the same sadness, Lil realized something else: He was ashamed of his Gypsy blood. Or mayhap resentful that she'd left him such a shameful legacy. Lil could hardly blame him for that.

"Do we know anyone who can read this?" she asked.

The vicar nodded. "Shelly lived with Gypsies for over a year, and she has a facility for languages. I'd planned to bring her here tomorrow, but now . . ."

"Now it's more important to her than ever, isn't it?" Lil pointed out. "But, maybe the scratches she suffered were superficial."

Ian snapped, "And maybe the moon won't rise tomorrow, and the tides won't match their rhythm to it. Will you never stop believing in miracles?"

Slowly, Lil stood, wishing, for the millionth time, that she was taller. Still, she met him look for look. "No. Not willingly. And maybe that's why I have a better chance at finding a cure than you do. Maybe if you believed there was one—"

With a tormented sound, Ian whirled and stalked off down the road, back toward the village. She started after him.

The vicar gently caught her arm. "No. In his present state of mind, it's better to let him deal with this in his own way."

"Why did he want me to see this?"

"To understand the gulf between you, I expect. Have you seen the Haskell crypt next to your mansion?"

Indeed she had. Pain pierced Lil, so acute she had to grab her side. The crypt was carefully tended inside and out. Every Haskell had a tombstone, a loving inscription, and some had a catafalque. She'd only been in the crypt early on when Mrs. McCavity showed her about the estate grounds, but even now, she remembered the ornate monument decorating the last male Haskell's grave.

Whereas the woman he'd wronged lay unmourned, unknown.

Oh, yes, Lil understood Ian's message and why he'd brought her here. Such was his fate—he'd die as he'd lived, alone, unloved. Either forever the lone wolf who roamed the moors until the day it died, or as the man who'd wandered the world to avoid sharing this fate he tried so desperately to shield her from.

The pain in her side grew so sharp she gasped.

Vicar Holmes frowned and peered into her face. "Are you well, my dear?"

By sheer effort of will, Lil dropped her hand and stood tall, staring blindly down at the neglected marker. She fell to her knees and began to frantically pull the rest of the moss away from the headstone. It had a century's head start on her, but she was young, and vibrant, and strong with desperation.

She felt the vicar's appalled gaze as, like a madwoman, she continued to yank at the moss until the headstone was totally clear. "Sir, could I trouble you for some strong lye soap and a sturdy brush?" She couldn't meet his eyes as she made the request. She couldn't explain, even to herself, why she felt such urgency. But she felt an urgent need to do all she could to redress the wrongs of her own ancestor.

"But you have an army of servants," the vicar protested.

"I don't know quite how to explain this, but it was Haskell hands that began this evil. Only Haskell hands can end it. Please, sir. I must do this."

He gave what might have been an approving smile, turned, and hurried back toward the parsonage.

Glancing over her shoulder to assure herself she was alone, Lil knelt by the headstone again and traced the name with a soothing fingertip. "Somewhere, you must be watching and listening. We're both women of the wilds, Gypsy girl. I don't like the airs and proprieties of this society any more than you did. But surely you see that if I suffer the same fate as the others, and Ian is cursed forever as a wolf, you perpetuate what you hated most. Male heirs will come again, and not just a Griffith and a Haskell will suffer. The entire village will be ruined. Is that your legacy for the child you labored alone to bear, and his children?"

Footsteps drew her to her feet. She took the warm water, strong lye soap, and brush the vicar handed her. "Please, I'll be fine. I'll return to the parsonage when I'm finished."

With only a nod, he left her to her self-imposed task. For what seemed hours, but was probably only minutes, she scrubbed. And, strangely, the harder she labored, the suds burning her hands, the more the pain in her side receded.

When she was done, she tossed the brush into the dirty water, stood again, and stared down at the now-clean headstone. The lettering, at least, was stark, and would be easier for Shelly to read. Feeling much better despite her chapped hands, Lil turned to leave.

But the same mysterious instincts that had been her only comfort of late compelled her. She moved back and stood over the remnants of what must have been a vibrant life, clasped her hands, and looked down at the gleaming headstone.

With only the urgent pounding of her own heart as witness, Lil closed her eyes and vowed softly, "I promise to come here every day. With my own hands, I will clean these stones one by one, and place flowers on your grave. And if there is a bridge left between this world and the next, perhaps a kindness, a daily good deed, can slowly supplant the wrong that was done you. Please, in return, show me how to end in happiness what you began in pain. Let Ian and me end this curse in the best way—by the ultimate bond of blood as we create a child of our love. We will protect her, and nurture her, and see that she knows as much of the Griffith heritage as the Haskell one."

For a blink of an eye, that bridge seemed to form. It seemed to Lil as if a sudden eerie stillness formed a link between the world she knew and the one she imagined. Even the wind paused in its gusting dance with the grass and flowers to listen.

In the distance, a dark, bushy plant seemed to shake its wild head defiantly. Was that a winsome face framed by black hair? Lil could almost believe the girl not only listened from her spirit world, but smiled. Approvingly.

As if she'd awaited just such a promise as this . . .

A soft gasp behind Lil made her whirl around.

Ian stood there, one foot forward, as if he'd frozen in mid-step. She saw from his expression that he must have heard at least part of her vow. He looked from the shining headstone to the dirty water, to her reddened hands, and finally to her face.

Darkness fled his eyes. Like a light turning on, they glowed with an amber radiance as welcoming as a home hearth bright enough to banish the night.

Or bridge two worlds. And meld two fates.

Ian held out his hand to her. "Come, Delilah. I have to show you my favorite place in all the world. Together, we will cleanse it. And if there's a bridge, as you so poignantly stated just now, between this world and the next, between light and darkness, and pain and happiness, together, we will find it."

Lil could have hesitated, or bristled at his temerity, for she knew he wasn't inviting her on a tour of the moors. He wanted to share with her that patch of earth he'd taunted her with back when they first met.

In exactly the way he'd described then.

Softness upon her backside, hardness at her front.

She didn't hesitate. In two steps, she met him, her hand clasping his.

Perhaps this was all they'd have. But it was enough, for now, to celebrate life with him.

While it was yet daylight, at least, good karma was strong enough to cheat death.

Chapter Nine

Ian and Lil left the village as they'd arrived, riding double. But this time, the shocked stares didn't bother Lil. Like everything else beyond the scent and touch of this man, the scandalized villagers had taken on an unreal quality. The streets soon faded behind the two riders and Lil noted, but didn't care, when Ian left the road to weave a tortuous path deep into the moors.

No one else existed in this sheltered world she and Ian made together.

The clip-clop of hooves was the only sound that broke the beat of two hearts pounding in tandem. Toward one goal.

To use their bodies' union as an expression of their merging hearts. Lil understood, finally, that Ian's odd behavior since their last joining made perfect sense if she cast it in the right light. He'd avoided her, then dragged her to the grave for one reason only: to protect her. In a peculiarly honorable way, he was determined to frighten her away. For her own good.

Just as the wolf had growled ferociously but hesitated to attack, the man acted fierce to cover his need.

For her. If not, why would a rake of his experience be so tender to a woman whose name he hated? She recalled the rude, suggestive way he'd called her "mistress" from the very beginning, and she realized that deferring to a little slip of an American girl, an outsider to boot, must have been a blow to his pride.

Yet his prickles had been stripped away along with her own. That night of the full moon had been the culmination of an obsession neither of them could resist. But why? Ian Griffith was the strongest, most independent man she'd ever met. Too strong to be led by the nether regions of his anatomy, no matter how much Delilah tempted him.

Her heart skipped a beat. Could he love her?

And did she love him in return?

Lil stared blindly ahead, examining her own feelings. Her fiancé had hurt her almost beyond bearing by going from her bed to another woman's, pretending to love her when all he cared about was her money. But she'd been a green nineteen-year-old, a headstrong only child, heiress to a fortune she neither relished nor knew how to manage. Her father had tried to warn her of her fiancé's shallowness, but she'd refused to listen, as usual. Now she knew that her fixation had been part defiance, part sexual fascination, and part infatuation.

When she broke off the engagement, her pride hurt

more than her heart. Still, for the next few years, she'd held all men at a distance. And then, when her parents both died in the same year, she'd learned to take over her father's affairs. She didn't have time to think of men.

Until she came here. To the land of her ancestors.

To be confronted with a man who appealed to all the womanly urges she'd deliberately stifled.

Quite apart from his lupine tendencies, Ian Griffith was as complex and unexplored as the terrain around them. A commoner with a tormented artist's soul. A practical leader of men with romantic notions he kept sacrosanct in his secretive heart. An intelligent, self-educated man who was a believer in mystical things like omens and blood bonds.

In short, he was as much a bundle of contradictions as was she. In many ways, he was her male counterpart, no matter the gap in their education, breeding, and wealth. But even if he'd been her polar opposite, she had only to look at him to think of shocking things.

Romping naked on the moors. Smoothing her hands over the hard angles and intriguing planes of his body that were so harmonious with his personality.

She looked down at Ian's strong hands holding the reins before her, the black hair on his wrists, and longed to feel again his soft body hair titillating her:

This time, she couldn't blame her madness on the moon, or his tempting nakedness.

This time, she went with him openly, willingly. To fornicate, as Pa would call it.

And she didn't feel one whit of shame.

She traced the fine black whorls on his wrist with a fingertip. Even that slight caress made him inhale sharply and draw back on the reins. "Don't. Or we shan't make it to my special place."

She kissed his hand in answer.

Cursing under his breath, Ian turned her in the saddle to face him and kissed her. Desperately, with all the passion of both man and wolf. As if he would, in truth, eat her, consume her, absorb her.

And she responded with equal hunger. She felt him grow erect, stabbing his need into her lower abdomen.

Breathing raggedly, he gripped her shoulders and pushed her gently away. "I've never made love on a horse before. What I have in mind will take much longer and requires total freedom of movement. Now behave, vixen."

His dark face brightened by a smile, he softened the command with a kiss on each of her palms. He froze, staring down at their redness. "Did you mean what you said at my ancestor's grave?" Ian asked softly.

Nodding, she tensed, expecting him to tell her not to clean the rest of the graves, to save her tender hands. Not even to herself could she explain why she had to keep her vow, so how could she expect him to understand?

Again, he surprised her, for he only lifted her palm and kissed it. An inch at a time. With a tenderness that honored her pain and made it his own, he trailed kisses over her hands from fingertips to wrists. And finally, when his soft, warm mouth had changed the stinging to a delicious tingling, using the very tip of his tongue, he delicately licked her lifeline.

Her fingers curled around the intimate caress, as if, with that simple movement, she could capture this moment and hold it forever in the palm of her hand. She was so moved she had to force herself to listen to his husky words.

"Gypsies believe that a lifetime is marked in the palm of the hand, if you know how to read it."

"And do you know how to read it?" she asked, caressing his tousled black head with her free hand.

His handsome face intent, he lifted his head and stared down at her palm. He traced the lines with his fingertip. "You have a heart too large for your small frame. You will have a long life, but see this break?" He indicated the sharp gap in the long, curving line that followed the base of her thumb to her wrist. "A terrible blow will befall you sometime soon, something you may not overcome."

Some of her enjoyment was spoiled, and he must have read that in her expression, for he turned her back around, tightened his arms about her, grabbed the reins, and nudged the grazing stallion forward. "Forgive my superstition. It's a silly habit I gained from my grandmother. Such things mean nothing."

"You'll never convince Safira of that. And it's eerie, the way her predictions often come true. I've never doubted the existence of phenomena we cannot understand. But our capacity to have faith in them is limited. We seem to be born doubtful, and die confirmed skeptics." She might have added she was living proof of that.

215

Had she not scorned the very existence of were-wolves when she first arrived here?

She knew better now.

Lil snuggled her shoulders against Ian's back. She was meant to come here, to meet and meld with this man. If that meant she loved him, then so be it. Whether she had a few weeks with him or a lifetime, she wanted to make the best of them. And if that made her a harlot, as some of her own servants whispered, well, Delilah Trent had never lived her life according to any mores but her own, and neither would Lil Haskell.

When they approached a rock outcropping, the stallion shied sideways, snorting. Ian soon had the horse under control, but for an instant, he paused, staring off to his right.

Lil followed the direction of his gaze. At first she didn't see anything out of the ordinary except something white. A scrap of ragged fabric was caught on a low bush, fluttering in the breeze. Feeling something odd in his reaction, Lil glanced up at Ian.

He was still as death for a moment, that bleakness back in his eyes as he stared at the fabric. But when he caught her gaze, he mustered a smile and turned the stallion sharply in the opposite direction.

For some reason, his reaction made her uneasy, but before she had time to pinpoint why, they were headed straight into a rocky slope. She gripped the saddle in alarm, but then she saw, almost hidden until they were upon it, a narrow opening in the rock. There was a jagged split in the huge outcropping, half grown over with reeds and scrub, so it was invisible until one entered.

Ian guided the stallion adroitly through the jagged-toothed walls, and at times the space was so narrow Lil felt stone brush her leg. But as they approached the end, and light split the tiny canyon's exit, Lil heard the rush of water.

They emerged into the little patch of Eden Ian had described to her so vividly that day in the salon. Ian's arms tightened about her midriff as he let the reins dangle. The stallion dipped his head and grazed on the lush grass surrounding this sheltered nook.

The tiny stream that trailed a serpentine path through Bodmin Moor must broaden through a huge gap in the rock above, for it tumbled in a merry waterfall into a natural spring below. The two water sources burbled, cavorting in a sylphlike dance, then merging into one fluid entity where neither waterfall nor spring had any separate identity.

Slipping off the horse, Ian held up his arms. Without hesitation, she reached down to him, and he carefully, gently, as if she were unutterably precious to him, lifted her down. After unsaddling the stallion, he held her back against his broad chest, clasping his arms about her waist, and let her look at his secret place.

"I finally understand why you love the moors so much," she whispered, noting the patch of soft moss growing to the edge of the spring, down its banks, to merge its destiny into the pool, too. "Who would have suspected such grace in such a bleak place?"

He turned her in the circle of his arms. "That's why

217

I . . . lust for you so much. Who would have thought a pampered, spoiled heiress could have the heart and spirit of my moors? No one will ever conquer you, Delilah. A man might lose himself in you for an hour, a day, a week. Even delude himself that when he beds you, he owns you. But he can only embrace you for the night and hope that by daylight, you still want to be held."

Lil slipped her arms around his neck and leaned back in his clasp to stare deeply into his eyes. "We are much alike, Ian. I only realized it a few minutes ago, but I think the connection between us has little to do with curses and blood bonds, and much to do with our own natures. In a way, we've both been lone wolves. Forging our own paths, under our own terms, alone rather than compromising who we are and what we want. We were fated to meet, and end our wandering here, in this perfect place, in this perfect way. No woman will ever hold you, either, Ian Griffith. Unless you want to stay . . ."

His brown throat moved as he swallowed harshly, but then he framed her face in his hands. "And what if . . . the next time I don't—?" His voice became muffled under her fingertip.

"No what if. Only what *is*. You. Me. A patch of Eden. And a memory neither of us will ever forget." Rising on her toes to kiss him, her breath mingling with his in a gentle caress, she whispered, "Give me a child, Ian. Then no matter what happens, the curse will end as it began. With a child and a new generation unhaunted by fear of the night."

She took his groan of denial and capitulation from

his lips. But just as he kissed her back, his hard mouth consuming her, stealing her self away, she had time for one last thought.

What if his malady was transferred into the child? Could the curse be passed on in that way, too?

But she had to chance it. She'd never met a man whose child she wanted, and she knew herself well enough to know that she might never meet such a man again. Be hanged to the whispers, the scandal. She had plenty of money and backbone if she had to raise the child alone. And forever after, she'd have something of Ian to cherish.

His fingers trembling, Ian undid the buttons of her dress and slipped the garment off. The corset, the petticoats, the chemise quickly followed. Then Lil was covered only by a blush, a breeze, sheer stockings gartered at her thighs—and by a passionate amber glow.

The look in Ian's eyes not only surrounded her, in some odd way it absorbed her, too. Forgetting embarrassment, who he was, who she was, even where she was, she knew only *why* she was. To mate with this wild man in a melding as elemental and natural as the merging of the waterfall and the spring.

Closer . . . she had to get closer. She squirmed against him, pulling at his own soft shirt with urgent hands. What were these strange barriers between them? She felt the roughness of fabric against all her exposed, sensitive areas.

She wanted skin!

She moved so close that he had to steady himself to keep from being driven backward. Shapely female

219

arms and torso sinuously brushed up against him, tempting him as her namesake had tempted Samson. Still he stood invincible, staring arrogantly down at her, fully dressed, only his hands resting on her shoulders.

Delicious anger quivered through her, for she knew what he was doing. Tempting her. Taunting her. Making her face her own need for him.

Two could play that game.

She undid the top two buttons of his breeches and slipped her fingers inside. So much for his act of invincibility. She couldn't quite clasp her fingers around the prize in the close confines of the fabric, but she felt enough to know that he was fully aroused. She used one forefinger and stroked along the length of that upthrust need.

A choked sound came from him. He pressed his palm against her hand, trapping her in the intimate caress. "You have it. Now what are you going to do with it?"

Blushing at her own boldness, but compelled by something beyond lust, beyond body, something that went deeper in both of them than they were comfortable admitting, she used her free hand to unfasten the rest of his buttons. She pulled him, pulsing with a passion no subterfuge could hide, into her palm. Clasping her fingers around the proud eminence, she purred, "Do with it? Why, I intend to use it well."

His mouth fell open. He blinked, and blinked again, the muted glow in his amber eyes dimming with confusion. She knew no woman had ever spoken to him so. He was the one accustomed to doing the leading, and he expected women to follow.

But a situation such as this didn't require either a leader or a follower—it required mutual cooperation. How she wanted to cooperate . . .

Smiling wickedly at her own thoughts, she brought up her other hand and gently brushed both palms against each side of his sensitive erection. He shuddered. His neck arching back, he blindly caught her hands to pull her away. As if he feared what he'd do if she continued to touch him so.

Finally, aroused beyond his formidable control, Ian clasped her wrists in one hand and tugged her down beside him to the welcoming bed of moss. Fully as possessive as a male wolf about to mate the female, he shoved her down and stood over her, slowly pulling off his shirt while he raked her with feral eyes. Lil stretched luxuriously against the moss, her back exquisitely sensitive to the sensual stroke of nature's hand.

And her front was equally aroused by hot amber eyes and the waterfall's fine misty spray. Then Ian was naked, too. For a moment he stood, primitive and unadorned, as much a part of nature as this secluded piece of Eden.

They ate one another with their eyes. In the darkness of their first joining, she'd only had one feeble lantern to show her the wonder of his presence. Now, in full daylight, she saw that his legs were long, lithe, and muscled. His stomach was flat, furred with a narrow line of black hair that broadened to a vee on his broad chest and flared again at his loins.

As she looked at him there, saw the rampant maleness that would shortly engorge the soft, aching center of her, Lil no longer knew who seduced whom. And it no longer mattered.

Unable to speak, she held her arms up to him.

With a soft sigh that might have been surrender in a weaker man, he knelt beside her.

Immediately she tried to latch on to him. The aching, empty void deep inside her desperately needed filling. But this time, he was firmly in control of the wolf. He caught both her hands in one of his and held them above her head.

Slowly, he stroked her with his other hand. Neck to collarbone, lightly tracing a curlicue path between, but not touching, her aching breasts. His hand gently traced every contour of her stomach, and then the heel of his hand pressed into the rounded curve just above her womanhood.

Flaring amber eyes spoke the wisdom of the ages, gleaned from both human and wolf instincts. She knew as surely as if he'd spoken that he, too, wanted that pulsing void filled. She began struggling in his clasp, trying to get free so she could end this torment.

He only gritted his teeth, gripped her wrists more firmly, and lowered his hand to trace the poetic contours of her hip, one side to the other. He didn't touch the feminine flower unfurled, waiting to be plucked.

And it was deliberate, damn him!

As his hand wandered down the length of her stockinged thigh, she said through her teeth, "I have some thumbscrews and an iron maiden you can use, too."

The tormenting caress stopped. His eyes leapt to her face, startled, but then white teeth flashed in a reckless grin. "Oh, I don't need them to torture you into submission. Every weapon I need to win this little battle of wills is attached to my person." He shifted his weight slightly, and for one maddening moment, she felt the silken slide of his manhood questing between her legs. He touched her exactly where she needed it most, at the aching kernel of her womanhood.

Instinctively, she moved her legs apart, her eyes drifting closed as she decided to let him win this artful duel of words and bodies. She might die, otherwise. . . . But to her intense frustration, as quickly as he pressed into her in the urgent caress, he withheld himself.

She felt teeth raking her leg. Her eyes popped open. Somehow, he managed to retain his hold on her wrists with his much longer reach and still catch her garter in his teeth. He pulled the garter down, and her stocking with it, inch by inch, his teeth grazing her tingling thigh all along the way.

But when he came to her knee, he couldn't move lower any more without letting her go. Amber eyes flashed up to meet her gaze, assessing how far to take her in this sensual journey before he gave her what they both wanted.

Playing along though every inch of her body burned with need for him, Delilah gave him a lazy smile. "Decisions, decisions. Are you going to feed me or eat me?"

He went very still, but then he saw the teasing

gleam in her eyes. He relaxed and replied huskily, "Both, I think." It was her turn to be shocked, but long lashes veiled his beautiful eyes as he smiled back. Secretively. Making her wait.

First he used the same torturous process on her other stocking and garter, but this time he flicked his tongue across the path along with his teeth. Then, finally, blessedly, he straddled her, the flaring, excited head of his tumescence a vanguard to his intent. With a will of its own, it pointed toward the prize it sought.

His effort obvious in the strained muscles of his neck, Ian still managed to maintain control. He rested his cheek between her breasts, listening to the frantic pace of her heart. "Sometimes I want to hold your heart in my hands and cherish it as a valiant talisman to ward off evil. And sometimes . . ." He finally let her go, but when she tried to grasp his manhood, he pressed her palms flat against his chest. "Sometimes I want to rip my own heart from my chest and watch it pulse to your touch. We both feed one another, Delilah. With every smile, every touch, we sustain who we are and grow a bit more into who we can be. Together."

Lil's arms felt weak, her bones melting beneath the impact of his words and touch. She could only caress his thick black hair and wonder what she had done in her lifetime to deserve such a moment. With a quavery laugh, she teased, "And how do you want to eat me?"

He sat up abruptly. A hectic flush of desire coloring his strong Gypsy cheekbones, he swooped down and purred against her breast, "Like this." He drew one excited nipple into his mouth and suckled so strongly and hungrily that her torso arched to meet him. He dipped lower to her belly, grazing it with his teeth. "And this."

"And this . . ." He ended the sensual whisper against her womanly triangle.

Gasping, Lil almost splintered with pleasure. First his hot breath proclaimed his intent, and then she felt the delicate brush of his tongue. Licking, tasting, sampling the kernel pouting for his attention. And Lil squirmed. She pulled at his thick hair.

When that didn't work, she reached down and clasped him.

It was enough. No games; no winners; no losers.

Only destiny, a man with a maid in the age-old way. Ian shoved her legs apart and plunged fully inside in one long, luxurious slide.

The feel of him questing so deeply into her was an intimacy so poignant that at first Lil could only lie back and enjoy it. The first time had been wonderful, but they'd both been a bit awkward, learning where to press, how to stroke.

Now they knew how to pleasure one another.

Pulsing at the very lip of her womb, Ian stopped and framed her flushed face in his hands. "I want to make my mark in you, to brand you mine, whether I end as wolf or man. Remember, Delilah: No matter what comes, or what they say of me, in this moment, we consecrate our bond. Nothing will ever break it, not even hell itself." He stared into her forest green eyes, amber flames blazing a path through her very thoughts.

Lil realized it was almost as if he knew something terrible was coming, and he wanted to give her this moment to counterbalance the unavoidable sorrow.

But there was no need. Could any woman forget such a moment?

Spread-eagled, invaded, vulnerable as only a woman can be to the power of a male, Delilah had never felt stronger. For Ian was equally powerless before the allure of her femininity. She felt it in the trembling of his hands, saw it in the passion in his eyes.

For this, they'd been created. And from this, they'd create the ultimate atonement for a century of wrongs: a child of their loins who would be the last, best reparation to the Gypsy girl. A mingling of Griffith and Haskell blood had begun this tragedy. The same mingling would end it.

Lil lifted her arms and clasped them about Ian's neck. "Mark me, my darling, now and always, as long as you are branded mine, too." She tilted her head sideways and nipped at the throbbing vein in the side of his neck. Not enough to hurt, just enough to show that she felt equally territorial about him. Perhaps she was becoming a bit lupine, too. . . .

When she licked the sting away, he gasped, clasped his hands beneath her hips, and let the wildness consume them both. Pulling out full length and then thrusting back inside until she couldn't hold any more, he showed her the dangers of tempting a wolf . . .

. . . and the joys.

Her eyes drifting shut on the incredible sensations

of that maleness blazing a trail inside her, Lil instinctively matched his primitive cadence. Her hips lifted on each downstroke. Awkwardly at first, for she had such myriad sensations to enjoy that she was almost overwhelmed.

The sound of the waterfall thundering into the pool; the scent of flowers growing close by; the feel of softness at her backside, hardness at her front. But as the urgent thrust and retreat quickened, all her senses narrowed down to the center of her body where they were joined. Instinctively, she tightened about him as she flung her hips upward. That made the strange pulsing in her core even more imperious, demanding that she give, and give some more.

For in this act, only in giving could one take in equal measure.

Filled with need, she used the strange inner muscles she'd discovered only through his touch. When she contracted about him on the downstroke, he groaned. The sound of his near surrender so enthralled her that she did it again.

And again, holding him tightly in warm velvet that stroked him end to end. And, as with all things worth cherishing, she found that, in giving, she received joy twofold.

Every clasp and retreat increased her own pulsations.

She felt him hardening even more as he coursed to the very depths of her. Still, it wasn't enough. Closer, she had to get closer, for only in total oneness with this man could she find the piece of herself that had always been missing.

Colleen Shannon

This, then, was what it meant to be a woman.

This, then, was what it meant to pleasure a man.

The joy she felt at her own rebirth was enough to push her over the edge into . . . ecstasy. The strange pulsations imploded deep inside where she cradled him, and then radiated outward. Through her arms and legs, to her very fingertips and toes, she quivered with the shock of her own fulfillment in this bonding.

When her inner contractions gripped him on that last masterful slide, he burst in exultation with her. Lil' reveled in the powerful release of his essence, feeling it bathe her womb in liquid warmth. Her own pulsations grew harder, stronger, and she tipped her hips up to him, the better to contain every drop. No matter what, she wanted his child. . . .

Their cries of joy met and mingled as slowly the wild darts of pleasure coursing through them faded to gentle pulsations, and passion finally gave way to tenderness.

Tenderly she cradled him in the depths of her body. Tenderly he nestled in her, stroking her in gentle adoration he obviously felt but could not voice. She felt him rest his hands on the ground beside her head, as if he were afraid his weight would hurt her, but she pulled him close, wishing she could climb inside him, too. Nothing in her life had ever been so heavy. So large. And so sweet . . .

For a precious moment that would be her best memory of all, he luxuriated with her in this total closeness. His lips drank of the throbbing hollow of her throat, and his hands caressed her, hips to knees.

Tears misted her eyes at his total—almost boyish—

absorption in this idyllic aftermath that was somehow more moving than the height of their pleasure. She didn't have to be told that he'd never felt this with any other woman. They would never be closer, in every sense, than now.

And there would never be a better time than now. . . .

"Ian," she said huskily, "tell me where to look for a cure."

Immediately, his caressing hands pulled away. He slipped out of her and rolled to his side, staring across the pond at the high walls above. Sitting up, he dipped his long legs into the water, bathing his loins, legs, and hands.

Almost, Lil was sorry she'd brought the matter up, but she had to broach this subject. And it was only a few weeks until the next full moon.

Wondering why she felt no embarrassment at her nakedness, Lil sat up and dropped her feet into the pool beside him, also dashing water over herself. But when the last trace of his scent was gone, she felt only sadness.

By unspoken agreement, they dressed. The lovely, bright day was tarnished as golden promise became the dross of despair.

Ian went straight to the saddle. Cursing herself for bringing up the cure, Lil stepped in front of him. He tried to go around her, but that only increased her determination. Lil said steadily, "There has to be a way. Why won't you let me help you?"

At first she thought he wouldn't answer, but then he dropped the saddle and looked at her. Torment had replaced joy, and Lil's sense of loss became acute.

He said, soft and low, "Because those who try to help me often end up dead."

Lil frowned, trying to figure out what he meant. "I do not believe that, even as a werewolf, you've killed anyone."

A laugh, half disbelief, half despair, escaped him. "You cannot understand what it's like, Delilah. You're trying to understand the savage mind of a wolf with a human brain. As much as you like to romanticize them, wolves are creatures of instinct, not reason. If they're hungry, they eat. If they're angry, they attack—"

"If they're threatened, they attack," Lil corrected him. "You forget, in Colorado, we have wolves, too. I used to go on fishing and hunting trips with my father into the mountains. We came across a pack that we often observed from a blind in the trees. Wolves have a social order that is too complex to be based on sheer instinct."

"Yes, this grand social order is based on pissing and fucking."

Lil gasped at his crudeness. His amber eyes had gone opaque. She couldn't see into him anymore. But still, she persisted. "If one of the pack is hurt, the others try to help it. If a she wolf dies, another she wolf will adopt her cubs."

"Sometimes. But if food is scarce—"

Lil propped her hands on her hips and glared at him. "Why are you being so stubborn?"

A smile curled the corners of his lips as his gaze raked her. "Because I've marked my territory quite

230

thoroughly today. Why waste more time wooing you? You wish to understand my lupine side, do you not? You'll return to my den any time I lead you to it. I believe we both know that now." And with that masterful insult, he turned to saddle the horse.

Lil's teeth ground together, but she exhaled slowly, quelling the anger he'd tried quite deliberately—and successfully—to incite. He'd brought her here to stake his claim, yes. But he'd been driven by a deeper need, too.

He'd tried too hard to pleasure her to be driven only by possessiveness or lust. He'd been moved at her cleaning of his ancestor's grave site, and he'd wanted to give her joy in return. Still, as much as she made excuses for him, she was also angry and hurt.

Couldn't he have more faith in her? She ran a small empire. Couldn't she find the solution to this dilemma, too, if he'd help her instead of fighting her?

When he mounted behind the saddle and held out a masterful hand, for an instant she looked at those soft black hairs and saw the manifestation of his other self. The sharp, curving claws scratching above her head while she shrank between the wall and the bed.

Banishing the vision back to hell where it belonged, she bit back more angry words and let him pull her up before him. He wound back the way they'd come, but was careful not to touch her more than necessary. And that hurt most of all. But was it himself he didn't trust, or her?

During the serpentine ride through the outcropping, past the edge of the moors, she stewed over that quandary, but she had no answer. One thing she knew, however: Whereas the journey there had been full of excitement and joy, on the journey back, she was leaving the best of what they offered to one another behind on that bed of moss. Alone together away from prying eyes, they were strong enough to conquer anything. Once they were back in the house, they'd be stuck in their roles of mistress and servant, heiress and werewolf.

She looked down at the break in her lifeline and wondered what it signified.

Above the stable, Shelly Holmes rubbed at the burning scratches in the back of her hand. She'd cleaned them; she'd put every salve in her considerable medicine chest on them; she'd even tried cauterizing them with the flat of a hot knife.

Nothing helped. They might harden over for a few days, but they were soon oozing again, a strange, milky substance unlike any pus she'd ever seen.

For the first time in her life, she was afraid.

Her mother was a famous chemist, her father, an Oxford scholar. Every immediate member of her family was brilliant, and they lived brilliantly respectable, if dull, lives. Shelly was the only exception. She was a wanderer, unable to stay in one place because she longed to make each new day an adventure, to discover a bit more about herself and her world with every border she crossed.

Her family didn't understand. She should marry, they often told her. Raise children as smart as herself, and she'd learn to be content with her lucky lot in being born English. Why waste that magnificent intellect on savages? To them and virtually everyone else she knew, she was the black sheep.

She smiled bitterly. More like a rogue wolf, now. She tried to picture her mother's face when she learned the fate of her only daughter, and the image so pained her that she bent again over the dusty tome she'd found on a trip into Falmouth. It was an ancient book of witchcraft, filled with spells, and potions, and cures for every curse under the sun.

Except the cures listed for lyncanthropy were worse than the illness. "Eviscerate the victim with a silver knife." Or "skin the werewolf by the light of a full moon and stake the victim out in the sunlight for the next week until the carcass has dissolved."

Furious at such nonsense, Shelly snapped the book closed. She wondered if there was something in the book on how to repel randy sailors. She smiled, remembering the last time Jeremy had invaded the stables to lay determined assault to her citadel with his unique blend of flirtation and coercion. She'd been courted in her time by a few men who were too strong themselves to be intimidated by her, but she'd never known anyone like Jeremy.

Once, inexplicably, she'd wanted to kiss that flapping mouth just to shut him up. She was seldom attracted to men, and Jeremy was considerably older than she, not to mention rude and ill-educated, and half a head shorter. And yet . . .

Sitting cross-legged on the floor, Shelly rested her hands lightly on her knees and inhaled deeply. Yoga made just about as much sense as the ridiculous attraction between two members of a species who could hardly be more different.

But somehow, the focusing of mind and body worked. Fifteen minutes later, she arose, feeling much better, and then heard a commotion below.

Shouts. A galloping horse. The crash of wood.

Shelly bolted outside into the stable yard. She took in the situation with a glance. The curricle Lil had driven that morning lay half on its side, the horse being cut from its traces. The animal was scratched, its nostrils flaring, as if it had been in an accident or unsupervised for some time, but it was the empty driver's seat that concerned Shelly.

"No trace of Lil?" she demanded of the groom holding the animal's bridle while the leads were cut away.

"No, ma'am. He come back alone, runnin' like he was bein' chased by somethin'."

Immediately, Shelly went inside and saddled her favorite gelding. The silly chit, why couldn't she learn that it was dangerous for those of Haskell blood to wander about the moors alone?

But in daylight? An even more frightening realization struck Shelly.

Ian Griffith was gone, too. . . .

Shortly after they left the tiny canyon, Lil realized the wind had risen. A putrid stench lay over the gusting grass like a pall. Lil covered her nose. "What is that smell?"

Ian tried to knee the stallion onward, but a piece of white cloth, tattered and bright with splotches of red, blew across its mane. It stuck to the animal's neck for a moment, and the stench grew stronger.

Ian grabbed the rag and tossed it away, but the stallion, agitated by the wind and the strange smell, whinnied shrilly and reared. Sitting behind the saddle with Lil before him, Ian didn't have a proper seat, and his feet came out of the stirrups. He went sliding down the animal's hindquarters.

Lil began to slide, too, but managed to stay seated by grabbing the animal's flowing mane. When the stallion's hooves came back down, she slipped back into place with a bone-jarring jolt. Her heart pounded in fear, and she knew the animal was about to bolt. Desperately, she grabbed the dangling reins and pulled them back as hard as she could, holding them despite the sting in her palms as the stallion tossed its head.

Her forethought gave Ian time to scramble up and get to the horse's head. He gripped the bridle, pulling with both hands, and between the two of them, they got the stallion under control. Quivering, but his ears pricked up as he stared toward a small mound in the near distance, the stallion finally went still.

Lil turned to see what the animal was staring at with such alarm. She saw scavengers, vultures and a scrawny wolf, fighting over something. She looked more closely and glimpsed a body, sprawled half in, half out of a shallow grave, arms spread out, face turned away. Even from here, Lil recognized the black hair, what used to be a full, lush bosom, obscene now in death, and the full, flirtatious red skirt of the barmaid.

Turning her head away, she gagged, forcing back bile. But when her gaze caught Ian's pale face, the gorge rose to her throat. He stared at his former lover's ravaged body, as limp now in death as it had been supple in life.

There wasn't a trace of surprise or mourning in his expression.

Only dread. And despair. And fear as he looked back at Lil.

The clues she'd tried to ignore fell into place: the way he'd quickly tried to distract her from that piece of white cloth; the look on his face as he led the stallion away.

And his comment to her by the pool finally made sense. *Remember,* he'd said, *no matter what they say of me, nothing will ever break our bond.*

Shuddering, Lil forced herself to meet those dark amber eyes. And the flash of guilt there was most telling of all.

The only way Ian Griffith could know about this girl's death, where she'd been interred, and the significance of that white flash of fabric, was if he'd buried her himself.

Chapter Ten

Turning away as if he couldn't bear the look in her eyes, Ian pulled a pistol from his saddle holster and fired at the vultures. Squawking, they flew off. The wolf yelped and bolted, too.

Lil looked from the scrawny wolf disappearing in the distance, to Ian, and back at the partially eaten corpse that had once been a beautiful woman. And she couldn't get the memory out of her head: Ian holding the waitress on his lap, nuzzling her.

As if she tasted delicious . . . Had he not said something similar to the last Haskell heiress in the heat of his passion only an hour ago? Lil's hands tightened on the reins. With a strength she didn't know she possessed, she backed the stallion away from the tall enigma standing silent under her accusatory gaze.

Make excuses. Give me a reasonable explanation.

Do something other than stand there in silence while you let me think the worst. But he didn't react except to release the stallion's bridle so she could back the animal another, safer, step away.

Maybe a glint of desolation flashed from his eyes for a bare instant, but then his cursed Griffith pride descended between them like a steel bulkhead. *Think what you like. I warned you to stay away.*

Why had she not listened? Lil wondered dully. She knew why, but the truth made this bitter conclusion to their loving no sweeter. She'd gambled everything she had because of her powerful need for this man. Her friends. Her good name. Her body. Her heart . . .

. . . and her life. Gambled on a steadfast faith that went beyond reason: that even as a wolf, he was not capable of killing except in self-defense.

Something far more tangible than faith mocked her: an obscene bundle of bones and rotted flesh. The stench from the body tainted everything, and the smell made her stomach queasy.

She backed the stallion another step. Only when she was certain she could wheel the animal about and get away if this ruthless stranger lunged at her, did she stop and say steadily, "If you tell me you only found the body, that you didn't bury her, that you don't know how she got there, that you didn't kill her, I'll . . . try to believe you."

"I buried her."

No hesitation. No regret. He might have been discussing the weather, or the price of corn.

Biting back a moan of pain, Lil reined the stallion about and kicked him. He bolted, and she had to hang on to his neck. Tears streamed from her eyes, trailing into her temples from the force of the wind as she flew across the moors. She had no thought of guiding Brutus, no fear they might stumble into a bog, and little care if they did. And no fear of riding any longer. Such foibles seemed foolish now in the face of this terror that wore her lover's face.

For Ian had made good on his promise. Symbolically, he'd held her heart in his hands and crushed it.

Perhaps he would do so in reality, next.

When, thirty minutes later, Lil found herself on the road, she looked around in vague surprise. Her hands ached from holding the reins, her thighs were bruised, but the stallion seemed to know where he was going without guidance from her. Ian rode on the moors every day, and Lil realized, with the small portion of her brain that seemed to be functioning, that she only had to give the animal its head to get home.

Home . . . A sudden poignant longing for Colorado almost overcame her. There were no bogs in her beloved mountains. No desolate, lonely brown spaces marked with spontaneous clusters of vibrant life.

No tall, taciturn, tempestuous man with a spirit as proud and free as the land he loved . . .

As Brutus began plodding toward home, Lil realized she was still crying. Odd that joy could so quickly turn to fear. But she had no one to blame but herself. Lil sat up straight in the saddle. This would not do. If anyone saw her like this . . . With a last hiccup, she swallowed back a month's worth of memories, trading them for a lifetime of regret.

This time, she'd face the truth, and not dress it up in silly romantic notions.

Her lover was a werewolf.

He was capable of killing.

And his lupine being hated no one so much as the last heiress of Haskell Hall. How could she have been so foolish as to think the man loved her? His human half turned the blood lust of the wolf into sexual lust for her body.

Just as she lusted for him, she tried to tell herself. But if her feelings were derived from only desire, why did she feel as if she were dying inside, where his claws struck deepest?

Tears came to her eyes again. A faint glimmer of hope couldn't be snuffed even by this dark denial. Her own feelings, at least, went beyond lust. She'd not been able to admit it before, but stripped of the veneer of pride and romanticism, she knew now that Ian Griffith, in both his personas, was more precious to her than any pile of moldy stone.

Which was why she'd risked everything she had out on the moors.

And lost . . .

Leaving her with the grimmest reality of all. She doubled over in the saddle while she clutched her abdomen.

Dear heaven, what if she carried even now the seeds of his madness within her?

Inside the parsonage's tiny salon, Shelly shared a solemn stare with her cousin. "So you think she went off with Ian?"

"I know she did. More than one villager saw them ride off together. But why does it matter? We're weeks away from a full moon, and it's daylight to boot. I'm sure Miss Haskell is in no danger. At the moment, anyway."

How could she voice her suspicions when they were only half-formed? The sudden urge to tell him of her own likely condition almost overcame Shelly, but she bit back the strange compulsion. He was family, true, but he was also the vicar here. His first loyalty was to his villagers, as it should be. And he was already worried enough about Ian. So she only stood, smoothed her glove over her burning hand, and smiled. "Very well. I'll make my way back on the road, look for a spot where a horse has entered the moors."

Her cousin cocked his head. "Is it really so easy as that to track them?"

"I learned much when I lived with the native American Indians. How to skin a buffalo. How to make moccasins. And a horse on a soft surface, especially one carrying two people, is very easy to track."

But when Shelly turned for the door, Vicar Holmes said, "Please, my dear cousin, before you forge boldly on your newest mission, I need you to translate something for me."

Mystified, Shelly followed him as he walked toward the far edge of the village. And tried not to notice the worried way he kept eyeing her gloved hands. Almost as if he knew.

*   *   *

When she arrived back at the Hall, Lil found it in a commotion. Horses, wagons, even a few work carts, anything that could move, were being marshaled by Jeremy into some sort of massive hunt. But for what?

Riding up quietly behind the barn on Brutus, Lil dismounted and led him into the empty stable. She led the tired animal straight into a stall, unsaddled him, and gave him a ration of oats. Then she walked into the front yard, where half the male servants were lined up, listening grimly to Jeremy.

"We don't come back until we find her. God willing, she only fell out o' the curricle somehow, and is even now walkin' home. And if ye see one o' them fiends of hell"—Jeremy brandished his shotgun—"call fer me and I'll dispatch him back where he belongs, as I should have the last time instead of listenin' to such drivel about bringing him home."

With a jolt, Lil realized Jeremy had organized a search party. For her. The carriage horse had obviously brought the curricle home, and they'd assumed the worst. But where was Shelly?

Ashamed that she hadn't thought of the reaction at the Hall in the midst of her own emotional turmoil, Lil hurried forward. "No need, Jeremy."

As one, every eye turned to her. A few of the men cursed in anger, a few smiled in relief. Jeremy reacted in typical fashion. First he hugged her fiercely, protectively, then he set her away and shook her slightly. "Ye madcap hoyden, ye added another ten years I cannot spare to me age. Where ye been?"

Lil looked at the attentive servants and back at Jeremy. "I'll explain later. But please, everyone, accept my apologies for causing needless worry. I'm . . . fine." Or she would be in another hundred years or so. She walked off, and she knew from the look on Jeremy's face that she had not heard the last of this.

As Lil entered her chambers, Safira was even more distraught, pacing up and down, muttering to herself in voluble Haitian while she cupped a strange amulet in her hands. Lil realized the mutterings were more of an incantation, and she wondered what spell Safira was casting now.

When she saw Lil, Safira swayed in place with such relief, Lil had to rush over to support her. Steadying herself, Safira immediately put the amulet, a hand-made combination of bird feathers, tiny bones, and a glowing moonstone, over Lil's neck. Lil's nose quivered, and it didn't take her long to realize the feathers had come from dead birds. A werewolf will probably be drawn to a moonstone, she thought to herself. But when she tried to take the amulet off, Safira covered her hands with her own.

"No, mistress. It will glow when a shape-shifter nears. And it will glow brightest, as blue as a sapphire, when the one who seeks your blood takes his true form to kill you."

Since the other werewolf had died in the bog, Lil didn't need such a warning device. She knew who the only werewolf was. In both forms. And no moonstone could ward off his power over her. . . .

But Safira continued. "Since you will not leave, at least you will be warned."

The words were on the tip of Lil's tongue: *Yes, you're right, let us leave this cursed place.* But she couldn't force them out. For the first time since her arrival, she was well and truly scared, but she refused to desert these taciturn people she'd grown to love because she was a coward.

Besides, a stubborn spark of faith danced, a firefly in the darkest reaches of her soul. Maybe Ian had killed the girl when the blood lust was upon him, but that didn't mean he'd strike again. And if she ran away, he'd haunt her ever after, waking or sleeping, four-legged, two-legged, until she, too, went mad.

My fate is your fate.

She had to *know* if he cared for her enough to take a vestige of her into the moon madness with him, even as she could now be carrying a vestige of him. "Thank you, Safira."

"Promise me you will not go about without it," Safira said sternly.

Lil grimaced. "How do you always read my mind?"

"Because, for a Christian woman, your thoughts are so clear. Your mind is as pure as your heart, mistress. Why else do I stay in this cold place where demons walk the night?"

Safira's faith in her caused Lil to collapse in tears again. Smelly amulet and all, Lil ducked her head against Safira's comforting bosom and wailed uncertainly, "Oh, Safira, what will I do?"

And out came the whole sordid story.

That night over dinner, composed but pale, Lil took one look at the long table swallowed by shadows and had the servants light more candles. She sent for both Shelly and Jeremy. And tried not to listen for steps too quiet to hear anyway. Surely even her arrogant estate manager wasn't bold enough to set foot in her household again. But where would he go? What would he do? What a fool she was to still care. But she did. However, before she had the right to ask about Ian, she had another duty to perform. To the girl who'd died . . .

When Shelly and Jeremy arrived, Lil waited until they'd been served their first course before she said bleakly, "Shelly, I would appreciate it if you'd send someone for the sheriff. I . . . know what happened to the serving maid who disappeared. Her family has a right to give her a decent burial."

Instead of gasping in shock, Shelly calmly wiped her mouth and looked at her employer across the table. Lil had seated Jeremy and Shelly both to her right, a whim Jeremy obviously appreciated and Shelly did not.

"Ian brought the body into town while I was still there," Shelly said mildly, as if she discussed nothing untoward. "That is one reason why I was late returning. I examined it, aided by my cousin."

"And?" Lil took a sip of wine to steady her voice. *Please, oh, please, a knock on the head, she was trampled, she was—*

"Like the others, I'm afraid. Scavengers had started on her, but not enough to hide the evidence. The tooth and claw marks match the other markings exactly."

Lil's glass tipped over and she watched, thinking how similar the port was to blood, as it dripped over the table to the floor.

Mouthing a salty oath under his breath, Jeremy

used his own napkin to blot the wine. "Steady there, missy. It's a rare storm that don't allow no port." His eyes twinkled at the bottle as he poured himself a hefty second serving.

Shelly even lost herself enough to smile in surprise at his play on words.

Lil stared blindly at the crimson stain. Like the stain on the girl's flesh—what remained of it. Like her vermillion skirt.

Like Lil's own sin. "And where is Ian now?" she whispered huskily.

Shelly held her own port up to the light, admired its clarity, and took a sip, before she said baldly, "In jail. You see, when he brought the body in, he confessed to killing her, too."

The room became a whirl of crimson drapes, wine carpets, and lamb far too bloody to be appetizing. There was a roaring in her ears, and Lil had to clutch the table edge, but the solid mahogany was rubber to her touch.

Jeremy's voice swam at her through a sea of red. "Mistress? Mistress!"

The next thing she knew, Lil awoke on the divan in the salon, Shelly fanning her, Jeremy bathing her brow with a clean, wet towel. Lil tossed the towel off and sat up, the fogginess in her mind replaced by crystal clarity: She had to get Ian out. If need be, they could lock him in the stall again, but he didn't deserve to be imprisoned in that dank, rat-infested cellar. She'd had to pay a fine once to get a drunken servant released, and she'd been horrified at the conditions of the town's only jail.

If the lycanthropy didn't kill him, ague from that terrible place would. But when she swung her legs to the floor, her head still swam and she had to lean back. "Jeremy, you must drive me to town. I want to pay the fine so we can bring Ian home."

Jeremy looked at her as if she had moon madness, too. "Aye, let's empty all the jails 'twixt here and Bristol, too."

Shelly said gently, "There is no fine for murder. He must stay in jail until his trial."

"Did he admit to his . . . condition? How else could he explain the state of the body? No man could . . . do that."

"From what I was told, no, not exactly. He said only that he awoke next to the body, blood all over him, and that he thinks he killed her in a fit of madness."

Lil's heart lurched with hope. Maybe he'd deliberately let her believe the worst, and he honestly didn't know if he'd killed the girl or not. If so, why would he implicate himself like that? Lil stood, one hand to her forehead, and said through her teeth, "I want to see the sheriff. I'll promise to keep him locked up, but I want him out of that awful place."

"The sheriff will not be disposed favorably toward your request if you awaken him at such an ungodly hour."

Lil glanced at her lapel watch. Almost eleven. How had it gotten so late?

"We let you sleep a couple of hours," Shelly explained gently. "My suggestion is that you eat, sleep, and arise strong enough to be an advocate for your

247

employee. If that's what you truly want to do. If you think it's . . . safe."

A pregnant pause grew as Jeremy and Shelly exchanged a glance, and then looked back at Lil expectantly.

Lil knew they wanted to hear details of where she'd been that day, and what had happened to send her home so distraught, riding the brute of a stallion she'd once feared. But Lil couldn't tell them the truth. Not that she was sure she knew it anymore, anyway. "Very well. First thing in the morning. Good night, Shelly. Good night, Jeremy." As she turned to the stairs, Lil noted that Shelly still wore her gloves, had not, in fact, taken them off even during dinner.

Something else to worry about, she decided as she wearily climbed the stairs. Oh, and she still needed to get Shelly to translate the Romany on the Gypsy girl's tombstone.

Tomorrow should be an interesting day, Lil decided wryly. She had a grave to clean, a potential killer-lover to release from jail, a curse to cure, and a ball to attend.

She'd missed having challenges to conquer when she came here. Another of her pa's old saws came back to her. "Be careful what you wish for. . . ."

But she'd apparently heeded that little homily no better than his other admonishments. She spent most of the rest of the night looking out the window at the mocking crescent moon.

Wishing . . .

As soon as Lil left, Shelly tried to duck out, but the door was blocked by a scrawny but very determined Jeremy. "Let me see yer hand, ducky."

She tried to ease around him, but he only blocked that direction, too. He was wiry and nimble for his age, so she used her best weapon to ward him off: her wits. "I didn't know you numbered a medical degree among your many accomplishments, my good little man." *There, that should do it. Prick a man's pride and he'd stomp off in high dudgeon every time.*

Instead, the little twerp smiled. Her calculated condescension bounced right off the steely demeanor of the only man she'd ever met with a confidence and independence equal to her own. "I got a good many accomplishments ye go not ideer about, me good big woman. But I can fix that, too." And with that calm retort, Jeremy shoved her against a wall, stepped between her legs, hauled her head down to his level, and kissed her.

She caught his shoulders to push him away, but his mouth was surprisingly soft and adept, the bulge in his breeches surprisingly hard and eager. She'd half believed his determined pursuit of her was his version of the "me big man, you little woman" game. But no man could fake this urgency of lips, hands, and sexual desire. Curious, she let him deepen the kiss, his lips slanting with both experience and gentle persuasion over her own.

Part of her brain, as always, remained detached. She tried to remember the last time . . . the Indian shaman who'd wanted to bind their spirits with the night, so that by the dawn, they'd each retain some of the strength and knowledge of the other. At least his approach had been unique.

And then there was the steel industrialist. But no one in the past few years. That must account for her slipping grip on composure, her sudden intense interest to see if Jeremy proved to be as unexpected in his lower quarters as he was in his upper. A small, simple man, with a big—

Shelly kissed him back. And when he groaned into her mouth, one of his hands fondling her breast, she opened her lips to the thrust of his tongue. When he reached around her to fumble with the lock on the salon door and lead her to the divan, she went meekly.

Well, perhaps it wasn't precisely meek to rip Jeremy's shirt and pants open, but he didn't seem to mind. In fact, he helped. And then it was his turn. In contrast, he very slowly, very sensually, unbuttoned her shirt.

With his teeth. Dabbling his tongue along the exposed skin as he went.

Before she lost herself in the only act that ever gave her liberty from the dispassion of her own thoughts, she realized four things. One, she was glad she didn't bother with such encumbrances as chemises. Two, she was glad she'd judged him correctly: of unusual size and virility for a man his height and age. Three, as she pulled him free of his breeches, she was glad she still wore her gloves. She'd have to be very careful not to scratch him in the heat of passion. Four, and most liberating of all . . . whether this was moral, or even smart, well, for once she'd act, not think.

Feel, not reason.

As Jeremy pulled her breeches down her long legs and kissed the vee already moist for him, Shelly stared blindly out the window, wondering why she felt the sensations much more keenly than usual. His scent whirling in her head, his gentle touch setting up a measured pulsing in her loins, Shelly smiled back at the moon, admiring the way Venus dangled bright from one crescent point, Antares from the other.

And then, thankfully, Shelly let her five senses sweep over her and carry her away. This, too, was as much a strange gift from this strange little man as a bequeathal of the moon: For the first time in her long, lonely life, Shelly Holmes didn't think at all.

From the moldy, dank, and dark cellar, Ian Griffith stared out at the same moon. He clutched the bars of the one tiny window above ground level and wondered why, even in mid-month, the crescent moon seemed to draw his spirit out of his body to prowl the moors. Biting his lip savagely until he tasted his own blood, he found strength enough to turn aside from that alluring glow and huddle in the corner.

His werewolf senses were becoming more acute with every month that passed, and even as he reveled in the sounds and scents of the night, he despaired. Perhaps this month, or the next, he wouldn't return to himself at all. He'd remain a werewolf until the villagers hunted him down and shot him through the heart.

At least, that would have been his fate, if he hadn't

wrested his destiny back in this last desperate act. Now, he'd be imprisoned in this tiny, foul-smelling place until the next change. Then all the whispers and gossip would end as villagers lined up to gawk at the curiosity they'd all suspected for many years but never truly believed in, good, practical Cornishmen that they were.

Ian wrapped his arms about his legs, rocking back and forth, but that was the only movement he allowed himself at the moment. He'd already paced a path in the mud floor, and pacing only made him more restless, the weight of his confinement even worse. The longing to run free almost made him choke, so he closed his eyes to rats eyeing him from opposite corners and visualized something more precious to him even than liberty.

Delilah.

Delilah as she'd been next to the pool, flushed and shyly eager with the passion neither of them could control. Not as she'd looked, ghastly with fear and accusation, judging him, like all the others, from atop his own horse.

He'd walked the moors for hours, trying to decide what to do. He couldn't go home. He had no home anymore save those barren wastes. He couldn't run away, for he would take this sickness with him and leave the people he loved helpless before the other werewolf. He could hide. Amongst the Druid stones and the ancient burial site that even the locals avoided, saying it was haunted.

But none of those options protected Delilah. As far

as he could see, only one act would safeguard the woman he loved as a man, and the heiress he was fated to kill as a wolf: He'd turn himself in.

Imprisoned, ridiculed, slated to hang, he'd end as he deserved, but at least Delilah Haskell Trent would be safe from her role in the curse.

And he'd never have to see that look in her eyes again.

Ian tried to find peace in what he'd done, for at least it was the act of a rational human being, not a wild beast. But the clawing need to get out of this stifling, enclosed space made his sacrifice seem more than he could bear.

And then distraction came, but not in a sound he welcomed.

A snarl. A vicious growling. And a scream.

Ian ran to the window, his head cocked, listening. Somewhere in the village, the other attacked. A boy, by the sounds of it. Screams that trailed off to a gurgle too faint for anyone with normal senses to hear.

Ian ran to the cell door, pounding on it until his knuckles were bloody, trying to raise an alert, but no one came running. He pulled with all his human strength at the bars, but he was too weak, the bars far too strong. He'd never get through them anyway, at least not without a powerful amount of digging.

The screams trailed off. Then there was only the sound of feeding.

Scents drifted to him.

Blood. Excrement. Death. And then . . . nothing.

Ian sank back to the floor, dully aware that at least this act proved his claim that there was more than one werewolf. It still wouldn't vindicate him, however.

But as the normal night sounds and scents soothed his senses again, calming him enough for reflection, Ian sat up straight in terror. "Idiot!"

Somehow, the other had found an ability to control the change. The full moon was two weeks away.

Even more frightening, he'd murdered a boy, someone who was not of Haskell blood.

The other killed now for sport.

Locked up in here, Ian hadn't a hope of protecting Delilah.

The next morning, Delilah felt much stronger. Equal to any task, even convincing the sheriff to release Ian into her custody. As she called for her second, more serviceable curricle at the stables, she saw Shelly leave her quarters, a strange smile on her face. Behind her came . . . Jeremy.

Having recently become, well, intimately familiar with how strong passion could be between the sexes, Lil didn't need more than the blush on Shelly's face to deduce that the two had spent the night together.

If Shelly's feathers looked a trifle ruffled, Jeremy definitely had a tomcat's satisfied grin as he watched his "ducky" blush. Lil could almost see feathers drifting from his mouth as he doffed his cap and wished his mistress a cheery good morning.

Lil smiled blandly back at them both, pretending she'd noted nothing out of the ordinary. "I'm off to the village. Are you coming, Shelly?"

Shelly nodded and hurried off with a sigh of relief. Jeremy watched her go, a gleam in his eyes Lil had never seen before, and then he offered his arm to Lil. She accepted his help into the curricle, but when he climbed up behind in the tiger's seat, she turned to him. "This may take the better part of the day, Jeremy. Are you sure you wish to come?"

"Aye. With murder and mayhem roamin' about, ye think I'd let me two gals go by their ownselves?"

And somehow, though she had no reason to be worried in the cloudless day, Jeremy's small but stalwart presence in the tiger's seat was a great comfort to Lil during the short ride into town.

When they arrived, they found the streets almost deserted. A dull, angry roar came from the direction of the grainery office that also served as the town's jail. Lil clucked urgently to the horse, her heart pounding with fear for Ian.

So many of the men from the countryside clustered at the door of the sturdy building that at first, Lil couldn't see what they were angry about. But several moved aside, and Lil saw a low cart near the steps, and above that, two old men holding ancient blunderbusses aimed at the crowd.

Lil had never seen a lynch party, but Jeremy obviously had. He grabbed the carriage pistol and leaped down, elbowing through the crowd. Terrified for both Ian and Jeremy, Lil tried to get down to follow him, but Shelly caught her arm.

"These men won't take favorably to interference from either of us. Remember, they consider us both outsiders. Let Jeremy handle this. It's obvious he's faced mobs before."

"But he's an outsider, too."

"Yes, but at least he's a man." Shelly's lip curled as she watched those of the opposite gender mill about like frightened cattle about to stampede. "The big question is, what's in that cart that has them so afraid?"

Lil stood on the tiger's seat, and she was finally able to peer down inside the cart. She gagged, covering her mouth.

Shelly's eyes darkened. Absently, she straightened her gloves over her own hands. "Pity," she murmured. "Can you tell who it is?"

"It looks . . . like a boy."

Shelly nodded without surprise. "I suspected the larger wolf didn't die. I went back the next day just to be sure there were no paw prints, but there were. Leading away from the bog. This is proof positive that this werewolf has the strength and ferocity of his lupine half and the cunning of his human half. Only a man would know that to escape a bog, you let it take you and swim into it instead of struggling to escape. It's still out there, Lil. Still killing."

Dumbstruck, Lil stared down into Shelly's hard gray eyes, trying to grapple with the fact that the other werewolf had survived, and was killing in mid-month now, too. Just then, a voice they both recognized came from the men agitating near the front of the crowd.

Thomas said, "We've evidence aplenty that this unnatural creature must be stopped. Let's do it now, before night falls and he kills again."

One of the guards on the stoop spat in the dirt. "He were in that cell all night long. I locked him in meself.

That blood's fresh, so some other critter did it. Mebbe even wolves, real ones this time. Stay back, all of ye. My eyes ain't too good, but this here cannon has enough shot to send half of ye home, butts a-stingin'."

Preston's voice came next. "How do you know this beastly hell hound can't shape-shift and get through the bars? He admitted to killing the girl. Ian Griffith is like all wild animals. Once he tastes blood, nothing else will satisfy him! We must stop him, now, before more of our people die so horribly."

Lil saw a swelling in the mob near the steps, and it reminded her of a vast, foul pustule about to burst. And then, blessedly, she heard Jeremy's voice.

Calm. Rock hard. "Go ahead, me hearties, take justice into yer own hands. But be willin' to face yer kids and wives this evenin', for ye'll go home the same as the critter ye claim to stop. Blood drippin' on yer hands."

Abrupt silence. But then the rabble-rousers safest in the middle shoved those in front.

One nervous guard got a bit too ready with his finger, and the BOOM! made Lil cover her ears and pray Jeremy wasn't hurt.

A few of the men near the steps groaned and backed off. But it was apparent they'd only gotten a bit of lead and were not seriously hurt.

Taking advantage of the startled break in the crowd, Jeremy shoved through them and climbed up the steps. He stood next to the guards, who really looked scared now.

Thomas's voice rang out again. "It's no different from shooting a rabid dog—"

But Jeremy's voice was stentorian, with the ringing authority learned by a man who'd shouted many a captain's order through a gale. "Avast, ye nodcocks! Cursed Griffith may be, but he's one o' ye, and he's risked his life fer ye more'n once. Can ye say the same o' these lily-livered lords tryin' to rile ye to do their dirty work? Griffith turned himself in. Be that the act o' a bloodthirsty fiend?"

This time, the mutters stopped altogether.

From her perch, Lil saw several of the men in back exchange chagrined looks. A few, eyes focused on the ground as they passed so they wouldn't have to look at her, slithered off in shame. And with their leaving went the support of the ones in the middle.

They, too, dispersed, and that soon left the ones in front exposed. With sympathetic looks at the farmer who, Lil saw now, had cried throughout the ordeal, they covered the lad's defiled body and carried him up the street.

Swiping his nose on his sleeve, the farmer followed. "What will I tell me missus?"

Lil's heart ached for him, and she became more determined than ever to find a remedy for this foul legacy that had begun to strike more than those of Haskell blood.

When the villagers were gone, Lil and Shelly approached the steps, where Preston and Thomas still glared up at the guards and Jeremy.

Startled, Thomas turned to her, and some of the anger faded from his face. "I'm sorry you had to hear this unpleasantness."

"And I'm sorry you had to cause it," Lil rejoined coldly. "Why do you hate Ian so?"

"An unsavory tale, I'm afraid, not fit for your tender ears. Now, my good man"—Thomas turned an imperious gaze on one of the cowering guards—"I wish to see your prisoner for myself, verify that his bars have not been tampered with."

The guards exchanged an uncertain look.

Jeremy inserted, "I'll go with them. Keep 'em peaceable."

Relieved at not having to escort the brothers themselves, the guards nodded eagerly.

When Jeremy and the brothers entered the small, dark office, Lil and Shelly followed.

The scent of rotten grain knocked Lil back two paces, but she covered her nose and followed the three men down a curving flight of stairs. As the dank, depressing place swallowed all the bright joy of the open countryside outside, she could only wonder how badly Ian's wild spirit must be suffering.

She deduced that, long ago, the cellar might have been a temporary storage facility, but this grainery had long since grown outmoded. It was seldom used for anything but a jail and an occasional customs house.

When they reached the cell, Lil heard a hoarse curse and what sounded like the growl of a wounded animal. A heavy thud came as Ian's full weight pressed against the sturdy door inset with a small grill. "You cowards! You're the lowest vermin, to always blame another for your own cr—" Ian broke off when he saw Lil and Shelly behind the three men.

Colleen Shannon

Using the key a guard had given him, Jeremy opened the cell door. "Back up, lad. We must inspect your window bars." Just in case, Jeremy pulled the pistol from his belt.

But the grill was blank now, the cell grimly silent.

Quelling her own sense of dread, and a deeper despair that Ian was trapped in this terrible place, Lil followed the brothers into the cell. Shelly crowded behind her, and Jeremy blocked the door, his pistol at the ready.

The cell was so full, Ian barely had room to back away, but he managed to turn his face into a corner and ignore them.

But Lil saw his trembling shoulders, and realized the effort it cost him not to attack these two aristocrats. What was the feud between them? One strong enough to make them want to kill each other?

She longed to go to him, to offer words of comfort, but now was not the time, and it most certainly was not the place.

As Shelly and Thomas stepped around Ian to carefully examine the bars on the tiny window, which was far too small for Ian to slip through, anyway, Lil was distracted by something else, something far more tangible to her than fear. Muttering a small oath of pain, Lil slipped her hand inside her dress to see what was burning her. Until she touched it, Lil had forgotten the moonstone. Turning her own back, Lil pulled the amulet from her dress.

It glowed. Pale blue. Eerily bright and luminescent as the moon it emulated.

A warning. The one who would try to kill her was present. . . .

Swallowing, Lil shoved the amulet back inside her gown. Positioning it outside her chemise, she turned back to the others, glad for the darkness. At least they couldn't see the tears in her eyes as she looked at the man she loved.

The one who would, in less than a month, probably try to kill her again.

But then, with an instinct that had little to do with reason and everything to do with desperate hope, she glanced at the brothers, both pulling now at the bars.

They were entirely too eager to implant the suspicion that Ian had escaped somehow last night. Could it be they were trying to cover their own crime? Maybe no one had ever seen any trace of the other werewolf's patterns because no one dared follow it to its lair. Or watch it take human form as it sought its den of iniquity.

The wealthiest estate in the district.

Clutching the warm moonstone again for comfort, Lil decided that tonight, during the ball, she'd have to do a bit of investigating herself. But she'd better not tell Shelly or Jeremy, or they'd have a fit.

Satisfied the bars were secure, Shelly finally turned aside, giving the two brothers a scornful look. Then she smiled over at Lil.

Lil's quick returning smile faded.

In the shadowy cellar, Shelly's eyes glowed greenish gray. . . .

Chapter Eleven

With a frustrated snarl, Thomas turned away from the barred window. "I don't know how he did it, but somehow he got out last night."

"Perhaps it's a phoenix we should be looking for instead of a werewolf," Shelly said sweetly. "For only a bird could flee this cage."

Thomas ignored her, watching Ian with an enmity as dark and dank as the cellar itself. "Perhaps you've fooled these *women*"—his tone implied idiots, but he didn't quite go that far—"but I know you for what you are, and before the month is out I'll prove it." Thomas turned on his heel toward the door, but Shelly stepped in front of him.

"From what I understand, the sheriff has been called for. Perhaps you should stay and share your evidence with him. After all, we can't have monsters roaming the countryside, now can we?" Shelly looked him up and down. "Especially when they're so thoroughly well disguised—or not."

To Lil's amusement, Thomas reddened at Shelly's implication. With her usual acuity, Lil realized Thomas had no interest in seeing the sheriff. Where the brothers were concerned, justice for Ian would come at a rope's end. Lil's gaze sought Ian, and she wondered at his total stillness. This subservience was most unlike him, especially since his own fate—and hers—hung in the balance.

Jerking his head at his brother, Thomas turned for the door.

Finally Ian came alive with startling swiftness. He caught Thomas's expensive jacket in both hands and shoved him against the wall. His eyes glowing amber, Ian growled like a wolf fighting to take over the pack, "The more carrion you eat, the fouler your breath becomes, and the more vultures will circle."

Thomas's eyes darkened to shiny agates sharp enough to cut, and for a moment it seemed as though he would attack Ian. But he glanced out the grilled window at Jeremy scowling, his weapon on the alert as he listened to every word.

Looking back at his enemy, Thomas used a verbal attack instead. It, too, was of the worst sort. "I leave the carrion for inferiors like you, Ian."

Every muscle in Ian's body stiffened, and for an instant, the wolf looked out of his eyes. Thomas's white teeth were bared in a challenging grimace, and Lil almost thought she heard snarling as they circled one another. Closer. Closer. Uncaring of who might be in the way.

But then, with a glance at her, Ian took a deep breath and his amber eyes went opaque. He backed off, turning his face to the wall again.

Wiping his brow in relief, Preston grabbed his brother's arm and shoved Thomas out the door Jeremy still guarded. Unable to hold herself, Lil caught Ian's arm. He quivered with reaction, and his wild scent in her nostrils was the same one she'd smelled during the full moon.

With a glance between Lil and Ian, Shelly also left. The door closed behind her. Leaving a lantern behind, Jeremy and Shelly gave them privacy.

Then Lil was alone with the half man, half wolf who haunted her, waking and sleeping, in both God-given and God-forsaken forms. Ever stronger with each breath she took, the unspoken but unbreakable bond of blood pulsed between them. In the quietude of her thoughts, Lil knew she had only to walk out of this grim, depressing place to be greeted by a day that made mock of such things as curses and murder most foul.

Yet she could not. She felt more than heard her heart pounding in her ears, felt more than heard his own strong heart echoing its response. Whether she excited him or made him hungry, whether he wanted to share his blood with her or consume her own, she honestly could not say.

Had any woman ever faced such a dilemma? This man was her lover and her predator. Still, she could not run.

Instead, in the power of that moment, Lil looked at Ian through human eyes and wished for lupine sensibilities. How much easier it would be if she could run by his side, her eyes seeing movement beyond human understanding and her ears hearing the subtle heartbeat of the moors. They'd be bound by no silly mores, foolish gossip, or restrictive laws.

But freedom always had a price, too.

She'd have to kill to eat, and she would enjoy that no more than Ian obviously did. She'd drink brackish water, sleep on the ground, learn to avoid all remnants of her former civilization.

She couldn't face that, either. Her lips compressed stubbornly. There had to be a way to bring him back to her world. First she had to get him out of here. "I'll speak to the sheriff myself. I'll post an astronomical bond, promise to keep you locked in the stables—"

Ian's voice was so hoarse she scarcely recognized it. "No, Lil, leave it be. For both our sakes. I need to learn to live within walls and you need to learn that some deeds are too dark for illumination."

"Nothing is too dark for understanding, Ian."

He reached out as if he longed to stroke the resolute curves of her mouth, but his hand dropped and clenched into a fist. "With understanding goes fear. You need to fear me, Lil. Never forget that. If you could see into my soul, and know what I see . . ." He trailed off, as if he couldn't finish the terrible thought.

Trying not to remember the pathetic sprawled figure of the girl who had once been Ian's lover, too, Lil brushed his tousled hair back. "Then maybe you're not looking in the right place. Look in your heart, Ian."

Some of the despair faded from his eyes. "You can say that to me after what you . . . saw?"

"How can I be certain you killed her since you're obviously not certain yourself?"

"You're willing to gamble your life on a guess?"

"No, but I'll gamble it on a belief. You see, I know enough of Ian Griffith to realize that no matter how many mountains he climbed, or countries he explored, the one thing he needed most could only be given to him. And that's why I'm still here. That's why I didn't go running home to Denver. Because I believe in you. Even if you killed the girl, you must have had a very good reason. The man I made love with, the man who risked his life for his miners, is not capable of capricious killing. And I believe when you look deep inside yourself and see the goodness that I see, the moon will have no more power over you."

With the soft growl of an animal in pain, Ian caught her shoulders and brought her into his arms. He didn't kiss her; he didn't caress her; he only held her. As if he wanted to absorb some of her goodness into himself. And Lil wrapped her arms tightly about his shoulders, wishing her faith in him were a magical cloak that could render them both invincible to all the evils yet to come.

Then Ian's warm breath was in her ear as he whispered, "I love you, Lil. I love you fiercely, as a wanderer who has known much passion, but little love. I love you as freely as a wolf who chooses his own mate. And I love you as deeply as a man who is not fit to kiss your hem, much less—"

"Kiss what's under it?" Lil hiccuped over a half laugh, half sob, knowing she had to relieve the emotion of the moment or fly to pieces in his arms. She felt his smile against her brow, but he tensed slightly. Waiting. And she knew what he wanted, what every man wanted when he offered his deepest affection.

Somehow, she couldn't say it yet. In her heart, she knew it to be true, that this wild fascination went beyond the sexual, but Lil Haskell was every bit as independent as Delilah Trent. If she was to believe in him enough to offer her sacred promise of love, then he must believe in her enough to let her find a cure. Maybe even to endanger her along the way, for only bold, decisive action would save them now. Why was it that only men were allowed to be champions on the field of valor? Courtly love meant just as much to women. No, even more.

When she didn't answer, his face went blank. He set her away from him and went to that secret place within himself where no one could trespass. She could reach out and touch him, but Lil had never felt the divide between them more acutely than now, across this mere five feet of space.

Lil hurried out the door to keep from bursting into tears. But as the door closed, Ian's desperate face pressed against the tiny bars.

"Delilah! Promise me you won't go to the ball tonight. Thomas and Preston are not what they seem."

"I beg to differ. They're exactly what they seem! Somehow I will find a way to prove that, too, along with the fact that cures exist for virtually any ailment, including sheer stubbornness!" Angry with his obduracy as well as her own, Lil left with his pleas ringing in her ears. Why couldn't he accept that she had the right to fight for his safety and happiness? For therein also lay her own. But then she hadn't admitted as much to him, had she?

As soon as she appeared on the floor above, Jeremy walked back down, locked the cell door, and followed Lil out.

Outside on the front steps, Lil and Jeremy found Shelly speaking to Vicar Holmes. They broke off when they saw her, but didn't remark on the tears in her eyes. Clearing her throat to steady her voice, Lil asked, "Have you had a chance to look at the inscription on the headstone yet, Shelly?"

Shelly replied, "Yes."

Lil waited, but when Shelly remained silent, Lil probed, "And what did it say?"

"Something too obscure even for me. The rough translation would be, 'When bright day steals the night, my heart is a stone. Oh, curse of delight, honor these bones. For this legacy I was born, and for death I wait. An eye for an eye, a hate for a hate.' "

Despite the bright beauty of the day, Lil felt an encroaching darkness consume her optimism. Even knowing the Gypsy girl's story, she found it hard to comprehend an enmity so complete that her very last words carry only venom, for all eternity. No wonder the curse was so strong.

Shelly patted her arm. "Romany nonsense! The Gypsies I've known were a merry lot. I wager this incantation has no more meaning than the senseless way the girl died."

"But where will we look now for the cure?"

"I'm going into Plymouth. I'll stop at the estate and send another carriage out for you, but I don't think I should delay this trip any longer. I know a seller of rare books there who dabbles in the arcane arts. Perhaps he will be able to suggest something. You promise not to attend the ball tonight?"

Quelling a twinge of conscience, knowing she didn't dare delay Shelly's search for a cure, Lil nodded. "I am fatigued. I will stay home." Tomorrow. And the next day. It wasn't really a lie, she told herself.

Shelly relaxed slightly. "Good. I wouldn't feel right about letting you attend alone."

Jeremy nodded. "Aye, mistress, if e'er two men stirred up a darker ill wind, I don't remember them. Ye don't mind waitin' fer the extra carriage?"

"Not at all. I have much to do in the village before I can leave, anyway," Lil said.

Decisively, Shelly turned for the curricle.

Jeremy glared at her. "Ye ain't goin' without me, ducky."

Shelly gave him a cursory glance, as she would a picayune obstacle, and walked around him.

To Lil's amusement, Jeremy stuck his pistol back in his belt with the air of a man about to go off to war, and scurried in front of Shelly to block her from climbing into the carriage. "We can decide this quiet-like or public-like. Which is it to be, ducky?"

Shelly said through her teeth, "If you call me ducky

269

one more time, it will be your feathers flying, not mine."

Her hostility flowed off Jeremy like, well, water off a duck's back. "Lord love ye, jest last night ye was a billin' and cooin'—"

Desperate to shut him up, Shelly shoved Jeremy onto the carriage seat. She was so overset that she even let him drive.

Smiling, Lil waved them off, wishing she could be present to hear the conversational barbs that would be exchanged all the way to Plymouth. Then, with a last longing glance at the grainery, she paused to purchase flowers from a stand.

She had a vow to keep, too. As she walked toward the Gypsy cemetery, she tried not to think of the curse, but it rang in her ears anyway. "For death I wait. An eye for an eye, a hate for a hate." And despite the warmth of the day, she shivered.

Some hours later, with darkness approaching, Lil stared at the sheriff over the rough table that served as a desk.

"Stuff and nonsense!" The bluff sheriff was a stolid, sensible man with stolid, sensible clothes and a stolid, sensible temperament. He goggled at Lil through bugged eyes. "If Thomas and Preston Harbaugh are werewolves, I'm a bloody vampire."

Quelling her frustration, Lil kept her voice even. "How do you explain the boy's death, then?"

"Doubtless real wolves."

"An entire pack came into the village and no one saw them or even heard them?"

The sheriff looked away. "That's a mite easier for me to believe than the notion that the richest men hereabouts are such vile, unnatural creatures. Ian Griffith, on the other hand, is known to have brought in one victim and to have confessed to killing her. He's always been an odd sort, too, roaming the moors day and night." The man bit the stem of his pipe as if to keep himself from saying something even more critical.

How could Lil justify Ian's innocence to a rightfully skeptical sheriff when she wasn't sure of it herself? Still, she tried. "I know my estate manager very well. Half the people in this village will vouch for his character. And surely my own isn't in question. I give you my solemn word that Ian will stay locked on my estate until the real killers are found, and brought to justice."

"From what I hear, Miss Haskell, you're in no position to make promises in regards to your own safety, much less anyone else's. Ian Griffith will stay here, right and tight, until I get to the bottom of this." He stood, the issue obviously settled in his eyes.

It was not, however, settled to Lil, but she swallowed back further protests and smiled as if acquiescing.

That night, haunted by the memory of Ian's despair at being locked up, Lil mechanically dressed for the ball. As Safira put the finishing touches on Lil's ensemble, Lil recalled the last time she'd worn this gown. That had not been a happy occasion either. Her first Denver society ball after the deaths of her par-

271

ents. Half the single men in Colorado, or so it had seemed at the time, had tried to win the new heiress's favors. Tonight, the Harbaugh brothers would doubtless do the same, and Lil intended to hold them at bay with the same skills she'd perfected then.

Sweet smiles. A full dance card. And an early exit. After she'd thoroughly investigated their home and grounds.

Lil appraised herself in the mirror, thinking this dress, which cost more than the yearly wardrobe allowance of most middle-class women, made a peculiar chain mail for a crusader against the forces of evil. But at least it would keep the brothers distracted.

Designed by a Paris modiste, the watered green silk perfectly matched Lil's eyes. The mutton sleeves were trimmed in gold braid that matched the fleurs-de-lis ornamenting the princess-style skirt. The heart-shaped bodice displayed her mother's emerald necklace to perfection. But Lil was enough of a woman of the world to know it wouldn't be the jewelry they'd be watching. Lil twitched at the bodice, trying to pull it up. It slipped immediately back into place, her generous cleavage also on dazzling display.

Quelling a stab of longing for Ian's strong presence, Lil collected her tiny beaded gold reticule—coincidentally filled with silver leaves and cinders. But it was the weight of the derringer inside the bag that she found most comforting.

Only when she turned to the door did Lil realize that Safira had dressed in her best finery as well. She wore a glittering silver turban that matched the silver stripes in her turquoise silk robes. Her bosom dripped with ornate turquoise silver jewelry that matched the four rings on each hand.

The look she gave her friend was not one most employers would have tolerated, but Lil and Safira were more than just employer and employee.

"Mistress, since Jeremy is gone, I'm attending the ball with you tonight." A statement, not a question. Still, for all her bravery, Safira's voice trembled slightly. "If I cannot convince you not to go, that is."

Lil stared blindly at herself in the mirror again, missing Ian even more acutely. The knowledge of why he couldn't go with her made it all the more imperative to beard the wolves in their den. Thomas and Preston would be too busy tonight to keep up with one small, wandering guest. She'd never have a better chance than now to investigate their study, look for some link to the Griffiths, or even search the grounds. Perhaps she'd find wolf hairs caught on a fence leading to the house, or maybe even the remains of one of their kills.

That would be an embarrassing climax to their party, she thought with satisfaction. Besides, surely even Thomas, as bold and brazen as he was, wouldn't risk transforming in the proximity of so many guests.

The memory of Ian cooped up in that foul place goaded her on. It was enough to counteract her own quite natural fear. As for Safira's . . . Lil looked back at her companion. The Haitian woman was terrified, but resigned. She opened the door for Lil.

Lil was touched by Safira's fierce loyalty. The moors were—in her eyes, at least—more savage than the jungles or mountains of the land of her birth. Lil kept her tone gentle and teasing. "Safira, if silver repels these creatures not a werewolf alive can come near you. I'm honored that concern for me would force you from the safety of the house for the first time since your arrival, but truly there's no need—"

"There's need aplenty. The visions grow worse, and I cannot sleep."

The teasing smile faded from Lil's face. She couldn't take any more dire warnings right now, so she didn't ask for details of Safira's latest visions. But since she was so hellbent and determined to face her own fears, she could hardly fault her companion for the same need. "Very well. We shan't be staying long, anyway."

On the way out the door, Safira caught Lil's arm. "The amulet?"

Lil patted her reticule. "The perfect accessory for a werewolf huntress. And I thank you for making it for me. It's already alerted me once." She couldn't quite bear telling her companion, who was almost as fond of Shelly as she was, that the stable manager was apparently in the early stages of lycanthropy herself.

An appalling thought struck Lil. What if Shelly transformed on the return trip, when she was alone with Jeremy? Jeremy would never shoot his "ducky."

But when Safira looked back at her expectantly, Lil quashed yet another worry amid a plethora of them and followed her companion downstairs, out the front door. As the coachman drove them over the moors and Safira kept her nose glued to the window half in fascination, half in fear, Lil tried to marshal her unruly thoughts into the proper frame of mind for attending a social event.

It was time to have fun. To dance. And to make merry.

But Lil's lecture to herself carried more than a tinge of irony, punctuated as it was by the comforting weight of the derringer resting on her knees inside her reticule.

With increasing desperation, Ian watched the three-quarter moon rise. He felt strength flowing through him, but this time he didn't back away from the challenging orb.

Earlier, he'd tried reasoning with the sheriff himself, warning the man that he needed guards at the ball, but the stolid sheriff was as intimidated by the Harbaughs as most people in the district.

The thought of Lil going to their vast estate alone chilled Ian's blood. Deliberately, he lifted his face to the mellow warmth of the beacon outside, letting it counteract his human fear. If Thomas could transform at will, so could he.

Ian concentrated on the sensations that foretold the change. The acute sensitivity, the feel of bone lengthening in his spine, the two rear legs forming. Even more importantly, for the first time, as he felt the prickling transformation begin, he didn't struggle against it. Instead, he ripped his shirt and pants off and shoved his bed to the tiny grilled window. He stood on the bed to better bathe himself in the basilisk gaze of the moon.

The change came faster then, delighted to be welcomed. And welcome it Ian did, with a peculiar exhilaration he'd never known. This time, the unnatural strength, the hearing and sense of smell offered hope, not despair. Perhaps that would make a difference in how much of his human self he retained.

These changes were his only chance to save Lil.

For Ian knew, with the instincts of both man and wolf, that Thomas planned to kill her that night.

And somehow make it look as if Ian did it. Griffith blood to Haskell blood, inflamed by the moonlight, Thomas would say. Of course, Ian could claim that Thomas Harbaugh was related to Ian Griffith by more than a common fate, but who would believe him?

Even as the change began to draw a curtain between Ian's two realities, some portion of caution remained in Ian's human half. He knew as a werewolf, he'd have strength enough to break the door down, but if Thomas succeeded in his plan, Ian also knew he might as well hang the noose around his own neck. No one would believe him innocent of Lil's death, especially when he was seen leaving the cell as a werewolf.

But fear for Lil was stronger than the instinctual need to preserve his own safety and freedom. For in truth, if Lil died, Ian Griffith wouldn't care to live, either. In any form.

The first time he took her he'd thumbed his nose at destiny; he'd reveled in the irony of an employed laborer, and a Griffith, too, enjoying the ultimate intimacy with a woman above his station, though certainly not above his touch. The second time, however, destiny made a mockery of such futilities as class warfare, and curses born of hatred.

Next to the pool, he and Lil had proved that the only force in the universe strong enough to counteract such age-old biases was . . .

Ian bit his tongue to distract himself from completing the thought, and only then realized that his fangs were almost fully extended. As he licked his own blood, he was relieved to find that his human thoughts, this time, hadn't been subsumed by the wolf's. He held onto memories of Lil, and they were talisman enough for the wolf to take the memories of the man into the darkness with him.

But this most recent memory was as painful to the wolf as it had been to the man. He'd confessed his love like the veriest schoolboy, and she'd not said a word in response. Besides, even if the last heiress of Haskell Hall so far forgot herself as to fall in love with her lowly estate manager, a cursed man who might kill her to boot, there was still the little problem of his malady.

A sardonic, lupine smile stretched Ian's still-changing countenance. He could visualize himself, with a cheery wave at the little woman, telling her, "I'm off on the hunt, darling. Oh, and by the by, do you prefer your deer heart cooked or raw?"

Ian's chuckle turned into a husky whine. He felt a tail whip against his back, tickling him to a sense of the ridiculous. Though his sense of humor was certainly more than a touch macabre.

As his spine finished its curve and claws formed on all four feet, Ian gladly ceded his mortal frailties for the superhuman strength of the wolf. He bunched his muscles and sprang against the door, knocking it from its hinges as if it were made of tin, not stout English oak.

As he loped upstairs in three giant leaps, both sides of Ian Griffith's personality empowered him to save the woman he loved. And somehow, before the night was out, he'd also prove that that rich whelp might be the most blue-blooded hound in the kennel, but he was also the most vicious.

Ian bounded into the office, knocking over two guards as he went, but the scent of their fear stirred nothing more in him than indifference. As Ian loped outside, he caught the sheriff's shocked expression, but he could scarcely pause for explanations. By the time the man fumbled out his pistol, Ian was already halfway up the street.

Freedom had never smelled so sweet. On the breeze that carried the scents of home, another memory lingered in the wolf's nostrils, the taste of it still seductive in his mouth. Lil's kiss. A powerful taste and scent strong enough to thwart the wild urge to bound onto the moors and be lost forever to the agonizing uncertainties and weaknesses of mankind.

But he couldn't. And he wouldn't. Tonight, no more hesitation. No more fear.

His amber eyes gleamed with savage excitement as, with great, soundless padded paws, he followed the path the man still remembered.

Tonight, he was the dominant male. He fought for his mate. And when he saved her from the other, she would be his. Always . . .

*   *   *

The lights blazing from the palatial mansion should have been welcoming, but Lil and Safira both paused as they stepped down from the carriage and looked at the guests streaming into the ornate portico. Lil had deliberately chosen to arrive fashionably late, so her hosts would be fashionably busy. But she wondered now if she'd been wise to come at all.

If Dante himself had tacked up a placard above the door that read, "Abandon hope, all ye who enter here," Lil could not have been more leery of entering.

The music echoing over the drive had a bacchanalian lilt. And many of the women wore gowns considerably more low-cut than Lil's own. Lil had met enough rakes in her time to recognize men of loose morals and manners, and it appeared that most of the roués in England had been invited to this secluded estate in Cornwall to revel in . . . what?

Watching a drunken couple stagger down the side steps, not even reaching the shadows before they passionately embraced, Lil said, "Safira, I'm not quite sure if we're going to be handed a menu or be *on* the menu at this feast, but I'm game if you are."

Safira's lovely dark throat moved as she swallowed anxiously. She kept both hands in her voluminous robe pockets, and Lil wondered how many of her own talismans she had hidden there. But Safira's reply was bold enough. "I have some concoctions of my own I can mix, if I'm forced to, mistress."

Why am I doing this? Lil asked herself as two quite disreputable-looking men eyed her and Safira. But still, she moved closer to the entrance. As another

279

couple sat down on a bench in the garden and shared a long, passionate kiss, Lil sighed, wishing, down to her slippers, that she could do the same with Ian. And afterward, stare right back at the moon, thumbing her nose at it, unafraid of its power.

But since she could do neither, she took the only course of action open. Doggedly, Lil climbed the steps, inching along in the crush of people, but looking inward in a discovery as difficult as it was painful.

She'd continued to dress up her feelings for Ian in pretty disguise, and some not quite so pretty. Though it was true that their relationship had begun in bed, she wasn't here risking her life because she wanted sex. She wanted what other women wanted, whatever their station. Love. Children. Happiness. And she could find them only with Ian because . . .

. . . she loved him. With a deep, passionate love all the more transforming because it began in lust. She loved the artist in him, the wanderer in him, the hungry intellect displayed by his love of books and travel. She loved the tenderness in him, the arrogance and the pride. She even loved the wolf in him.

Why couldn't she admit as much to him, too? Because deep inside, she still feared him. And love gave him another power over her greater than the bond that brought her here tonight. They were at the top of the stairs now. Lil looked at that brilliantly lit doorway and took a deep breath. It was too late to change her mind.

It would be too late for Ian, too, if she didn't somehow find proof that more than one werewolf preyed on the moors.

Linking her arm with Safira's, she entered the Inferno. In the vast foyer tiled with white marble and lit by glittering sconces, the Harbaugh brothers greeted guests. Thomas wore a navy blue silk jacket above formal pantaloons. Preston wore the more modern white tie and tails, but both were handsome.

And both were quite aware of it.

As Lil and Safira moved down the receiving line, Lil cast a quick look around, trying to get her bearings in the huge house. With the rooms so packed, it shouldn't be difficult to melt into the crowd and do some quite rude, but quite necessary, spying. Then it was her turn to shake Thomas's hand.

Thomas clasped both his large warm hands around her white silk glove. "I'm delighted you could come, but what happened to your male guest?" His teeth gleamed, as dazzling as the polished marble beneath their feet, but Lil wasn't fooled. He had no doubt deduced that she had intended to bring Ian as her guest.

But Lil made sure her own smile would shame the haughtiest Denver debutante. She only hoped it didn't look as false to him as it felt to her. "Safira has been bored of late, and I knew you and your brother would welcome any guest I chose to bring as warmly as you've welcomed me."

The appalled look Preston had been sending Safira's exotic and dark good looks and strange dress was quickly shuttered behind politesse. "Quite so, Miss Haskell. Do remember now that you promised me several dances."

As the brothers were forced to turn to the next

guests in line, Lil gave a noncommittal nod and hustled Safira toward the refreshment table. There was food aplenty to feed an army of dilettantes. But strangely, the artful array of canapes, exotic fruits, and pastries of every type that had looked so appetizing from a distance only turned Lil's stomach as soon as she smelled them. By unspoken agreement, the two women sought the ballroom next.

Here, too, the Harbaugh brothers had spared no expense. The parquet floor gleamed, and a string quartet that could have graced a London concert hall played dainty airs. More scandalously clad guests waltzed to the music, some couples much too close to each other for propriety.

Several handsome bachelors veered toward Lil, but she saw them coming in time to make a graceful escape to the ladies' receiving room set up behind several partitions. Fanning herself with her hand as if she were hot from dancing, Lil pretended to fuss over her hair before a mirror. If she dawdled, the men would give up and seek more available game.

Safira straightened her turban and walked outside with a conspiratorial look that said, "I'll let you know when it's safe to come out."

A flock of giggling young women, with condescending glances at Lil, put the finishing touches on their own ensembles. One remarked loudly, "If I'd known Thomas and Preston were going to invite upstarts from all over the county, I would not have attended. Some people have no notion of their proper place in the world." The young lady shared an acidic glance equally between Lil and an ashen-faced Miss

Farquar, who left one of the makeshift water closets, her cheeks streaked with tears.

Lil had always despised social climbers. One glance at the young cat, who was dressed with the excessive ornamentation of the newly wealthy, told Lil that she was on the prowl. And not just any old tomcat would do, so she was digging her claws into the competition. Lil was tempted to hiss that she had this particular alley all to herself, but since the cat had already spent part of her night tormenting Miss Farquar, Lil wasn't going to let her off that easily.

"And some people have expectations of a life they don't deserve. And too little sense to realize the cost." Lil offered an equally catty smile in return as the young woman's back all but arched. They battled with their eyes, and then the cat raced outside as if her tail were on fire.

"Happy hunting," Lil muttered after her. And then she added, "Tally ho, Thomas," wishing she could see the look on his face if he caught her glee at siccing the unpleasant young woman on him.

Miss Farquar gave a giggle. "She's quite insufferable, isn't she?"

"Yes. And she and Thomas deserve one another. Are you feeling quite the thing now or should I look for your mama?"

Miss Farquar had the grace to look ashamed, and both women knew she was recalling her earlier behavior when she and her mother had called on Lil. "Miss Haskell, would you forgive me for my own brand of insufferableness? It's just that the other heiresses of the Hall were quite snobbish, and we expected you to be the same."

"That's quite all right. I suspect I might have been a little snotty myself that day."

Amiably, the two women left the receiving room, agreeing that they'd have to meet for tea again. But as Miss Farquar turned to look for her mother with the obvious intention of going home, Lil stopped her. She lowered her voice. "Have you lived in the area long?"

"All my life."

"Have there been any . . . rumors about either of the Harbaugh brothers?"

Miss Farquar looked away so quickly that Lil realized she must have heard something. But the girl tried an evasive laugh, and said lightly, "Nothing more untoward than is spoken of other wild young men of Cornwall."

"Wild is perhaps the exact word I'm looking for." Lil pounced on her choice of words. "Is there any possibility that either Preston or Thomas could share Griffith blood, ah, perhaps on the wrong side of the sheets?"

Miss Farquar gave a halfhearted attempt to look shocked at Lil's boldness, but then she leaned forward and confessed, "Well . . . there were some rumors whispered when I was in leading strings, but my mother told me that those who carry tales often end up being carried away by them."

Her expression said there had, indeed, been a scandal. With a nod and a cheery wave, as if she'd noticed nothing, Lil wished Miss Farquar a good evening.

But the hints gave Lil motivation to keep looking. And look she did, for the next few hours, deterred by neither suitor nor suitability. With Safira at her side, Lil stayed with the flow of humanity through the downstairs rooms when she could, but separated from the tide when she couldn't.

Finally, well after midnight, in the downstairs study, Lil came across the single constant in both poor and wealthy families alike. An enormous black Bible reposed on a stand in pride of place, with generations clearly labeled in various hands.

With Safira guarding the door, Lil lit a candle and read the spidery writing.

She repeated the names in a whisper, and was disappointed to see no Griffith name. But what had she expected? The Harbaughs would no more admit their by-blows than the Haskells had. But then, near the end of the entries, Lil saw a familiar name. She looked at her companion, recalling that Safira had helped Mrs. McCavity sort the family books in the library, some of which had belonged to the Griffiths.

"Safira, what was the name of Ian's sister? The one who died many years ago?"

"Lydia, if memory serves me."

Lil's finger paused on the same name. "Wasn't she much older than he?" Unlike most of the entries, here only the forename was listed.

"Yes, according to the dates of her death and birth."

Thoughtfully, Lil closed the Bible. Lydia was not such an unusual name, but the fact that her name appeared in a branch that looked as if it had been erased and then inked in by a different hand, both marked next to Thomas's name, certainly warranted further investigation.

That chance came much sooner than Lil anticipated. Or wanted.

A smooth voice came from the doorway. "My dear Miss Haskell, if you'd told me you liked to snoop, I would have been happy to oblige. I see several, ah, areas I might enjoy investigating myself."

Lil froze in the act of putting the Bible back. The way Thomas quietly closed the door and then locked it was as expressive of his intent as the look in his bottomless black eyes. The music suddenly sounded very far away.

As the Bible plopped back in place, dropped by Lil's numb hands, she realized she'd seen those eyes before. They'd stared at her with just the same lustful intent. For flesh. And blood. And humiliation.

For such base lusts were all that Thomas Harbaugh knew, now that she saw him stripped of his veneer of civilization. Same look, same eyes, only in a different, longer face. A face even now changing, the snout lengthening . . .

With a half moan, half sob, Safira stuck both hands in her pockets and began a strange incantation, but Lil suspected it was far too little, far too late.

As Lil fumbled desperately for her derringer, pulling at her reticule strings with fingers numb with fright, vaguely she wished she'd lit more candles. She didn't need the sudden warmth of the moonstone to realize, beyond any shadow of a doubt, that Thomas Harbaugh did indeed have Griffith blood.

Blood that was stirred to kill her.

Chapter Twelve

What did it say of her, Lil wondered, that she wasted precious seconds when she could have run, or screamed, or pulled the pistol? Instead, she watched.

In fascination. Her curiosity was so strong that it overwhelmed her natural survival instincts. What she witnessed, after all the speculation and lurid rumor, was not legend. It was fact. How she wished Shelly could be here . . .

First the spine began bowing, lengthening, and Thomas bent over like a runner at the starting line. When he crouched, the change came more rapidly. His legs, bent at the knees, became strong canine limbs that matched the front legs his arms were forming. Lastly, a tail sprouted from the end of his spine, and his growing snout began to fill with sharp, menacing teeth. The human's well-shaped ears formed into furry ones already pricked, as if this Thomas, his true self revealed, heard things—and understood things—no mere human could comprehend.

"Mistress!" Safira pulled harder at Lil's arm. "My spells—they do nothing. We must run!"

Finally galvanized into a sense of the danger she was in, both by Safira's urgency and by the savage gleam in those black eyes, Lil realized she had only seconds left to react. She shoved aside the glowing moonstone and the silver leaves she realized would be useless, and pulled out the tiny derringer. Even to her own eyes, the pistol looked minuscule and harmless. But she'd hardly been dressed to carry her father's favorite revolver on her person.

Thomas blocked the door, so Safira ran to the French doors that led onto the patio. The doors rattled. "They're locked," Safira wailed.

With more bravado, than courage, Lil held the tiny gun steadily on the werewolf. "Break the glass, Safira," she suggested coolly, never taking her eyes off Thomas.

Her eyes began to water slightly, but still she didn't blink. By choice? she wondered. Or did he have her mesmerized? His gaze was fixed on her with a primitive intensity that went beyond rancor, or hunger, or even hatred.

And finally Lil understood why she'd always been wary around him, with that instinctive sense of distaste many women feel around male predators. Thomas Harbaugh, half Griffith on his mother's side, was obsessed. But his sickness went far beyond the curse of the Griffith males. He was filled with contempt for all women, not just Haskell women. He liked to toy with them, compliment them, and when they were charmed, he struck. He attacked as a man, in the worst way a man could dishonor a woman . . .

. . . by rape, just as Ian had said. Lil wished now she'd believed him.

When the ultimate act of dominance was denied him, Thomas let the lupine instincts take over. Lil sensed movement behind her, and realized Safira had picked up something heavy and heaved it at the leaded glass in the French doors. But the object bounced off the glass and clattered to the floor. With a rustle of silk robes, Safira frantically banged desk drawers, obviously looking for something heavier.

Lil's faint hope that perhaps someone would hear the commotion and investigate died as soon as it was born. The dull roar of laughter, music, and many voices were the clef notes to the mournful dirge of Lil's requiem.

No one would hear. No one would come. She and Safira were alone.

Thomas was fully formed now. His back legs shifted restlessly, and his claws, forming last, were so sharp they left scratches in the gleaming parquet floor.

Still, Thomas waited. Simply staring at her, his lips curled back in a soundless snarl.

And Lil finally fulfilled his unspoken but nearly tangible wish: She began to be afraid. Her own curiosity could well be her last act of hubris on this earth.

And her death would be horrid not because she was killed by a wild animal, but because her killer acted with the calculation and animosity of superior intelligence. An intelligence perverted from its normal higher order into an obsession with dominance and destruction.

First, Thomas would toy with her, frighten her, humiliate her.

He would feed on her terror before he fed on her blood.

And then, he'd wound her. Slowly, tearing into her flesh delicately at first, to cause the maximum amount of pain and the least amount of damage. Only when he'd gorged himself on her fear and anguish would he rip her rib cage open and . . .

The rattling of glass broke the spell of those pitiless black eyes. Lil heard a crack form in the panes, but she knew it was too late. Even if Safira broke enough glass for them to squeeze outside, Thomas would run them down in three strides.

Run *her* down. A new resolve steadied Lil's shaking hand. If she ran in the opposite direction from Safira, perhaps the Haitian woman would live to return to her beloved island.

As Thomas crouched to spring, Lil leveled the pistol carefully, knowing she'd get only one shot. Maybe she could hit him in the eye.

As she aimed, carefully squeezing the tiny trigger, she wondered how many times the barmaid screamed before she died. *He'll get not so much as a groan from my lips*.

Safira screamed, startling Lil so much that her careful aim was spoiled.

The small gun's report sounded like a cannon in

the enclosed study, but the slug missed Thomas's eye and struck him in the shoulder. He roared, more in fury than in pain, his bellow not quite loud enough to disguise the shattering glass. *Good, at least Safira can get away.*

But Lil didn't dare take her eyes away from Thomas as she backed slowly in the direction of the French doors. The slight wound was barely a pinprick to that mass of muscle and malice.

Thomas licked the spurting blood away and turned on his prey. He stalked her, step by lethal step. This time, when he growled, his fangs were crimson with his own blood. But curiously, he froze in mid-step. His head turned in the direction of the terrace.

Lil's hips came up against the desk. Just as she realized her miscalculation of the room's arrangement could cost her her life, she realized she heard no retreating footsteps; Safira hadn't run. In fact, Safira seemed to be keening in abject terror, frozen beside the French doors.

Even cornered against the desk, Lil had to risk a look over her shoulder at the terrace. Her pounding heart lurched in her breast.

Ian! Ian in his wolf form had broken the glass. And the moon was only three quarters full. He, too, had figured out how to control the change! But how had he gotten out of the cell? And why had he risked it?

Stunned, Lil assessed Ian's predicament.

Trapped. They were both trapped.

He was so large he was half caught in the sturdy wooden door frame. He was struggling furiously to

free himself, and Lil saw that both sides of his rib
cage were bleeding from cuts made by the glass when
he burst through. More blood dripped from his snout
and jaw, which must have taken the brunt of the
heavy glass. Lethal shards glittered on his coat and
the floor. Lil knew they'd lacerate his pads when he
walked over them. But the growls issuing from his
throat were at least as savage and determined as those
coming from Thomas.

Lil realized Thomas had scented Ian before she had
any inkling of his presence. Lil glanced between the
two werewolves, wondering how much of the rancor
vibrating from Thomas was aimed at his enemy. And
how much was directed at her . . .

Thomas tossed back his head and gave the long, low
howl that had mesmerized Ian that night when Lil
awakened in the tower. Easing to the side of the desk
now that Thomas's attention was fixed elsewhere, Lil
waited, nerves taut, to see what Ian would do.

Would he respond again?

Or had Thomas's dominance been broken when Ian
embraced his other identity?

The thought scarcely left her before Ian stopped
struggling. His amber eyes met and held their own
against bottomless black.

Lil took advantage of the distraction by rounding
the desk and dashing to the side of the room to hold
a shivering Safira in her arms. Still too close for
safety, Lil watched the strange, silent battle.

Her own life, and possibly Safira's, hung in the
balance. Her heart pounding against her ribs, Lil saw

the habits and personalities of the men eerily played out by the wolves.

Thomas rested on his haunches, his head erect, ears pricked forward, lordly. *Bow down to me, inferior,* he said with posture and eyes.

And Ian, still trapped in the door, started to hunch his shoulders. His ears flattened in automatic obedience. His gaze strayed away as he started to pay his obeisance to the dominant male.

"Please, oh, please, oh, please," Lil whispered. "Ian, he's evil. But good can be as strong as evil. If you try."

Confused amber eyes flicked toward her. Lil realized Ian's hearing was so acute that he'd heard her mumbled encouragement. Ian's nostrils flared, and she knew he'd picked up the scent of her sweat and fear. He looked from her to Thomas, who still sat calmly on his haunches, sure of Ian's subservience.

After an endless moment of breathless anticipation, Ian lowered his head.

The sweet flavors of life and love on Lil's tongue turned to the bitter ashes of defeat. Good couldn't overcome evil. Thomas was still stronger.

With a husky growl that sounded uncannily like a smirk to Lil, Thomas turned his attention from his inferior back to the women. Shoving the paralyzed Safira behind her, Lil raised her two-shot derringer again. Maybe she'd aim better this time. . . .

Thomas rounded the desk in one bound. His malevolence was almost palpable as he gathered himself to spring.

With a burst of power that startled Lil almost as

much as it did Thomas, Ian pushed mightily at the door frame. The wood cracked like kindling. He was free. He shook himself, glass specks flying off his thick coat, and leaped over the wicked shards on the floor. He landed two steps behind Thomas, apparently unhindered by the blood trickling from his various cuts.

A whuffle of disbelief escaped Thomas as he was forced to turn his attention from prey to pack. The ruff on his neck bristled with hostility. The two were-wolves started circling one another. Low, savage growls broadcast their intent.

There was nothing submissive about Ian now. His ears were alert, his teeth bared in a threat. Every muscle in his body was tense as he tracked Thomas with all his acute senses.

Lil almost fancied she saw amazement in Thomas's sulfurous black eyes, but fury soon consumed him. Arching his long neck, Thomas howled. But this time, when Thomas attacked, forepaws off the ground, Ian rose to meet him.

Their snarls grew in volume as they snapped and bit. Lil peeked at the broken French doors, but the two wolves battled in the only clear path to the exit.

Lil glanced at the door leading into the hallway. For the moment, it was clear. "Safira, run!" Lil gave her a little push, but Safira clung to her.

Lil glanced at Safira's hands. They were coated with a powdery residue and feathers. All of Safira's voodoo magic had been as ineffectual as Lil's own silver leaves and cinders. A flash of despair made Lil wonder if she would ever discover a power in the universe strong enough to overcome a century of evil.

When Lil pushed Safira again and her companion balked, Lil said frantically, "Safira, I've endangered you enough. Go now. Get help. I want a witness present to see Thomas regain his human form."

"But mistress—"

"No argument. I couldn't live with myself if you should be killed. And I . . . can't leave until I know Ian is safe." Lil ignored the look in those liquid dark eyes that posed the question: What of your own life? Reluctantly, Safira made a dash for the door.

When she was safely away, Lil turned her attention back to the fight. The two werewolves were poised on their hind legs, clawing and biting. Thomas's neck also oozed with blood, but there were so many new scratches on Ian's back and chest that his fur looked more red than black. Lil glanced at the hallway door, her survival instincts urging her to run, but then she looked back at Ian.

She'd made the conscious decision long ago to stay in Cornwall, even if it meant risking her life. Now that she was about to solve the mystery of which werewolf was stronger, and whether or not Ian could control his blood lust, she couldn't bear to run from the room. And if her life was forfeit, so be it.

Yet again Lil aimed her tiny pistol, but looking from the lethal mass of muscle and bone to the tiny pearl-handled derringer made her realize the futility of such a puny defense. Nevertheless, she warily eased around the combatants, trying to get a clear shot at Thomas. But no sooner did she get in position than the fight veered in a new direction.

Never in her life had Lil felt more helpless. The two werewolves were so smeared with blood that Lil couldn't tell which was wounded worse. Despite the fact that Thomas was slightly larger, the combatants seemed evenly matched.

Perhaps Ian was more desperate. Perhaps he was tired of being subordinate.

Or, and this sent a dart of pain through Lil so severe that the pistol wavered in her hand, perhaps Ian hadn't learned to control his urges at all. Perhaps he'd broken out of his cell for the same reason that Thomas had followed her into the study. Perhaps . . .

. . . Ian hadn't come here to fight *for* her, but to fight *over* her.

The thought was scarcely formed before, with a savagery that made Lil wince, Ian's jaws locked down on one of Thomas's ears. Howling, Thomas clawed viciously at Ian's back, but Ian only bit down harder, until blood flowed into his mouth. The taste of it seemed to give him strength, for, with a mighty heave, Ian threw Thomas across the room into the roaring fireplace.

The yowl of pain that came from Thomas as the fire seared his fur almost made Lil feel sorry for him.

Almost.

The andirons clattered, and Lil wondered if perhaps the impact had broken a rib, for when Thomas stumbled to his feet he favored one side. He shook his head, dazed with pain. For once the menace in those cold black eyes faded to gray murk. Unpleasant, but not as terrifying.

Her fingers trembling around the derringer butt, Lil

looked at Ian. His muscular chest moved in and out with his heavy breathing, but it was the demand in those amber eyes that glued Lil to the floor.

Possession.

Hunger.

Desire.

For—what?

Lil was afraid to move forward, and afraid not to. But her ambivalence was part and parcel of the duality of their entire relationship. She had come this far and she couldn't back away now. Lil glanced over Ian's shoulder at Thomas, but he was harmless for the moment, standing as though even breathing pained him. She looked back at Ian.

His nostrils flared as he stalked toward her, his great padded feet soundless on the floor. Still Lil held her ground despite her own fear. She'd prayed for this, that God would make him strong, but how could he defeat something as evil as Thomas and not have some remnant of savagery left himself?

She told herself to be still, to wait and know for sure. But when he was close enough to strike, the wild scent of him, sweat and blood, and wolf and man, made her react on an instinctive level. She backed away, her hands up to ward him off. From a very long distance, Lil noted that she pointed the derringer directly at his eye. She couldn't say herself whether she did so deliberately or not.

But Ian froze, one foot still raised. The images of his battle with Thomas were still too vivid, and for a moment Lil thought that great paw was about to slash at her. Wincing in fear, she dodged to the side. Amber eyes darkened with what might have been pain, but then the sounds of running feet in the hallway alerted them to the fact that help was on its way.

Ian's lips curled back from his teeth in a soundless snarl blatant with contempt. With a powerful thrust of his hind quarters, he leaped over Lil's shrinking figure, out the broken door to the terrace.

There was a slight rustle of leaves and then nothing. Not even the moon peered past the clouds, as if Diana herself were ashamed of a kindred hunter.

Trembling with the force of her warring emotions, Lil looked over at Thomas. To her fury, she realized the wordless confrontation with Ian must have taken longer than she'd realized. Thomas was already fully a man again. He kicked his tattered clothes into the fire, shrugging into a silk dressing gown he must have left lying over the sofa for exactly this emergency. Lil stuck her derringer back in her reticule, and used the precious seconds before the door opened to straighten her clothes and hair.

She knew what inference Thomas would put on this situation, but she held the man's black eyes as steadily as she had held the wolf's. "You can lie all you like, but how will you explain your burns and your broken rib?"

"Quite easily. Even better, it will be more or less true. The vicissitudes of passion, my dear."

Lil had time for only one quick step toward the French doors before the room filled with people. Preston, of course, led the way. He took one look at Thomas and glanced toward Lil. From the smirk that twisted his full mouth, Lil deduced that Preston either shared Thomas's malady or knew of it.

Settling a fake look of embarrassment over his handsome face, Preston pretended to try to block the door, but only after some of the worst gossips in the county pressed into the room. "It seems my brother has been . . . well, entertained this evening. I suspect we're a trifle de trop."

It took every ounce of possession Lil retained to stand erect and dignified under the salacious glances, but her equanimity was her only remaining ammunition against the Harbaugh brothers. And she used it well, with a dismissing glance shared equally between Preston and Thomas.

Drolly, she said, "Indeed, it might have been a most entertaining interlude, had his lordship been . . . up to the challenge. But I suppose I shall have to leave as I arrived, in full possession of my faculties, my reputation, and I might point out, my clothes. Pity. But some reputations are so difficult to live . . . up to, would you not agree, Thomas? Come, Safira."

Haughtily, Safira and Lil walked through the shocked party-goers. Thomas hadn't spoken a word, but Lil felt his enmity as a tangible thing against her back as she exited. She only wished she'd had nerve enough to rip his dressing gown away and make him explain his wounds. She didn't relax her pose until they were safely in the carriage and away.

Then, reaction setting in, Lil collapsed in tears. "Oh, Safira, what am I to do? I'd like to believe Ian was trying to protect me . . . but the curse is so strong, and I feel so weak. Somehow, I betrayed him."

"Mistress, every woman deserves to cry after such an evening." Safira drew her mistress close and patted her back.

The exotic scents of Safira's potions and her own personal perfume lulled Lil to a dull torpor. "Is that a voodoo belief?"

"No. It's a female right. Haitian or American."

"Thank you for coming to my aid. But I fear no one can help me with what I have to do next."

Safira stiffened slightly. "It will do no good to go to the authorities about his lordship. I am sorry I couldn't get help faster. Before he transformed again."

"It doesn't matter. I don't know how I know this, but somehow, this comedy of terrors can only be resolved by myself and Ian and Thomas."

"And the other brother?"

"I am not sure about him yet, but I suspect he's in collusion with his brother, though not a werewolf himself."

"And you will risk your life on this assumption?"

"I've already risked it several times over tonight alone. We are lucky to be alive, Safira."

And they wouldn't be, without Ian.

"Luck had very little to do with it this time, mistress."

The two women shared a weak smile. But as the carriage clattered through the gates and Lil looked up at the dark tower, she knew her dilemma couldn't be solved with bravado. She and Ian each had their demons to face. The ones outside. And the ones inside.

Did she love Ian enough to trust him in his were-wolf form as much as she trusted the man?

This time, the pain driving Ian had nothing to do with his physical form. For the first time in his cursed existence, Ian enjoyed his fleet, four-footed form. Even if by some miracle they found a cure, Ian hoped some portion of his sharpened senses would remain.

No rigidly erect human being could comprehend the joy of flying over marshy pond and low grasses on four feet. At times, he seemed a part of the wind itself, as elemental as the mist dampening his tongue. And yet, now that he had embraced the change, and better, learned to control it, he felt simultaneously weakened and strengthened. The wolf paused and licked at his wounds with a healing tongue.

But the man's wounds lay deep where they could not be touched.

Even when he'd burst out of his cell, endangering both of his personas, and then risked his very life in fighting the strongest, vilest werewolf who had ever walked the marshes, Lil hadn't trusted him. Despite all her posturing, all her little homilies about how wonderful it would be to be a wolf, Lil did not look upon his lupine form with anything but disgust and fear. She had not only backed away from him when he moved forward to comfort her, dripping with the blood from his near-mortal battle to save her, she'd even brandished that ridiculous pistol at him.

Why had he believed her different? More courageous than the other heiresses?

He must have been blinded by sexual desire. A lust

so strong that his own latent romantic tendencies had dressed up nature's base call in the frills and follies of "love."

Or perhaps . . . the curse had changed Lil's own softer feelings into disgust. For surely that had been disgust he'd seen in her green eyes.

Perhaps it would be best if he remained out here. It was certain he couldn't go back to the tower or the village. Now everyone from the sheriff to Lil's companion knew him as a werewolf.

Ian stopped on a tor overlooking the Druid ruins, which had always held a strange attraction for him. Most of the stones had fallen in antiquity, but the altar remained upright.

It was here, according to family legend, that the last male Haskell heir had first taken his Gypsy paramour. Normally Ian avoided the place, but for some reason, tonight his feet had led him here. Ian lifted his snout and sniffed the wind. He took in the familiar scents of rotting vegetation, salty breeze, and the bogs themselves.

And something else.

Beneath the comforting smells, Ian sensed something more ephemeral. Ian sniffed more deeply, closing his eyes, using the way of the wolf. Instinct, not logic. It was almost as if, alone in this sacred place of his Druid ancestors, Ian scented the whiff of destiny. Here the curse began. Here, perhaps, it would end.

Snarling, he turned away from the peaceful, slumbering stones. The wolf could not afford to be as foolish and weak as the man. There was no magical elixir to cure lycanthropy. He had no choice but to squelch his softer human feelings, for they led to disaster.

Lil's revulsion had stolen his last feeble hope. When she looked into the eyes of the wolf, she didn't see the man. She saw a hairy, smelly, dangerous beast. So be it.

Be damned to the stones of his ancestors. Be damned to the Gypsy girl who began this.

And be damned most of all to the last female of Haskell blood.

For a brief, heady period, she had been his solace, his companion, and his only joy. Now, when he'd finally embraced this benighted form, she had changed, too.

She was no longer his deliverance.

She was his curse. And he would avoid her accordingly. The wolf flung back his head and howled, a long, lonely lament echoing with despair.

But even as he began loping over the moors again, trying to enjoy his hard-won freedom, memories haunted the wolf. And the wolf knew its keen instincts that saw so much more clearly than human sight, whether Lil Haskell was still his chosen mate or not, he couldn't let Thomas kill her.

Now that he'd proved he could defeat Thomas, the wolf would watch. Wait. And with his new skills combining the knowledge of man and the power of wolf, Ian Griffith would yet find a way to control his destiny.

He'd save Delilah Haskell.

Then he'd walk away, still werewolf, but cured nonetheless.

As proud as the moors he loved. And as desolate.

*   *   *

After the night of the ball, Lil's already tattered rep-utation was reduced to shreds. But Lil had always been subject to whispers, and the Cornish folk were not as bold and brassy as those in Colorado. Besides, if Lil had lived her life according to the precepts of her social rank, she never would have come to Corn-wall. She had no doubt that the source of the rumors came as much from the hosts of the ball as from the revelers. Thomas wasn't done with her yet. But his bloody lordship would learn that Delilah Haskell Trent wasn't finished with him, either.

It was Ian she brooded over.

Days passed, and still he didn't come home. Since he'd transformed without the full moon, and could control the change, she assumed that he stayed away by choice. Of course, the fact that the entire district now knew his terrible secret would make him wary. But couldn't he trust her to help him?

The thought sliced her like a lash, knocking her back into the chair in the salon, where she'd stood in contemplation. Why should Ian trust her, when she had not trusted him? Surely if he had been intent on killing her in Thomas's stead, he could have dragged her out the broken door by the scruff of her neck. Or ripped her throat out with one bite of those dagger-sharp teeth.

Or clawed his way past her fragile bones to her heart. Fulfilling their macabre destiny. But Ian had railed against the fate as hard as she.

Her sight blurred by tears, Lil stared at her almost complete sampler. The amber silk she'd used for the wolf's eyes seemed to gleam at her accusingly. Now that it was too late, Lil realized Ian had fled from her fear, not from the people running down the corridor. The grimace had not been born of menace, but of pain. At the look on her face.

Ian had endangered himself in every way when he broke through that door. Three times now, he hadn't killed her when he'd had the chance.

He hadn't failed her.

The brutal truth was she'd failed him.

Miserably, Lil rose to pace the salon, wondering what to do. Perhaps Ian had decided to remain a were-wolf, finding the ways of the wild more civilized than the hypocrisy of humanity. If so, how would she ever find him? Especially if he didn't want to be found.

A knock sounded at the salon door. Lil dashed her tears off on a scrap of handkerchief. "Come in."

"My dear Miss Haskell—" Shelly broke off when she saw Lil's face. The aloof stable manager meta-morphosed into Lil's mentor and friend. Hands out-stretched, Shelly hurried forward.

The touch of those strong but sympathetic hands brought new tears to Lil's eyes. "Oh, Shelly, things are in such a muddle."

"Then we shall make mud pies."

A tearful laugh betokened Lil's appreciation of Shelly's understanding. "That shall be a neat trick. If I dare to set foot on the moors again, I may have two werewolves out to kill me now instead of one."

"Whatever do you mean?"

When Lil's incipient tears became a flood, Shelly pulled her to the divan. "If you mean the commotion at the ball, I shouldn't concern myself overmuch about that. Safira told me what happened."

Lil blew her nose fiercely. "Everything? That's not possible because she wasn't in the room when I betrayed Ian."

Shelly sighed heavily. "That's a very strong word."

"It's a very ugly act," Lil replied, and went on to explain what she'd done. "I fear I shall never see Ian again in any form. It's been four days since the ball and I haven't see hide nor—"

"Hair of him?" That honking laugh was somehow reassuring to Lil's bruised feelings. "Judging by the furor the Harbaughs have stirred up in the village, Ian is wise to stay away. But Lil, I've seen his expression when he looks at you. Though I have no doubt that your quite understandable caution upset him, if I know anything of men, and I know quite a lot, we have not seen the last of the Wolf of Haskell Hall."

Putting her kerchief away, Lil resolved to dispose of her useless grief with the same alacrity. "For my part, I'd wager that if you spent the last four days in Jeremy's company, you know quite a bit more of men now than when you set off."

Shelly nodded ruefully. "As usual, you are correct. If you share my dreadful secret with anyone else I'll deny it, but I must admit I admire men more now than when I set out. Do you know I have so far forgotten my own mature, hard-earned dignity that I've grown accustomed to his dulcet Cockney tones calling me 'ducky'?"

The shared laugh made them both feel better. "Jeremy does grow on one," Lil teased.

Shelly shrugged. "One can grow accustomed to eating worms if one has to. But it's still not a taste I would willingly cultivate."

"The question is, what are we both going to do about our odd afflictions?"

Briskly, Shelly patted Lil's hands. "Do? Why, we will be as sensible as is our wont. We shall have a hot bath, a comfortable coze in front of a fire, and a good night's sleep. In the morning, things will not be so bleak."

And for the next few hours, it seemed as if Shelly's prediction would come true. Lil did indeed feel much better after her bath and her talk, but as Shelly yawned and made as if to rise to seek her own bed, Lil blurted out, "Shelly, are you a werewolf too?"

Her stable manager froze, half sitting, half rising, her awkward position revealing her state of mind. Shelly never did anything halfway. Green eyes met gray, and now Shelly's lids did not droop with tiredness. "How ever did you know?"

Lil was touched at Shelly's immediate capitulation, for it spoke highly of her trust in her employer. "When we were in the cell, your eyes glowed in the darkness. Now that the full moon is almost upon us, how are you feeling?"

"Like a wild woman." And indeed, Shelly's eyes took on a peculiar glow in the shadowy room. Just as Lil began to ease slightly away from her, Shelly chuckled and patted her friend's hands. "One still quite in control of her baser urges."

"Have you . . . changed yet?"

307

Colleen Shannon

"Yes. Once. Luckily, Jeremy was in a tavern at the time."

The strange sense of unreality that had been creeping up on Lil for days almost overcame her. If anyone had told her a few months back that she would be sitting in her mother's ancestral home chatting with a werewolf, Lil would have laughed herself senseless. But as she looked at Shelly, Lil was overcome with the old curiosity. "What's it like?"

"I shall try to describe it to you. It is at the same time a joy and a tribulation, a blessing and a curse. Never have I felt the vibrancy of life more acutely, and yet never have I been so certain of its fragility. I have spent my entire life in the pursuit of knowledge and reason. And yet only when this malady makes me shake as if with an ague, do I understand that the true joys of life are found not in the mind's control of who we are, but in its synergy with our entire beings. Mind. Body. Senses. Heart. And instinct. If you wish to understand what it is like to be a werewolf, focus not on who you are, but *why* you are."

Lil was much struck by Shelly's words, for she spoke so eloquently the same feelings Lil had sensed in Ian's touch. He had obviously wanted to both embrace and reject the terrible power that had him in its grip, and yet it was a power that gave as well as took.

One more thing Lil had to know. "Shelly, are you able to control not only your actions, but your instincts and your fears? Do you keep your sense of self even when you walk on all fours instead of erect?"

"Not only do I keep my sense of self, I have a

much better sense of my surroundings and the presence of others."

Lil considered this, but realized Shelly was without a doubt the most powerful intellect Lil had ever encountered. If anyone could harness the power of the werewolf, and make of its savagery something wonderful by sheer force of will and mind and spirit, it was Shelly Holmes. Lil stared out the window at the moon playing hide-and-seek with the clouds. Ian was very intelligent, too, but he'd lived with the terrible weight of his fate his entire life, so it was only natural that it would be much more difficult for him to see anything positive in his destiny. If only she had followed him out of Thomas's study, done as Shelly recommended and listened to her instincts rather than her mind, she'd know the answer to this gnawing question.

But as she gazed up at the moon, her persistent rational side taunted her, *Yes, and the price of trusting your instincts could be your life.* But did that really matter? The life she'd have if she ran home to Colorado now would be a living hell. There was too much of her father in her. Papa had inhaled the scents of seawater and bilge in steerage for the entire Atlantic crossing—on a hunch. On a gamble as he set out for the gold fields of America.

The same hunch that prompted his daughter to make the same crossing in the opposite direction, in much greater comfort. For a better life. Happiness. A way of fulfilling one's destiny that would also improve the lot of others in some small way. Papa had succeeded because of the odds, not in spite of them.

After her repeated brushes with death, Lil knew she carried the legacy of her braw Scots ancestors as much as her mother's analytical English ancestors.

Run away? Never!

Lil looked back at Shelly's attentive face. "I can't say I fully understand what you are trying to tell me, but I promise to try to heed your advice. And you? Did you have any luck finding a cure?"

The animation faded from Shelly's expression. Looking away, she shook her head. "At least not anything I understand. Now, my dear, if you'll excuse me, even werewolves need sleep, and I've been mastering my urge to run naked across the moors with increasing difficulty. I had heavy black shutters nailed over my windows upon my return, so with any luck, I'll awaken safe and secure in my own bed. Good night. I can't wish you sweet dreams, but I can certainly wish you ones you can remember. And heed." The door closed gently behind Shelly.

Lil sat on the edge of the bed, staring out at that curiously eloquent Cornish moon. It soon drew her to a chair by the window. And for the remainder of that night, she stared out at the moors, trying to feel what Ian felt.

Listening to her instincts, not her mind, or even her heart.

For therein lay their salvation . . .

Chapter Thirteen

The next day, when Lil kept her vow of putting flowers upon the Gypsy girl's grave, she felt watching eyes upon her. She glanced up at her shadow—Jeremy—who stood alert over her, armed with shotgun, rifle, and pistol, but he was looking toward the village, not the woods.

Bowing her head again, Lil told herself she was imagining things. But her reverie was broken. She stood, dusted off her dress, and looked down at her handiwork. She'd cleaned the last headstone today. Tomorrow, she'd bring extra flowers. Put them on each—

"Good afternoon, Miss Haskell."

Lil gasped at the sound of that smooth voice, looking over her shoulder at the source.

Colleen Shannon

Jeremy spun around, alarmed, and pointed his shotgun toward the woods.

Thomas stood there, fair hair gleaming in the sunshine, broad shoulders impressive in Bond Street tailoring, legs well formed in tight breeches and tall boots. A blue-blooded nobleman through and through, by all appearances. Gallant. Handsome.

And as deceptively harmless as the moors themselves. Beneath the peaceful facade lurked seething hungers that had consumed many an unwary traveler.

Except Lil was no longer unwary. She had only to look in Thomas's eyes to see him for what he was. But for some reason, maybe because she was backed up by Jeremy's stalwart protection, maybe because it was daylight, or maybe just because she hated Thomas so for what he was trying to do to Ian, Lil wasn't afraid.

In fact, she took a quick step toward him before she was able to leash her anger. "Lowering yourself to visit the family grave, my lord? If you're truly the rightful heir, that is, and even deserve the title. Or did you snatch that up the way you do everything that strikes your fancy?"

"Oh, my father made me rightful heir, all right."

"I cannot believe your father embraced you as his heir if you were . . . illegitimate."

Anger flashed in his eyes. "He loved my mother far more than his legal wife. But he was already married when they met, and had been for some time. My stepmother was an invalid, believed to be barren. When Lydia went away to have me, and no one saw my stepmother for almost a year, well, few dared

312

question my birth. She was a Griffith, poor and un-
wed. She loved me enough to give me away, knowing
I'd have a better future as my father's heir."

"Preston surely questioned the inheritance when he
got older."

"Preston idolizes me. He was a surprise baby, and
he came along only after my mother died and there
was something of a reconciliation between my father
and my stepmother. Preston is glad to be a second
son, and I am always generous with him. But it is to
my mother that I owe the legacy that means more to
me." He glanced at Lydia's headstone.

She found Thomas's hypocrisy distasteful, for
Lydia's grave had been as neglected as the rest. "Then
why don't you embrace her legacy fully? Stay out on
the moors with the other ruthless animals where you
belong." Lil glanced at the road into the village, teeming now with mobcapped maids running errands,
farmers fetching supplies, and housewives meeting to
knit and gossip on one another's porches. "Better yet,
embrace it now, at this moment."

A nasty smile that reminded Lil of the wolf's smirk
curled Thomas's full mouth. "You'd like that,
wouldn't you, to have half your villagers see me
transform? I ever aim to please a lady—oh, excuse
me, in your case, perhaps I should say fallen
woman—but even I haven't figured out the art of
changing in full daylight. Luckily for you."

"And you. How would you explain all those fright-
ful tears to your tailor?" She'd never admit it, but his
insult had stung a little. Lil turned a haughty shoulder
to him and began to walk back toward the village.

When Thomas kept step, there wasn't much she could do to stop him, but Jeremy walked behind him, his hands gripping the shotgun firmly, not quite pointing it, but ready to, if necessary.

Thomas certainly caught the hint, for he was very careful not to brush against Lil as they walked. "Don't you want to know why I followed you?"

His words only angered Lil more. "No. But I'm sure you'll tell me anyway."

"Quite so. To be blunt, my dear Miss Haskell, your quest is at an end. Unhappily so. You see, Ian's cure was always literally at his feet. The answer lies in the inscription on our ancestor's grave. One neither of you is capable of deciphering, apparently, or you would already have done so."

Lil stopped in mid-step. "Do you honestly think I'd believe anything you tell me? If you know the cure, why haven't you used it yourself?" Even as she asked the question, Lil knew why merely from the look on that handsome, detestable face.

He didn't want to be cured.

He was a man who lived for the thrill of power and dominance, so why would he willingly cede his advantage over mere mortals?

"Perhaps I want to help you see the futility of your goal. Consider this your last warning, your last chance to run back to America. I have seldom met a woman I respected, much less admired, but you face adversity with the bravery of a man, so I will accord you a similar courtesy. In a word, Ian Griffith will die a werewolf, a member of my pack, subservient to me— or he will die two days from now, neither wolf nor

314

man, and I shall reluctantly put him out of his misery. Either way, he is lost to you. Though I much admire your refusal to leave him the other night while we were . . . occupied, your loyalty is misplaced."

"You tried to kill him at the ball and failed."

"Are you so certain? How do you know I didn't mortally wound him? No one has seen him since."

Lil's lashes flickered as she tried to hold those cold, dead eyes, but that was the only hint that she'd worried about the same thing. "I'd know if Ian were dead." And she would, somehow. She'd hurt him, yes, but there was still a bond of blood between them that could never be broken in this world, and probably not in the next.

Her steadfast faith seemed to anger Thomas, for he clenched his fists, taking a step toward her. The nudge of Jeremy's shotgun in his back calmed him quickly enough, however, for he stopped.

Hands thrust into his pockets, he used his tongue as a weapon instead. "The only reason I haven't killed him yet is because my mother loved him, and because he followed where I led. Your arrival spoiled the balance of power between us. If I'm forced into killing him, you'll have only yourself to blame."

Lil knew he'd intended to hurt her, so she didn't give him the satisfaction of seeing that he'd struck at her most vulnerable weakness: guilt. She struck back without hesitation. "If you kill him, I'll hunt you down like the dog you are, if it takes me to my dying day." Lil could have kicked herself—and him—at her careless choice of words.

Naturally, he pounced on them. "Which could

come very soon. If you persist in this foolish defiance. And yet, I should regret it if you forced me into such violence. Even the other night, I only intended to frighten you."

Lil couldn't squelch a scoffing sound.

"Truly. Why do you think I'm facing you in full daylight, on my best behavior, to warn you if I wish you ill?"

That was a good question. This time, Lil wisely remained silent. Listening always garnered more information from men of his stamp, for they so liked to talk about their own superiority.

"When we were boys, Ian and I used to play together on occasion. He couldn't best me then at any of our harmless little contests of skill and strength. And he certainly shan't best me now. I am much stronger than he."

"And more ruthless."

He nodded that lordly head. "You can accept this, give up and return to America, or . . ." He leaned so close that his breath stirred the hair at her temples, and for a moment, the chill in those stygian eyes warmed a few degrees. "You can join us. Two nights from now. At the Druid ruins outside the village. So we can complete what destiny began." He tipped his hat to her. "Good day, Miss Haskell." And he walked off, his steps soundless on the cobblestones.

Jeremy put Lil's feelings into action. He spat on the spot where Thomas had stood. "I've met some devious shysters in me time, but that 'un"—Jeremy spat again—"he could give an eel lessons on bein' slippery. Ye won't go near them heathen remains, me

316

girl. If I have to hog-tie ye and sit on ye."

"Of course not." *Not unless it's strictly necessary.* "That's exactly what he wants." Lil led the way toward their carriage, but when she passed the vicarage, on impulse she turned back around and tapped on the door.

One part of Thomas's boast she believed: He knew the cure for the Griffith lycanthropy. And if the secret lay in deciphering that inscription, then she'd spend every waking hour of the next two days, and part of her sleeping hours, if necessary, on the puzzle. And who better to help her than a brilliant man who loved puzzles?

When Vicar Holmes himself came to the door and ushered her inside, Lil turned to Jeremy. "Somehow, we have to warn Ian, tell him Thomas is planning something at the Druid stones in two nights. Will you look for him again?"

"But—" At Lil's expression, Jeremy bit back his protests and nodded shortly. "Aye. Again. But how will ye get home?"

"I'll bring her myself, after tea," the vicar offered.

Lil hesitated. Despite her urgency to find Ian, she'd never supplied any of the search parties with directions to his own private Eden. That was sacrosanct, and he'd never forgive her if she gave away its location, even to help him. But now she was worried about more than his dignity, or even his trust.

She feared for his life. Lil whispered in Jeremy's ear the directions to the cleft in the rock face and pressed the note she'd hastily scribbled into his hand. "If you find him, give him this. And please, tell no one else. Go alone. Ian won't hurt you, but take Shelly, just in case." If need be, Shelly could help protect Jeremy. Lil almost smiled, wishing she could be there when Jeremy's "ducky" became a wolf. The look on his face . . .

Jeremy scowled. "Shelly's acting right queer enough, lately, without chasin' after werewolves who 'won't hurt you.' " Jeremy raised his voice, imitating Lil's higher tones on the last few words, and then he was gone.

Lil had the grace to flush under the vicar's steady gaze. "Truly, I don't believe Ian will hurt Jeremy. Jeremy's not of Haskell blood, and he's the best man I've ever seen at emerging unscathed in dangerous situations. Besides, we've little time to waste. . . ." Quickly, Lil filled the vicar in on Thomas's threats.

"This cure. Do you think it will help my cousin, too?"

For the first time, Lil saw fear in those pale blue eyes, but not fear for himself. He must truly love his cousin. She replied, "I honestly do not know. And until we decipher the words on that headstone, we're helpless." Musingly she repeated the gypsy's curse, "When bright day steals the night, my heart is a stone. Oh, curse of delight, honor these bones. For this legacy I was born, and for death I wait. An eye for an eye, a hate for a hate.

"Was she an educated girl?" Lil asked after a moment's thought.

"Yes. A rich matron from the parish took a liking to her and even sent her away to finishing school. The old Gypsy woman from the village told me only one person in her family had ever been able to solve the riddle."

"Who?" Lil braced herself, half expecting the answer. It came quickly enough.

"Lydia. Ian's older sister. But he was still just a boy when she died, far too young for anyone to know if the curse would fall on him or not, so I suppose that's why she didn't share her knowledge with him."

"Did you know Thomas is actually Lydia's son, and that he's a Griffith, too?"

The vicar hesitated, and then nodded. "I suspected as much. He's the other werewolf, isn't he?"

"Yes. I think Lydia must have told him her interpretation of the headstone on her deathbed. But do you think he'll share it with Ian? Not for a king's ransom, or the cost of his own soul, which he's obviously already bartered to the devil." Agitated, Lil stood to look out the window. The bright new day seemed obscenely picturesque in her frame of mind.

Day . . . How could day steal the night? Bones. Stones. Wait. Hate. There was no commonality to the references at all, as far as Lil could see. And yet there must be some significance to them. Thomas seemed so certain of the date, two days away when the full moon was at its zenith. And since the moon was the source of all the trouble, maybe that was what the Gypsy girl had meant by night. What could block the moon?

Lil whirled, her dark green eyes sparkling again. "A lunar eclipse! Do you know if there's a lunar eclipse expected two nights hence?"

"Why, yes. I subscribe to the publication of the

Royal Astronomical Society, and it will be this part of Cornwall's first lunar eclipse in almost . . ." The vicar's mild blue eyes widened to saucers.

"A century!" Lil filled in for him. "This has to be it! The wait—a hundred years. The day steals the night—the lunar eclipse. Now where would one find stones and bones . . . the Gypsy cemetery?"

"The poor Gypsy lass was the first Griffith buried there. No, I don't think she would have invoked her curse upon a place so close to the village she loved."

"Where was she found? Out on the moors, I know, but could it have been near the Druid ruins?"

"I don't know the exact location, but from all accounts, it could have been there."

"Are there any graves near it?"

"Not that I know of, at least not of any Gypsies. There was an ancient tomb found beneath the altar stones some years back, but it held no remains. The Gypsies, in fact, avoid the place, believing it cursed."

"And if that's where she lost her virtue to my not-so-esteemed ancestor," Lil pointed out, "then she'd have every reason to despise the place. Where better to end the curse than where it began?"

"Yes, but how? Merely exposing Ian to the eclipse is surely not enough."

"I have to find Ian. Between the two of us, we can figure out the last clue." *An eye for an eye, a hate for a hate.*

"Are you sure that's wise?"

His concern stopped Lil with her hand on the doorknob. Slowly, she turned back to look unflinchingly into those penetrating eyes that reminded her so much

320

of Shelly's equally astute gaze. All the feelings she'd bottled for days, a volatile mixture of hope and despair, poured from her. "Wise? No. What do you wish me to say? That I'm afraid? That the savagery Ian used in defeating Thomas the other night terrifies me? That I dread the very thought that perhaps, now that he's learned to accept what he is, he'll learn to like it, too, as Thomas has? All these things are true. I'd be wise to barricade myself in my mansion and not show my face again until the eclipse is passed. Wiser still to run straight back to Colorado. Wisest of all to forget such a wonderful man as Ian Griffith even exists, especially as he seems to have cast off his humanity with his clothes. But the Trents are no wiser than the Haskells, and we could well have the same motto: I will neither yield to the song of the siren, nor the voice of the hyena, the tears of the crocodile, nor the howling of the wolf." Quietly, Lil went out and closed the door.

Just as quietly, she eased back in, blushing at the vicar's laugh. "In my high dudgeon, I forgot I have no carriage. Do you mind taking me back to the estate?"

The vicar pretended to consider the request. "And be alone with a firebrand such as yourself?"

"I guess I deserve that. But I promise I shan't eat you."

"My dear Miss Haskell, you deserve the best good fortune that can be bestowed upon a person. I find your bravery and your resolve an inspiration, and I shall do all in my small power to help you find your happiness. Let us hope that whatever cures Ian shall also cure my cousin." He escorted her outside, up into his old but serviceable barouche.

But as they drove back to the estate, Lil didn't have heart to tell him that she had her worries about Shelly's state of mind, too. Shelly hadn't seemed any too upset at her malady, nor overly concerned about finding a cure.

Keeping a good distance back from the barouche, Ian covered the marsh in a ground-eating, effortless lope. The longer he remained in this lithe form, the more appealing it became. Odd how the fate he'd wandered the world to escape now seemed so alluring. Since the night of the ball, he'd watched Lil from afar. Close enough to see, and smell, and sense it if she were in danger, but far enough away to evade the search parties. Some Lil sent, some the sheriff sent, but a man's brain combined with the agility of the wolf offered huge advantages for an escapee. It was ridiculously easy to disguise his tracks by doubling back on them, or swimming through a bog, or climbing a tree.

A few days ago, he'd clung to the upper trunk of a dying oak and watched the sheriff and the dozen men he'd recruited from the village walk beneath him. If they'd bothered to look up . . . but they didn't expect a wolf to climb trees.

Only once had Ian been tempted to assume human form again. When he watched Delilah clean the last headstone. She did so with an expression of such aching loss, and loneliness, as if she felt, through her contact with the graves of his people, their own ostracism. Occasionally, she'd look up, through the woods, seeming to peer straight into the reeds where he hid, and once, even from that distance, he saw tears catch an errant ray of sunlight.

In that moment, it was as if she'd reached out to touch him. It was for him that she did this humbling task. The richest woman in the county was on her hands and knees scrubbing to honor the forgotten remnants of a despised race. His people, she said with every movement of that brush, were her people. And he'd so longed to believe her, to hope that despite their differing social ranks, the curse, and her fear of him, that somehow love could form a bridge between them.

Before he paused to think, or remember his own hurt, Ian felt himself changing, his forelegs beginning to form into arms again. On the conscious human level that was becoming increasingly more difficult for him to heed, he was surprised at his own ability. Even Thomas hadn't figured out the way of shape-shifting in daylight. What this meant for Ian's future, he couldn't say, and for the moment, he didn't care. He only wanted to hold Lil again, maybe for the last time. As a man.

He'd have to go to her naked, but she'd seen him that way before, and Jeremy would certainly feel less inclined to use his gun on a fellow male's vulnerability. But he was only half transformed when he scented the other.

Ian froze, half man, half wolf, and watched Thomas try to ingratiate himself. They were too far away for Ian to hear their conversation, but Ian let the wolf take him again, concern for Lil paramount now. For once, Ian found Jeremy's marksmanship a comfort. Ian tried to ease closer, but a bare patch of grass separated them. He could only watch, his heart pounding with alarm, as Thomas and Lil walked toward the village.

Ian knew every tilt of Lil's head and every sway of those supple hips. She walked martially, head erect, spine straight. At least she wasn't fooled by Thomas anymore. She despised him, Ian was relieved to see. But he could only wonder what Thomas said to leave her staring after him, white-faced, as he strode off in his customary, arrogant way.

And then, shortly after Lil entered the vicarage, Jeremy emerged. Ian watched him get on the carriage and cluck to the horse. Ian hesitated, but he had to know what Thomas had said to Lil. She was safe with the vicar for the moment.

Ian took the shortcut through the woods. But to his dismay, Jeremy turned off the main road back to the estate, onto the dirt track that led but one place.

Betrayal was rank upon Ian's tongue. Lil had told Jeremy about their secret place! How could she? She knew she was the only one he'd taken there. Furious now, his lips pulled back in a snarl, Ian trotted behind the carriage. He'd subsisted on plump rabbits and greasy water fowl for the past week, and Jeremy's scrawny figure suddenly began to look very tasty. . . .

In her quarters above the stables a short while later, Shelly nodded vigorously at Lil's interpretation of the curse. "Of course! We made something quite simple overly complex, cousin."

The vicar smiled. "A failing in our family, as I'm sure you'd agree. Therefore, shall we then make something quite complex overly simple?"

Shelly's smiled faded. She turned away from the tea service sitting on the table in her tiny sitting room and fetched the pot off the stove. "More coffee, Lil?"

Lil held her cup out. She shared a glance with the vicar and gave him a little nod in answer to his wordless plea before saying to Shelly, "If it's true that the cure for lycanthropy can only be found in two nights, what do you plan to do? Will you go with me to the Druid stones?"

Warming her hands around her teacup as if she were chilled, Shelly sat back down at the table and said quietly, "I hope that will be true, for Ian. But you forget one small but critical fact. I'm not a Griffith. The cure for his curse will quite likely not work for me."

Vicar Holmes stared down into his cup as if he couldn't bring himself to look at his cousin while he pried so mercilessly into her heart and mind. "Are you sure you wish to be cured, Shelly?"

For a moment, silence seemed an oppressive weight in the room.

"Yes. This malady is like a sleeping sickness. At its height, I feel it least. Only when it's in remission do I realize its seductiveness. The other night, well, the feelings came upon me at a most inopportune moment." She buried her nose in her teacup.

Lil didn't need her blush to know what she was

talking about. "But I thought you said you could control it."

"Not entirely. And controlling how the change transforms me is particularly difficult. My mind remains clear, but my instincts get more primitive. The wolf's instincts are to hunt, and they are much stronger than our veneer of civilization."

"So if you were already venal—"

"I'd become more so."

"And if you were gentle?"

"I'd find that gentleness becoming tinged with savagery."

Lil surged to her feet, her eyes wide. "My God! Jeremy! I sent Jeremy after Ian!"

The cup fell out of Shelly's hand, shattering on the floor.

Jeremy drew the carriage to a stop. The track had all but disappeared, but that rock outcropping in the near distance should lead to the pool, if Lil's directions were correct. Jeremy stuck his pistol in his belt and jumped down, the shotgun in his hand. He'd leave the rifle. Ian had become a ghost, and wasn't likely to show himself.

Jeremy hadn't taken two steps before he smelled it. He stopped, lifted his head, and sniffed the wind. His sensitive sailor's nose had timed the tides by the scents on the breeze, and now it picked up something that alarmed him. It smelled like a wet dog.

Gasping in alarm, Jeremy spun. Before he could get the shotgun into position, a brutal paw knocked it away. And then Jeremy was flat on his back, with the werewolf's front paws pressing on his chest. The marshy ground oozed up around Jeremy, and for a moment, he thought he'd dug his own grave. Then the beast propped its feet astride his shoulders, and he could breathe.

And wished he couldn't. Now he could see clearly, too. The fangs were inches from his face, saliva making them glisten in the brassy afternoon sunlight. Sunlight? He'd thought himself safe enough during the day. *More fool I,* he thought, raising his hands to the werewolf's neck, forcing those fangs back from his face with his puny strength.

And mayhap that would be a fitting epitaph.

More fool I. To come to this cold land with its cold people. To fall in love again with a woman he'd never truly win when he was far too old for such foolishness. To traipse around the moors carrying love letters for werewolves.

He felt tension increasing in the beast's spine, and a low growl shook that muscular frame. Jeremy thought about reaching for his pistol, but to do that he'd have to release the creature's neck. Those teeth could rip out his jugular with one bite.

Besides, he recognized those amber eyes. Perhaps the madness had fully taken Ian Griffith, but some part of the man remained in that mixed-up brain, and Jeremy couldn't kill the only being Lil had ever truly loved. And so, as had been his wont throughout his life, Jeremy gambled. Not on Ian, whom he admired but did not know very well.

On Lil. Whom he knew well indeed. She could not

be so smitten by a man who lacked goodness and mercy in his heart.

Jeremy's hands fell away. He went lax, closing his eyes, and turning his head away. "Get on with it, then, matey. Ain't hardly enough of me to fill yer belly, but I'll go down choice, I reckon."

Jeremy felt that great head come so close it blocked the sunshine. Breath, hot and hungry, seared the side of his neck.

By the time Lil, Shelly, and the vicar reached Jeremy's empty carriage, the grazing horse had dragged it off the path. It was near dark, and the moon was almost full, but Lil was too frantic with fear for Jeremy to worry overmuch about her own safety.

While the vicar worked the carriage wheel free, Lil ran toward the rock outcropping, glad that Shelly was with her. If anything had happened to Jeremy, she'd never forgive herself. And he? If he had to, would he shoot Ian in the heart? Dear God, what if she lost the two men she loved best in all the world through her own selfish, heedless actions?

She ran through the fissure in the rock so fast she scraped her side, but still, she didn't slow down. When she burst into the clearing by the pool, she stopped abruptly. Blinked. And looked again.

Jeremy sat on a fallen log by a fire, turning a rabbit on a spit. And next to him, lying down, his paws around the remains of a bloody carcass that looked to be, thank God, an animal, lay Ian. As Lil watched, his massive jaws crunched into bone as if the hard substance were one of Mrs. McCavity's scones. As

328

he chewed, Ian looked at her. His muzzle was dappled with blood.

Firelight caught in those amber depths. The reflected heat burned her where she stood, and she felt his thoughts as clearly as if he'd spoken. *See? This is what I am. Run away again. Or stay. The choice is yours.*

Jeremy, quite unafraid, quite unmarked, turned the spit with a steady hand.

Had Jeremy shot the deer Ian was eating? Never in Lil's life had she seen a stranger feast, or a more cavalier attitude in the face of danger, even from a man as bold and stubborn as Jeremy.

He saw them, and gave a cheery wave. "Join us, duckies. We've plenty to go around."

Lil's knees felt wobbly as she crossed the clearing. Shelly followed more steadily, but her grey eyes were luminous, too, in the firelight, as she looked at her lover with hunger in her eyes.

Jeremy was too busy ripping off a rabbit leg for Shelly to see the look in her eyes. He watched her fall on the meat as if she were famished. "It were a close one, I don't mind telling you," Jeremy said. "But when I backed off, the blood lust faded from him. When I offered to bag his dinner for him, he accepted. He even stripped the rabbit hide away for me since I'd forgotten me knife."

"Jeremy, you could bargain with the devil," Lil said, collapsing next to him on the log, trying to squelch the vision in her head that the meat she was currently eating had been cleaned by a werewolf's jaws. One couldn't catch the ailment from saliva, surely?

Out of the corner of her eye, she watched Ian continue to grind the deer's bones with a disgusting crunching sound. Finally, knowing he did it deliberately, driven as both man and wolf to taunt the mate he felt had betrayed him, Lil turned on the log to face him.

"I'd ask if you'd read my message, but you've obviously been busy."

Ian only bared his teeth at her, and then went back to his feast.

"I can only wonder, watching you, if you still want to be cured."

Those teeth stopped grinding. Those amber eyes fixed on her, alert. Merciless.

Lil swallowed back her fear, telling herself he hadn't killed Jeremy when he'd had the chance, but then Jeremy was not a Haskell. "Thomas plans to subdue you, or kill you, in two nights. At the Druid stones. That's why I sent Jeremy after you. To warn you."

That great head lowered and rested on tired paws. Ian's eyelids dropped.

Panic seized Lil. Was the man already lost to the wolf? He didn't act as if he heard her, much less comprehended her. "Ian, you have to listen!" She surged to her feet, taking a step toward him. "Be angry with me all you want. In truth, I can't blame you, but you can be cured, or killed, in two nights. . . ." She trailed off, rearing back at his reaction.

He leaped up, hair bristling, growling.

"Sit down, calm-like, me girl," Jeremy said quietly.

Lil collapsed back onto the log so hard her teeth jarred together. Tears came to her eyes, as much born of frustration as pain, but she tossed her half-eaten rabbit into the fire and folded her dress over and over in her fingers until she'd won a measure of calm again. Outwardly, at least.

Ian sank back down and began to lick his paws. He seemed uncaring of her pain, or even her presence. When was the last time he'd taken human form?

When the rabbit carcass was bare, Jeremy wiped his hands and sighed. "Mayhap I should let him bite me. This is a better life than most people know."

Shelly looked at him sharply. She glanced at Ian's drooping eyelids, and then at Lil. Lil nodded. Her heart pounded in her throat with fear, but still, she had little choice. She had to try to reach Ian.

"Come along, Jeremy," Shelly said briskly. She kicked dirt over the fire. "We'll wait at the rock-face entrance, Lil. If you need anything, just yell." Jeremy's feet dragged as she led him off. Lil knew he was worried about leaving her alone with a werewolf.

Feeling only slightly reassured that help was close at hand, Lil stood. Slowly and carefully this time. "Ian, please, listen. Don't you understand? If you remain a wolf, Thomas plans to brutalize you into submission. If you try to find the cure, he'll attempt to kill you. We have to make plans. We have to be ready. I've solved part of the riddle of the curse, but—"

A snort came from the wolf. Ian's head lifted, and

331

amber eyes, glowing brighter than the dying embers of the fire, fixed on her.

Lil mastered her own trepidation and forced herself to hold out her hand toward him. "Please, Ian. You have to fight this, or you will become what you hate most!"

Perhaps it was the scent of her hand, hovering almost within biting distance of those sharp fangs. Perhaps it was the sight of her, silvery hair shining with a purity reflected in her face as she pleaded with him under the siren moon.

A siren for a siren . . .

But before she had time to react, before Jeremy, watching at a distance, could do more than raise his shotgun, Ian pounced on Lil.

Catching the back of her dress in his teeth, Ian dragged Lil with him into the darkness.

Chapter Fourteen

All the gruesome tales Lil had heard about werewolves, the horrid deaths of the other heiresses, her memories of Ian's savagery with Thomas, flashed through Lil's stunned mind as Ian dragged her off. Jeremy's roar of alarm, his bootsteps running after them but fading fast, at first made Lil's weak struggles to get away more desperate.

But she only scraped her elbows and legs against the grass, and the wolf only growled and dragged her faster. She stopped. Trying to run would anger him more. Following Shelly's advice and listening to her instincts, she forced herself to go limp.

Immediately, he released her. With a small growl and a shove of his nose into the small of her back, he forced her ahead of him up the rocky slope near the waterfall.

As her feet scrambled for purchase, she felt all the truths she'd taken for granted on equally slippery ground. It was as if the gentle but strong man she'd fallen in love with was lost forever inside the elemental power of the wolf. And she was partly to blame, for she'd driven him to embrace his destiny.

As she climbed the cliff face, Lil looked down at what remained of Ian Griffith. As she watched him bound up the slippery slope as if he were not limited by the normal physical realities of gravity and exhaustion, the most frightening truth of all came upon her.

Upon this moment, this night when an almost full moon scowled down on them, hung the balance of their lives. This creature, half man, half wolf, was, in a way, her own creation. Ian had let the wildness take him to save her from Thomas, and she'd repaid him by hurting him.

The heiress had called up the animal in the Wolf of Haskell Hall.

Only the heiress could win back the man.

And suddenly, clearly, gifted to her by instinct instead of insight, she knew what to do.

The cold spray in her face was a welcome shock of reality. Over the twin thunders of her heartbeat and the waterfall, Lil couldn't hear Jeremy and Shelly searching for her, as she knew they must be, but she wanted no witnesses to what was to come. She'd pushed Ian to his limits, hurt him so badly that he'd remained a wolf for almost a week. Whatever it took to win him back to her world, she'd risk it.

Resolved now, but no less afraid, she extended her

hands, balancing her weight against slick, smooth rock, wondering why he kept pushing her closer to the waterfall. Then she felt it. A gap in the stone. Blindly, she ducked behind the spray into what she realized was a cavern. She entered it, and darkness enveloped her, thick, smothering. She felt the wolf's presence behind her. He was so enormous his breath was hot on the back of her neck, so it was with relief that she knocked against something that clattered. It gave her an excuse to kneel. Her trembling fingers felt a lantern.

She lit it. She saw a stash of clothes, a few books, a trunk, dishes, food. This, then, was where Ian hid. But the fruit was old and dried, the clothes neatly folded and with the beginnings of mold growing in the folds.

These supplies hadn't been used recently. This further proof that Ian had forsaken both her and her world shook her to her half boots. With nothing left to distract her, she stood and faced him. And backed away a step before she could stop herself. How was it possible to love and fear, idolize and despise, all at the same time?

In the leaping shadows cast by the lantern, her demon took the worst face and form possible for any woman: that of her lover. Even as she watched, the wolf rendered itself down to the puny essence of the man. The rapidity of Ian's change astonished her. It was far faster than Thomas's and took no more than a few seconds.

One moment he snarled at her, lips back over his fangs, the ruff on his neck bristling with aggression.

The next, Ian stood there, lips curled equally grimly, beautiful male body glistening with spray in the lantern light, but that only accentuated muscles that were surely more defined than the last time she'd seen him thus. Worst of all was the look in those amber eyes. It was the same in both males—accusatory, pitiless.

"Which of us do you hate more, Delilah?" Ian asked, his voice husky with disuse. Holding her gaze, he started to change again, but she held her hands out pleadingly.

"Don't!"

Ian let the man take over again, but Lil sensed the effort of will it took for the wolf to allow the weakness. Lil rushed into speech, acutely aware that time was running out, for both of them. She had to make him understand that it was seeing his power unleashed that had made her afraid. "I could never hate you, or the wolf. Fear you? Yes. I am a Haskell. You are a Griffith. Can you blame me when you dragged me here against my will? How can I know your intent when I'm not sure you know it yourself?"

His nostrils flared, and then, in one spring, he was upon her. Ian had always been strong, but this man now was so much more than mortal. He had a power only a beast could unleash. He shoved her back against the cave wall, pressing his naked warmth into her. He was so warm, and she was so cold. For a forgotten moment, she remembered. How it had been, not how it was now . . .

His jaw flexing, he caught her wandering hands and held them above her head. "Do you not enjoy what you helped create?"

She should have been comforted that, even now, their thoughts were so similar, but hearing her words in his voice only made her pain more acute. "Yes, perhaps I romanticized the qualities of the wolf. But I also romanticized the qualities of the man. The man I"—her voice broke but she forced herself to go on— "cared for would never frighten me."

He inhaled sharply at her near-admission, and for a moment, his free hand ran down the supple curve of waist and hip, so beautifully delineated in the clinging dress. But then his hand fell away and his teeth showed as he snarled, "Cared for? Even now, you can't say it. You pointed a gun at me after I risked my life to save you!"

"I didn't mean to, you startled me, I acted on instinct. . . ." She trailed off, wishing she'd chosen some other excuse.

"What do your instincts tell you now, Delilah Haskell?"

The words were so soft and deadly that they made her shiver with more than the cold. Resentment looked at her from behind those pitiless amber eyes. And hunger. Hunger so ravenous that if he consumed her, limb by limb, right down to her beating heart, he still wouldn't be satiated.

But was it hunger for her body as food, or her body as pleasure? Lil closed her eyes, cringing away, still afraid of the answer.

With a guttural sound that could have been made by either wolf or man, Ian released her in disgust and turned his back. "Leave me. Go. While you still can."

Lil's eyes opened. Even from the back, he was

beautiful. His muscles had adjusted to the ways of the wolf, even if his mind had not. She wanted to touch him, to know him, to learn this new Ian Griffith all over again. But before she could take a step toward him, he whirled upon her.

"I brought you here to tell you my decision. I took this form because it frightens you less, but its weakness displeases me. It will be the last time you see it."

"No, Ian, please—"

"Don't beg. I once wanted you for my mate, but no longer. I need a mate to protect my back, not hide behind it. Go back to your soft bed and your safe world, Miss Haskell. It was always too small and confining for me, even when I was only a man. I will trouble you no more. The curse drew us together. And now the curse will separate us."

She saw the hairs lengthening on his body, and knew what fate he'd chosen. She wanted to cry out a warning, but there was no time, or breath in her, to plead. Again, with the power of her instincts instead of the rationality she'd always trusted, she knew she had only seconds to act. If the man left without her helping him recall the best of his humanity, the wolf would reign supreme.

Only one lure drew man and wolf equally.

Covering the small gap between them in two desperate bounds that made his eyes widen and his transformation stop, Lil flung herself against him. Linking her hands behind his neck, she pulled that strong head down to her level. The hairs receded, and in the shock of his stare, she saw Ian, not the wolf.

Right before she kissed him, she whispered, "Tell me if the wolf remembers this." The moment her lips felt the familiar warmth and hardness of his, the residue of fear left her. His height, his touch, the feel of unencumbered male skin, the soft hairs on his chest prickling the exposed vee of flesh in her dress, loosened by the way he'd dragged her here . . . these were powerful bonds that nothing could break.

Not the curse. Not her own fear. Not even the call of the wolf.

She felt his emotional tug-of-war tremble through him. Slowly, the seductive warmth and feel of the woman as mate, not food, pulled the man back from the brink of the wolf's lair. She felt the change in him, for he quit resisting and embraced her in return.

Exultation thrilled through her, blazing a trail for the hungry caress of his hands. Ian remembered, too. She sensed it in the sudden tenderness of his kiss, his reciprocal need for intimacy. An intimacy only humans could know.

The power of this feeling came not from the body, but from the heart.

Ian dragged his mouth away and nipped at the pulse in the side of her neck. "Yes, Temptress Delilah, even when I howl at the moon, I remember. And I regret. Why torment us both with the beauty of something past? This changes nothing—"

"It changes everything. Don't think, Ian. My thinking too much was what led us to this. Feel." Lil took his hand and brought it inside her half-open dress.

He stiffened. Breath left him in a sigh. This time, when he looked at her, she saw the best of Ian Griffith in those amber eyes. He could not touch her there without thinking of her as a woman, remembering himself as a man. The last of his resistance faded as his hand cupped her gently.

Whether it was she or he who led the way to the blankets spread in a corner, she could not say. She'd long since forgotten that outside, Jeremy searched for her. Forgotten that in two nights, Thomas had a plan that would spell supremacy for him and death to Ian. Forgotten, even, to be afraid.

The man who pressed her back on the blankets was her lover, her lover as remembrance of times past and hope for times yet to come. Eagerly, she helped him open the rest of her bodice, but when their torsos brushed together, they forgot themselves.

His fumbling hands desperate with hunger, Ian lifted her skirts and pulled down her drawers. She parted her legs for him, as eager to banish the darkness with the roaring fire of passion as he.

With two fingers, he tested her readiness. When he found her receptive, he positioned the proof of his maleness against the gate to her femininity. Lifting her hips, she met his downthrust, and the intimacy and stretching had never been so moving.

Emptiness, filled.

Loneliness, banished.

Fear, vanquished.

Deep within her, he paused, his eyes closed. Luxuriating, too, in this ultimate intimacy stronger even than the bond forged by the curse. For long seconds he stayed still, and the rush of blood through their veins, their heartbeats, their very lives themselves, joined into a oneness completed by this embrace.

But soon, aroused by the feel of him filling her so well, Lil couldn't remain still any longer. She lifted her head to watch their joining, undulating her hips.

His eyes opened. He looked down, too. With an explosive little gasp that transmitted itself from him to her and back, he lost himself in her. He pulled out and shoved deep, over and over in a syncopation surely more primitive, and more fulfilling, than ever before. Even then, the possession didn't satisfy him. Turning her around, he lifted her to her knees and filled her from behind.

The position was new for Lil, and at first the strangeness of it broke the spell. With his hands on her hips and his knees braced so he could shove more of his maleness into her, she sensed his need to dominate, to possess her, now and forever. Then he pressed her legs together between his own, and she felt his reaching as never before. One of his hands cupped a breast, and the other thumbed the dewy bud of her burgeoning fulfillment.

And then thought fell away to a maelstrom of light and darkness flickering behind her eyes. The earth rocked beneath her knees. The night died, and with it, the moon's power over her life, for this last, best instinct told her she'd won. No man could want her the way Ian wanted her, shoving into her with powerful strokes she felt at the very tip of her womb, and not care for her still, despite the wolf's lure.

The woman's lure was greater.

Gladly Lil surrendered herself to him, for if he dominated her, she, too, dominated him. And in her giving, she took the ultimate gift. With a last thrust that took them both home, he filled her with his manhood. With the spilling of his virility that mingled with her own feminine fulfillment, he found himself, and her, again.

Lil collapsed beneath him. He drooped against her back, but rolled quickly aside and drew her into his arms instead, using a clean towel to dab away the evidence of their union. Their heartbeats slowed gradually, but still their feet and legs remained entwined. Lil knew he didn't want to break contact any more than she did. Or to face the world and the challenge awaiting them.

He continued to caress her bosom. She tilted her head back on his shoulder and smiled her satisfaction at the look on his face. Even if they succeeded in breaking the curse, something of the wolf would always remain in him. Wolfish was the only description for his appreciative smile.

"You do have a way of making a man remember what he was fighting for," he teased.

"And you have a way of making a woman remember why she'll always have a fondness for wolves."

"Vixen."

"That's a female fox, I believe."

"And you are equally sly."

"No, but equally hungry." She nipped his shoulder. "Besides, it worked, didn't it? Tell me if the wolf can know a pleasure like that."

"Only with you for a mate."

Lil went very still, her hand resting upon the mat of hair on his chest. She felt the acceleration of his heartbeat, and sensed his urgent interest in her response. But she had her own question that must be answered. "Do you wish to remain a wolf, Ian, even if we can cure you?"

His stroking hand stopped. "There was a time when you claimed to want to be a wolf in another lifetime," he said. "It is not such a bad fate. Things are much simpler. No pretty lies wrapped up in smiles. No tiresome hypocrisy or gossip."

"No food but raw meat. No books to read. No doctors."

"Life is always a series of exchanges. In the wild. And in *civilization*." His intonation on that last word spoke loudly of his contempt.

The residual glow of their union faded back to the dull gray of choices. For such would be life without Ian. Unrelieved hues of gray, with no black or white, no hope or despair. Yet her alternative was equally dreary. How could she turn her back on this life she'd fought so hard for, abandon the legacy to uncaring male relatives? So she could run over the moors with Ian, and be subject to the rules of the wild instead of the rules of society? So many people depended upon her for their livelihoods, and she'd fought so hard to be master of her own destiny. How could she give it all up now and embrace the ailment that had taken the man she loved?

No. Far better to win back her lover. Then they could set their own rules. But her lengthy silence was apparently answer enough to Ian, for he stood. Stretching himself, his muscles flexing with grace and power in the lantern light, he moved to his clothes.

Lil sensed his indecision as he stared down, but finally, jerkily, as if he had to force himself, he shook off the worst of the mold and began to garb himself in the symbols of the world he'd so nearly forsworn. Lil went limp with relief. Then, energized, she leaped to her feet and straightened her clothes as best she could. Two buttons on her dress were hanging by a thread, but she pulled her chemise closed and tugged the ripped bodice over it as best she could.

When they were presentable, they faced one another. The scent of their union lingered on the air. His nostrils quivered, as if only that whiff gave him strength enough to do what humanity demanded. He held out his hand. "Come. I will go back to the estate with you. For tonight."

"And tomorrow?" Lil took his hand, feeling ambivalence surging through him as he blew out the lantern and led her to the cave entrance.

"Will have its own demands without our creating more. Leave it be, for now, Lil."

And they didn't discuss their plans again until they reached the campfire glowing before the fallen log. Shelly and Jeremy sat, shoulders brushing, heads together while they talked quietly, and neither of them looked overly concerned.

Shelly and Jeremy eyed them up and down, and then exchanged glances in grim agreement. "I told you he wouldn't hurt her," Shelly said to Jeremy.

Lil had to look away from Jeremy's disappointed stare, wondering if *harlot* was written on her forehead, but he only kicked dirt over the fire and led the way out of the clearing. Shelly, however, squeezed

344

Lil's shoulder in wordless understanding. Her steady gray eyes approved, and then, she, too, turned to leave. Ian hurried out as if he couldn't bear to look back.

At the rocky opening, Lil paused to glance over her shoulder. Things were indeed much simpler here. She hoped that, in a week or so, she and Ian could return and bless this little piece of Eden with the joy God gifted to men and women. In all its strange, tormenting complexity.

And if she had to resort to the tactics of the wild and fight tooth and claw, she'd find a way to convince Ian simpler was not necessarily better.

The next day, from dawn to dusk, Shelly and Lil huddled together, trying to solve the last clue on the Gypsy girl's headstone. Ian remained in his tower, secluded, refusing even to breakfast with Lil. She understood the battle raging within him, and knew it was a choice he had to make alone, but still she was hurt. And worried. He knew how to transform even in daylight. In seconds he could leap to the ground and . . .

"He won't desert you as long as Thomas is still a threat," Shelly said quietly as Lil stared out at the deceptively calm and quiet summer day. "Even this past week, as a wolf, he watched over you."

Lil's gaze snapped to her face. "How do you know that?"

"I found his tracks one day after I sensed his presence. In both forms, he loves you, Lil."

Despite the warmth of the room, Lil shivered. As she remembered the menace in that mass of muscle and mayhem, she doubted if such a creature could know the softer feelings of love. Dominance. Possessiveness. Loneliness. Even the way he took her spoke of the habits of the wolf. "He's asked me to be his mate, if he remains a wolf," said Lil.

"And your answer?"

"I've spent my entire life learning to make reasoned decisions. As have you. We are not silly, emotional, impulsive women, Shelly. How can I give up everything I've worked so hard for and live by instinct alone? Before I saw what the sickness did to Thomas and is about to do to Ian, I could romanticize it, but now I know that transforming force for what it is. Bestial. Seductive. It endows great power, but exacts a terrible price."

"What if that's the only way you'll win Ian? What if we fail tomorrow night? What if he chooses to remain a wolf?"

Lil closed her eyes, wrapping her arms around herself, but still she shivered. She couldn't supply the answer because she simply didn't know it. She loved him, yes, would follow him to the ends of the earth if she had to. But on two legs. Not four.

Sighing, Shelly turned back to the note sheets filled with criss-crossed writing.

But there was something Lil had to know, too. "And what if tomorrow doesn't cure you, Shelly? What will you do?"

Shelly tossed her pencil down. "Go back to my wandering, I should imagine. And hope to find a miracle in some forgotten corner of the earth."

"At least you still wish to be cured. But don't you want to go . . . home?"

Shelly gave a hollow laugh. "My family has always found me something of a wild woman. If they should discover that I am, indeed, exactly that . . . well, my father is such a stickler for propriety, I wouldn't put it past him to lock me up himself."

"And what about Jeremy?"

"He still doesn't know. And if I have to leave, I should prefer you don't tell him. Where I go, he cannot follow. He'd never leave you, anyway. I've been but a diversion for him. But I cannot regret it. Unlike most men, the little banty cock makes me laugh. I shall always remember him fondly. Now . . . back to the business at hand."

Lil accepted Shelly's change of subject, but she saw past her friend's show of calm. Despite Shelly's careless words, there was pain in those acute gray eyes. She'd miss Jeremy. And Jeremy's feelings for her were far deeper than she realized.

Lil wrote out the last line yet again. "For death I wait. An eye for an eye, a hate for a hate." And she shivered again, staring at the words, wondering if they would be the last puzzle she struggled with on this earth.

The most important day of Lil's life dawned cloudless and serene. As she dressed in a serviceable serge gown, she stared out the window, wishing for some of the weather's calm. She and Shelly had worked well into the night, but still, the missing puzzle piece eluded them. It was almost as if . . . the Gypsy girl had deliberately set in place all the answers they needed, save the most important one.

That one they had to find themselves. But how? How could hatred counteract the dark power driving Ian? That unholy urge only seemed to give the wolf more allure, at least where Thomas was concerned. He thrived on hatred.

Thomas. Lil's eyes narrowed. He knew the answer. Wasn't there some way to weasel it out of him by guile, if not by force? She should at least try. By his own admission, he didn't know how to change in the daylight. If she took Jeremy, she should be safe enough.

But if she took Jeremy, Thomas would never admit anything.

Still fighting between good sense and desperation, Lil traversed the long path to Ian's tower door. She knocked. Waited. And knocked again.

Finally his voice came, strained, hoarse. "Go away, Lil."

"Ian, we have to face this together. If you come out now, maybe tonight it won't be so bad."

"It's never been this bad. Especially by daylight. I can't answer for what I might do if you come in. Stay away!"

Dear heaven, was he about to transform again? She rapped harder on the door, and finally his voice came again, but if she hadn't known it was Ian who spoke, she wouldn't have recognized it. So quiet and desolate. A wolf's lament in a man's defeated intonation. "I am weary of fighting. I am weary of feeling. I'm even weary of thinking. I only want to . . . be. In whatever form God decides, for my fate is no longer in my hands. It's too late for us, Lil."

Tears sprang to Lil's eyes. It was as if the wolf had sapped all the energy and fire from the man. Like an incubus that beguiled with a beauty hideous beneath the allure. Despair almost took Lil, too, but she cleared her throat and said, "If you truly believe that, then all is lost." She waited, but silence prevailed on the other side. "I . . . have an errand to run. I'll see you tonight at the Druid ruins. Promise me you'll be there."

Still no answer. Trembling, she stared at that stubborn portal, and then she turned on her heel and tromped downstairs. Very well, if he was so determined to do this alone, then so would she. He'd left her no other choice. She was going to find the cure, whether he willed it or not.

He wanted a mate to protect his back, not hide behind him, didn't he?

Some hours later, when the rosy hue that presages dusk colored the sky, Safira ran downstairs, panic-stricken. "The mistress! She's gone! HELP!" And then she lost herself in the musical rhythm of her native tongue, heedless of the butler's shocked stare.

It wasn't until they fetched Jeremy from the stables that she finally calmed enough to say, "She said . . . she wished to take a nap. Rest . . . tonight. But when I went in to set her clothes out . . . noticed the lump in the bed was in the same position. I moved it, and . . ." She swallowed harshly, leaning back in the chair they'd pushed forward for her. "This is very bad. She has gone to *him*. The rich one who is so poor in spirit."

Jeremy bit off an oath more intelligible to the butler, but no less shocking. "That's canned it." Jeremy glared at a footman. "You there. Go to the village and fetch the sheriff and as many men as he can collect. Tell them to meet us at the Harbaugh estate."

Gentling his tone, he turned his gaze upon Safira. "Me dusky beauty, calm yourself. How long has she been gone?"

Safira mumbled something in Haitian, caught herself. "Three hours. At least."

Jeremy exchanged a grim glance with the butler. "Just in case the sheriff don't bother hisself, ye'd best arm what men can shoot and be ready to go with me in a trice." He went below stairs to fetch his weapons.

The housekeeper rang every bell in the mansion, and soon more servants crowded into the foyer. The butler clapped for silence and explained what had happened. A few of the men knew how to shoot, and they stepped forward readily. Even a few who didn't joined them, but several dour servants cast resentful glances up the stairs, toward the tower.

One grizzled footman who'd been a family retainer long enough to speak his mind folded his arms over his chest. "Why should we risk our lives chasing after a mistress who's so busy cleaning someone else's house she cannot look to her own?"

Several fervent "ayes" came from other quarters. There were more furtive glances toward the tower.

Emboldened, the footman added, "Let her baseborn

lover do the dirty work. He's more fit for it than any of us."

The butler scowled and opened his mouth, but a cool voice came from the front door. "The only disgrace upon the Haskell name comes from ungrateful wretches like you." Shelly strode inside, her eyes snapping with anger. "You wouldn't have a job if she hadn't risked her life to stay here. This is how you repay her?"

The footman glared at her. Jeremy came back upstairs, bristling with weapons, but he stopped, glancing at the combatants.

The butler moved between Shelly and the footman. "I can handle this, Miss Holmes." He looked back at the footman. "You, sir, are discharged. As for the rest of you, I cannot make you go to the aid of our mistress. She is a stranger, true, but one who has tried to deal more than fairly with all of us. The Hall has not been in such good shape in years. The mine has a new pump, the school your children attend has new desks and was recently painted. Myself, I believe that if Miss Haskell says the Harbaughs are somehow involved in these deaths, then they must be investigated. And since she has not returned after visiting them, it is our duty to look for her."

A couple of tentative cheers answered him, and then a more enthusiastic one that echoed to the rafters. There was a surge toward the door.

Protectively, Jeremy moved next to Shelly. He whispered, "Didn't know the stiff-rumped jackanapes had it in him, stab me if else."

Shelly gave him a wry glance. "I shall hope that won't be necessary. Come along."

In the tower, Ian heard the ringing bells, the raised voices. He tried to ignore the noise, to focus on fighting the need to burst free of this stifling room and this stifling life.

He sat, his back turned away from the darkened shutters, sweat dripping from every pore, and tried not to think about the damp earth beneath his paws, the swift rush of wind carrying the scents of freedom, even the joy of chasing down a rabbit. Only one thing kept him imprisoned in this room, only one image gave him strength to fight the madness that seemed his only sanity.

Lil. Arms upheld, lips sultry, legs spread to welcome him. Giving herself to him to show him what he'd be missing if he stayed a wolf. And if she hadn't done that, risked her safety and her dignity upon the hard cave floor, he knew that he wouldn't be having this battle now.

The lycanthropy would have won. If he could defeat this terrible sickness now, when the moon was at its zenith and temptation had never been greater, perhaps he could learn to live with the malady even if he couldn't conquer it. For Lil, he told himself over and over, the words a benediction that soothed him as much as a church's quiet sanctity. But with that thought came the next, a natural extension of his own love.

Did she love him? If she didn't, her sexual fascination with him went beyond fixation to obsession.

And yet, she wouldn't say the words. She was a proud woman, he tried to tell himself. Why should she admit she loved him when he talked of leaving her forever? Yet on the hope of her love teetered the fate of the Haskells and the Griffiths. Without it, they were both doomed.

Images flickered in his tormented brain, the man's love for the woman mixed up with the wolf's urge to secure territory and win his mate. The need to transform grew greater as the rosy glow outside the shutters began its twilight meandering to gray. Ian bit his own tongue, biting back the urge to scream for Lil, but the trickle of blood in his mouth tasted so sweet. . . .

The scream came despite his best efforts. He blinked sweat from his eyes, shocked at his own lack of control. And then a sound penetrated his concentration. It wasn't a scream, but a cheer from many different voices. Down below, in the gravel drive, his acute senses heard the clomp of feet.

Horses being saddled. Carriages creaking as they were encumbered with more weight than they were designed to take. It sounded as if every servant in the mansion had decided to go on an outing when the entire village knew the worst night to wander about was the night of the full moon.

Which meant . . . Ian surged to his feet and ran to the window. Taking a deep breath, he flung the shutter open. Shelly and Jeremy, in one carriage, led the Haskell servants down the drive toward the gate. And beneath the brassy sunset that was even now ceding to the night, Ian saw the glint of many weapons.

Truth hit him like a blow to the stomach. Lil. Lil had gone to Thomas to try to force the truth about the curse from him. Ian released his pent-up breath. With it went his resistance. Lifting his face to the moon rising with a death-mask grin over the horizon, Ian let the madness take him.

Lil awoke, groggy, afraid, and alone, on a fresh, new mattress that was wasted in this tiny hovel. Why was the feather bed covered with luxurious linens in stark contrast to the rusty, iron bedstead her wrists were tied to? Lil shoved back with her hips and was able to lever herself upright, looking around what appeared to be a deserted hunter's cabin.

One room. A cold, tiny hearth. A battered cupboard against one wall, which was filled with fresh delicacies like cream, and scones, and jam, and expensive brandy and French cheese, even a tin of caviar on ice. The oddity of the expensive victuals in this hut was not lost on her. As she watched, a rat ran across the floor, whiskers twitching, and bolted into a hole.

Lil wished she could bolt as easily. Why had she believed Preston harmless?

She took deep, calming breaths, and gradually, the buzzing in her ears quieted. She tried to collect her scattered wits. The last thing she remembered . . .

She'd arrived in full daylight at the Harbaugh estate, glad to see it filled with busy servants. The butler offered to take her cloak in the warm day, but Lil smiled and shook her head. "I've been rather chilled of late. Would you give his lordship my card?"

The butler bowed and ushered her into a sitting

area full of light. Keeping her back to the light so she'd have the advantage of seeing her enemy clearly while her own expression remained in shadow, Lil held her hand inside her cloak on her father's pistol. Her precautions seemed absurd while she was surrounded by the pomp and splendor of this country estate, but the power behind this show only made Ian's danger—and her own fear for him—worse.

If she was going to accuse one of the wealthiest men in the county of lycanthropy, she had to have proof. Proof that even the sheriff couldn't refute. Lil had stopped in the village on the way here and visited that worthy herself, hinting of interesting goings-on this evening at the Druid ruins.

If the sheriff came, and watched with his own eyes as Thomas transformed under the full moon, if she could somehow save Ian, then her own danger at this moment was little enough cost. All she had to do, Lil decided grimly, was bribe if possible, force if need be, the last clue from Thomas. Then she'd lure him to the ruins right around the time of sunset, and . . .

The door opened. Lil's breath left her lungs in a whoosh when she saw Preston instead of Thomas. She glanced hopefully past him, but there was no one with him but a servant carrying a tea tray. He positioned the tray before the settee and left without looking at her.

Preston came forward, his hands outstretched. "Miss Haskell! What an unexpected surprise. Welcome. Thomas is away for the day, but I hope you'll make do with my company instead. Tea?"

Of necessity, Lil had to take her hand out of her

pocket to accept his clasp, but she wasn't frightened of Preston. He was all bluff and very little boldness, unless backed up by his brother. Half brother, she corrected herself. She suffered his polite kiss on her cheek, and pulled her hands away as soon as she decently could. "I admit I'm disappointed. I was so looking forward to seeing him." No one had to teach her the rules of ruthless parlor games.

"One lump, or two?"

With extreme effort, she managed not to make a snide retort, but she couldn't avoid a calculating glance at his thick skull. Her fingers tightened around the pistol butt, but she only gritted her teeth in a smile. "Three, actually." Maybe that would help disguise the taste of the dismal stuff. One thing she would simply have to change if she remained in Cornwall. Tea time would offer a new civilized alternative: coffee.

Sniffing suspiciously, Lil hesitated. The tea looked and smelled normal. Thomas she might believe capable of drugging her in his own drawing room. Not Preston. Lil sipped twice, thinking that was all she could bear, and stood. She had a very good idea where Thomas was. Likely already on his way to the stones.

Before she could speculate on what that meant, she was overwhelmed by dizziness. Her eyes grew unfocused, and a roaring grew in her ears. She caught the edge of a table, but it tilted, and her world tipped on its axis. As she collapsed to the rug, Preston's face filled her field of vision.

Blinking rapidly, Lil tried to get up, but her limbs

wouldn't cooperate. She could only lie there and stare up at Preston's blatantly false concern. Soon she wouldn't have to look at him. For he seemed to be receding down a dim tunnel.

As he knelt over her, she was too weak even to cringe away as he took the pistol out of her cloak. Her last thought before unconsciousness seized her only added to the nausea caused by whatever foul potion Preston had served: He was more like Thomas than she'd realized. Right down to his detestable smile . . .

. . . which taunted her now. He entered the hut, dressed in country attire very different from the formal garb he'd worn—Lil glanced at the lowering sun—an hour or so ago. He had her pistol in his belt, and the object she'd intended to use to bribe Thomas rustled as he pulled it from his pocket.

Lil stared at the deed to the tiny parcel of land that the Harbaughs had been trying to purchase from the Haskells for almost fifty years. It bordered both properties, but was a straight path through the moors to the coastal road, instead of the circuitous route the Harbaughs' miners had to take to get their ores to the foundry on the coast.

Preston put the deed back in his pocket, patting it. "Thank you, Miss Haskell. Most kind of you."

"I haven't signed it yet. Nor shall I."

"Oh, you shall." Thomas entered, six feet of walking, talking arrogance. "In a few days, after we've gotten to know one another very well, you'll admit that we suit. In every way. Our lands adjoin. You have money. I have a title. You need respectability. I need a strong woman—one so much more interesting than these simpering misses."

Lil glanced at the supplies, but somehow, she knew he lied. He'd never be able to hide her so close to the stones when so many people knew that tonight the Griffith legacy would be written in the shadow of the monolith of their ancestors. He was lying. He wanted her dead.

But she played along. "You were setting up your little love nest, were you not? That's why you weren't home."

"Of course. I intended to fetch you myself, shortly before nightfall, but Preston so thoughtfully brought you here to save me the bother."

The two brothers shared a look of genuine affection. At least, on Preston's part. Obviously, he idolized his half brother. Thomas gave him an approving smile, and Preston all but rolled over for his belly to be rubbed.

Was he a werewolf, too? No, she didn't think so. But he was still very much under the sway of the leader of the pack.

Then those acquisitive black eyes turned in her direction. Lil felt his urge to dominate even before he took a step toward her. Instinctively, she began pulling at her bonds. Thomas came closer, closer.

She used her only weapon, one that had proved effective against him before. Her tongue. "Really, I thought better of you. A man of your wealth, breeding, and looks having to resort to force? How very . . . ignoble of you. Perhaps, with the right motivation, I might be swayed. Release me, and after we have a bite to eat—"

"Quite so. I'd rather have my bite first." Thomas began to remove his clothes as he talked. "The sooner you begin the change, the sooner you shall be fully mine."

And Lil realized, as he stripped so matter-of-factly, with no hint of seduction or lust, that she had miscalculated again.

Thomas Harbaugh knew how to change in daylight, too. He undressed not to ravish her as a man.

He undressed to ravish her as a wolf. And begin her sacrifice.

Chapter Fifteen

The moors had always called to Ian, even when he was halfway across the world. Now that he'd surrendered to their bleak grandeur, they bestowed upon him a measure of their elemental energy. He was invincible, immortal.

His bounds were so swift that he scarcely felt the giving warmth of his mother soil. The scenery was a blur, and he'd long since veered around the humans on the road. They were going in the wrong direction, anyway. His mate wasn't at that ugly place where humans dwelled in false splendor. Ian Griffith might be useful another time, but tonight, the wolf didn't need his human insecurities or weaknesses.

The Wolf of Haskell Hall knew who had taken her. And why.

The other.

Weaker he might be, but nevertheless, the human part of Ian enjoyed the moon glow with a fanciful admiration beyond the grasp of the wild. The wolf loped, but Ian watched, and wondered if this glorious sunset would be the last he'd ever see.

A crimson rim on the western horizon was the only relic of a dying day. Far too feeble to depose the pomp and splendor of the night's royal court. A midnight velvet cloak stretched to encompass the sky, its majesty deified by the full moon, which glowed like an orb topping the scepterlike tor Ian climbed. Below stretched the palace: the Druid ruins. The strongest wolf would rule it and all the moors, after this night.

Ian sat for a brief moment, his breath scarcely quickened by the long run, and surveyed his surroundings with all his acute senses. At first he saw no movement, heard nothing, even with all his heightened awareness channeled toward saving his mate.

Voices carried to him, taunting on the dancing wind.

An angry male voice, shouting. And then Lil! Afraid. There, behind the trees.

He scrambled down the slope toward the sounds. The man, caught in the wolf's hide, held his vow before him like a talisman. *Keep Lil safe, keep Lil safe. Make her love you. Make her love you.*

But as he burst through the trees and saw the tiny cottage, window glowing brighter as the last of the sunset faded, the wolf's primitive urges drowned out the pale human voice. *Protect. Kill the other. Take mate back to den. She will be your life mate when you possess her again.*

361

In a mass of sinew and synergy with the night, both aims became one as Ian ran through the thick growth toward the glowing window.

Some minutes earlier, inside the cottage, Lil had tried to compose herself. If Thomas intended to kill her, he would have done so by now, surely. He merely sat on his haunches, staring at her. Waiting. For what? He was fully a werewolf, had been for quite some time, yet he merely licked his paws, casting her an occasional possessive glance before returning to his ablutions. A few times he glanced out the window, looking at the rising moon, lips curling back in the canine version of a smirk, but then he continued his bath. It was as if he wanted to look his best for the biggest event of his life.

And the last event of Lil's . . . she knew it with those instincts that had been as important to her as logic of late. But she wouldn't go easily.

Pulling harder at her bonds, Lil cried to Preston, who calmly cut himself a hunk of cheese and bread, "Don't you fear for your immortal soul, to be his . . . familiar like this? How many people has he killed? At least he has the sickness. Whereas you—"

"Do it for enjoyment." Preston took a big bite of his sandwich. "And do Cornwall a favor by ridding it of more squalling brats suckling on Mother England's teat."

"You sicken me," Lil whispered, unable to watch him eat with such gusto despite their gruesome conversation.

His only response was to polish off the rest of his

sandwich. "Have to fortify myself, you know. If you have any sense, you'll eat, too. Your night will not be exactly . . . relaxing."

The last thing Lil wanted was food, but he'd have to untie her hands for her to eat. She nodded. "A piece of fruit, some cheese, and a glass of wine, please."

To her immense relief, he untied her when he brought her the food. She ignored the caviar he offered on toast, wondering if this was her last meal, and sipped absently. She watched the moon climb a bit higher. As it rose, Thomas grew more agitated.

He was pacing now, casting ever more frequent glances outside.

Draining the last of her wine, Lil looked outside, too. She'd never seen the moon so full and bright. So far, at least, there was no sign of an eclipse.

The sunset had passed minutes ago, but she'd heard no sounds indicating the sheriff, or anyone else, had arrived. So much for his belief in her honesty and passion. He certainly couldn't deny the existence of werewolves anymore, but Thomas Harbaugh a werewolf? Nonsense.

Thomas was beginning to quiver, ears pricked forward, listening intently, too. And Lil knew he wanted Ian to arrive almost as much as she did. Wolf or man. It didn't matter. Thomas wanted to subdue or kill both of them.

But it mattered to Lil. Very much. If Ian came as a wolf, would he be able to pull back from the madness this time? Yet if he came as a man, he'd have little hope against Thomas.

For the third time, Preston looked at his pocket

watch. He seemed uncommonly interested in the eclipse, too.

Lil gave Preston a dismissive glance. "Half brother or not, you're expendable, too, if you don't cower well enough. Why not let him make you a werewolf, too? Or are you too afraid?"

"Shut up, you little bitch!" Preston shouted, taking an angry step toward her.

Thomas glanced up.

"I'd be surprised if you even knew his plan," Lil continued in a contemptuous tone. "He doesn't trust you, that's apparent. I'm certain he's never told you what his mother said about the way to cure the Griffith malady."

Raising a clenched fist as he came, Preston hurried toward her.

Lil gave a little cry of alarm and scrambled off the bed.

Thomas growled a warning, and that was all it took.

Preston stopped, his fist dropping, and to Lil's vast relief, he channeled his anger into his retort. "Typical female, you think you're the answer for everything. As usual, you're wrong. Dead wrong."

Thomas gave a louder warning growl, glaring at his brother.

But this time, Preston ignored him, his cheeks red, his words hammering at Lil relentlessly. "You'll help end this power struggle, indeed, you stupid little ninny, but not as the heroine. You're the prize." When Lil paled and shook her head, backing away again, he gave a nasty little laugh. "Tonight, when the moon is fully blocked by the eclipse, Ian Griffith, as the last Griffith male, can choose his own fate. He can be fully a man again, or fully a werewolf, remaining so forever, subject to my brother's dominance."

Lil's heart pounded so hard she barely heard her own question. "And what is the deciding factor?"

"You. What a disappointment you are, Miss Haskell. Despite all your posturing, it's quite obvious you're as stupid as the other heiresses after all. Let me spell it out for you. Ian will feast on your heart during the eclipse and seal his fate, or—" Preston's head snapped to the side, blood gushing from his cut mouth, as Thomas's paw slapped him across the room.

His eyes rolling back in his head as he struck the wall, Preston sank, limp, to the floor.

Lil scarcely noticed, for the last clue fell into place so easily she was shocked she hadn't seen how well it fit before. "An eye for an eye, a hate for a hate," ran the last line.

The only force in the universe strong enough to counteract hatred? Love. Deep love. Selfless love. A depth of feeling Lil had not been able to muster before now. She was the last Haskell heiress; Ian was the last Griffith male. She'd quite logically been afraid to offer him even more control over her.

But logic offered no solace in this situation, for it was a choice, quite literally, of the heart. One way or another, from the day she set foot in Cornwall, Ian's destiny had been to consume her heart. And her destiny was to save them both by offering it to him.

As terrified as she was at the thought of facing Ian

as a werewolf again, of trying to prove her love for him even when he took such a fearsome form, for a moment, Lil was saddened at the pain that had led to such a curse. Simple. Grisly. And irrevocable. It must have seemed appropriate to the dying Gypsy girl, but Lil had sensed her presence, and wondered if her hatred kept her from finding peace in the next world, too.

Lil glanced outside. The moon was high, and a sliver of it was missing.

The eclipse had begun.

Thomas, too, looked outside. This time, when he glanced at her, his fangs showed. His waiting was over. He intended to drag her outside and toy with her, make her bleed, so the scent of her blood and fear would permeate the Druid stones by the time Ian came.

Praying Preston still had her pistol in his pocket, Lil leaped over the bed as Thomas bunched to spring. As she fumbled in Preston's jacket, Thomas stopped, nose lifted, to sniff the air. The ruff on his neck bristled. He growled and began to turn.

Too late. Something blocked the moon, something dark, and powerful, and angry, leaping through the window to knock him flat.

Ian! Lil was half relieved, half terrified that this time, he wouldn't be able to change back into a man, but she wasted no more time. She heard the two werewolves engage with savage growls, but Preston's left pocket was empty. *Please, oh, please.*

She went limp with relief when she felt the pistol in Preston's right pocket. By the time she turned, holding it at the ready, the battle had taken the huge combatants through the closed door, reducing it to splinters.

Lil ran out, but stopped abruptly, squinting. After the lantern light in the cabin, and with the growing darkness of the moon, an eighth of it missing now, she couldn't adjust to the darkness. But she stumbled over rocks and dead growth to follow the sounds.

She wondered if she'd have to shoot Thomas. Or herself . . . for if she thought Ian's lycanthropy was too strong, she'd die by her own hand before she'd let Ian eat her beating heart. Maybe then, at least, he'd survive.

"Is that love deep enough for you, Gypsy girl?" Lil whispered, casting a furious glance at the dark moors. Beneath the soft sigh of the wind, she might have heard sobs of someone else caught between life and death, good and evil. . . .

A half mile away, Shelly lashed the carriage horse to a gallop, her sensitive ears picking up the sounds of a vicious battle long before Jeremy heard a thing. She wished now she'd come straight here, but an hour or so ago, she'd been more concerned with Lil's safety than Ian's tormented soul.

She'd known immediately that the Harbaugh butler lied when he said Lil hadn't been there. As she and Jeremy had turned to leave, the sheriff had arrived.

When he, too, was told the Harbaughs were not at home, his eyes narrowed. Shelly didn't take time to debate with him the truth or falsehood of Lil's warnings about the dire goings-on likely this night, or that the Harbaughs would be intimately involved. Truth to tell, she wanted to get away and make it to the ruins long before the sheriff even thought to follow. He'd only get in the way.

But as she left, she heard Lil's butler conversing quietly with his Harbaugh counterpart and the sheriff. She smiled. If there was one person local law enforcement trusted to know the truth about the gentry in the area, it was their butlers. Shelly fervently hoped the Haskell retainer would convince the Harbaugh servant that he'd protected his vile masters long enough.

And she and Jeremy had driven off helter-skelter for the track that led to the ruins.

During the drive, it had been increasingly hard to ignore the moon's lure. Jeremy was frantic with fear for Lil, unaware of the sweat on Shelly's brow, or the fact that her eyes had learned to pierce the veil of night. She knew they must be glowing. . . .

But when she lashed the horse into a gallop, Jeremy clutched the sides of the carriage. "What ails ye, woman? On this rut, we're likely to kill ourselves long afore we can help Lil."

"If we don't arrive soon, it will be too late. Possibly for both Lil and Ian."

"Oh, ye can foretell the future now, too, ducky?"

Shelly hesitated. She hoped she'd find some clue to the cure for her own sickness, but if she didn't . . . Did she want Jeremy to know? Shelly, most unusually for her, couldn't answer that.

On the last straightaway that led to the ruins, Shelly said out of the side of her mouth, "I heard the fight, Jeremy. Two werewolves battle. For Lil." She felt his shock, but didn't have more time to explain. Down the slope, the Druid ruins shone white in the waning moonlight.

A shot rang out. And then a scream.

When Lil's eyes adjusted to the growing darkness, she almost wished they hadn't. The two dark, writhing figures, fighting in the clearing made by the ruins, were locked in mortal combat. The battle had separated them briefly, and Lil had tried a shot, but she was shaking so much it went wide. And then the two werewolves were locked in fierce combat again. Since Lil couldn't be sure of hitting Thomas without shooting Ian, the pistol in her hand only weighed her down with its false sense of security.

The huge granite monoliths glowed ghostly white, silent witnesses.

Lil swallowed, telling herself that Ian was too good and kind to let the madness take him to the point that he'd want to kill her. But this Ian frightened her, even more than the wolf at the ball. Reared up on his hind legs, silhouetted against the waning moon, tail whipping viciously, he snarled and bit at Thomas, who was weakening from blood loss.

Thomas had a piece of flesh missing from his shoulder. Claw marks gouged him in numerous seeping wounds. More torn flesh gaped from his neck and back.

Aside from a gash on his chest from the rake of Thomas's teeth, the Wolf of Haskell Hall was unmarked. A new dominant male was about to reign supreme.

As Lil watched, the pistol trembling in her hand, Ian slammed into Thomas with both paws, and Thomas tumbled, rolling in the grass, landing on his back. Ian leaped atop him, biting and snapping. Thomas yelped and howled, trying to bite back, but Ian's teeth were fastened in his neck, holding him still.

Lil heard footsteps run into the clearing. She looked over her shoulder at the familiar outlines of Shelly and Jeremy. They tried to pull her back, away from the fight.

She resisted. "No. One way or another, this ends, tonight. By my hand. Or Ian's."

Unable to do anything else to help them, Shelly stood a silent bulwark on one side of Lil, Jeremy on the other. The light was fading rapidly now. Lil glanced up. The moon was three-quarters covered, its glowing aura adding a peculiar radiance to the cosmological duel between moon and earth, burnishing good and evil down below.

Thomas weakly tried to throw Ian off, but Ian clamped down harder on Thomas's neck. Blood spurted into his vicious jaws, and when Thomas swiped at him with a paw, he shook Thomas like a dog's toy.

Thomas howled, clawing at Ian's back, scoring deep furrows that glistened even in the dim light. Ian bit harder.

Thomas's black eyes began to lose their glow. More feebly now, he struggled to get away, but blood spurted, and then gushed in a stream as Ian bit through the jugular. Thomas collapsed, his eyes closing.

The pistol sagged in Lil's hand. Ian had won. What now?

But Ian still wasn't satisfied. He slapped Thomas with a brutal paw and rolled him over. Then, his magnificent strength limned against the sliver of moon, he clawed and bit at Thomas's chest.

Gagging, Lil turned away, unable to watch. The sounds were bad enough. The crunch of bone, a squishy ooze as tissue was ripped open. And then feeding sounds.

Lil pressed her face into Shelly's strong shoulder, unable to watch Thomas meet the gory fate he'd wished upon Lil.

Even Jeremy turned away. Only Shelly watched.

And then darkness. Total eclipse. Complete. Frightening. Relieved only by those horrid sounds. Finally, they stopped.

Lil sensed movement. She shook with terror. This was worse, far worse, than the battle in the study. Lil knew it had to be done, that Ian was protecting her. Only when Thomas's heart was pierced would he die. And who better to kill him than the man he'd tried to destroy?

But it made Lil's own task no easier. Every logical sense she retained urged her to run. This beast she couldn't see was so vicious that surely he was lost to any humanity or finer feelings she might once have inspired in him. The thing that remained was roused by blood, and his final prey was close and defenseless. She was a Haskell. He was a Griffith.

But something deep inside Lil, where not even logic or reason could touch, made her pull away from

Shelly's protective clutch. She glanced up at the moon. A faint rim of light was already breaking through in one corner. The peak of the eclipse was almost over.

If Preston had spoken true, Lil knew she had only seconds left to act. Lil moved away from Shelly and Jeremy, her pistol lax at her side, and took two steps forward. Toward the dark energy hovering only ten feet away. Toward destiny.

She sensed that Ian, too, waited to see what she'd do. Run? Scream? Beg? Or trust him. Love him. Even when he was in such a terrifying form.

In one leap he could knock her down and tear into her chest. Lil quelled her vivid terrors, shutting off her insistent mind and letting her instincts rule. In the ancient way, the best way, the only way God, man, or even Gypsy wronged had ever found to cure hatred and evil.

Letting the pistol drop from her hand, Lil moved forward another step, hearing Jeremy's bit-off curse, and Shelly's soft command to him to wait.

Still Ian didn't move. She saw him only by the twin spots of living amber fire glowing in the darkness. She smelled blood on him, and the acrid scent of dogs after fighting, but she was thankful for the eclipse. At least she didn't have to see what she was about to embrace.

With a last step, Lil reached out, gambling all she was on what she wanted to become. Just as the curse foretold, this werewolf would have her heart this night. "Ian, please. Hear me out. And then, if you

372

want to kill me, well, perhaps that was my destiny all along."

She sensed that he stood and padded closer. She felt the heat of his body now. Those twin glowing amber eyes were so close, on a level with hers because he was so large; she knew she would touch him if she reached out again. "My fate is your fate. We can both fulfill the curse this night with my death and your eternal damnation. Or we can end it here. Now. With the one thing your ancestor wanted most and never got."

Lil's trembling fingertips touched the ruff on his spine. The fur was warm, but slick, and she knew she touched blood. She bit her lip over the urge to back away, but it was too late. Either she reached Ian's heart and mind, lurking still inside the wolf, or . . . Lil ran her hand over the strong neck, her voice tight with tears. "I love you, Ian. I have for days, weeks, but I was afraid to tell you and give you more power over me. I'm proud, too. I admit it. But I believe in you. Even after seeing you eat another's heart, I believe that the man I love, the artist, the lover, the man who risked his life for me, is stronger than the wolf. If you believe it, too, the moon will have no more power over you. Please, darling. Hold me in your arms. Change one last time. For me. For us. Forever."

Lil continued to stroke him gently. She felt him tremble, and fear gripped her. Was he about to bite her hand? Her touch knew the truth before her eyes. She felt the change. Lush hair began to shorten, the spine to move upright, broad shoulders form.

And then her reward. Warm male flesh touched her,

tempted her, instead of fur. Lil's knees weakened, and she would have fallen if he hadn't caught her in a passionate embrace. A man's embrace.

Then he was holding her, kissing her cheeks, her eyes, babbling little love words meant only for her. "Lil, Lil, I feared I drove you away . . . never lose you . . . keep you with me . . . den or tower . . . four feet or two . . . couldn't kill you. I killed him to protect you. Nothing hurt you. Ever. Wolf or man, I mate for life." He ended on her lips.

As the eclipse faded and the moon began to peek again at the changes wrought when it was helpless, Eros held sway instead of Diana. Sheathing her arrows, Diana faded away into the heavens, leaving a growing, glowing orb that could have been green cheese for all the heed Ian gave it.

Jeremy shook his head as he stared at the naked man embracing his charge. Ian was still covered in blood. It smeared Lil's clothes and hands, even her face. But she was oblivious, lost in his embrace, until they broke the kiss, gasping for breath.

The eclipse faded more, and the moon grew brighter above their heads. Ian Griffith smiled down at his employer, but there was nothing subservient about him. With the wolf's possessiveness, he promised to make her glad she'd chosen him. But his amber eyes were still alight.

From within.

With love.

Lil buried her cheek against his chest, listening to the strong thump against her ear, wondering if she'd ever hear anything else as wonderful. And then, carried on the breeze of forgetfulness and forgiveness, Lil fancied she heard the soft crying stop.

Lil lifted her head and looked across the moors. Perhaps that was a swath of black hair flipping over proud shoulders, the ghostly image rising as Lil watched, to join the heavens she'd cursed. A release gifted to her by the descendant of the bloodline she hated. That, too, had a continuity and justice that pleased Lil. Cornwall, finally, felt like home.

"What are you looking at, darling?" Ian asked her, turning to follow the direction of her gaze.

"Nothing. We made our own fates, Ian. That's why we were both strong enough. We'll continue to make them, every day of our lives, and our children will know nothing of curses or evil, or fear." Lil pulled his head back down to her level and sealed her vow with a kiss.

Shelly sniffed and fumbled for a handkerchief.

Jeremy glared at her. "Ducky, if ye become a watering pot, I'll enter a monastery fore I'll see ye become as silly and sentimental as other females."

"Jeremy, stop your yammering. Do you think I'm blind?" She handed him her kerchief.

With another glare, Jeremy wiped his own tears away.

Shelly turned her back on the moon and went toward the glowing cottage. "Now come along. We've another Harbaugh to account for and take to the sheriff." She and Jeremy dragged a dazed, grieving Preston out of the cottage, tying him securely to the carriage. "Bribe your way out of kidnapping and attempted murder, Preston," Shelly said sweetly.

Preston stared at the two figures still embracing against the backdrop of the moon. His face twisted at the bloody remains of his brother on the ground, and his shoulders shook with silent tears. Then he turned away as if he couldn't bear to look any longer, and Jeremy and Shelly gave the two lovers privacy.

The standing stones were the only remaining witnesses to the death of the Wolf of Haskell Hall. But they saw only a man holding a woman.

Above, the moon was merely a satellite of the earth.

A month later, the new master and mistress of Haskell Hall met their retainers in the foyer. Lil handed out gifts for all, purchased on her honeymoon trip to Italy. Ian passed out cigars.

As she took her present, Safira hugged her mistress. When she pulled away, her hands brushed against Lil's abdomen. She nodded reassuringly and shared a secret smile with Lil. *She's a strong girl. She'll be the best of Griffith and Haskell.*

Safira and Lil both looked at Ian, conversing quietly with the butler about Italian politics. He looked no different from the estate manager Lil had met when she first arrived at Haskell Hall.

He'd refused, as he told Lil, to change his attire along with his marital status. He liked the way he dressed, rich or poor, and that was that. Secretly, Lil had been glad to see that something of the wolf remained in Ian, after all. Ian caught her glance, nodded at the butler, and returned to his wife's side.

"Are you feeling well, darling?"

"I'm fine, Ian."

Safira looked from Lil's trim waist to Ian's protective clasp around his wife's shoulders. "You'll both need me, in about eight months' time. I will return. When winter is over." She shuddered distastefully at the growing nip in the air.

Scowling, Jeremy took her bags to the portico. Safira nodded her turbaned head regally at the servants and followed.

The servants returned to their duties, and Lil turned toward the study. The door was still closed, and it was very quiet inside. As she and Ian exchanged a concerned glance, the door opened.

The vicar ushered his cousin outside with his usual courtesy, but he was pale, his pale blue eyes dull with concern as he watched Shelly.

She, however, was resolute. She glanced at her bodice watch and picked up one of her bags waiting in the hallway. "Jeremy will be even more furious if I don't get on with it. We'll never make it to the train station by morning if we don't leave now."

"You will send me your new address when you've rented a flat in London, correct, Shelly?" the vicar insisted.

"Certainly." But she didn't meet his eyes. Shelly walked toward Lil, her hands outstretched. "You will let me know about the baby, yes? Then, for all time, the curse will truly be broken."

"Of course. And you, Shelly?" Lil whispered in her ear as she hugged her former stable manager. "What will you do?"

"Seek. Read. Learn." Shelly glanced around, but

she, Ian, the vicar, and Lil were alone in the foyer. Shelly looked back at her friends and said solemnly, "It's not such a difficult trick, you know. The instincts of the wolf are actually far less brutal than the instincts of humankind. I long ago learned to control my baser impulses. I actually find this shape quite malleable, forming and disappearing at my will. In short, I control it. It doesn't control me. It is not so different, after all. I have always been alone." But her gray eyes turned sad as Jeremy stomped inside and glared at her, holding the door wide.

Daring her. He wasn't happy with her for leaving.

"Did you ever tell him?" Lil asked quietly as she walked Shelly to the door.

"No. Since I'm leaving . . . no. It's best this way."

Waving, the vicar climbed aboard his own carriage and clucked to his horse, rattling down the drive, but not before Lil saw him cast a last worried glance at his cousin.

Lil watched Jeremy help Shelly into the carriage. Still in high dudgeon, he avoided Shelly's pleading glance and snapped the door closed. He mounted the seat. "I'll be back in a few days, mistress." Jeremy lifted the reins, but waited for Lil's final leave-taking.

Lil leaned through the open window to take Shelly's hand. "I'll miss you. Please, write often. And if I find anything myself, well . . . send us your address."

Shelly nodded. She glanced at Ian. "Take good care of her, Ian. You're a very lucky man."

Ian pulled Lil under his arm. "I know. And I wish the same luck for you." They stepped back.

378

The carriage pulled away, but the last picture Lil had of her indomitable friend was the doubt in Shelly's face. She didn't believe much in the power of luck.

As they watched the carriage rattle through the gates, Ian pulled Lil closer. He kissed her tears away. "Don't mourn for her, darling. If any person on this earth can turn something so horrible into something useful, it's Shelly Holmes."

Lil wiped her tears away. Her green eyes grew slumberous and smoky as she looked at her husband, still indomitably powerful with only two legs, instead of four. And equally virile. "And what if I miss my wolf?"

Ian glanced around. They were alone in the drive, with a full moon rising. "Would you like a midnight feast at our secret place? I am a bit . . . ravenous. I'll prove I still know how to howl at the moon. I might even teach you before I'm done. And we'll see if we can't shock the county even more than we have already."

Arm in arm, the master and mistress of Haskell Hall went in to tell cook to prepare a basket.

Above the estate, the moon cast its silvery glow.

And in the carriage turning onto the London road, Shelly Holmes's eyes glowed in return.

Enter a tumultuous world of thrilling sensuality and chilling terror, where nothing is as it seems, and dreams and nightmares blend into heart-pounding encounters too enticing to be denied, too frightening to be forgotten. In our new line of gothics the most exciting writers of romance fiction explore dark secrets, forbidden desires, the hidden part of the psyche that is revealed only at the midnight hour by . . .

Candleglow

Coming in March . . .

The Scarletti Curse

by Christine Feehan

Strange, twisted carvings and hideous gargoyles adorned the *palazzo* of the great Scarletti family. But a still more fearful secret lurked within its storm-tossed turrets. For every bride who entered its forbidding walls seemed doomed to leave in a casket. Chosen by her feudal lord, Nicoletta knew she must accept her fate as Don Scarletti's bride-to-be. The only question was whether he would be her heart's destiny or her soul's demise . . . .

Available March 2001   0-505-52421-X

THE
SCARLETTI
CURSE

CHRISTINE
FEEHAN

There was complete silence in the room. A cold draft seemed to come out of the very walls and swirl around Nicoletta so that she shivered. Deep within her heart, she heard her own cry of unspoken protest. There was evil walking in the *palazzo*. She stared up at Don Scarletti, her gaze locked with his. Fierce. Intense. Soul to soul. She couldn't even feel the hand of her companion, Maria Pia, in hers. She and the don were the only two people in existence. He was watching her closely, his mind in hers. She *felt* him there. He was waiting in silence for her to condemn him.

Unbidden came the image of his scraped knuckles, the small, incriminating droplet of blood on his otherwise immaculate clothing. Nicoletta felt her heart pound. His gaze continued to bore straight into hers, and she couldn't turn away from him. She knew he was waiting for it, knew he expected her to denounce him. Don Scarletti, *Il Demonio* of the *palazzo*. The curse. The whispers. The rumors. Still Giovanni Scarletti stood tall and straight, his black eyes fathomless, his features carefully expressionless.

Nicoletta took a breath and let it out slowly. "Will you send your men to search the maze for Cristano? It is possible he wandered in and could not find his way out."

Was that what had happened to her former suitor?

The don bowed slightly. "At once, *piccola*. And I will send them into the hills to see if the young man was injured on his way home." He said the words deliberately to remind her of the numerous times others had set out traveling and fallen victim to wild animals, the harsh terrain, or even to robbers. But his voice sounded incredibly gentle, and a warmth brushed at the walls of her mind, so that she felt almost comforted.

Nicoletta swallowed the hard knot in her throat. It was difficult to think straight with the don watching her so intently. She could sense Maria Pia's gaze on him now, accusing.

"Don Scarletti, you were the last person to see Cristano alive." Maria Pia said what Nicoletta would not. Her very tone was a declaration of his guilt.

"We do not know that he is dead, Dona Sigmora," Giovanni pointed out softly. His voice held a thread of menace, as if his patience were fast wearing thin. "If the young man met his demise in the maze, the scavengers would be present overhead."

Relief swept through Nicoletta. "That is true, Maria

Pia," she said. But a terrible dread was slowly creeping into her mind and heart and soul like a dark shadow. She would know if someone was hurt, wouldn't she? Surely she would know.

Maria Pia faced the don bravely. "The wedding should be postponed until the young man is found," she challenged. *If you are exonerated.* The words were left unsaid, but they shimmered there in the room, as vivid and alive as if Maria Pia had uttered them aloud in condemnation.

The black eyes gleamed ominously. "Nothing will stop the wedding, Dona Sigmora. Not you, not this rebellious young man. For all I know, he disappeared with every intention of bringing a halt to the wedding plans. We are to be married on the morrow." It was a decree, Giovanni's dark features an implacable mask.

For a moment Maria Pia looked mutinous, but the don's words seemed to sink in. She knew Cristano well. He had a shocking temper and, if humiliated, could sulk for days. He was quite capable of disappearing and causing alarm to get back at Nicoletta for not marrying him as he had demanded. Maria Pia looked at her young charge. She had the feeling Nicoletta was in terrible danger, and she wanted desperately to drag her from the *palazzo*. "It is possible I am worrying over nothing," she said softly, looking at the floor in defeat. Her fear for Nicoletta had caused her to rashly condemn the don. But Giovanni Scarletti was not going to give up her beloved Nicoletta; she could see that in his masculine aggressiveness, his possessive posture each time he was near the young woman.

Giovanni reached out to capture Nicoletta's hand, taking it right out of Maria Pia's firm clasp. He carried her fingers to the warmth of his mouth. It was a blatant gesture, claiming her, branding her as his own.

His black gaze was locked on hers so that Nicoletta had a strange feeling of falling forward, to be trapped for all eternity in the depths of his eyes. Time stood still. Her heart beat for him. She felt the rush of blood, of heat, of liquid fire.

Don Scarletti released her reluctantly, his touch lingering for a moment before he glided away. "I have kept my visitor waiting far too long, and I must arrange for my men to begin the search for your young friend."

Nicoletta stood dazed, as if in a trance, staring at the closed door after the don left the room.

Maria Pia sighed heavily. "Do you believe him, Nicoletta? Really believe him? Because I am not certain I do. It is possible Cristano is hiding out in the hills. When he was a boy and angry with his *madre,* he did such things. Or it is possible he is hurt and needs help." She was watching Nicoletta closely as she spoke.

Nicoletta's teeth teased nervously at her lower lip. She should know if there was someone in need, and Maria Pia was well aware of it. Nicoletta had always known. And the bird would come to her. She looked at the older woman. "I must go outside, where I can feel the wind on my face. I want to look at the sky."

"What do you have in your hair?" Maria Pia

reached around her and picked strands of a spider's web from her long tresses.

"Something is wrong here, *piccola*. When I am in this house I feel the echo of your *madre*'s screams as she was thrown over the balcony to her destruction. I can feel the spirits of the dead. They are uneasy in this *palazzo*." She made the sign of the cross and kissed her crucifix. "May the good Madonna save you from your enemies."

Nicoletta did not protest. She knew she had enemies at the *palazzo;* she just didn't know why. She felt eyes staring at her in disapproval each time she left her bedchamber. "I must go outside," she said again. Her heart felt heavy in her chest. She opened the door, turning back toward Maria Pia as she did so. "How did all of this start, so long ago? When did they first start to whisper of the curse on the Scarletti *famiglia?* Is it possible there's a strain of madness in the Scarletti blood?"

Maria Pia glanced past Nicoletta to the waiting guards. "It is not a good thing to speak of in this place where the walls have eyes and ears." She lifted her chin. "Come, let us go out to the courtyard. We will see if the don kept his word and sent his men looking for Cristano."

"I can imagine many things about Don Scarletti, but he lives by his word. He would not tell me one thing and do another," she said, to her own surprise defending him.

Maria Pia looked at her sharply. "It is possible you are already falling under his spell. I told you to be careful. He can make you say things you do not wish

387

to reveal. You must be strong, Nicoletta. Until you know more of the don . . ."

"The man who is to be my husband," Nicoletta whispered. "We are to be wed on the morrow. I will live with him, and this *palazzo* will be my home. I have no choice in the matter. You said even the Holy Father would not go against him."

Maria Pia twisted her hands together as they moved down the long corridor to the stairs. She leaned on the banister and uttered a soft cry, once more crossing herself devoutly. "Look at this, Nicoletta! The artwork on his stairs. A serpent coiled around a tree branch! What manner of man is he?"

"He inherited the *palazzo* and the title from his *padre*. What should he have done? Refused to live in it because he did not like the artwork on the stairs? It is beautiful, Maria Pia. If you look at some of the work, it is truly remarkable."

Maria Pia resorted to clucking as she often did when she was agitated. "He has cast a spell over you, *bambina.*"

Nicoletta glanced over her shoulder at the silent guards following them at a circumspect distance. "Where is little Sophie?" The don's niece, who had doted on Nicoletta since she came to the palazzo to help heal her, would be upset that her beloved mentor had been trapped in the palazzo's maze of secret passageways while looking for her.

"The child was sent to her room, *signorina*," one guard replied instantly.

Nicoletta looked at Maria Pia. "Come along with me. I must go to Sophie. She will be so frightened.

By now she will think *il fantasma* has gotten me."

As they started back up the stairs, the guard shook his head. "The child was removed from the nursery and is on the first floor."

Nicoletta smiled at him. "Thank you." She knew the exact hideous room the child had been banished to. She ran along the corridor toward the chamber, Maria Pia trailing behind and waiting outside the door.

Sophie lay facedown crying on the big bed, so small she could barely be seen among the covers. Nicoletta rushed to her and pulled her into her arms, rocking her while the child sobbed as if her heart were breaking.

"I thought I killed you!" The child hiccupped the words, her tears soaking Nicoletta's neck. "I am sorry, Nicoletta."

"Bambina." Nicoletta hugged her even closer. "You did not do anything so wrong."

Sophie lifted her head, looking forlorn. *"Zio* Giovanni told me never to go into the passage. He said it was dangerous. Now I have to stay in this scary room forever. I have to be punished." She wailed the last dramatically and looked as pathetic as possible.

Nicoletta laughed softly. "Maria Pia shall stay with you, and I will go talk to your *zio*. Perhaps he will think you have been punished enough. But you must heed his warnings. I do not think *i fantasmi* guard the passageways, but you could get lost in there and endanger your life. You must promise me you will never go in there again."

Sophie nodded vigorously, willing to promise Nicoletta anything at all.

"Dry your tears, *bambina*. I will get you out of your prison." She ruffled the child's hair and beckoned Maria Pia into the room to comfort Sophie while she was gone.

Nicoletta hurried back along the hall, but outside the don's study she hesitated, her courage suddenly faltering. She was interrupting his work, intruding on his time. She was all at once unsure of herself. Don Scarletti had been kind to her, but he had a certain reputation, and, a very powerful man, he had probably earned that reputation many times over. She bit her lip in an agony of indecision. He and his important visitor had already been interrupted once so he could rescue her from the secret passageway.

She glanced over her shoulder at the guards, then rapped on the door quickly before she completely lost her nerve.

Giovanni opened the door to find a very nervous Nicoletta gazing up at him. He wrapped one large palm around the nape of her neck as he moved out into the corridor, closing the door to his study behind him, obviously affording his visitor privacy. His thumb tipped her face up to his. "Once again I find you without your companion, *cara mia*. How is it you manage to elude Maria Pia so often? She looks quite capable to me."

That faint betraying shiver began again, from deep within her. Helplessly she glanced at the guards. They were no help, moving away to give the don privacy in dealing with his errant bride-to-be. Giovanni urged her closer to the hard strength of his body. "What is so urgent, *piccola,* that you would dare *il demonio* in his lair?" His thumb was now feathering along the delicate line of her jaw, lingering over her frantically beating pulse.

Her dark eyes were enormous as she looked up at him. "I do not think of you as *il demonio,*" she denied.

He quirked an elegant eyebrow at her. "Is that so?"

"I might have before I met you," she conceded reluctantly, unfailingly truthful.

His black eyes gleamed at her, a wicked amusement dancing in their depths. "I may have become one since I met you," he answered her suggestively.

She frowned at him. "I think you like to scare me with your wickedness, Don Scarletti, but in truth, I am not so easily frightened." It was almost the truth. No one else seemed to frighten her in quite the way he managed. He looked so implacable. Dare she argue with him? "I . . . I have a need to speak with you . . . about your order to have your men taste my food and drink. I would not wish anyone to be inadvertently ill on my account," she said haltingly.

Giovanni shook his head gravely. "I will not rescind my order, *cara mia*, not even to please you. But you already knew that. I suspect you had another reason to seek me out."

He was watching her with such intensity, she wasn't certain she would be able to think straight much longer. "I . . . I would like to take young Sophie with me outside into the courtyard. She is very sorry for her disobedience, and I have lectured her on the danger of the passageway."

He stared down at her for so long, Nicoletta thought she might melt. She was mesmerized by the hot intensity in his black gaze. She was very aware of his powerful body so close to hers; she could feel the heat of his skin. There seemed to be a current arcing between them like a lightning bolt, sizzling and dancing so that her skin became sensitive and ached with an odd, unfamiliar need. His gaze dropped to her mouth, and her knees went weak. Butterfly wings brushed at her stomach, and heat pooled deep within her.

Then suddenly, his mouth fastened to hers, hot and exciting, sweeping her away. It was a dark promise, erotic and sensual, his tongue demanding rather than asking for her response. She melted into him, boneless and pliant, her body molding to his, so that she felt his fierce arousal. Instead of pulling away as she should have, Nicoletta reveled in her power, wanting more, suddenly craving his dark secrets, aching with a need so strong she burned with it. Liquid fire. Molten heat.

Her breasts swelled with need, pushing into the heavy muscles of his body, straining for his touch. The thin material of her blouse seemed all at once too much of a barrier between them. Her mind was suddenly filled with sensual images—her hands on his skin, his palm cupping her breast, his mouth blazing fire along her throat, lower, across bare skin to close, hot and moist, over her aching breast. She wanted him more than she had ever wanted anything in her life.

Giovanni lifted his head, his hand still curled around the nape of her neck, her body resting against his. "I need you, Nicoletta." His voice was husky and sensual. "*Dio,* I do not think I can wait one more night. Go take the child into the courtyard, and do not get into any more trouble. Keep Donna Sigmora with you at all times. She is your only protection from me."

She could feel his strong body trembling with the effort to allow her to go. A good girl would have been appalled at his conduct, shocked and horrified at her own conduct, but Nicoletta suspected she wasn't as good as Maria Pia would have liked. She wanted the don's hands on her body. And she knew he wanted her. She made him nearly as weak with wanting as he made her. She gazed up at him, trying desperately to find a way to breathe.

He groaned softly. "You cannot do that, *piccola.* You cannot look at me with such need in your eyes." He kissed the top of her silky hair. "I am not to be trusted. . . ."

Dark Gold
CHRISTINE FEEHAN

*They were masters of the darkness, searching through
eternity for a mistress of the light . . .*

Alexandria Houton will sacrifice anything—even her life—to
protect her orphaned little brother. But when both encounter an
unspeakable evil in the swirling San Francisco mists, Alex can
only cry to heaven for their deliverance . . . And out of the
darkness swoops Aidan Savage, a golden being more powerful,
more mysterious, than any other creature of the night. The
ageless Carpathian male snatches them from a hideous fate.
But is Aidan Alex's salvation . . . or her sin? If she surrenders
to Aidan's savage, unearthly seduction—gives him the color,
the light, the family he craves—will Alex truly save her
brother? Or sacrifice more than her life?

___52375-2 $4.99 US/$5.99 CAN

Dorchester Publishing Co., Inc.
P.O. Box 6640
Wayne, PA 19087-8640

Please add $1.75 for shipping and handling for the first book and
$.50 for each book thereafter. NY, NYC, and PA residents,
please add appropriate sales tax. No cash, stamps, or C.O.D.s. All
orders shipped within 6 weeks via postal service book rate.
Canadian orders require $2.00 extra postage and must be paid in
U.S. dollars through a U.S. banking facility.

Name_____
Address_____
City_____State_____Zip_____
I have enclosed $_____ in payment for the checked book(s).
Payment <u>must</u> accompany all orders. ❏ Please send a free catalog.

DARK DESIRE

CHRISTINE FEEHAN

The stranger silently summons her from across the continents, across the seas. He whispers of eternal torment, of endless hunger…of dark, dangerous desires. And somehow American surgeon Shea O'Halloran can feel his anguish, sense his haunting aloneness, and she aches to heal him, to heal herself. Drawn to the far Carpathian mountains, Shea finds a ravaged, raging man, a being like no other. And her soul trembles. For in his burning eyes, his icy heart, she recognizes the beloved stranger who's already become part of her. This imperious Carpathian male compels Shea to his side. But is she to be his healer…or his prey? His victim…or his mate? Is he luring her into madness…or will his dark desire make her whole?

___52354-X $4.99 US/$5.99 CAN

The Steadfast Heart

Colleen Shannon

Though it has been nearly ten years since Vincent Anthony Kimball's first and only love, Chantal, disappeared from his life, memories of her sweet face still haunt him. Then he sees her at the ballet, and is engulfed by waves of need and longing. But is she really his long-lost Chantal, or the prima ballerina Papillone? Whatever the case, Vince knows that, like the brave tin soldier of the fairy tale, he will do anything to return his true love to him, give anything to unite their hearts as one.

___52271-3 $5.99 US/$6.99 CAN

Heaven's Hero

Colleen Shannon

At the turn of the century, anything can happen....

Once upon a time former cop Nick Escavido believed in heaven and heroes. Until he lost his job, his wife, and his self respect by doing the right thing with the wrong people. Then a magic mirror and a whirlwind journey through time lands him in a bygone age . . . at the feet of the most dangerously alluring female he's ever met. Lady Isabella Catherine Giovanni dresses like a man, but he soon learns she acts every bit a woman. And as she holds his heart at sword point he discovers that at the dawn of a new age, miracles do happen. To those who believe. To those who dare to be heaven's hero.

___52373-6 $5.99 US/$6.99 CAN

HEAVEN'S ROGUE
COLLEEN SHANNON

His is timeless perfection, molded by a genius. He stands magnificently tensed for action, noble, confident, and invincible. His firm hips cradle superior masculinity. His body reflects the heroic ideal of an age; once every thousand years such a flawless man exists. And Honoria Psyche Fitzhugh recognizes in him the soulmate she'd always pined for and the champion she sorely needs. Too bad he is a stone-cold statue… a statue on which Honor has staked her career as a museum curator. But when the white marble turns to warm flesh under her fingertips, Honor knows she will risk more than her future in the art world for the man she has liberated with her touch. At the dawn of a new millennium, Honor has awakened a true Renaissance man, but has she found a love to carry her into the next century?

___52340-X $5.99 US/$6.99 CAN